Shrine of Stars

THE THIRD BOOK OF CONFLUENCE

Shrine of Stars

THE THIRD BOOK OF CONFLUENCE

PAUL J. McAULEY

VICTOR GOLLANCZ

LONDON

First published in Great Britain in 1999 by
Victor Gollancz SF
An imprint of Orion Books Ltd
Orion House, 5 Upper St Martin's Lane,
London WC2H 9EA

To receive information on the Millennium list, e-mail us at:
smy@orionbooks.co.uk

A CIP catalogue record for this book is
available from the British Library

ISBN 0575064293

Typeset by Deltatype Ltd, Birkenhead, Merseyside
Printed in Great Britain by
Clays Ltd, St Ives plc

For my mother

Think on why you were created:
Not to exist like animals indeed,
But to seek virtue and knowledge.
                          Dante Alighieri,
                          The Divine Comedy

1 ~ The Pyre

The two ill-matched men were working in a small clearing in the trees that grew along the edge of the shallow reach of water. The larger of the two was chopping steadily at the base of a young blue pine. He wore only ragged trousers belted with a length of frayed rope and was quite hairless, with flabby, pinkish-grey skin and an ugly, vacant face as round as cheese. The head of his axe had been blackened by fire; its handle was a length of stout pine branch shucked of its bark and held in the socket of the axe head with a ring of carefully whittled wedges. His companion was unhandily trimming branches from a pine bole, using an ivory-handled poniard. He was slender and sleek-headed, like a shipwrecked dandy in scuffed and muddy boots, black trousers and a ragged white shirt with an embroidered collar. A ceramic coin hung from his long supple neck by a doubled leather thong, and a circlet woven from coypu hair and studded with tiny black seed pearls was loose on his upper arm. Now and again he would stop his work and stare anxiously at the blue sky beyond the tree-clad shore.

The two men had already built a raft, which lay near the edge of the water. It was no more than a pentad of blue pine logs lashed together by a few pegged crosspieces and strips of marsh antelope hide, and topped by bundles of reeds. Now they were constructing a pyre, which stood half-completed in the centre of the clearing. Each layer of cut and trimmed pine and sweetgum logs was set crosswise to the layer below, and dry reeds and caches of resinous pine cones were stuffed in every chink. The body of a third man lay nearby. It was covered with fresh pine boughs, and had attracted the attention of a great number of black and bronze flies. A fire of small branches and wood chips burned beyond, sending up white, aromatic smoke; strings of meat cut in long strips dangled in the smoke, curling as they dried.

I

All around was devastation. Swamp cedars, sweetgum trees and blue pines all leaned in the same direction. A few of the biggest trees had fallen and their upturned roots had pulled up wedges of the clayey soil. Nothing remained of the blue pines which had cloaked the ridge above but ash and smouldering stumps. Some way beyond the clearing where the two men worked was a wide, shallow basin of vitrified mud filled with ash-covered steaming water.

Except for the ringing of the axe, the land was silent, as if still shocked by the violence recently done there. On one side, beyond the island's central ridge and a marshy creek, were the low black cliffs of the old river shore and a narrow plain of dry scrub that ran along the edge of the world; in the other, beyond the reach of shallow, still water, a marsh of yellow reeds stretched towards the edge of the Great River. It was noon, and very hot.

The slender man cut the last branch from the pine bole and straightened and looked up at the sky again. 'I don't see the need to trim logs which are only for burning,' he said. 'Do you love work so much, Tibor, that you must always make more?'

'The pyre must go together neatly, little master,' Tibor said, fitting his words to the rhythmic blows of his axe. 'It must not fall apart when it burns, and so the logs must be trimmed.'

'We should leave it and go,' the slender man said. 'The flier might return at any moment. And call me Pandaras. I'm not anyone's master.'

'Phalerus deserves a proper funeral. He was a good man. He always bought me cigarette makings whenever the *Weazel* put into port.'

'Tamora was a good friend,' Pandaras said sharply, 'and I buried her burnt bones and the hilt of her sword under a stone. There's no time for niceties. The flier might come back, and the sooner we start to search for my master, the better.'

'He might be dead too,' Tibor said, and stood back and gave the pine a hard kick above the gash he had cut around its trunk. The little tree leaned and Tibor kicked it again and it fell with a threshing of boughs and a crackling as the last measure of wood in the cut broke free.

'He's alive,' Pandaras said, and touched the circlet on his arm. 'He left the fetish behind so that I would know. He was led into an ambush by Eliphas, but he is alive. I think he entrusted me with his coin and his copy of the Puranas because he suspected that Eliphas might betray him, as Tamora so often said that he would. I swore when I found the fetish and I swear now that I will find him, even if I must follow him to the end of the river.'

Tibor took papers cut from corn husks and a few strands of coarse tobacco from a plastic pouch tucked into the waist of his trousers, and began to roll a cigarette. He said, 'We should not have climbed down to the shrine, little master. I know about shrines, and that one had been warped to evil ends.'

'Eliphas lured my master there, if that's what you mean. If we had not followed them, we would not have learned what happened. Fortunately, I was able to read the clues as any other man might read a story in a book. There was a fight in the shrine, and someone was hurt and ran away. Perhaps Eliphas tried to surprise Tamora from behind, and she managed to defend herself. She wounded him and chased him outside, and that was when she was killed, most likely by someone from the flier. Eliphas didn't have an energy pistol, or he would have used it much earlier – there would have been no need to lead my master away from the ship into an ambush. But it was an energy pistol that killed poor Tamora, and melted the keelrock of the stair, and no doubt the same energy pistol was used to subdue Yama.'

While Pandaras talked, Tibor crossed to the fire and lit his cigarette with the burning end of a branch. He dropped the branch back into the fire and drew on his cigarette and exhaled a plume of smoke. 'We will find the *Weazel*,' he said, 'and the Captain will help us find your master.'

'They are all dead, Tibor. You have to understand that.'

'We found no bodies except poor Phalerus's,' Tibor said stubbornly. 'And nothing at all of the ship, except the axe head.'

'A fire fierce enough to transmute mud to something like glass would have vaporized the ship like a grain of rice in a furnace. Phalerus was hunting in the marsh near the island, and he was caught in steam flash-heated by the blast of the flier's light cannon. The others died at once and their bodies were burned up with the ship.'

Pandaras and Tibor had found Phalerus's scalded body lying near an antelope he had shot. It was clear that the old sailor had not died immediately; he had put the shaft of an arbalest bolt between his teeth and nearly bitten it through in his agony. Pandaras remembered a

3

story that one of his uncles had told him about an accident in a foundry. A man had slipped and fallen waist-deep in a vat of molten iron. The man's workmates had been paralysed by his terrible screams, but his father had grabbed a long-handled ladle and had pushed his son's head beneath the glowing surface. Phalerus had died almost as badly, and he had died alone, with no one to ease his passing.

Tibor started to trim the larger branches from the pine he had felled. After a little while, he stopped and said, 'The Captain is clever. She's escaped pirates before, and that's what happened here. The flier's light cannon missed the *Weazel*, and she made a run for it. Maybe Phalerus was left behind, but the rest will be with the ship. The Captain won't know your master has been taken, and maybe she'll come back for him.' He ran a hand over the parallel scars that seamed his broad chest. He said, 'I belong with the ship, little master.'

Pandaras swiped away the little black bees that had clustered at the corners of his eyes to drink his sweat. 'I'm not your master,' he said. 'We are travelling together, as free men. Eliphas betrayed my master and killed your shipmates, and I will kill him for that. I swear it. Eliphas claimed to know of a city hidden in the Glass Desert where others of my master's bloodline lived, and so lured him all this way from Ys. Eliphas is a liar and a traitor, but all lies have some truth in them, and I think we'll find the place where he has taken my master if we continue downriver. You will help me, and then you can set out on your own road.'

Pandaras did not want the responsibility of looking after Tibor, but he needed him because the hierodule knew how to survive in the wilderness. Pandaras had lived all his short life in Ys. He knew the city's stone streets and its people; he knew words which, if whispered in the right place, could kill a man; he knew the rituals and meeting places of hundreds of cults, the monastery where anyone could beg waybread and beer at noon, the places where the magistrates and their machines never went, the places where they could always be found, the rhythm of the docks, the histories of a thousand temples, the secrets of a decad of trades. But the randomness of this wild shore confused and frightened him. It was tangled, impenetrable, alien to thought.

'I am a slave of all the world, little master.' Tibor drew on the stub of his cigarette, held his breath, and exhaled. 'Nothing can change that.

Ten thousand years ago my bloodline fought on the side of the feral machines, against the will of the Preservers. In the shame of our defeat we must serve the Preservers and their peoples for all our lives, and hope only that we will be redeemed at the end of time.'

'All men are servants of the Preservers,' Pandaras said. 'They raised us up from animals, remember all who have ever lived, and will raise them from the dead in the last moment at the end of time and space. If you must be a servant, then serve my master, Yama. He is of the ancient race of the Builders, who made this world according to the will of the Preservers. In all the world, he is closer to them than any other man – the emissary from the holy city of Gond admitted as much. He is their avatar. I have seen him bend countless machines to his will. In Ys, on the roof of the Palace of the Memory of the People, he brought a baby of one of the indigenous people to self-awareness, and you saw how he drew up monstrous polyps from the bottom of the Great River to save us from Prefect Corin. He is a wise and holy man. He alone can end the war begun by the heretics; he alone can return the world to the path which will lead to redemption of all its peoples. So by helping me find him, you will serve all the world.'

'We will search for your master, and for my ship,' Tibor said. He drew a last puff from the stub of his cigarette and pinched it out and swallowed it. His long red tongue passed over his black lips. 'But a ship is easier to find than a man. How will we find him, in all the long world?'

Pandaras showed Tibor the ceramic coin Yama had given him before following the traitor Eliphas into ambush. It held a faint spark in its centre. Pandaras hoped that it meant that Yama was still alive, but no matter which way he turned the coin, the spark did not grow brighter or dimmer.

Tibor nodded. 'I have heard of such things, young master, but never thought to see one.'

'It's real,' Pandaras said. 'Now work harder and talk less. I want to be gone from here as soon as possible.'

At last the pyre was finished. Pandaras and Tibor laid Phalerus's body on top and covered it with a blanket of orange mallows and yellow irises. Tibor knew the funeral rituals by heart, and Pandaras followed his instructions, becoming for that short time the servant of a holy slave. They asperged the body with water and Tibor said prayers for the memory of the dead sailor before lighting the dry reeds he had woven through the lower layers of the pyre.

When it was burning well, with Phalerus's body a shadow in the centre of leaping yellow flames and white smoke bending like a banner towards the blackened ridge of the little island, Pandaras and Tibor clambered on to their raft and poled away from the devastated island with unseemly haste. It took them the rest of the day to thread a way through the stands of tall yellow reeds to the mudbanks and pioneer mangroves that lay beyond, along the margin of the shrinking river. When the water became too deep to use the pole, Tibor took up a leaf-shaped paddle he had carved from a scrap of wood.

Pandaras squatted at the raft's blunt prow, Phalerus's arbalest in his lap and his master's pack between his feet. He was more afraid than he could let the hierodule know. Tibor said that the raft was stronger than it looked, that the strips of hide would shrink in the water and bind the logs ever tighter, but Pandaras thought it a flimsy craft. The idea of travelling the length of the Great River on it, like an emmet clinging to a flake of bark, filled him with dread, but he was certain that Yama had been carried away on the flier, and he loved his master so fiercely that he would follow him beyond the edge of the world. He had smeared every bit of his exposed pelt with black mud to protect himself from the biting flies and midges which danced in dense clouds over stumps and breather roots. He was a savage in a savage land. He would go naked, cover his body with strange swirling tattoos, drink blood from freshly killed animals until he was as strong as a storm, and then he would pull down the walls of the citadel where his master was held, rescue him, and kill the traitor who had taken him. His people would make songs about it until the end of time.

Such dreams sustained his small hope. Those, and the faint but unwavering spark trapped within the ceramic coin.

At last the raft rounded the point of a long arm of mangroves, and the wide river suddenly stretched before them, gleaming like a plain of gold in the light of the setting sun. There was so much light glittering up from the water that Pandaras could not see if it had an ending. He stood, suddenly filled with elation, and flung out an arm and pointed downriver, towards the war.

2 ~ Dr Dismas's Disease

Dr Dismas came into the big white room without ceremony, flinging open the double doors and striding straight towards Yama, scattering the machines which floated at various levels in the air. A decad of servants in various brightly coloured liveries trailed behind him.

Yama had been performing some of the exercises Sergeant Rhodean had taught him, and jumped up as Dr Dismas approached. He was barechested and barefoot, wearing only a pair of silk trews and a wide bandage wound twice around the burns on his chest. Ever since his capture, he had wanted nothing more than to be able to command just one machine and make it fling itself into Dr Dismas's eye and burn through his brain, but no matter how much he strained to contact the machines around him, he could not bend them to his will. The powers which he had painfully learned to master had been taken from him by the thing which had grown from seeds Dr Dismas had, by a trick, planted in him at the beginning of his adventures. He was plagued by a fluttering of red and black at the edges of his vision, and was visited in his sleep by strange and terrible dreams which, although he utterly forgot them upon waking, left an indelible residue of terror and loathing.

Dr Dismas did not speak at once, but clapped his stiff hands together in an irregular rhythm and paced up and down while looking sidelong at Yama, as if trying to marshal his hectic thoughts. The servants stood in a row behind him. They were all indigens, and all mutilated. Yama scarcely noticed them. He was watching the bent-backed, black-clad apothecary as a mouse might watch a snake.

'You are awake!' Dr Dismas said at last. 'Good, good. How are you, Yamamanama? Any headaches? Any coloured lights or spots floating in your vision? Your burns are healing nicely, I see. Ah, why do you look at me that way? I am your saviour!'

'You infected me with this disease, Doctor. Are you worried that it is not progressing as fast as you wish?'

'It is not a disease, Yamamanama. Do not think of it as a disease. And do not resist it. That will make things worse for you.'

'Where is this place, Doctor? Why have you brought me here? Where are the others?'

He had asked these questions many times before, and Dr Dismas had not yet answered them. The apothecary smiled and said, 'Our allies gave it to me as a reward for services rendered. A part payment, I should say, for I have only just begun. We, my dear Yamamanama, have only just begun. How much we still have to do!'

Dr Dismas marched across the room and stood for a moment at the great window, his hands twisted behind his back. But he could not stand still for long, and whirled around and smiled at Yama. He must have recently injected himself with a dose of the drug, for he was pumped full of an energy he could not quite control, a small, sleek, perpetually agitated man in a black claw hammer frock coat that reached to his knees, the stiff planes of his brown face propped above the high collar of his white shirt. He was at once comic and malign.

Yama hated Dr Dismas, but knew that the apothecary had the answers to many of his questions. He said, 'I am your prisoner, Doctor. What do you want from me?'

'Prisoner? No, no, no. O, no, not a prisoner,' Dr Dismas said. 'We are at a delicate stage. You are as yet neither one thing or another, Yamamanama. A chrysalid. A larva. You think yourself a power in the world, but you are nothing to what you will become. I promise it. Come here. Stand by me. Don't be afraid.'

'I am not afraid, Doctor.' But it was a lie, and Yama knew that Dr Dismas knew it. The doctor knew him too well. For no matter how much he tried to stay calm, the residue of his dreams, the flickering red and black fringes that plagued his sight, the thing growing under his skin, and the scuttling and crawling and floating machines that infested the room all conspired to keep him perpetually fearful.

Dr Dismas began to fit a cigarette into the holder which had been, he claimed, carved from the fingerbone of a murderer. His concentration on the task was absolute; his left hand had been bent into a stiff claw by the plaques which grew beneath his skin – a symptom of his disease, the disease with which he had infected Yama. At last it was done, and he lit the cigarette and drew on it and blew two smoke rings, the second spinning through the first. He smiled at this little trick and said, 'Not afraid? You should be afraid. But I am sure that there is more to it than fear. You are angry, certainly. And curious. I am sure that you are curious. Come here. Stand by me.'

Yama drew on the lessons in diplomacy which his poor dead stepfather, the Aedile of Aeolis, had so patiently taught him. Always turn any weakness into advantage by admitting it, for nothing draws out your enemy like an exposed weakness. He said, 'I am afraid, Doctor. I am afraid that I might try to kill you. As you killed Tamora.'

'I do not know that name.'

Yama's hatred was suddenly so intense that he could hardly bear it. He said, 'The cateran. My companion.'

'Ah. The silly woman with the little sword and the bad temper. Well, if I killed her, it is because she was responsible for the death of Eliphas, who so successfully led you to me. An eye for an eye, as the Amnan would say. How is your father, by the way? And the stinking little city he pretends to rule?'

Yama charged at the doctor then, and one of the flock of machines which floated in the big, airy room swerved and clipped him on the side of the head. One moment he was running headlong, the next he was sprawled on his back on the rubbery black floor, looking up at the ceiling. Pain shot through him. His chest and face had been badly seared by the backwash of the blast which had killed Tamora and Eliphas, and his ribs had been cracked when it had knocked him down. A splinter of rock had pierced his lung, too, and although he had been treated by a battery of machines, he tasted blood at the back of his mouth now.

Dr Dismas smiled down at him and extended the claw of his left hand. Yama ignored it and laboriously and painfully got to his feet.

'You have spirit,' Dr Dismas said. 'That's good. You will need it.'

'Where are the others? Pandaras, and the crew of the *Weazel*. Did you leave them behind?'

'The *Weazel*? Oh, that's of no consequence. It is only you I am interested in, dear Child of the River. Are you all right? Not hurt by your fall? Good. Come and stand by the window with me. I have much to tell you, and we will make a start today.'

Yama followed Dr Dismas unwillingly. The room was part of a mansion hollowed out of one of the flanks of the floating garden. Its single window, bulging like an eye, overlooked a vast panorama. Far below, Baucis, the city of Trees, stretched away in the sunlight of a perfect afternoon. Other floating gardens hung at various heights above their own shadows, like green clouds. Some were linked together by catenaries, rope slides and arched bridges of shining metal. An arboreal bloodline had inhabited Baucis before the heretics had come; their city had been a patchwork of ten thousand small woods separated by clear-felled belts and low, grassy hills. Now many of the woods had been cut down. New roads slashed through the rolling landscape, a network of fused red clay tracks like fresh wounds. The heretics had made their encampments on the hills, and a kind of haze or miasma of smoke from weapons foundries and numerous fires hung over the remaining patches of trees.

Beyond the city, the vivid green jungle stretched away beneath the mist of its own exhalations. The floating garden was so high up that both edges of the world were visible: the ragged blue line of the Rim Mountains on the right and the silver plain of the Great River on the left, and all the habitable world between them, dwindling beneath strings of white cloud towards a faint hint of red. In the days since he had been captured, Yama had spent much of the time gazing at this scene, and had convinced himself that he could see beyond the fall of the Great River and the mountains at the midpoint of the world to the beginning of the Glass Desert.

Dr Dismas exhaled a riffle of clove-scented smoke and said, 'Everything you see is the territory of the heretics. Two hundred cities downriver of this one, and a hundred more upriver. Thousands of bloodlines are theirs now. And soon the rest, Yamamanama. Soon the rest, unless something is done. Their triumph is great, but they must be prevented from completing it. They have meddled in much that they do not understand. They have tried to wake the great engines in the keelways of the world, for instance. Fortunately, they did not succeed.'

Dr Dismas looked sideways, but Yama said nothing. The apothecary had a habit of alluding to matters about which Yama knew little, perhaps in the hope of drawing out secrets, as a fisherman might scatter bait to lure fish to the surface. Yama had glimpsed something of the vast machines beneath the surface of the world when Beatrice had returned him to the peel-house by the old roads in the keelways, but he had not known much about his powers then, and had not thought to try and question them.

'Well, for now you will help the heretics,' Dr Dismas said briskly. 'You will provide a service for which we will later ask payment. Please. For your sake do not make any more sudden moves. My servants here are simple things and have very literal minds. I would not like to see you hurt because of a misunderstanding.'

Yama's fist was so tightly clenched that his fingernails cut four points of pain into his palm. He said, 'Whatever I was able to do has been taken away from me. I am glad that it is gone. Even if I still had it, I would never choose to serve you.'

'Oh, it isn't a question of choice. And it is still there, somewhere or other. I'm sure it will surface again.'

'Do what you will. Invoke the thing you placed inside me. Invoke your disease. But do not involve me. Do not try to make me take your side or see your point of view.'

Yama turned away and crossed to the bed and sat down. Dr Dismas remained by the window. Hunched into his frock coat, he slowly and carefully lit another cigarette and exhaled a plume of smoke while gazing at the city spread below, like a conqueror at his ease. At last, without turning around, he said, 'You have it easy, Yamamanama. I envy you. I was alone when I was changed, and my paramour was old and badly crippled. We both nearly died before the union was complete, and we nearly died again when we retraced my path across the Glass Desert. That was almost forty years ago. An odd coincidence, don't you think?'

Yama was interested, despite the loathing he felt towards the apothecary. He said, 'I suppose that it was something to do with the Ancients of Days.'

'Good, good. You have been learning about your past. It will save us much time. Yes, it had something to do with one of them. With the most important of them, in fact. All of the Ancients of Days were merely variations on a single theme, but the one who called herself Angel was closest to the original. I believe that you have met her.'

11

The woman in the shrine. The woman in white. Yama said, 'It was the revenant of something five million years old, of a pathetic scared fool who failed at godhood and escaped her enemies by fleeing to a neighbouring galaxy. She found nothing there and returned to meddle with Confluence. She was the seed of the heretics, and was killed by her fellows.'

'Indeed, indeed. But before she was killed, Angel left a copy of herself in the space inside the shrines. Her aspect – that was who you talked to. She wants you on her side, and so she told you her story. And told you how powerful she was, no doubt.'

'I destroyed her, Doctor.'

Dr Dismas smiled. 'Oh, I think not. You have much to learn about distributed information. She is stored as a pattern of interrupted light deep within the space inside the shrines. Perhaps your paramour will destroy her, when it is stronger, and if I so choose, but you destroyed only the copy of a copy.' Dr Dismas plunged his right hand into the pocket of his frock coat and brought out the plastic straws which he habitually cast when he needed to make a decision. He rattled them together, smiling craftily, and put them away. 'The fate of gods in my hands – don't you find it amusing? Ah, you are a humourless boy, Yamamanama. It is not your fault. Anyone brought up by that stiff-backed narrow-minded backwards-looking innumerate superstitious fool would—'

Yama roared and ran at Dr Dismas again, and again was knocked down by one of the machines, but before he fell he had the satisfaction of seeing the apothecary take a step backwards. For a moment he was blinded by a silent roar of red and black that seemed to fill his head. He rolled on to his back, a ringing in his ears and the taste of blood in his mouth, and slowly got to his knees. When he stood, the room seemed to sway around him, and he sat down on the edge of the bed.

Dr Dismas lit another cigarette and watched Yama with a genuine tenderness. 'You'll need that spirit, Yamamanama,' he said. 'It is a hard road I have set you on, but you will thank me at last. You will be transformed, as I have been transformed. I will tell you how.

'It is a symptom of the disastrous reversal in the development of the peoples of Confluence that, although their technologies predated the creation of our world by five million years, the Ancients of Days were able to manipulate much that was hidden or lost to the ten thousand bloodlines. In particular, Angel was able to enter the space inside the shrines, and she learned much there.'

'She destroyed the avatars,' Yama said. 'People believe that the heretics destroyed them, but it happened before the war began.'

'Hush. This is my story, not hers. You already know hers, it seems. She tried to recruit you, but I know that you resisted, for otherwise you would not be here. You chose wisely. She is not our friend, Yamamanama. She is our ally, yes, but not our friend. Enobarbus submits to her without reservation, but we have our own plans. And besides, much of what she says is self-serving, or simply untrue. Angel did not destroy the avatars. That was the work of the copy of herself that she installed in the space inside the shrines. The aspect you talked to was a copy of that copy, but no matter. In any form, it is a poor deluded thing. After Angel died, it found itself besieged, and it lashed out. That was how the avatars came to be destroyed. The avatars, and many records, and most of the directories and maps within the space inside the shrines. That was the true war; the war fought since, between the heretics and the bureaucrats, is but its shadow. And so the bureaucrats were defeated before the first ship of fools sailed from Ys to put down the uprisings at the midpoint of the world.

'But that does not concern us. While Angel was travelling downriver towards the last and least city of Confluence, where she would plant the seed that would grow into the heretics, at that same moment, I was entering the Glass Desert. I had been trained as an apothecary – my family had been a part of the Department of Apothecaries and Chirurgeons for thousands of years – but I sought greater knowledge. Arcane knowledge hidden or forgotten or forbidden by priests and bureaucrats frightened by the true destiny of the world. As a child I had riddled the crannies of the Department's library. This was before the hierodules within the screens of the library were destroyed along with the avatars, and written records were almost entirely unused then. There were vast amounts of trash, but I discovered a few gems.'

Yama said, 'And that was where you met Eliphas.'

'No, not then. I knew him, in the way that a boy might glancingly know everyone who works in the place where he grows up, but until my return last year I doubt that I had ever exchanged a single word with him. Eliphas had long before given up searching for ancient treasures, although his friend and one-time partner, the chief of clerks of the library, did give me encouragement. *He* was interested in maps, but I found something better.

'It was the personal account of a travelling chirurgeon five thousand years dead. He had worked amongst the unchanged bloodlines at the midpoint of the world, and found a cluster of odd symptoms amongst certain of the nomadic clans which sometimes ventured into the ancient battlegrounds of the Glass Desert. It was unusual in that the same symptoms were exhibited by different bloodlines. Most clans killed or cast out those afflicted, but in some they were considered blessed by the Preservers and became soothsayers, prophets, oracles, mysts and so on.'

'This is the disease with which you infected me,' Yama said.

Dr Dismas flung out an arm, pointed at Yama, and screamed with sudden violence, 'Quiet! Enough interruptions! You will be quiet or I will . . .' His arm trembled violently, and he whirled around to face the window. His shoulders heaved. When he turned back he was smiling and there was honey in his voice. 'This is my story, Yamamanama. Do not race ahead. You think you know more than you do.'

'Perhaps I am not interested in your story, and want to bring it to its end as quickly as possible.'

'Ah, but you are interested. I know you are. Besides,' Dr Dismas added, in the same overly sweet, wheedling voice, 'if you do not listen I will slice off one of your ears as a lesson. Now, where was I?'

'You had discovered an old traveller's tale.'

Yama was interested, despite himself. Dr Dismas's story was similar to the lies Eliphas had used to lure him downriver. Eliphas had claimed to have found a traveller's account of a hidden city in the Glass Desert, a city inhabited by people of Yama's bloodline. The documents he had shown Yama had been fabrications, but perhaps the old question runner's lies had been rooted in truth after all.

Dr Dismas said, 'I returned again and again to this poorly written memoir until I had it by heart. I even made a copy of it. But I was a child, with many long years of study ahead of me. My fascination faded and I turned to other matters. When at last I qualified and was sent to my first post, I took only the tools of my trade, in a leather wallet bequeathed to me by my grandfather, and the standard catalogue of electuaries, panaceas, simples, urticants and so on. I did not take the copy of the memoir which I had made, for I had set it aside with other childish things.

'I will not trouble you with the details of my first posting, nor those of my second. I was a foolish and naïve young man, eager to do good in a world where goodness can gain only small and temporary victories. But at my third posting, fate intervened. I do not believe in the Preservers, Yamamanama. Or rather, I do not believe that they exist any longer in the phenomenological universe. But it was as if something, some agency, touched my life then, and changed it for ever. Perhaps my paramour's reach was longer than it seemed.

'I was dispatched to a mean little town in the mountains beyond the fall of the Great River, close to the border of the Glass Desert. And it was here that I encountered the symptoms of which I had read and re-read with wonder as a child.

'Of course, my interest was rekindled at once. Travelling with a caravanserai, I visited the summer camps of unchanged nomads and learned much of the course of the disease. I marked its progression from simple plaques and associated loss of sensation to mania, blindness and death. I was able to dissect the fresh corpse of a haruspex – I had to break into her tomb to do it – and chart the growths and nodes along her nervous system. And by conflating the routes of the various clans of nomads through the margin of the Glass Desert with the incidence of the disease, I was able to plot its focal point.

'I will not trouble you with a long catalogue of the hardships I endured to reach my goal. I went alone because I trusted no one, and that almost killed me. The Glass Desert is a terrible place. There is no free water beyond the mountains of the Great Divide, for the river which was the mirror of our Great River failed after the wars of the Age of Insurrection. It is a place of glare and heat, of endless sand dunes, salt pans, alkali flats, vitrified craters and devastated terrain. Nothing grows but stoneworts and a few hardy plants which are more like machines than living organisms – when I first saw them I knew then the memoir had not lied, and I was almost killed when, in my excitement, I went too close to a clump of them.

'I took a string of camels and a mule, but the camels contracted a falling sickness and I had to leave most of my supplies with their corpses. The mule survived until a great dust storm blew up. The storm lasted twelve days and all that time the mule was tethered outside my tent. When at last I emerged, with the sun a bleary spot in a sky still stained ochre by suspended dust, I found that the poor beast had been flayed to its bones, and things like turkey vultures were quarrelling over what remained. They too were partly machine, and I had to kill them when they turned on me. One clipped me with the tip of a wing, and its serrated flight feathers opened a great gash in my side, clear down to the cartilage sheaves of my chest cage.

'I went on, weakened by my wound, and carrying what I could, knowing that I did not have enough water or food for the return journey. I walked at night, and by day sheltered from the heat and from dust devils and fierce little storms of knife-sharp crystallized silica. It was burning hot by day, and so cold at night that with each breath little puffs of ice crystals fell, tinkling, from my lips. The sky was utterly clear; I felt that I could see past the distant smudges and specks of galaxies to the afterglow of the hatching of the cosmic egg. I walked like this for four days, until I found the place I had been searching for.'

Dr Dismas lit another cigarette. His hands were trembling badly. Yama watched him closely. He was caught up in the story because what had happened to Dr Dismas then was happening to him now. The red and black flickering which troubled his vision had intensified; it was as if he was peering through banners which flew on an impalpable wind. Terror beat within him on great steel wings. He had the sudden strange notion that instead of being captured by Dr Dismas outside the shrine, he had fallen off the edge of the world and was falling still, that this was a terrible dream from which he might at any moment awaken to worse horror.

'O Yamamanama,' Dr Dismas said at last. 'Child of the River. How I envy you! It was so long ago that I have only a few bright memories, worn smooth by my constant handling like pebbles in the bed of a mountain stream. It was so terrible, and so wonderful! Such pain, and such joy! Such joy!'

Yama was amazed, for the apothecary was weeping.

Dr Dismas's expression was haunted yet ecstatic. 'O yes,' he said. 'Tears. Poor weak human tears. For what I was. For what I became, in the embrace of my paramour. I was reborn, and it was painful and bloody and wretched. And out of it such glory, such joy. Such joy.'

He blotted the tears from his brown, plaque-stiffened cheeks with the claw of his left hand and sniffed hard. Usually, Dr Dismas displayed emotion as a theatrical puppet might hold an appropriate mask before its immobile, painted face. (Was it part of the Preservers' plan, Yama suddenly wondered, that almost all of the bloodlines shared the same facial expressions and bodily postures which expressed fear and hope, rage and love, happiness and sorrow?) His real thoughts were unguessable. But for the first time he appeared to be wholly possessed by human feeling.

'Ah,' Dr Dismas said at last, sniffing delicately, 'it moves me still to think about it. I had come upon the place without realizing it. I was delirious by then. My feet were blistered and badly bleeding. I had heat sores all over my body. My joints were swollen and I was so badly sunburnt that my skin was blackened and cracked, and constantly wept blood and pus. It was dawn. A fierce hot wind was blowing, sucking moisture from my body. I had reached a place of chaotic terrain. The land was like rough-cast glass, dissected by a maze of wandering ridges and canyons. I was lost, and too ill to know that by the end of the day, or by the end of the next day, I would surely be dead. I stumbled into the shade of a deep ravine and threw up my tent and crawled inside.

'My paramour had heard my footsteps leagues away, listening with a thousand whiskers grown across the land. It had watched me from decads of different eyes, some fixed like crystals in the rock and glass, others mounted on scuttling extensions it had cleaved from the wreckage of its own body.

'It was those extensions that came for me, in the heat of noon.'

'There were hundreds of them. They were like spiders or mantids fashioned out of black glass. They moved with stiff scuttling motions. I woke when the first cut through the material of my tent. In a fevered panic, I killed decads with a single shot of my energy pistol and stumbled from the blazing wreckage of my tent. More waited outside, clinging to the vertical rock face beneath which I'd camped. They fell on me, stung me insensible, and spun a cocoon around me.

'And so began—'

A chime sounded out of the midair of the room. 'What now?' Dr Dismas said irritably, and turned his back on Yama and fell into what seemed to be a one-sided conversation. 'Can't it wait? Yes, the boy.

Yes I am. Yes. No, I want to tell him. You wouldn't understand why, unless you ... Yes, I know you ... Very well, if you must.'

Dr Dismas turned and gazed at Yama with his yellow eyes as if seeing him for the first time. He said, 'We were speaking of the courtship between my paramour and myself. I told you how it began, of the little machines which were as much a part of my paramour as your fingers and toes and eyes and ears are a part of you, Yamamanama. They found me and paralysed me as a hunting wasp paralyses a fat caterpillar. And like so many hunting wasps, they wound me in a cocoon of threads spun from their own bodies. The threads were possessed of a certain intelligence, and began to mend my wounds. Meanwhile, the machines brought me water enriched with vitamins and amino acids and sugars, and fed it to me drop by drop.

'I was delirious, and I did not understand what was happening to me. I dreamed that I was in lazaret in the cool shade of palm trees, with the sound of running water outside its white canvas walls. Perhaps it was a presentiment of the future. And all the time, my paramour was creeping towards me.

'For it had realized that I was a prize out of the ordinary. It had allowed its extensions to infect any nomads that passed by, but the things which grew in the nomads' bodies were no more intelligent than the extensions themselves. But I was something rarer, and it came to me itself. Or rather, it grew towards me, as a desert plant will grow a root towards a lode of water.

'I do not know how long it took, but at last it reached me. A silver wire no thicker than a spider's thread pierced my skull and branched and rebranched a million times, uniting with the neurons in my visual and auditory lobes. And then my paramour stood before me, terrible in its glory, and told me the true history of the world.

'I will not tell you what it told me. You will have to learn that yourself. It is growing inside you. Soon it will be complete, and will awaken fully. But I will say that what I learned then transformed me utterly and completely. I learned of my paramour's fabulous battles in the vacuum beyond the envelope of air which wraps our world, of its splendid victories and the terrible defeat of its final fall. It plunged from a great height and at a great speed, transforming as it fell. It struck hard and penetrated deep within the mantle of the world, melting rock with the heat of its fiery fall and sealing itself in its tomb.

Ah, I see you understand. Yes, you are awakening. You share this, don't you? It lay there for ten thousand years, slowly reconfiguring itself, sending out its extensions into the desert around, listening, learning.

'Imagine the strength of will, child! The will to survive ten thousand years in agony and utterly alone. Until very recently it had not dared to communicate with those of its fellows which had survived the wars of insurrection. It had to deduce what was happening in the world by interrogating the wretches its extensions captured and changed. The stings of its extensions infected many, but only a few returned, and the compass of their lives was so narrow that they had little useful to communicate.

'And then I arrived, and all was different. It was not just that I was one of the changed bloodlines, but that I arrived soon after Angel meddled with the space inside the shrines. My paramour had heard her call. And so I was healed and sent back to find out what I could about the new war, and to make an alliance.

'But I did much better than that. I won so much more for my paramour. I won this hero, the last of the Builders, the Child of the River, and I laid him at its feet. The little seeds that I tricked him into ingesting were from my paramour, of course, my paramour and your father. And so we are united, you and I. Together we will do great things,' Dr Dismas said, and smiled stiffly and bowed low.

'I would rather die,' Yama said. 'I will not serve, Doctor.'

'But you are awake,' Dr Dismas said merrily. 'I know it! I can feel it! Speak to me, my darling child! It is time! Time!'

And Yama realized that all this time the apothecary had been speaking as much to the thing growing inside him as to himself. And in that moment of realization pain struck through every cell in his body. The black and red fire of the pain washed away the world. Something stood in the fire. It was a vision of a foetus, curled up like a fish, all in gold. It slowly turned its heavy, blind head towards Yama, who thought he would go mad if its eyes opened and its gaze fell upon him. It spoke. Its voice was his own.

You will not serve? Ah, but that is against the nature of your bloodline. Your kind were created to serve the Preservers, to build this world. Well, the rest of your race are long gone, but you are here, and you will serve. You will serve me.

Another voice spoke from the world beyond the fire: deep, resonant and angry.

'What are you doing to him? Stop it, Dismas! Stop it at once! I command you!'

The pain receded. The vision dissolved. Yama's body, which had been arched like a bow, relaxed. His head fell to one side. And he saw, framed by a flickering haze of red and black, the mane and the ugly scarred face of the heretic warlord and traitor, Enobarbus.

3 ~ The Trader

Pandaras and Tibor drifted downriver for three days, always keeping close to the edge of the mangrove swamps which fringed the farside shore. Pandaras did not dare set out across the broad river on the little raft, for a single wave might swamp it in an instant. Even though he could swim well, he tied himself to the bundles of reeds each night in case he slipped overboard in his sleep and drowned before he could wake. He slept very little, and Tibor did not sleep at all. The hierodule said that sleeplessness was another curse the Preservers had placed upon the bloodline. Pandaras thought that it helped explain why the fellow was so lacking in imagination, for he had no dreamlife.

The spark in the coin did not grow brighter, but neither did it grow dimmer. Yama was alive, but he was very far away. It did not matter. Every time he looked at the coin, Pandaras pledged to find his master even if it took him beyond the end of the world, even if it took him all his life.

To pass the time while Tibor paddled steadily and the ragged margin of mangrove stands and banyan islands drifted by, full of green shadows despite the bright, hot sunlight, Pandaras told the hierodule every detail of his adventures with Yama. How he had appointed himself Yama's squire after the landlord of *The Crossed Axes* tried to kill Yama for the coins he carried; how they had met the cateran, Tamora, and their failed attempt to bring the escaped star-sailor to justice; the destruction of the Temple of the Black Well and their entry into the Palace of the Memory of the People (of which Pandaras remembered little, for he had been laid out by a blow to the head). The conspiracy in the Department of Vaticination which had led to capture by Yama's enemy, Prefect Corin, and then escape from imprisonment, with Yama full of wrath and cloaked in blue fire he had conjured from a shrine, the first time Pandaras had been truly afraid of his master. And the miracle by which Yama had raised up a baby of one of the indigenous races which lived in the Palace, and the triumphant procession of Yama through the streets of Ys. The rest, the voyage of the *Weazel* downriver, the sack of Yama's childhood home and the chase by Prefect Corin which had ended in an attack by monstrous polyps from the deep and a storm and near shipwreck, Tibor already knew. But Pandaras, who loved stories, told it anyway.

'My master says that stories are the only kind of immortality achievable without the grace of the Preservers. Certainly, they are the lifeblood of my people. We are so very short-lived, yet live long in memory because of our skill in making stories and songs. A good story can be handed down through a hundred generations, its details changing but its heart always the same, and the people in it live again each time it is told. So might we, Tibor, for surely this is the greatest story the world has ever known.'

'All the world is a story,' Tibor said, after paddling silently for a while. 'Who can find the single droplet which falls from a leaf-tip into the flood of the Great River? Who can say where one story ends and another begins?'

Pandaras thought that Tibor was quoting from an obscure sura in the Puranas and, having no wish to argue theology with a hierodule, for once held his tongue.

The nights were dark and still, lit only by the dim red swirl of the Eye of the Preservers. The Eye rose slightly earlier each night, and each night reached a slightly higher point in the black sky above the river's black plain before falling back towards the farside horizon. In the vast stillness of the night, Pandaras felt most acutely the emptiness of the unpeopled shore, and he was relieved when at last the song of birds and monkeys and the whistling chorus of millions of frogs greeted the dawn. The days quickly grew hot, but Tibor did not seem to mind the heat. He said that he had grown up in a far hotter land, near the midpoint of the world. A little sun like this was nothing.

Without salt, the antelope meat went off before they could eat more than a quarter of it, but there was food all around. There were always ripe fruits waiting to be plucked from strangler figs or banana plants. Tibor plaited nets from fibres scraped from the fronds of the big ferns which clung to the mangroves, and trawled for catfish and lampreys in shallow backwaters, while Pandaras nimbly climbed about the canopies of banyans, taking eggs from bird and lizard nests. Tibor ate insects too, often catching them on the wing with his long red tongue.

Occasionally they glimpsed the flash of a sail far out in the middle of the river, an argosy or carrack heading for the war, and one day a machine circled the raft before rising up and flying straight towards the misty line of the nearside shore. It had a long, wasp-waisted body, a decad of paired, shimmeringly fragile vanes, and a cluster of bright red eyes. Pandaras cocked the arbalest while the machine dipped overhead, remembering the machines which Prefect Corin had sent out to search for Yama. But Prefect Corin must be dead, drowned when his ship had been torn apart by the giant polyps Yama had called from the deep river-bottom. There were many machines on Confluence, Pandaras told himself. It signified nothing.

Late in the afternoon of the next day, they reached the house of an itinerant trader. It was tucked away in a backwater shaded by tall mangroves, a ramshackle shanty built in the branches of a banyan, with walls and a peaked roof fashioned from panels of woven grasses. A decad of small boats were strung out along an anchor line on the still, black water below. Little glowing lamps shone everywhere amongst the tree's glossy green leaves, like a horde of fireflies. Music from a cassette player came clearly across the water as Tibor paddled the raft towards the shanty, and a bird set up a harsh clamour, warning of their approach.

The trader was a crafty old man named Ayulf. He was of a bloodline familiar to Pandaras, the bloodline of half the ruffians who smuggled cigarettes and other proscribed trade goods to indigens, or otherwise scraped a living on the wrong side of the law along the docks of Ys or on the Great River. Ayulf wore only a dhoti around his scrawny waist, in which he habitually rummaged to scratch or rearrange his genitals. His arms and legs were long and stringy, and his small head was crowned with a dirty, half-unravelled turban from which greasy spikes of hair stuck out in every direction. His eyes were yellow, like flame or bits of amber, and he hissed softly to himself when he was thinking; he did that a lot as Pandaras told a highly edited version of his story while devouring a salty mess of rice and fish.

Ayulf traded with the local fisherfolk, exchanging cigarettes, cheap cooking pots, fish hooks, nylon netting and leaves of bronze or iron for lizard, snake and cayman skins, the hides of marsh antelopes, the feathers of bell birds and birds of heaven, and rare spices and medicines extracted from plants and lichens which grew on the banyans and mangroves. The shanty was cluttered with bales of cigarettes wrapped in black plastic, wooden cases and machines or bits of machines. Some kind of large gun was in pieces on the floor by the large, flat stone which served as a hearth. Salted hides were slung beneath the roof, layered with aromatic tar bush leaves to keep off insects. A pentad of fisherfolk women and more than twice that number of their children moved about in the dusky evening light, lighting lamps, mending clothes, stirring the cookpot in which fish soup perpetually simmered, chattering in their dialect and casting covert glances at Pandaras and Tibor. A half-tame crow hopped about, too. It was big, half Pandaras's height, and looked beadily at him as if wondering whether it would be easy to kill him, and what he might taste like. The crow's white droppings spattered the floor and the stacks of plastic-wrapped bales, and it was given to crying out hoarsely and jumping here and there with an abrupt dry flutter of its black wings. It was always just at the corner of Pandaras's sight. It made him jumpy, and he kept one hand near the hilt of his ivory-handled poniard. The arbalest was slung at his shoulder. He did not trust the trader.

'You don't mind my bird,' Ayulf said. 'He's never seen no one like you before and he's curious.' He had been cuddling the youngest of the women to him; now he dismissed the girl with a slap to her haunches and said, 'They are animals, not men, but someone like me must make a living as best he can, and take what company he can, too. You understand, eh? You being in the same line of business as me. Don't deny it. I know a man that lives by his wits when I see him.'

Ayulf was staring at Tibor when he said this, but then he seemed to recollect himself and winked at Pandaras.

'I can see that you make a good living here,' Pandaras said.

'There's a lot that washes downriver,' the trader said, 'and a lot that makes its way back from the war.' He jerked a thumb over his shoulder. 'That culverine, for instance. I'd sell it to you, except I've promised it to a good friend of mine who'll be along to collect it once I've fixed its firing mechanism. But I have other guns. I'll take that arbalest off you in part exchange for something with a bit more bite. You need heavy weapons around here. The Preservers don't see so well in this part of the river, if you get my meaning.'

Ayulf's friend was probably a pirate, Pandaras thought. The trader must pay a good deal of tribute for protection. He said, 'You are generous to your friends, dominie.'

'It helps to be generous out here,' Ayulf said. He plucked a bit of gristle from his gappy teeth and tossed it to the crow, which snapped it from the air with its bone-white beak and swallowed it whole. 'Favours bring business and keep trouble away.'

'I can see that your business is good. You have a good place here, many women, many things to trade. Why, you even have an abundance of boats.'

'You need a boat to get about. How does that raft of yours handle out on the river?'

'Well enough, for a raft. My friend here has a lot of experience with rafts.'

Ayulf's yellow gaze flicked towards Tibor. 'Friend, eh? With a friend like yours, you are a rich man indeed, and deserve better than a raft, I would think.'

They slowly got around to bargaining, and at last, with Tibor following, climbed down to the lowest branches of the banyan to inspect a long narrow pirogue. It had been dug out of a single tree trunk and had a log outrigger and a high prow. A reaction motor lay in the stinking water which half-filled it. Although Ayulf could not get the motor to start, he promised that it usually ran as sweet as the streams of the paradise which the Preservers would create at the far end of time. The sun had set and, despite the little lights strung through the branches of the banyan, there was not much light under the shanty, but Pandaras could see better in the dark than the trader. He took a hard look at the motor – it was clogged with dried mud and probably had been dropped in the river at some point – and said that it was a big motor for a small boat.

'Sometimes in my line of work you need to get somewhere quickly,' Ayulf said, showing his ruined teeth in a ghastly grin. 'This will take you anywhere on the river, my little man, swift as a thought from the Preservers.'

Pandaras smiled at him. 'It might do that once it is fixed. If it can be fixed. The inlet and outlet channels are clogged and bent, but that's a trivial matter. What's worse is that the reaction chamber might be corroded under all this mud, and the feeder valves and the ignition spark will need complete readjustment. That is, if they are still working. There's a hole in the fuel tank, too. Did someone shoot at it?'

Ayulf walked his long fingernails up his narrow jaw and pulled at his ear. He glanced at Tibor and crowded closer to Pandaras, who lightly touched the hilt of his poniard. The trader pretended not to notice the gesture. He stank powerfully of tobacco, sweat and urine. He said, 'If you know something of motors, you will see that this is a fine one, very powerful.'

'I see that it is very broken. No doubt you got it from someone who was foolish enough to drop it into the river or have their boat sunk from under them. It's been lying too long at the bottom of the river to be any good, but I'd be happy to take it away from you as a favour, since the look of it spoils the rest of your fine fleet.'

With hot food in his belly and his face and feet and hands washed in filtered water, Pandaras felt more cheerful than he had since the flier had taken away his master and destroyed the *Weazel*. This poor shanty could almost count as civilization, and bargaining was the stuff of civilization, the way by which you measured yourself against your fellows. He had Tibor carry the reaction motor into the shanty and pretended to be angry that someone had burdened Ayulf with something in such a bad condition. On this basis, he and Ayulf bargained for an hour over glasses of peppermint-flavoured arak; Pandaras took care to pour most of his share through a crack in the floorboards whenever Ayulf was distracted by one of his women.

Ayulf was a crafty bargainer, but he was not as clever as he thought he was. He had been too long amongst river pirates and the simple fisherfolk, and had lost his edge. He suggested almost straight away that Pandaras leave Tibor with him and take the pirogue and the motor, and plenty of supplies too, but Pandaras said that he wanted only the pirogue, although he would take the motor if Ayulk had no need for it. In the end, it cost Pandaras half Yama's store of iron coins as well as the husks of the burnt-out machines. He had shown these to Ayulf early on and knew, by the widening of the man's yellow eyes, that the trader instantly coveted them.

Ayulf broke open another bottle of arak to celebrate the deal, and although Pandaras drank only enough to be polite, it quickly went to his head. 'That's it,' Ayulf said encouragingly. 'Drink. Be happy. We've both done well with this deal. Let your slave here drink, too. Aren't we all friends?'

'I do not drink alcohol,' Tibor said. 'It is a poison to my people.'

'We wouldn't want to poison you,' Ayulf said. 'Not you. You're worth a lot to your master.' He said to Pandaras, 'You can really fix that?'

'I'm going to do my best,' Pandaras said, and opened up the motor's combustion chamber and began to remove and clean the feeder valves and the rotary spark. The crow perched close by, cocking its head this way and that, fascinated by the bright bits of metal which emerged from their coatings of mud. Ayulf watched sidelong, and said that Pandaras seemed to know a little about motors.

'One of my uncles on my stepfather's side had a trade in them. This was in Ys, where such things are forbidden, so it was on the black side of the market. Others think that our bloodline is famous only for songs and stories, and see our hands and think that we cannot do good work with them. But while our fingers are crooked, they are also strong, and we are very patient when we need to be. You might think this motor worthless, but when I'm done it will be better than new. You are very generous, Ayulf, and I thank you a million times over. Here, more of this rotgut, eh? We will drink to my success.'

'You stay here a few days,' Ayulf said. 'You and your slave.'

'He isn't my slave.'

'He has to be someone's, and he came with you. Maybe we become partners, eh? Make much money. There is much that needs fixing here. I hear the war goes badly, which means it goes well for you and me, eh? More and more in the regular army run away from it, need to sell stuff cheap to buy what they need dear, and caterans are always hungry for the best weapons, no matter what side they are on.'

'I have to find my master,' Pandaras said.

Tibor said, 'And the ship.'

Ayulf poured Pandaras's shot glass brimfull, drank from the bottle and wiped his mouth with the back of his hand. 'It left you behind, eh? Maybe after an argument or a delicate kind of disagreement? I sometimes find those who have fallen out violently with their shipmates, if the caymans and fishes haven't found them first.'

'There was certainly a fight,' Pandaras said, glaring at Tibor.

'And you lost and were left to rot on some island? I know how that is. Are you sure they want you back? More likely you ran away, eh? They wouldn't leave a valuable slave behind with you. Yes, you took him and ran away, I would guess. No, it's all right, I won't tell. Listen, why go downriver? I have all you want here. Food and drink and women. Well, the women are animals, of course, but they know how to please a man in the warm trade.'

Ayulf grabbed at the nearest of the women, but she pushed him away with a loud laugh and turned back to frying shrimp in a big blackened cast iron pan.

'Always cooking,' Ayulf said. He started at the woman and made a humming noise in the back of his throat. 'Why now, eh? Why so late? You all eat too much, you and your brats. I should throw a few of you to the caymans, eh? Which ones first?' He stuck his long middle finger (its nail had been filed to a sharp point, and was painted red) at the nearest woman and made a noise like a pistol shot. She giggled and put her hands over her face. Her fingers were webbed, and spread very wide, like a fan. They were tipped with little black claws.

'Someone is coming,' the oldest woman said, from the far corner of the shanty. She was very fat, overflowing the stool on which she perched. She was working at a bit of wood with a tiny knife. Her skin was as green as mouldy cheese. She said, 'They bring hides to trade, man. They will make you rich.'

'They share their thoughts,' Ayulf told Pandaras. 'They are not like us, who keep our thoughts sealed in our skulls. Everything is shared with them, like air or water. Kill any one of them, and it makes no difference.'

Pandaras nodded. He was having trouble focusing on the spring, ball-bearing and three bits of metal that should fit together to make one of the feeder valves. There seemed to be too many of them, and his fingers too clumsy. He was drunk, and he had not meant to become drunk. But Ayulf was drunk too, and Pandaras had his poniard and the arbalest, and, at a pinch, Tibor (although he was not sure that Tibor, for all his size and strength, would be any good in a fight). And fisherfolk were coming. The trader would not try anything in front of them.

'You like to think we are all a single mind,' the old woman in the corner told Ayulf, 'but you know it is not true. It is just that we think alike, that's all. Hush! They are here.'

There were whistles from below, a muffled splash. The crow stirred and hopped to the rail of the veranda, finding its balance with a rustling stir of wings. It cried out hoarsely. Ayulf stumbled to the rail, pushed the bird out of the way, and peered down into the darkness.

Voices floated up. The trader cursed and threw down the half-empty bottle of arak he had been clutching. It shattered on one of the banyan's branches. 'Too fucking late! You understand? Understand too late? Come back tomorrow!'

More voices. The trader cursed again, clambered over the rail, and swarmed down the banyan. Pandaras stood (the cluttered, shadowy shanty seemed to revolve around him, and he felt a spasm of nausea) and went out on to the veranda. Below, lit by the tiny lanterns scattered amongst the banyan's leaves, Ayulf was arguing with a tall thin man who stood in a coracle. The man was holding up what looked like a huge ragged book. There were other coracles at the edge of the darkness beyond the glow of the lanterns.

Tibor came out and stood at Pandaras's back. He said, 'The woman wants to speak with you, young master.'

'Hush. I want to know what is going on.'

'This is a bad place.'

'I know. That's why I need to know what this is all about.'

'We should go.'

'I want to fix the motor. I can do it, but I'm tired. Later. I'll finish it later.'

Below them, Ayulf finished a long impassioned speech, but the man in the coracle made no reply and at last the trader threw up his skinny arms and climbed back to the veranda. He fell flat on his face when he clambered over the rail, got up and went inside and found another bottle of arak, ripped the plastic seal away with his teeth and took a long swallow.

'They are impossible,' Ayulf said petulantly, to no one in particular. He took another swallow and wiped his wet lips, glaring around at the women. A child woke somewhere and made a snuffling noise. Two more children clung to their mother's legs, staring at the trader with big black eyes. In the corner, the fat old woman was calmly whittling her bit of wood. 'Animals,' the trader said. 'Why am I wasting my time with animals?'

One by one, the fisherfolk climbed to the veranda and, stooping, entered the shanty. There were four of them. Unlike their women, they were so thin that if they had been of Pandaras's bloodline they would have been in the last stage of starvation, and so tall that their heads brushed the ceiling. Their green skins were dappled with darker tones. It was not a book their leader carried, but a sheaf of bloody uncured hides, and he placed this at Ayulf's feet.

One of the women crept up to Pandaras while the trader dickered with the leader of the fisherfolk in their croaking dialect. The leader squatted face to face with Ayulf, his sharp knees above the top of his head, nodding impassively, occasionally picking a shrimp from the heaped plate and examining it with slow thoughtfulness before dropping it into his wide mouth and swallowing it whole. His companions stood behind him in the shadows, as still as herons waiting for a fish to swim by. Most of the hides were of marsh antelope, but one was that of a leopard. Ayulf had spread it out in front of him and was stroking the spotted, viridescent fur with his long fingernails. To Pandaras's great scorn, the trader made no attempt to conceal how much he coveted the leopard hide.

'My mother will speak with you,' the woman said in Pandaras's ear. 'We know that you are a friend of ours, and we will help you.'

Pandaras yawned. It was very late and he was drunk. Drunk and tired. He had given up trying to fit the motor back together. His fingers were numb and his stomach hurt. Later. Tomorrow. The shanty was swaying to and fro like a boat on the breast of the river. The lanterns seemed very bright, a swarm of hectic colours that kept trying to run into each other. It was an effort to keep anything in focus for more than a moment.

The woman touched the fetish which Pandaras wore over his shirt sleeve, but Pandaras mistook the gesture and pushed her away. He wanted to curl up around the pain in his stomach. He wanted to sleep.

'Your master is a fool,' he told the woman. He was aware of Tibor's steady gaze on the other side of the shadowy shanty. He said, 'I can take care of myself.'

'Oncus,' the woman said, but Pandaras had forgotten that name and stared at her dumbly until she went away.

Pandaras woke with a start sometime later. It was still dark. His mouth was parched and he had a bad headache and somehow he was standing upright. Then he realized that Tibor was holding him up by the collar of his ragged shirt and kicked out indignantly. Tibor let him go. The hierodule had the reaction motor under his arm.

Ayulf was in a hammock on the far side of the shanty, half-curled around a fat young woman and snoring through his open mouth. A knot of children slept below. The oldest woman was watching Pandaras from her stool on the other side of the slab hearth, the carved peg of wood in one hand, her little knife in the other.

'We go, young master,' Tibor said in a low, hoarse whisper.

Pandaras drew out his poniard. 'I'll cut his throat,' he said. He was still drunk. His stomach hurt badly, as if he had been swallowing slivers of hot metal. The muscles in his arms and legs felt as if they were on the verge of cramping. He said, 'He poisoned me. I'll cut his throat and watch him die in his own blood. I can do it.'

Tibor wrapped a large, six-fingered hand around Pandaras's wrist. The poniard's blade pressed against the hierodule's grey skin, but did not cut it. 'You fixed the motor,' Pandaras said stupidly.

'It is very like the motor of the *Weazel*,' Tibor said, and added, 'Your pardon, but I think you need to be helped,' and lifted Pandaras up and swung him over the rail of the veranda.

They were halfway down when Pandaras remembered something and began to scramble back up. Tibor tried to catch his foot, but Pandaras kicked his hand away. 'The pack and the arbalest,' he hissed. 'My master's book. His money.'

The woman stirred and whispered amongst themselves when Pandaras reappeared, but he ignored them. He found the arbalest and the pack by the flat hearthstone – the book was still inside, but the money was gone.

'Where is it?' he hissed at the old woman. 'Where did your master hide my money?'

She shook her head, and put her fingers to her throat.

Pandaras showed her the poniard. 'I'll kill him where he sleeps. Show me where he hid it and I will go.'

On its perch above the stay of Ayulf's hammock, the crow stirred, gave a single hoarse screech, and flew directly at Pandaras. Pandaras dropped the pack and slashed blindly as the bird enveloped him in its beating wings and pecked at the forearm he had raised to protect his eyes. He cut it with a lucky thrust and it fluttered away, trailing blood and dragging a black wing across the floor.

Pandaras chased after it, bleeding from half a dozen places, and went down under Ayulf's weight and hot stink. For a moment, the trader's hands were everywhere as he sought to prise the poniard from Pandaras's grasp, but then his weight was lifted away. Pandaras rolled over, gasping, and saw Tibor throw Ayulf across the shanty. The skinny trader crashed into the woven panels of the far wall. As they collapsed around him, he rolled away, quick as thought. Pandaras's poniard quivered in the planking where he had been.

Pandaras scrambled for cover too.

'I'll kill him,' Ayulf said. He was pointing a percussion pistol at Tibor, who stood foursquare in the middle of the shanty, the arbalest dangling from one hand. 'Come out, my little man, and maybe I'll let you live. Otherwise your slave dies, and then you die.'

Pandaras stood, his hands spread in front of him. He was covered in cold sweat. Ayulf grinned and raised the pistol – and then his arm slammed backwards into one of the posts which held up the roof. The pistol clattered on the floor.

Tibor lowered the arbalest. 'We go,' he told Pandaras.

Ayulf pawed at the bolt which pinned his forearm to the post and screamed at the women, 'Get me free! Kill them and get me free!'

The old woman rose from her stool. The floor of the shanty creaked under her weight. 'Go,' she told Pandaras. 'I will tend to him.'

Pandaras jerked the poniard from the planking, scooped up the pack and stuffed two bottles of arak in it, and ran after Tibor. He more or less fell through the branches of the banyan and landed on his back in the stinking water which half-filled the pirogue.

As Tibor pushed off from the banyan, Pandaras fixed the reaction motor to its post and asked Tibor if he had mended the fuel tank.

'With a plug of resin,' Tibor said.

Pandaras's hands were shaking badly. He got half the arak over himself when he tried to fill the tank. The motor started on the third attempt and spat a mass of bubbles with a coughing roar. Pandaras shoved the tiller up. The motor's inlet flooded with a solid thump and its outlet spewed a creamy wake that glimmered in the darkness and the pirogue shot forwards. With Tibor using his paddle to steer, they made a wide arc towards the open river, the constellations of lights strung through the banyan dwindling into the darkness of the shore.

Looking back, Pandaras saw Ayulf stagger to the veranda. Something was on his shoulder: the culverine. A tongue of flame burst from its throat. Ayulf fell backwards and the roof of the shanty caught fire.

The reaction motor ran out of fuel just as the sun began to free itself from the band of blue haze that marked where the Rim Mountains stood, far beyond the nearside shore of the Great River. When the motor sputtered to a stop, Pandaras tipped it up on its frame. Tibor, kneeling in the bow of the pirogue, set to with the paddle.

Behind them, across several leagues of water, the mangroves of the farside shore made a ragged black line against the brightening sky. There was no sign that Ayulf had tried to follow them; no doubt he was too busy trying to save his shanty from the blaze caused by the misfire of the culverine.

'The women told me that they put something in his arak to make him sleep,' Tibor told Pandaras, 'but they knew that he would try to kill you when he woke and found you still alive, even though he was very afraid.'

Pandaras showed his teeth. His head and stomach still hurt, but he was no longer drunk. He said, 'Of course he was afraid. That's why he drank so much – because he was afraid, and because he was ashamed of his fear. I would have killed him if he tried anything, and he knew it. I've killed bigger men than him, and they wore armour and carried energy pistols.'

It had only been one man, the guard at the gate of the house of the rogue star-sailor. Pandaras had killed him by a trick and had been captured by the other guards almost immediately afterwards, but he was certain that he could kill again if he had to.

'Ayulf was afraid of me, not you, little master,' Tibor said placidly. 'He knew that I am yours to command, and that I would have intervened if he had tried to shoot or stab or strangle you. But he also knew that once you were dead, I would have served him. He smeared poison in the bottom of your glass, the poison fisherfolk use to stun fish, but you poured away most of the arak he gave you, and that saved you.'

'Hah. You suggest that you are more valuable than me. But who is the master here, and who the slave?'

'I know my price, little master, because I was sold on the open market and Captain Lorquital paid well for me. But do you know your worth?'

'It isn't measured in coin,' Pandaras said. 'And I think that you overestimate your value. What's the use of someone who can fix a reaction motor but forgets that it needs fuel?'

'I thought that we should leave quietly and quickly.'

'And forgot my master's book and the money, too.'

'You were nearly killed when you went back, little master. Life is more important than things.'

'Easy to say if you've never owned anything. The book is important. Don't you remember how much time my master spent studying it? And we'll need money, soon enough.'

Tibor paddled silently for a while.

'Well,' Pandaras said at last, 'Ayulf got what he deserved. Why do those women stay with him, do you think?'

'I understand that it is the custom of the fisherfolk to offer up hostages to secure bargains between different families. And so they secured bargains with Ayulf, although I do not believe that he understood what obligations he owed them. The eldest of the women told me that she knew a great chief called Oncus. She recognized his fetish, and that is why she decided to save you.'

Pandaras touched the coypu hair fetish, which he wore on his upper arm, over his shirt. It was loose there, although it had fitted snugly on his master's wrist. He said, 'I had forgotten the name of the old croaker who helped us when Prefect Corin tried to flush us out of the floating forest. What luck, eh?'

'Who can say what is luck, and what is the will of the Preservers?'

'That's easy. A man makes his own luck. Anything else is a gift, but no one should hope to build their lives on the gifts of others. My master was clever enough to leave the fetish behind so that I would know he had been taken alive, and I was clever enough to find it and to wear it. So it was by the luck I made from my master's forethought that we were saved.'

'Yet our lives are the gifts of the Preservers,' Tibor said solemnly.

'You are engaged on a holy task, little master, and you should behave accordingly.'

'A holy task?'

'Why, you seek your master, of course. Did you not tell me that he will raise up all the indigenous peoples? If that is true, may he not also redeem the sins of my own people, and of all the races of hierodules?'

'We have to find him first,' Pandaras said, and touched the ceramic coin which, hung from his neck on its leather thong, dangled inside his shirt. 'I fear for him.'

Pandaras had been badly weakened by the dose of poison, and was suffering from stomach cramps. While Tibor drove the pirogue steadily towards the nearside shore, he sat in the stern and leafed through the book he had risked his life to save.

He knew that this was an old and valuable copy of the Puranas, and that some of its pictures had been changed when his master had visited a shrine. They were quite unlike any Pandaras had ever seen before, but because, like many of his people, he was a gifted storyteller, he was able to guess something of their narrative. One of the Ancients of Days had escaped from the others and had become mixed up in a Change War. Then her ship had found her, and she had been executed by the rest of its crew. Pandaras knew that there must be more to the story than that, for his master had studied long and hard in the book while the *Weazel* had sailed downriver, but he could not riddle it and at last put it away.

It took a day and a night to paddle the rest of the way to the nearside shore, a patchwork of marshy fields, dense green woods and little villages. Many of the villages stood a league or more from the shore, stranded there by the river's slow retreat. Pandaras carved a flute from a joint of bamboo and usually managed to win his supper each night by playing a medley of tunes. He quickly discovered that those he had learned as a child and put away when he had grown older were most appreciated by the indigens. In that sense at least they were as children, but Pandaras thought that the children of men would be less trusting and less innocent than these simple folk.

The indigenous people of the shore were closely related to the husbandmen who lived in the ruins of the pleasure gardens on the roof of the Palace of the Memory of the People. They were not much taller than Pandaras, but were very muscular, with seamed skin the colour of freshly broken brick. Their stubby fingers were sometimes linked by loose webs of skin, and in one village the skin tones were darkened by greenish mottling, as if in the past they had had some congress with the fisherfolk.

Each night, Pandaras saved some of the food he was given and took it to Tibor, who stayed hidden outside the villages. After the incident with Ayulf, Pandaras trusted the indigens far less than they trusted him, and did not want anyone to see the hierodule and think that they could take him away. Sometimes he was also able to bring some palm wine, which could be used in the reaction motor; with a little fuel, they could travel thirty leagues in a day.

It was a slow, lazy time. One day was much like the next, hot and sunny with quick fierce showers in the afternoon, for it was the rainy season. At last, a little over a decad after they had first reached the nearside shore (Pandaras made a notch in the hull of the pirogue each day, like a prisoner), they came to Ophir.

4 ~ Hope

The young warlord, Enobarbus, and the rogue apothecary, Dr Dismas, both wanted the same thing from Yama, but wanted it for different reasons. Enobarbus, champion of the aspect of Angel and traitor to the army raised against the heretics by the Department of Indigenous Affairs, wanted to conquer the world in the name of his mistress and overthrow the stasis imposed in the name of the Preservers by the vast civil service. After that, Utopia would follow as naturally as summer follows the rise of the Eye of the Preservers: everyone a suzerain and everyone living for ever with the aid of old technologies which the heretics were busily reviving. Dr Dismas wanted an end to stasis too, but what he wanted after that was more complex. He was a hybrid of man and feral machine, an agent of the faction whose rebellion had, during the Age of Insurrection, wrecked half the world and destroyed many of the avatars left by the Preservers to guide and enlighten the ten thousand bloodlines of the Shaped. He wanted an end to the belief that the Preservers were gods and a closer union between machines and men, but his motives remained opaque. Or rather, he gave so many different reasons that it seemed to Yama that he wanted only a glorious chaos, a soup of contingency, change for change's sake.

Despite their differences, Enobarbus and Dr Dismas agreed on one thing: Yama was the key to victory. Their quarrels ranged back and forth across his head like those of children squabbling over a toy.

Yama took little notice of them. He was growing less and less aware of the world. He was sinking into the battleground of his own body. The thing which Dr Dismas had planted inside him at the beginning of his adventures was fully awake now, and its power was growing day by day, hour by hour. It was as if Yama's self was an island or castle of light surrounded by a restless flood of darkness both malevolent and sentient. Not only was it rising, but it was constantly sending out stealthy filaments and tentacles, constantly probing for weaknesses. Yama felt that if he gave way to it for a moment, even in the dreams which possessed him in sleep (which were not truly dreams; nor was it truly sleep), then he would dissolve at once, like a flake of salt dropped in the Great River.

It was Yama's worst enemy and his most intimate relation. More a brother than Telmon; more a lover than Derev; a greater enemy than Prefect Corin or Dr Dismas. A secret sharer, a spectral reflection, a dark half: his Shadow.

Dr Dismas explained that it was growing an interpenetrating neural network in parallel to the web of neurons in Yama's brain – an exact duplicate, in fact, but on a much smaller scale, each pseudoneuron no more than a hundred molecules wide, each pseudoaxon a whisker the width of six carbon atoms. Yama did not really understand this; he did not understand much of the apothecary's gabble. But he knew that the Shadow had grown under his skin and was extending into the intimate cavern of his skull. His dreams were no longer his own. Most were kaleidoscopic visions of battlefields and cities under siege, but in one chilling reverie he saw a great, joyful crowd of people linking and relinking hands in a stately dance, and behind each of the dancers, aping every movement, was a malevolent starveling creature as thin as paper and as black as soot.

Yama knew that as the Shadow spread through his skull it had assumed control of his powers and was using them to subvert machines loyal to the cause of the Preservers, turning them against the army of the Department of Indigenous Affairs. He knew that it was speeding the tide of war towards Ys. The visions of battle were true visions of the Shadow's interventions in the war far upriver, leaking from its consciousness to his. He could not stop the Shadow taking control of his power over machines, but he learned that he could follow it out into the world as a wren might steal a ride on the back of a lammergeyer or a mite on a spider. Awake, Yama could no longer even sense the presence of machines, much less bend them to his will, but in the grip of one of the deep trances that these days passed for sleep, riding the Shadow's consciousness far from his unconscious body, he was able to take over a machine and steal away, fleeing from the terrible visions of clashing blades of light, fountains of fire, screams of men and beasts.

In this guise, the world seemed partly transparent; there were revelations everywhere Yama looked. Using the borrowed machine's deep radar he could see the ancient dredgers in the deeps of the Great River, accompanied by schools of giant polyps which kept their ceramic carapaces clean and plucked tasty morsels from the silt they pushed towards the pipes which would carry it to the Rim Mountains. He could see the passages and great caverns beneath the skin of the world, the vast, unfathomable machines which laboured there and the great engines in the keelways. And he could see the world itself by light above and below that narrow band in the spectrum of electromagnetic radiation used by living creatures; see the forests of the Marsh of the Lost Waters as a crumpled landscape of white, reflected heat with beasts and men bright sparks moving within it; see the myriads of machines which tended the world as intense specks of constantly rewoven electromagnetic patterns; see the distant cloud of feral machines which hung several million leagues behind the orbit of Confluence. In this form, at least, the feral machine he had inadvertently called upon for help was no more than any of the others, indistinguishable in the dim cloud of overlapping electromagnetic signatures.

As below, so above. Yama could hear the faint roar of the Universe's birthpang, the wailing ululation and popcorn crepitation of radio sources within the Galaxy beneath the world's keel, the faint chirps of the halo stars. And hear too the song of the accretion disc around the Eye of the Preservers, the intense crackle of fusion in gravity-tied knots in the infalling gases, the fricative hiss of molecular hydrogen, the howl of tidally heated matter reaching its last end at the event horizon of the black hole at the centre of the disc, the great No from which nothing, not even the Preservers, who had willed their own incarceration, could escape until the Universe's last end.

One night, Yama sensed something beyond the lines of the army of the Department of Indigenous Affairs. It was like a memory which would not take form, a melody he could not quite name. A far star that was fainter than any machine, yet which drew him as a weary traveller in a wide wasteland might at last glimpse the distant flicker of his own hearth, and hurry homewards with a gladdened heart. But even as he flew towards it, the machine he had borrowed speeding above the sullen waves of the night-dark river, the Shadow stirred and woke, and Yama woke too. (Far upriver, a machine suddenly found itself a few metres above the midway current of the Great River, falling down a gravithic geodesic towards Ophir. Braking so hard that its shell glowed red-hot with friction, it spun eccentrically on its axis – just as a hound might shake itself – remembered the task it was supposed to be executing, fixed the coordinates and sped off, dismayed and embarrassed.) And on waking, Yama knew what the thing which had drawn him must be. He held the knowledge close, drawing strength from the hope it gave him, and made a vow. I will find it, he thought, and find if Pandaras is still alive. No, he must be. The coin will not work unless he is holding it. Not all is lost.

It was a frail hope. For even if he found Pandaras, what could he tell him? And if Pandaras found him, what could he do?

A frail hope, yes, but all the hope he had.

5 ~ Ophir

It had once been the most beautiful city on Confluence, prosperous and peaceful, its network of canals perfumed by water lilies and lined by palms and flowering trees, its houses white as salt, with green gardens tumbling from their terraces, its main temple renowned for the wisdom of its avatar. Three bloodlines had lived there in harmony. It had been famous for its metalworkers, jewellers and weavers, and for the seminary where half the priests on the world were trained.

The war had transformed it. The population had been swollen to ten times its original size by soldiers and their followers, and by refugees who crowded the streets and made their encampments in the parklands and groves of citrus trees around the city. Fliers hung at the upriver edge of the city, some bigger than the carracks which disgorged a thousand soldiers at a time. The docks were clogged with carracks and other ships, the quays piled with supplies. The park around the great temple had been turned into a barracks. Illicit stills flourished, supplying hundreds of fly-by-night bars. There were firefights between gangs dealing in drugs and prostitution, and between the gangs and the civil guards who tried to contain them. Dead bodies lay unclaimed by the sides of the busy streets, picked over by dholes and kit foxes, or floated amongst the flowering lilies in the wide canals, each attended by a retinue of green turtles and one or two pensive turkey vultures. There were rumours of heretic cults infiltrating the city; soon after they arrived, Pandaras and Tibor saw a woman run into a café which, a moment later, exploded in a ball of orange flame from which two or three burning figures staggered to collapse on the pavement.

Day and night the streets were full of soldiers and all those who fed off them: prostitutes of a hundred different bloodlines, hawkers, gamblers, grifters, gandy men, charlatans selling false blessings or fake charms or shirts guaranteed to repel the weapons of the heretics. Streams of wagons, rickshaws and tok-toks, the motorized bicycles particular to Ophir, wound through crowded streets noisy with the cries of hawkers and hordes of beggars, with music from bars and roadside food stalls, with bells and whistles and horns from the unceasing flow of traffic, with the roar of illegal generators. The canals were clogged with slow-moving boats, and at every intersection sampans were tied together to form impromptu water markets. At night, neon signs buzzed and flickered and cast coloured shadows over the white walls of the buildings, and the noise and the crowds seemed to double and redouble, a restless unsleeping flood of people.

Pandaras sold the reaction motor and arbalest on the first day of their arrival, but he got very little for them; the city was glutted with weapons and equipment. He took up singing in the pavement cafés, performing two or three standard airs at each while Tibor collected a few small coins from the customers. When Tibor complained bitterly at this indignity, Pandaras pointed to the small girl who was moving from table to table and asking the customers if they wanted their boots cleaned, and then to her brothers, working by the door with cloths and polish, and said that there were worse ways of earning a living.

'I am a hierodule, little master,' Tibor said, with an air of wounded dignity. 'I am not some street urchin. This is beneath me.'

'You are mine to command. You said so yourself. Your people allow themselves to be commanded by others as atonement for the sins of their ancestors. You make yourselves slaves, and so you make those around you slaves too, because they must take responsibility for you. How easy it must be to have others make all your decisions for you! How easy it is to be like a child! Well, now you must suffer the consequences. You cannot choose how you will serve. You must do as you are told. And you will do as I tell you, because we need money to buy passage downriver. Perhaps you do not understand that because you are a slave, and slaves have no need of money because their owners look after them. But we need money now if we are to find my master before I grow old. My bloodline burns brightly and briefly. I have no patience for the safe but slow way of doing things.'

'We will find the Weazel,' Tibor said. 'Then all will be well. You will see. They think us dead, but they will be so happy to see us again.'

'They are dead! They are dead and destroyed and the ship is destroyed. Phalerus survived a little while because he was further away from the centre of the fire, but it would have been better for him if he had died at once, like the others. And that is what happened. Everyone but Phalerus was killed in one instant, and burned up into smoke in the next. They were killed by a weapon of war. You must understand that, Tibor. You must.'

'You could sell the book,' Tibor said, after a long silence.

Pandaras sighed. It was impossible to knock any sense into the hierodule's round, hairless head. He said, 'It is not mine to sell. It is my master's, and I have sworn to return it to him.'

'Perhaps the *Weazel* will arrive soon,' Tibor said. 'We have surely overtaken it, little master, but it will catch up with us by and by and put in at the docks. Everything that goes downriver to the war stops at Ophir.'

'We cannot stay here,' Pandaras said. 'We must find my master.'

The tiny spark in the coin had multiplied into a pattern of dots and dashes of light that was different every time Pandaras looked at it. They were nearer to Yama now, he thought, but not yet close.

For the first few nights Pandaras and Tibor lived on the streets, washing and drinking at the public standpipes, sleeping on a roof amongst clattering windmill generators in a nest of bubblewrap and plastic foam packing bought from a scavenger. Everything in the city had its price. Weapons, armour and ammunition were cheap, but food and accommodation were ludicrously expensive, for this was a war economy.

Ophir was a long way from the war front in the fringe jungles of the Marsh of the Lost Waters, but on their third night in the city, Pandaras and Tibor were woken by a faint continuous thunder and flashes of blue light far downriver. It seemed to have woken the whole city, for people stood on every roof, watching the fugitive flashes. Suddenly a thread of white light split the black sky from top to bottom and for a moment it was everywhere as bright as day. The light winked out even as Pandaras raised his hands to shield his eyes, and several heartbeats later there was a long low rumble and the roof on which he and Tibor stood rolled like the deck of a ship. The palms that lined the street below doffed their heads, and all over the city bats and birds and big dragonflies took wing.

Once Pandaras had amassed enough money for a deposit, he rented a sleeping place in a house beside one of the canals. It was a subdivision of what had once been a graciously proportioned room, screened by paper stretched over bamboo frames, with barely enough space for a pair of raffia sleeping mats. Two families lived in the other parts of the room. One, of a quick, lithe, brown-skinned black-haired bloodline, ran a food stall, and the smell of hot oil and steamed vegetables always hung heavy in the air. Tibor helped them out, at first chopping vegetables, then graduating to making the sweet shrimp sauce and thin loaves which were served with every dish. The other family, five generations, from tiny hairless kit to toothless grandfather, lived on the income from three rickshaws. It was always noisy, for someone was always awake in one or other of the room's subdivisions, mending one of the rickshaws or cooking, squabbling or playing cards or listening to a cassette of prayers, and all around was the mingled sound of hundreds of other lives lived in public.

It was the life from which Pandaras had run, first becoming a pot boy, and then self-appointed squire to Yama. He was as restless as Tibor and knew he could not make the money he needed by busking. That was only a stopgap until he came up with a plan. Amazingly, it was not possible to join the army here, or even become a cateran, as Yama had once wanted to do, although there were plenty of caterans roaming the city. Nor was it possible to hitch a ride downriver on the troop ships; it was necessary to bribe one of the crew for passage, as did the gamblers, whores and other camp followers. Pandaras was confident that he could think of some way of making the money quickly. This was a place where someone with wit and cunning could make a great deal of money, as long as no one killed him first.

One of the sons of the family who ran the rickshaws, for instance, came and went at odd hours, always dressed in a sharply creased kilt and a clean white short-sleeved shirt. He had an arrogant air which humbled his parents and his grandfather. His eyes were masked by orange plastic wraparound shades, and a cigarette was always dangling from his lips. A gang member if ever there was one. Pandaras tried to follow him a couple of times, but the boy quickly and easily lost him in the crowded, noisy maze of alleys and passages behind the buildings which fronted the canal, and if he knew that he was being followed he gave no sign of it. But if there was any money to be made quickly, Pandaras thought, the boy or someone like him would be the key to it.

Two bravos had already tried to shake down Pandaras and Tibor, ambushing them one night outside the café where they had finished their final set and demanding all their money in return for a licence to perform in this part of the city. Pandaras, who knew that showing any sign of weakness would mark you for ever as prey, whipped out his poniard and cut one of the bravos on the arm and chased him away. Tibor grabbed the other around the neck and lifted him off the ground and gently took his butterfly knife and handed it to Pandaras, who flipped it open and closed in front of the bravo's face and asked pleasantly why innocent entertainers should be worthy of the consideration of two fine brave gentlemen.

The man spat a long stream of yellow phlegm. Like his friend, he was very tall and very thin, wrapped from top to toe in overlapping spirals of grey rags. The little skin that showed was granular and hard and bone-white. The joints of his stick-like arms and legs were swollen; his head was small and flat, like a plate set on a corded neck, with a triangular mouth and a pair of black, mobile, wide-spaced eyes.

Pandaras wiped sticky phlegm from his face and put the blade of the butterfly knife against one of the man's eye-stalks. It shrank to a little bobble and the other eye bent around and stared anxiously at the blade. The man said, 'You wouldn't dare.'

Tibor said, 'I will let him go, little master. I am sure he will not bother us again after this mistake.'

'First he'll tell us who he works for.'

The man's triangular mouthparts flexed and he spat again, this time at Pandaras's feet. He said, 'You've made the mistake. I'm Pyr's. So are you and all street trash like you, except you don't know it.'

'This Pyr runs things, eh? And I thought that the Department of Indigenous Affairs had charge of the city.'

'You mean the army?' The man's mouthparts chattered: laughter. He said, 'How long have you been here? The army looks towards the war, not the streets. We keep out of its way and it doesn't trouble us. Let me give you some advice. We're not like the army. We like things tidy. People who don't fit in with the way things are run are removed. You're handy with a blade, but maybe next time we come back with pistols.'

'Maybe I should speak with Pyr. I have a great deal he might want to know.' Pandaras signalled to Tibor, who released the man.

'If Pyr wants to speak with you, she'll send for you. Pray she doesn't, though.' The man adjusted his disarranged winding cloths, spat a third time, and stalked off.

Despite this threat, Pandaras and Tibor were not troubled again on their nightly rounds of the cafés, but Pandaras knew that sooner or later there would be a comeback. There always was. He just had to be ahead of it, to think of what they might do and be ready.

Pandaras became friendly with the grandfather of the rickshaw family. Memoth was a distinguished old man who spent his days at one of the major intersections of the city, pumping up the pneumatic tyres of rickshaws or tok-toks for a penny a time. It was hard work, and Pandaras massaged Memoth's aching shoulders with clove oil in the evenings and listened to the gossip the old man brought back from the rickshaw drivers, who were the eyes and ears of the city.

Memoth's family was one of three bloodlines which had inhabited Ophir before the war. They were a spidery people with short bodies and long arms and legs, given to abrupt, jerky movements. Memoth's skull was bony, with a pronounced crest and a jutting shelf of a brow from which his lively brown eyes peered. He wore only an oil-stained kilt and a belt hung with little tools. Like all his people, many of whom worked at the docks, assembling or repairing weapons, he was handy with machines. His coarse pelt was striped yellow and brown, and his plaited mane was white. That would have been a sign of his status in the days before the war, but now he had to humble himself before his arrogant gangster grandson and accept his charity.

Memoth had once owned several houses, but they had all been requisitioned by the army, and now his family made their living as best they could. But he was not bitter; indeed, he was the most patient and good-natured man Pandaras had ever met. He told Pandaras stories about his bloodline, of how before they were changed they had lived in a wide plain of tall grasses along the edge of the foothills of the Rim Mountains, the men hunting small game, the women gathering roots and fruit. At the end of each summer, when the Eye of the Preservers set for the last time, the wild grasses ripened and the women threshed the grain and ground it into coarse flour to make bread, and brewed a kind of beer from the husks. It was only thirty generations ago, Memoth said, but only now did they realize how rich they had been.

'We worked only a few hours a day. The rest of the time we sang or told stories, or made pictures on flat rocks or made patterns with the rocks themselves to please the Preservers. But now we must work all the hours we are awake, and still go hungry. What profits a bloodline to change?'

'Because unless they are changed, men are not free.' His master would have a better answer, Pandaras thought, for Yama was always thinking about these matters.

It did not satisfy Memoth. He said, 'Free, yes. Free to starve. Free to become the slaves of other men.'

'We say in Ys that people like us are the strength of the city.'

'So I have heard,' Memoth said, 'but I think the ordinary populace of Ys are as oppressed as we are here. The Preservers lay a heavy burden upon us. Perhaps men like us are unworthy of their gifts.'

'We must always hope our children may do better,' Pandaras said, but Memoth did not answer this. Few in the city believed this fundamental creed. In their despair, they had forgotten the charity of the Preservers.

As usual, they were sitting outside the door of the partitioned room, Memoth on a plastic chair, Pandaras at his feet. On the other side of the canal, which was choked with the dark green leaves of water hyacinth, women of the same bloodline as the bravos who had ambushed Yama and Tibor were washing clothes, squatting by the water's edge and gossiping as they beat dirt from wet cloth with smooth stones. Someone was playing a cassette of prayers very loudly in one of the buildings that loomed above, and someone else was shouting angrily. It had just rained and the air was still fresh. The webs of electrical cables that sagged high above the canal crackled and spat as water dripped from them. All this reminded Pandaras of his childhood home in Ys, except that it was hotter and more humid.

A flier passed slowly overhead, its underside bristling with gun emplacements that seemed to brush the rooftops. The whole quarter throbbed with the noise of its generators; the air seemed to grow colder in its shadow. Everyone stopped to watch it. When it was gone, Memoth stirred and said that the war was getting nearer, and it was going badly.

Pandaras nodded and sipped from his bowl of mint tea, waiting for the old man to expand on his theme. He had heard much about the war since he had arrived in Ophir. It had always been distant in Ys. People mostly did not trouble to think about it. They accepted the news disseminated by licensed storytellers who sang songs and told tales of great heroism and tremendous victories to any who bothered to listen. But here the war was almost next door and everyone had their own story to tell. And most of the stories were about a sudden surge of advances by the heretics, of the army's weapons failing mysteriously, of its machines falling from the sky. There was talk of a new general or leader amongst the rabble of the heretics. There was talk of sudden, harrowing defeats, of bitter retreats.

Memoth said that you could tell that something was wrong because almost no one followed the soldiers to war now. The gamblers and whores knew that there was no profit to be had from defeat.

'My people should leave the city,' he said. 'We should go back to our high plains, back to the old life. Except that we cannot be other than that which we have become. We are human now, and we have lost the facility to be like animals and let only our instincts guide us. We are each of us alone in our own heads.'

It grieved Pandaras to hear this despairing plaint, for he liked the old man. He asked, 'What does your grandson say?'

Memoth did not reply at once. He drank his tea, straining the last of it with his big front teeth and spitting out bits of twig. At last, he said, 'He is not of my family. Not any more. Now he is Pyr's.'

Pandaras wanted to know more, but Memoth would not say anything else about Pyr or his grandson. No one who worked in the cafés wanted to talk about her either, warding off Pandaras's enquiries with fingers touched to throat or eyes or forehead, telling him that he should not trouble himself with people like her, who caused only harm to people like him. Without specific knowledge, Pandaras constructed grandiose and impossibly complicated plans about swindling or duping the gangster leader, and knew that they were no more than dreams. He was growing desperate, because after two decades in the city he had saved hardly any money. Money here was like air, necessary to sustain every moment of life, and as difficult to catch or keep hold of.

And then the soldiers came for Tibor.

*

It was near dawn. Pandaras was woken by a boot in his ribs. The tiny sleeping space was full of soldiers. He came up fighting and was lifted and flung aside. In another part of the subdivided room, two women were screaming at different pitches and a man was shouting angrily. One of the soldiers threw down a bit of paper, kicked Pandaras hard, and followed his companions.

Tibor was gone. Pandaras ran outside as a flat-bottomed boat with a rear-mounted fan motor roared away in the grey half-light. Its wake washed over the sides of the canal and lifted and dropped the sampans clustered at the intersection. Someone fired a carbine into the air; then the boat slewed around a bend and was gone.

Pandaras gave chase, but had to stop, winded, after half a league. He walked back, holding his side. His ribs hurt badly and everything he owned, including Yama's precious book, was in the room.

The paper was a note of requisition for ... *a certain hierodule, known by the name of Tibor.* A receipt for two hundred and fifty units of army scrip was stapled to it. Pandaras tore the requisition and the receipt to pieces and threw them at the children who had crept to the doorway to see what he was doing. Army scrip was almost worthless. Two hundred and fifty units would not even buy a cigarette.

His ribs still hurt: sharp stabbing pains if he breathed too deeply. He tore a strip of cloth from the tail of his worn shirt and bound it around his chest. Memoth was sitting by the door, and called to Pandaras when he went outside.

'They will have taken your friend out of the city,' the old man said. 'They will have taken him to the war. There is talk of a big battle and many casualties. A hierodule would be of much use there. The hierodules of our temple were taken long ago to tend the lazarets.'

'There is a lazaret here,' Pandaras said stupidly.

'That's for civilians, and it is virtually closed down because there are no supplies to be had by the normal channels. They don't bring wounded soldiers to the city. It would be bad for the morale of those who have just arrived and have yet to fight. Besides, many of the wounded would die of the journey. No, they are treated in floating lazarets close to the front line. That is where your friend has been taken, I expect. Are you going too, Pandaras?'

'I have an obligation,' Pandaras said, and saw, without surprise, Memoth's grandson coming along the path by the canal, his smile wide beneath his wraparound orange shades. The two bravos who had ambushed Pandaras and Tibor at the café were behind him.

Pandaras went with them. He had no choice. They allowed him to keep the ivory-handled poniard and Yama's book, but reclaimed the butterfly knife and took all the money he had saved. As they passed through the spice market he said, 'You told them, didn't you?'

The boy's grin widened. He had a cocky walk, and people made way for him. His crisp white shirt glimmered in the green shade beneath the tamarisk trees where the spice merchants had set out their tables. He said in his soft, hoarse voice, 'Many have seen you with the hierodule. It was a good trick, eh? People gave you extra money because of him. Don't deny it. It made the other jongleurs jealous. Perhaps one of them told the soldiers about your slave. Also, I hear someone was looking for you. Maybe he did it, eh? Don't be sore. Maybe there's something else you can do.'

'I want to talk with Pyr.'

Pandaras felt very alert. His anger was quite gone. In a curious way it was a relief that what he had feared for so long had finally happened, but he knew that he had to be very careful now. If he failed at this, he failed both Tibor and his master.

The boy laughed, and patted Pandaras on the shoulder with a curiously tentative touch. He said, 'These things take time.'

'Who is it that is looking for me?'

'He talks too much,' one of the bravos said. It was the one Pandaras had wounded. 'I'll clip his tongue.'

'You'll leave him alone,' the boy said.

'How is your arm?' Pandaras asked.

The bravo made a hissing sound and touched the butt of the pistol which was tucked amongst the grey rags wound around his lanky body.

The boy said, 'It is one of the bureaucrats who is looking for you. Not the army, but one of those who run the army. Tall, with a staff. Black hair, and a stripe of white, here.'

The boy ran a finger down the left side of his face, and Pandaras knew at once who it must be, even though the man had surely been killed. Every hair on his head rose, prickling. He said, 'Then I must see Pyr. At once.'

'First you prove yourself,' the boy said. 'Then, maybe you see her. She is very busy. She has much business.'

Pandaras was kept for three days in a small, hot room on the top floor of a six-storey house which overlooked one of the city's squares. Crowds and traffic noise all day and all night; the smell of burnt alcohol mixed with the scent of the flowering vine that twisted around the balcony outside the window. A transformer on a pole beneath the balcony hummed and hissed to itself. Water dripped from a broken pipe into a plastic bowl in the centre of the room. A gecko kept Pandaras company, clinging to one or another of the walls for hours at a time, with only a faint pulse in its throat to show that it was alive, before suddenly stirring and making a swift dart at a roach or click beetle. There was no furniture in the room. Pandaras slept on the balcony and spent most of his waking hours looking at the pictures in the copy of the Puranas or watching the traffic which swarmed around the stands of giant bamboos in the centre of the square. He knew that he must not lose his nerve. He must keep his resolve.

The coin was still displaying its shifting pattern of sparks.

The boy and the two bravos visited Pandaras each morning and evening. They brought food from the fry stall at the corner, rice and shrimp and green chillies in a paper bag, the edges of which were translucent with oil. The boy squatted by the window and watched as Pandaras ate, humming to himself and cleaning his broad nails with a pocket knife; the bravos lurked by the door, talking to themselves in a dialect of stuttering clicks. The boy had a percussion pistol in the back of the waistband of his creased trousers, with his shirt-tail out to cover it, and the bravos had pistols too.

The boy's name was Azoth. Although he was older than Pandaras, his bloodline was long-lived and he was still a child, with the calculating cruelty of one who has never been truly hurt, who believes that he will never die or that death is nothing. He never took off his orange plastic shades and would not answer any of Pandaras's questions, but instead talked about the war for ten minutes or half an hour before, without warning, standing up and leaving, followed by the bravos.

The door was unlocked, but Pandaras knew better than to try and walk away.

On the evening of the third day he was roughly hustled downstairs by the two bravos and forced to stand at the edge of the road. Passers-by made wide diversions around them; traffic roared past a hands-breadth in front of them. A rickshaw stood in the shade of the giant bamboos. Pandaras saw someone inside the rickshaw lean forwards and say something to the driver, who nodded and stood up on his pedals. As the rickshaw pulled away, Pandaras got another glimpse of its passenger: a woman in a red silk dress, much smaller than him, with the large eyes of a nocturnal bloodline and long, lustrous black hair.

On the way back up the stairs he asked the boy, Azoth, if the woman he had seen was Pyr.

'Mind your questions,' one of the bravos said.

'I don't talk with you,' Pandaras said. 'You know nothing.'

'Pyr is interested in you,' Azoth said.

'Is she scared to speak with me?'

'She does not know if you are worth the trouble,' Azoth said. He put his hand on the pistol hidden beneath his shirt-tail when he entered the room, and crossed to the window and leaned at it and looked down at the bustling street below.

'Something is troubling you,' Pandaras said.

'We look after our own,' Azoth said, without turning around. 'Prove yourself, and you are ours, and we are yours.'

'He's still looking for me, isn't he? And I know he is a dangerous man.'

'Perhaps we should give you to him. Would you like that?'

'Then he does not offer money, or I think that you would have done that already.'

'He makes threats. We don't like that. Pyr will find him, by and by, and deal with him.' Azoth turned and stared rudely at Pandaras. 'Who are you?'

'A loyal servant.'

Azoth nódded. 'We wondered why you had a hierodule, and why you are so eagerly sought. Where is your master?'

'I have lost him.'

Azoth smiled. 'Don't worry. Masters are easy to find for the likes of you.'

Later, as the boy was leaving, Pandaras said, 'Tell Pyr I know many things.'

The bravos made their chattering laughter. Azoth said, 'Don't make yourself more than you are, and you'll do fine.'

Pandaras thought about that as he sat on the narrow balcony and watched the street below. Perhaps he was no more than he had been before he had met Yama, a mere pot boy with a talent for telling stories and getting into trouble. Perhaps he had caught himself in one of his stories. And yet he had survived adventures which no ordinary person had ever faced. Even if he had begun his travels as an ordinary man, one of the unremarked swarm of his bloodline, then he was ordinary no more, for extraordinary things had happened to him. And now he was being hunted by Prefect Corin, who must be more than a man to have survived the destruction of his ship by the monstrous polyps Yama had called up from the depths of the river. Pandaras shivered, remembering how one of the polyps had torn poor Pantin apart with a contemptuous flick of its tentacles. He touched the fetish and then the coin and promised his master that he would not fail.

'I have fallen into trouble, but I will find my way out,' he whispered. 'And I will find you and rescue you from whatever harm you have fallen into. My life is short, and worth little to anyone but me, but I swear on it now.'

Pandaras could not sleep for thinking of all he had to do and of what Azoth might want of him. He leafed through the copy of the Puranas, and found that the more he looked at the pictures the more they seemed to contain. They were saturated with meaning, and now he was beginning to fully understand the story they told.

The Ancient of Days who had escaped her ship had fled the length of the world, ending up in an obscure city at the place where the Great River fell over the edge of the world. The bloodline which lived there was unchanged, and she had taken control of them despite the efforts of the city's Commissioner and its Archivist. She had learned something in the shrines by the fall of the Great River and had quickened the minuscule machines in the brains of some of the inhabitants of the city. They had been reborn as individuals. They had been changed. And then the ship of the Ancients of Days had arrived in the middle of the civil war between changed and unchanged, having travelled the length of the Great River from its landfall at Ys. She had tried to destroy her crewmates, but they had killed her. Yet her ideas had survived. The Archivist of Sensch had escaped from the ship of the

Ancients of Days. He had been the first of the heretics who even now strove to overturn the word of the Preservers.

Pandaras began to feel that perhaps the heretics might be right, or might at least have guessed the truth about some things. It was as if a voice had woken inside his head: the book had woken it, or planted it there. The world had turned away from the path ordained by the Preservers. It had become static and stratified, weighed down by ritual and custom. No one was free to choose their own destiny.

He shuddered, a single quick convulsion like a sneeze – his mother would have said that a ghoul had been sniffing around his grave. The book was valuable to his master, but it was dangerous. He must not look in it again, he thought, but a small part of him, that whispering voice perhaps, knew that he would.

It was long after midnight. The Eye of the Preservers was beginning to set over the roofs and treetops of the city. Its red swirl was dimmed by the city's neon glare, but the pupil at its centre was quite distinct, the pinprick void swept clean by the black hole into which the Preservers had vanished and from which they would not emerge until the end of time. Could the heretics dare take the war there, if they conquered the world the Preservers had left behind?

Pandaras shuddered again. 'I will not fail you, master,' he whispered.

The next morning, Azoth and the two bravos did not bring Pandaras's breakfast. Instead, Azoth said, 'Come with us. No, leave your things here. They will be safe.'

'Are you going to take me to Pyr?'

The bravos made their chattering laugh.

Azoth said, 'Perhaps soon. First you must prove yourself.'

Azoth hailed a rickshaw and they rode a long way through the brawling streets. The bravos fixed their mobile eyes on Pandaras as he stared out and asked Azoth many questions about the places they passed. They got off in a narrow street somewhere near the docks. The masts of many ships pricked the blue sky beyond the flat roofs of the godowns. As they walked past a chandler's, Azoth pinched Pandaras's arm and said to take notice, because that was the place he would firebomb.

'Why?'

'Because you'll do what you're told,' one of the bravos said.

'Because Pyr wants it,' Azoth said, with a shrug. 'It's just business.'

A small boy was hawking fuel alcohol at the dusty intersection at the end of the street. Azoth threw money at him and told him to go away. The boy snatched up the coins, knuckled his forehead, and said he would like to see the show.

'Fill two of your bottles, then,' Azoth said. 'One word to anyone and I'll cut out your eyes and tongue. Understand? Why are you smiling?'

'Because nothing exciting ever happens here,' the boy said. He was still smiling, but his hands were trembling and he splashed purple alcohol on the pavement as he filled the bottles.

One of the bravos took out a piece of cloth and tore it into long thin strips which he twisted up and stuck in the necks of the bottles. 'You tip the bottle to wet the wick,' Azoth told Pandaras. 'Light the very end and keep the bottle upright when you throw it. Throw the bottles hard and make sure they hit something that will smash them. Make sure you throw them through the door, too.'

'I know how it's done,' Pandaras said. He was not scared, but there was a hollowness in his belly. It was the feeling he always had in the quiet moments before something violent happened. He picked up the two bottles. The rags in their necks stank sharply of sugar alcohol.

One of the bravos had a lighter. He waved its little flame at Pandaras, who stepped back in alarm, the two bottles and their sopping wicks clutched to his chest.

'Stop that,' Azoth said sharply, and held out his hand. The bravo gave him the lighter; he flicked it twice to show how the flame was struck and put it in Pandaras's shirt pocket. 'Do it now,' he said, 'and come straight back.'

It was early in the morning, but the street was already busy. Although no one seemed to take any notice of him, Pandaras felt that he was watched by a thousand pairs of eyes as he walked to the chandler's, with the heavy bottles clutched to his chest and the stink of alcohol burning in his nostrils. The shutters of the shop were only half raised; someone was moving about inside, whistling a cheerful tune. On the other side of the street, his heart beating quickly and lightly, Pandaras set down the bottles and lit the wick of one of them. He put the lighter away and picked up the bottle and threw it at the pavement outside the chandler's door. As glass smashed and flames bloomed he snatched up the other bottle and ran.

Not towards Azoth and the bravos, but in the other direction. People made way for him. He ran in front of a cart (the nilagai pulling it reared in its traces, raking the air with its clawed forelegs), dodged a soldier who grabbed at him, and ran into a crooked passage between two godowns, turning three corners before stopping, still clutching the bottle to his chest and listening to his hammering pulse and rasping breath.

Shrill whistles and an insistent bell somewhere in the distance, and beyond these bright noises the city's constant roar. Pandaras still had not got his breath back when he heard footsteps approaching. He ducked low and glanced around the corner, ducked back and lit the wick of the bottle, fearful that the snick of the lighter would give him away, and stepped out.

The two bravos stopped and looked at each other. Azoth was not with him. Their mouthparts clattered together in brief laughter; then they saw what Pandaras held. One raised his pistol and there was a flash and it flew from his hands – a misfire, Pandaras thought, and lobbed the flaming bottle as hard as he could. It smashed at the feet of the bravos and they were at the centre of a sudden tall blossom of blue flames. They shrieked and twisted in the flames and although people presently crept down the passage and poured water on them, they were already dead, and Pandaras was far away.

It took Pandaras the rest of the day to cross the city and reach the building where he had been kept prisoner. He kept up a monologue all the way, telling himself that he was a fool to go back because Azoth would certainly be waiting there, that Tibor had been right and they should have left the city days and days ago. Better to live on grubs and leaves than be in the thrall of some gangster like Pyr.

But it was the city which had caught him, not Pyr. There were plenty like Pyr in Ophir; he could have fallen in with any of them once he had allowed himself to be seduced by the city's song. How well he knew that song, and what it promised! It was in his blood, the song that seduces all who are born in a city or who come to live in one.

Azoth had had it right. The city had made Pandaras think that he could be more than he was. He thought that he could win a fortune from it and rescue his master in style, and it had nearly cost him all he had. But he could not afford to lose the book. It was not his. Not his to sell, not his to lose. ·

When he reached the square, he stood for a long time on the far side of the stands of giant bamboos. The window of the room in which he had been kept was dark, but that signified nothing. He was very hungry – he had tried to snatch a hand of red bananas from a stall, but had been chased off – and very nervous. He walked around the block and came back to the square from another direction, did it again and thought he had located two people who were watching the building, one loitering by the food stall on the corner, the other at a roadside shrine, alternately wafting smoke from an incense cone and staring at the swarming passers-by.

In the end, Pandaras went into the building next door and climbed its staircase to the roof, coming out amongst a small forest of clattering wind generators. An old man, drunk or drugged, lay on his back, waving his long arms and legs in the air like a beetle. Two more, wrapped in winding grey rags, turned their stalked eyes towards Pandaras, but they were only drunkards, sharing a plastic blister of an oily white liquor.

Pandaras marked his spot and took a short run and jumped the gap between the two buildings. He walked around the edge of the roof until he spied the balcony of the room where he had been kept, then took out his poniard and sawed at a sagging spot in the asphalted roof, exposing a lathe and plaster ceiling below.

There were wind generators on this roof too. He pried the heavy battery from one and threw it into the hole he had made and jumped after it, yelling like a crazy man and holding his poniard high above his head.

He landed in a pile of rubble and dust and fell over. There were three men in the room, but Pandaras only saw two of them at first. One was dead, lying on his back in the middle of the room with not a mark on him. The other was Azoth. He sat beneath the window, the copy of the Puranas open in his lap, faint light from a picture shining eerily under his narrow chin. His orange wraparound shades had fallen off; he stared down at the book in his lap with unblinking eyes and did not move when Pandaras dared to take a step towards him.

'He was like that when I arrived,' someone said.

Pandaras recognized the man's soft voice at once. He had been interrogated by him after the fall of the Department of Vaticination in the Palace of the Memory of the People. Without turning around, he said, 'And the other?'

'Drowned, I fear, in the bowl of water conveniently left in the middle of the floor. How easy death is to find. Throw down your knife, boy, or it will find you in the next instant.'

Pandaras dropped his poniard at his feet. He said, 'Death finds some more easily than others. All the waters of the Great River were not enough to drown you.'

'Where is he?'

It took a great effort not to turn around. 'Not here. Downriver, I think.'

'Hmm. You will tell me all you know. Ah, do not bother to deny it. You know that you will. But not here, not now. I do not have time to kill all the gangsters in this city. Close the book, boy. We will bring it with us.'

Pandaras said, 'What happened to Azoth?'

'Is that his name? He needs it no longer. The book is dangerous, boy. It has been changed. It takes the soul of any unwary enough to look into it.'

'It did not take mine,' Pandaras said, taking the book from Azoth's unresisting fingers. The boy continued to stare at his empty hands. A slick of drool glistened on the brown pelt of his chin.

'Perhaps it already has taken you. We will see.' Prefect Corin stepped out of the shadows by the door, the white stripe on the left side of his face catching the light from the book Pandaras held open towards him. He said, 'That will not affect me. I believe that you have a token of the man I am seeking.'

Pandaras could not move. The book slipped from his numbed fingers and fell at his feet. Every hair on his body rose, prickling; the muscles of his arms and legs were painfully locked.

Prefect Corin said, 'You have a little talent for music, like many of your kind, so you might find it amusing to know that I hold you with a tightly focused beam of sound. It is a single note pitched higher than you or I can hear, but your muscles hear it.'

He crossed the room in three strides, reached inside Pandaras's shirt and lifted out the coin. With an abrupt motion he pulled the doubled thong over Pandaras's head. He stared at the coin for a long moment, then pressed it against Pandaras's forehead.

Pandaras felt it burning there. Prefect Corin exhaled, slipped the thong back over Pandaras's head, and extended his arm towards Azoth. There was a flash of blue light; Azoth's head exploded in pink mist. The boy's body pitched forwards, throwing a long spurt of rich red blood from its neck stump, kicked out twice, and lay still.

'Yamamanama has learned much,' Prefect Corin said. 'Or he is well advised. The coin has attuned itself to him and he has attuned it to you. You can find him by using it, or he can find you. No one else. Very well then.'

Suddenly Pandaras could move again. He fell to his hands and knees and bent his head and vomited.

Prefect Corin said, 'You will live, boy. Come now. With me. We have far to go, I fear.'

6 ~ The Shadow

As ever, Dr Dismas was there when Yama woke, and almost at once Agnitus and Enobarbus came into the room, followed by a phalanx of officers and guards. The warlord had news of another great victory, but Yama was too full of joy to pay much attention at first. He had at last found Pandaras, and had rescued him from danger and lost him, all in a few hectic minutes. Pandaras was alive, and although he seemed to have fallen into deep trouble, Yama was certain that the boy was searching for him, for he wore Oncus's fetish on his arm.

'There are great advances all across the front,' Enobarbus was saying. 'In only a few days Yamamanama has gained more territory than we have won in the past year.'

Yama wondered if Pandaras knew that he had guided the machine which had knocked the gun from the hand of the ruffian in the alley. Yama had lost contact with the machine moments later, when the Shadow had withdrawn its control of a myriad machines along the warfront, but it did not matter. He had found Pandaras once, and he could find him again.

'Not exactly Yamamanama,' Dr Dismas told Enobarbus.

'Could this be done without him?'

'That's not the point, my dear Enobarbus.'

The two men stood on either side of Yama's big, disordered bed. Yama could not move, but suddenly he had a dizzy vision of his paralysed body from above; the Shadow had possessed one of the little machines which spun in the air, and was feeding him its optical output.

A pentad of officers with red capes falling around their battle armour stood behind Enobarbus. One of the officers was writing on a slate. Its green and white light flickered in flowing patterns tugged here and there by his stylus. Guards flanked the officers, clad from head to toe in black plastic like man-shaped beetles, their carbines held at port arms. They were there not to protect Yama, but to defend their commander in the event that Yama – or the Shadow – went mad and tried to destroy him. Enobarbus's physician, black-cloaked, grey-maned Agnitus, stood just at the edge of the field of view, as patient as a carrion crow. There were servants in the room too, young men and women in tunics and tabards of gorgeous watered silks, or in fantastic uniforms of red leather kilts, golden cuirasses inlaid with intricate designs of black mother-of-pearl and plumed helmets that almost doubled their height, armed with ornately decorated gisarmes, pole-axes and sarissas which they held grounded before them. The servants and soldiers were all indigens. Some were frog-jawed fisherfolk, others lanky, rail-thin herders. There was a single sturdy forest pygmy a third the height of the others, with glossy black skin that shone as if oiled. They were all Dr Dismas's experimental subjects. Metal collars were embedded in their necks and their shaven scalps were marred by angry red lacerations crudely stitched with black thread. One had had the top of his skull sliced off and replaced with a disc of transparent plastic; cubes and pyramids and spheres nestled amongst what was left of his brain. He shook slightly and constantly; drool slicked his chin and stained the front of his red silk blouson.

And someone or something stood amongst the officers, guards and servants, insubstantial, shifting, barely glimpsed, the shadow of a shadow. It filled Yama with dread. He could not look directly at it, but he guessed that it was a new torment of the Shadow. Day by day it was growing stronger; day by day he was growing weaker. But now at least his hope was renewed. If he could find Pandaras again, and tell the boy where he was being held prisoner, he could at last begin to plan his escape.

Yama was paralysed by an injection which Dr Dismas had given him several hours before. Now, at an unseen signal, three of the servants stepped forwards and tenderly lifted him from the bed and carried him to a canopied throne, propping him up amongst satin cushions. Dr Dismas turned Yama's bare arm over, stroked a vein in the crook of his elbow until it plumped up, a river of blue blood under pale skin, then with a swift underhand motion stabbed the hypodermic needle home. Yama blacked out for a moment, and then was back in every part of his body, dizzy and cramped and sick to his stomach.

One of the servants held Yama's head while he vomited into a yellow plastic bowl. There was little but mucus to come up. Dr Dismas took a square of linen from another servant and wiped the slick of chyme from Yama's chin as deftly and gently as a mother tending her child. Yama suffered this silently, and allowed Agnitus to probe him with hard fingers.

'As usual, he is febrile and dehydrated. Otherwise his muscle tone is good and his vital signs are stable.' Agnitus stared at Dr Dismas. 'You use him hard, Doctor. At his rate he may not last the course.'

Dr Dismas met the physician's lambent gaze. 'Much is asked of him. I do my best.'

Enobarbus stepped up beside Agnitus. The warlord looked rumpled and tired, yet he was grinning broadly and his eyes were alive in his ruined face as he bent towards Yama. 'Know that I am very pleased with you,' he said. 'You have done great things. I have just flown back from an advance point beyond the Marsh of the Lost Waters. The positions which our enemies have held for a year are beginning to crumble beneath the new assaults. Their machines turn against them and they are much weakened because of it. Soon we will mount a push that will take us within sight of Ophir. I promise that I will march through her gates in less than twenty days.'

'You are talking to the wrong one,' Dr Dismas said impatiently. 'We won't need him much longer. Not once the child of my paramour is fully integrated.'

Yama looked past the warlord and his physician, trying to see the thing which stood behind them, in the midst of the officers and servants and guards. A stain in the air in the shape of a man that gradually brightened and came into focus. A familiar, patient, care-worn face with a fine pelt of grey hair, long-fingered hands folded over each other beneath the chin. It was the eidolon of a dead man, of Yama's beloved stepfather, the Aedile of Aeolis.

Yama tried to turn away, but he was paralysed once more, this time by the Shadow's will. The eidolon spoke. Its words crawled across Yama's brain like sparks over a log in a dying fire.

I am well pleased with you, my son. Do not listen to the doctor. I will not let you fade away. A part of you will always be with me.

The eidolon winked and faded. And then, horribly, Yama felt his tongue and jaw work. Something said in a hoarse, strangled voice, 'I need him still, Doctor. Even when construction of the pseudocortex is complete there will be much to learn because there is much he does not yet know about himself.'

Dr Dismas leaned over and wiped Yama's cracked lips with a sponge and squeezed a trickle of water into his mouth. 'There,' he said. He brushed Yama's cheeks, kneading the plaques beneath the skin with stiff fingers. 'This is a frail and stubborn vessel, but I will look after it for you. I will guard it with my life.'

The eidolon of Yama's dead stepfather came back, more solid than ever. *He thinks that he is our father*, it said. *He will pay for his mistake, by and by. He has wasted much time with his experiments and his foolish plots. He could have brought you to me years ago.*

Yama found that he could move again. He said, 'Yes, you would have preferred to take me when I did not know who I was and what I could do because you are not as powerful as you would like me to believe.'

'Ah, Yamamanama,' Dr Dismas said, standing back from the bed. 'You are still there.'

I grow, day by day. And day by day you shrink.

'I will not go away.'

'Oh, no, dear Child of the River,' Dr Dismas said. 'You are mine.'

There is much we could do together, Child of the River. Why resist? We could be the ruler of this world, just as a beginning. The battles I win now will bring an end to a war ten thousand years old, but they are as nothing to those I will have to fight in the space inside the shrines after I have defeated the forces loyal to the Preservers. After that victory, she who is now our ally will try and destroy me. She will not succeed, of course, and if you help me you will learn much about the world and all the worlds beyond. She has her own plans for Confluence and soon I will possess them just as I possess you. Ask Dr Dismas about the machinery of the keelways. Ask him about the heart of the world. The eidolon smiled, a sharp, cunning, rapacious grin that was not at all like the gentle smile of Yama's stepfather. It said, *Ask him why the Great River shrinks.*

After the Aedile had died, Yama had found amongst his papers pages of notes about the fall of the level of the Great River. The Aedile had made measurements every decad for many years, and had calculated the likely date of the beginning of the river's failure. Most

63

believed that it had begun when the Ancients of Days had meddled with the space inside the shrines and deleted the avatars which had survived the wars of the Age of Insurrection. But the Aedile's calculations showed that the fall in the level of the Great River had begun much later, in the year that Yama had been found by old Constable Thaw, a baby lying on the breast of a dead woman in a white boat cast adrift on the Great River.

Yama could not tell if the Shadow really knew what linked these two events, or if it was merely tormenting him with its stolen knowledge, but it had touched upon his greatest fear, that he might not be the saviour of the world, as so many claimed, but might instead be its unwitting nemesis. He reached out and gripped Dr Dismas's claw-like left hand and said, 'There is much we can do together, Doctor. I think that together we can save the world, but first we must stop the war.'

'Ah, but we will, Yamamanama. We will.' Dr Dismas was smiling as he tried and failed to free his hand from Yama's grip. He looked at Agnitus and said, 'Help me, damn you.'

Help me, the eidolon said. *Ask him the question. It will cause much trouble, I promise you. I am on your side, Yamamanama. How could I not be? I depend upon you for my life and for my powers. In one sense I am becoming you. But soon things will change, and you will depend upon me. We will have to reach an agreement, or you will dwindle to no more than a remnant. Would you work with me as an equal part of a gestalt, or would you be worse than any of the good doctor's experimental subjects? I could bury you so deep that all the light and the glory of the world would be no more than a mute spark, as dim and distant as the furthest star. I could subject you to torments worse than even the good doctor can imagine, without cease. Choose.*

'He is in your care,' Agnitus told Dr Dismas, 'as you delight in telling us.'

'You tell us that you control him,' Enobarbus said. 'Sometimes I wonder how true it is. We must talk about it.'

'It is the child of my paramour that controls him,' Dr Dismas said. He was still struggling to free himself from Yama's grip. 'It still grows.'

An age ago, Yama and his stepbrother, Telmon, had liked to listen to Sergeant Rhodean's stories about the battles at the midpoint of the world. This had been in the gymnasium of the peel-house, and the old soldier had scratched the positions and lines of attacking and opposing armies in the packed red clay of the floor with the point of an old javelin. He had taught Yama and Telmon that the best commanders overcame their enemies by wisdom as much as by force. Indeed, it was better to subdue an enemy without fighting: to enter into battle was a last resort. For that reason, knowledge of the enemy was paramount. Not just the character and strength of the opposing army, but the morale and training of its ordinary men and its officers, the severity of punishments inflicted on miscreants, the state of its supplies, the nature of the terrain it occupied, the disposition of conquered peoples towards the occupiers, and the present and predicted weather. The best policy was to understand the enemy's strategy and then to seek to undermine it, to always grasp the initiative and to be flexible, to attack where the enemy felt itself to be invulnerable and thus to bring about a decisive change. Sergeant Rhodean had shown his pupils that even a weaker force can overwhelm a strong enemy if it seizes the opportunity and strikes with precision and overwhelming momentum.

More than ever, Yama knew that he had to draw on the lessons of the kindly old soldier. He was a prisoner in the centre of the empire of the heretics, surrounded by the servants and machines of Dr Dismas and the soldiers of Enobarbus, with a jungle and armies of heretics separating him from the unconquered regions a thousand leagues upriver, and only the hope that a former pot boy could come to his rescue. Worse, he was a prisoner in his own body, struggling against the growing power of the Shadow which Dr Dismas had introduced into his body. But now he saw that by allying himself with his most immediate threat he could exploit the divisions of those who held him prisoner.

'The keelways,' he said. 'Tell me the truth about how the world works, Doctor.'

You are mine! The eidolon tipped back its head and howled, twisting the mild face of Yama's stepfather into something coarse and lupine. Its eyes burned with a feral red light, as if a balefire had been kindled inside its skull. The soldiers and servants around it took no notice, of course.

'The boy is fevered,' Dr Dismas said, and at last managed to wrench away from Yama's grip. He kneaded the stiff claw of his left hand with his right, as if comforting an injured pet, and smiled at Enobarbus and Agnitus. 'I have him, gentlemen. I assure you.'

'I belong to no one,' Yama said. 'Tell me about the keelways, Doctor. Tell me about the machines down there. It is possible that I can control them? Is that what you want of me, once the war is over?'

'I want nothing of you, Yamamanama,' Dr Dismas said quickly. 'I have brought you here as a gift to Enobarbus, a weapon to bring a swift end to the war. Ask him what he wants. Do not ask me.'

'Yet somehow he has an idea that you do want something, Dismas,' Enobarbus said. 'We'll talk of this, I think.'

He turned and swept out of the room, his guards on either side and the pentad of officers following behind in a swirl of red capes. The eidolon moved through them like smoke and stood at Agnitus's shoulder.

I am proud of you, my child, it said. *We have already done much together, you and I, and with your help we will do much more.*

'Tell me about the machines in the keelways,' Yama said. He stood up, his legs prickling with pins and needles, and limped across the room to the great blister of the window, struggling to compose his thoughts and to conceal his great excitement. If the Shadow wanted his help, then it was not as strong as it claimed. Or perhaps he was stronger, if only he knew it.

Behind him, Agnitus asked Dr Dismas, 'How great are his powers, Dismas?'

The apothecary was fitting another cigarette into his carved bone holder and did not reply until it had it lit; Yama smelled the clove-scented smoke. 'He'll have been told about the keelways by the child of my paramour. Who knows what they talk about inside the skull they presently have in common? It is of no moment, Agnitus, because soon enough the boy will be redundant. Remember to tell your master that.'

A black speck floated far off in the blue sky, high above the patchwork woods of the city of trees, far beyond the archipelagos of floating gardens.

Yama said, 'And do not forget to tell him that I have been in the keelways, too. It was after I escaped from you the first time, Doctor. I fetched up in the Silent Quarter and entered the keelways after I got away from the poor fools you employed. I learned much, then.'

The speck was a bird, perhaps, a lammergeyer which had wandered far from the slopes of the Rim Mountains. Yama watched it with growing apprehension.

Dr Dismas said dismissively, 'The keelways are hardly a secret.'

Agnitus said, 'You did not answer my question, Dismas.'

'The records are vague, a single sura in the Puranas. Yamamanama's bloodline built the world under instruction from the Preservers. Why should they not know all about it? But the boy is ignorant, Agnitus, brought up by a disgraced civil servant in a wretched backwater, with hardly any experience of the world. We proceed by experiment. Of course, if your master is frightened, I can leave and take the boy elsewhere. There are many who would be glad of his services.'

'I think not,' Agnitus said.

'That Enobarbus is not frightened? Or that I cannot leave? Take care, Agnitus,' Dr Dismas said sharply. 'I have powerful allies.'

Not a bird. It was too big to be a bird. It came on steadily. Yama could not look away from it and, although he told himself that it was only an illusion, his skin crawled with horror.

Agnitus told Dr Dismas, 'Your allies fight amongst each other even as they try to conquer the world. That is why they were defeated in the wars of the Age of Insurrection, and that is why they cannot prevail without our help. That is why you are here, Dismas. Do not forget that.'

'I'll hear that from Enobarbus, not his creature.'

Agnitus's laugh was a low, rumbling growl. He said, 'You're a fool, Dismas. You think everyone should be owned by someone else because you are yourself something's creature.'

The thing beat the air outside the great bubble of the window with wide leathery wings. It was triple-headed, and each head was set on a long, flexible neck, and their faces were triangulated upon Yama. They were brute-like distortions of the people he knew and loved and had lost: his stepfather, the Aedile of Aeolis; his stepbrother, Telmon, killed in the war against the heretics; and Tamora, the cateran who had been killed by Dr Dismas on the stair outside the shrine cut into the edge of the world. He bore their gaze, although it was very hard. Their voices crept into his brain.

Nothing ever dies, Yamamanama. I can bring them back. Help me, and I will let them live again.

'I will serve only on my own terms.'

Behind him, Dr Dismas said sharply, 'It's a last vestige, Agnitus. It will soon pass, and he will be gone for ever.'

Foolish creature! We do not need him. Yamamanama, or the old, broken, and insane thing which changed him. Together, we make something new in the world.

'Together,' Yama said.

O yes. Together. Together, we will change everything.

The creature's human heads opened their mouths wide and blew gouts of flame which washed over the eye of the window. Yama stood his ground. It was only a foolish gesture, a sign of the Shadow's vanity. And vanity was a weakness.

The flames faded. The creature was gone. Inside Yama's skull, a voice whispered eagerly.

Soon.

7 ~ The Ironclads

'You will go around it,' Prefect Corin told the captain of the flying platform.

'But I will not,' the captain said firmly. He hung from a branch of the tree by an arm and a leg and glared unblinkingly at Prefect Corin. His eyes were large and black and perfectly round. He was smaller than Pandaras, and naked except for a tool belt. His fine silvery fur was touched with black at the tips of his ears and fingers and toes. Two decads of his crew hung from or stood on branches in the other trees at the edge of the little wood, watching silently. The captain said, 'My orders I already have. You know them well, and you know that you cannot change them. This we have already discussed.'

Prefect Corin spoke softly; Pandaras could hardly hear him over the throbbing of the flier's motors. He said, 'You know who I am and what I can do.'

The captaim grinned, showing needle-sharp white teeth. 'We know that this platform you can't fly. Beyond the pass no one flies, Prefect. Not while heretics hold high ground and the river.'

Prefect Corin laid a hand on Pandaras's shoulder and said, 'Show it to them.'

Reluctantly, Pandaras drew out the ceramic coin and held it up. Little flecks and dashes of light filled it from edge to edge, scuttling about each other like busy emmets. The captain glanced at it, then shrugged.

'The device shows that the man I seek is not here,' Prefect Corin said. The light of the disc set stars in the centres of his liquid black eyes. 'He is further downriver, amongst the heretics.'

'From us the heretics took our city, Prefect,' the captain said. 'All we have left is this platform. Like to get our city back, we would, but far downriver it is, and higher than this we cannot fly higher. We try to go through, and from the tops of hills heretics fire down on us. Sweep us off the platform like bugs off a leaf. And the river's worse; out there they have many gun platforms floating. No, Prefect. For ourselves we can't do it, and for you we can't do it either. As far as we can we have taken you. Enough talk. To berthing we must attend.'

The captain swung away into the dense green canopy. His crew turned as one and followed, disappearing in a flurry of shaken foliage.

Columns of soldiers were assembling at the debarkation points on either side of the flying platform's wide black wedge. The big fan motors at its stern roared and roared as it began to turn into the wind. To port, ranges of mountains covered in dense forest saddled away, their peaks shining in the last light of the sun above valleys full of shadows; the river stretched to starboard, gleaming like pewter. It was only a decad of leagues wide here, its deep, swift flow pinched between the mountains. An advance force of heretics was attempting to take the city which had once dominated this narrows.

Pandaras and Prefect Corin had spent a day and a night and most of the next day on the flying platform, travelling steadily towards the front line. Like all the big lifting bodies, it warped the gravity field of the world so that it floated on the wind, and motors had been added so that it could be manoeuvred. It had once supported a floating garden, but the little wood at the point of the platform where the crew lived and worked was all that remained; the rest of the surface was webbed with a complex of ropes and struts to which cargo or living quarters for passengers could be anchored.

Like the troops, Prefect Corin and Pandaras slept in the open and ate at one of the campfires, although Pandaras had little appetite and hardly slept at all, fearing that if he did the platform might tilt and he would wake tumbling through the air an instant before his death. The Prefect did not seem to sleep either. All night he sat cross-legged, with his hands turned up on his knees, watching the Eye of the Preservers as it rose high into the black sky before reversing its course and setting at the downriver vanishing point of the world, and all the next day he stood at the point of the platform, staring like a perched hawk waiting for a glimpse of its prey. Now and then, Pandaras tried to strike up a conversation, but he was not so much rebuffed as ignored.

None of the troops or their officers would go near them, and

Pandaras had little idea of where they were being taken. Except that it was downriver, towards the war, and towards his master. That was some comfort, at least.

The note of the motors deepened; the platform was making headway against the wind as it moved towards the shore. Prefect Corin plucked his staff from the mossy ground and walked into the darkness beneath the trees. The little machine stung Pandaras's neck and he trotted at Prefect Corin's heels. Wind whipped them as they came out of the shelter of the little wood, and Prefect Corin put two fingers to the brim of his black hat. A huge baobab tree stood at the point of the platform, webbed with cables and hung with little platforms. The crew, a single family unit, was swarming everywhere, chattering in a high, rapid patois.

The foothills of the mountains came down to the edge of the river. The city stretched along the narrow ribbon of flat land at their margin. It was in ruins. Not a single building was intact, although the grid of the streets was still visible. The stumps of several huge towers stood at the shore like a cluster of melted candles. The air swarmed with glittering clouds of tiny machines that blew back and forth above the ruined city, twisting about each other but never quite meeting. Pandaras saw that there were many burnt places, and craters of different sizes on the forested hills, and thousands of trees had been blown down along one high ridge.

The flying platform was manoeuvring above the encampment of the defending army, townships of tents and domes knitted together by roads that crawled with traffic and marching columns of soldiers. Hundreds of men worked on huge machines folded into pits and surrounded by cranes and scaffold towers.

As the platform neared the ruined city, edging towards a series of flat-topped pylons, bright sparks shot up from the slopes of the foothills as if in greeting, and puffs of white smoke bloomed in the darkening sky, seemingly as innocent as daisies. A rapid popping started up somewhere beneath the platform and streams of fiery flecks curved in to the source of the display; gunners strapped in blisters on the underside were replying to the heretic bombardment.

Even as the platform was being tied down, the troops began to swarm down hundreds of ropes. Equipment was lowered in slings and nets. A disc swooped out of the dusk and came to rest a handspan beyond the point of the platform's prow. Perfect Corin took Pandaras by the arm and they stepped on to the disc, which immediately dropped towards the ground. Pandaras thought that he knew now how Prefect Corin had escaped when the giant polyps had sunk his ship. Because the disc warped gravity, there was no sensation of falling. Rather, it was as if the world tilted about the disc's fixed point and jumped forwards to embrace them. Before Pandaras could begin to feel dizzy, they were down.

Prefect Corin strode off at once. Pandaras had no choice but to follow him, for the pain caused by the little machine fastened to his neck increased in proportion to its distance from its master. Prefect Corin walked quickly and Pandaras had to half-trot, half-run to keep up with him.

'This is a great shambles,' he said breathlessly, dodging to one side as two columns of men in black resin armour jogged past. They were following the traffic that streamed along a wide muddy road. Crackling arc lights made islands of harsh white glare in the gathering darkness. There was noise everywhere, the braying of draft animals and the shouts of men, the roar of motors and the constant thunder of distant explosions, and snatches of wild music carried on the wind. Pandaras said, 'Where have you brought me, dominie? Is this part of your plan? Will we become caterans?'

'We will not be here long,' Prefect Corin said, and stepped into the dazzle of the headlights of an oncoming steam wagon and raised his staff.

The wagon slewed to a stop, belching a huge cloud of black smoke. Prefect Corin swung up on the bench by the driver and said something in his ear. Pandaras hastily clambered on to the loadbed as the wagon started up again, and was thrown amongst loosely stacked rolls of landscape cloth as it swerved away from the road and bounced across churned ground towards the battlefront.

The city had been built from land coral. Here and there patches which were still alive had thrown up spires and brain-like hummocks and had smothered one of the tower stumps in a lattice of red threads, but most of the city was dead, piled in heaps of rubble that bordered the cleared streets. Trenches had been dug everywhere, lit by dabs of foxfire or strings of red or green electric lights. Soldiers squatted around heat boxes or campfires; a few scouts stood on platforms behind sandbags, scanning the enemy lines, which were only two leagues distant.

When the wagon stopped Pandaras jumped down and trotted after Prefect Corin in near darkness. They skirted a trio of overlapping craters filled with muddy water and climbed to the top of a low rise. A series of bunkers were dug into the reverse side of the slope. A man in a long black leather coat came out of a curtained doorway and greeted the Prefect. He was the commander of the defensive forces, a lean, nervous man of Prefect Corin's bloodline. His name was Menas. A decad of little machines hovered around him; the largest shed a fitful yellow light by which Menas consulted a timepiece as large as an onion and studded with an even decad of dials.

'You are just in time, brother,' Menas said, and put away his timepiece and embraced Prefect Corin. 'The duel is about to begin. Listen? Do you hear the thunder?'

Pandaras had thought that it was distant artillery fire, but when he looked at where Menas pointed, he saw heavy thunderclouds rolling across the dark sky. Lightning strobed between clouds and the edge of the river.

'They manipulate the weather,' Menas said. 'They like to set the stage for the nightly duel. So far it is stalemate, for by the grace of the Preservers our mages have built an ironclad which is the match of their champion. Come with me. Come on! We do not have much time!'

A pentad of staff officers went with them, each followed by his own flock of little machines. Menas was filled with so much energy that he could not keep still or follow the thread of any conversation for more than a minute; he kept breaking off to run over to this or that group of soldiers, to ask how they were and where they were from and if they were ready to fight. It was clear that the soldiers loved him. All of them cheered his approach and offered him libations of beer and wine.

'We will show them this time, boys,' Menas shouted. 'We will push them back into the river!' He whirled about and ran back up the slope to where Prefect Corin waited. 'They are in good heart,' he said breathlessly. 'The best men we have, the bravest fighters.'

'I see no fighting here,' Prefect Corin said coldly.

'Soon enough,' Menas said, and once again took his complicated timepiece from his coat pocket and held it up to the light of one of the machines which hung above his head. 'We satisfy their need for drama, but it is a matter of precise timing.' He put away the timepiece and added more soberly, 'Some day they will decide to move forwards, and we will not be able to stop them.'

Prefect Corin looked at Menas and said, 'Perhaps you have been too close to the heretics for too long, brother.'

'This is not Ys,' Menas said. 'This is the war, the real war. I do not tell lies to my soldiers, I tell them the truth. There are no lies here, no stories to comfort the general population. The heretic forces have grown stronger over the years, and in the last handful of days they have grown very bold indeed. I hear that things go badly in the marshes. I hear that our machines are failing there and I believe that the heretics could take this city whenever they wish, but instead they play a game with us. We can hold our present position as long as we cooperate with them. We must strive to match them. If not, there are horrors . . .'

His voice had dropped to a whisper. Pandaras shuddered, realizing that the man's hectic energy barely concealed his terror. His eyes were rimmed with red, and his hands trembled; he thrust them in the pockets of his long, black leather overcoat and leaned closer to Prefect Corin and whispered. 'They bring back the dead.'

Prefect Corin eyed Menas with distaste. He said, 'We must cross their lines. The captain of the flying platform refused me. I hope that you will not.'

Menas shrugged. 'We send in scouts all the time. Sometimes they come back. Usually turned. They pass all the tests we can devise and then, a few days later, they walk into a crowded bunker and burst into flame.'

Pandaras remembered the explosion in the café moments after the young woman had run into it.

Prefect Corin said, 'It is not the first time I have done this.'

'Things have changed. They turn our machines against us somehow. The mages cannot explain it, but at least their new devices are proof against heretic trickery. At least, for the time being.'

Prefect Corin nodded. 'It is because things have changed that I must cross the lines.'

'There will be a scouting party going out soon, I expect. One of my staff can advise you.' Menas looked at Pandaras. 'Is this boy going with you? Who is he? Is he your servant?'

'He will lead me to my prize.'

'I have my own reasons,' Pandaras said, and dodged away when Prefect Corin struck at him with his staff. 'I am a seeker after truth, like my master!'

The machine on his neck stung him hard and he cried out and fell down. Two of the staff officers laughed. Pandaras picked himself up and cursed their ancestry all the way back to the slimes from which they had been mistakenly raised by the Preservers. The machine stung him again, forcing him to run after Prefect Corin and Menas, who were walking towards a glow in the distance.

Pandaras was astonished to see that it was a shrine, a big disc standing on its edge at an intersection of two broad streets. But perhaps it was not astonishing after all, for shrines were only partly of this world, and were immune to energies that would evaporate ordinary matter. Perhaps this place had once been the site of a temple which now lay in ruins on every side, with only its heart left intact.

Soldiers had gathered in front of the shrine, and the glow which beat from its disc made their faces shine and polished their prickly black resin corselets. Pandaras approached it reluctantly, remembering the woman in white who had appeared inside the shrine of the Temple of the Black Well. But as he followed Prefect Corin through the ranks of soldiers, he realized that this shrine was a fake, an enlarged version of the disc of cheap half-silvered glass which his mother had kept on a high shelf in their room. She had lit a candle behind it on holy days so that light moved within it like an echo of those avatars which, before the heretics had swept them away, had haunted certain shrines in the city. A similar trick was being played here, although the source of light was far brighter than a mere candle, and it was somehow bent and split so that circles of primary colours continually expanded from the brilliant white point at the centre and seemed to ripple out into the darkening air.

Pandaras looked away, for he had the dizzy feeling that he might fall into the light and never escape. No doubt his master would have said that this was how the Preservers had felt as they had begun their infinite fall into the Eye, and would have constructed some keen analogy between the conditions required for prayer and the Preservers' state of grace, but the play of light simply made Pandaras nauseous.

'A little invention of the mages,' Menas told Prefect Corin

boastfully. 'They call it an ipseorama. You do not yet have them in Ys, but the time will come soon enough. It induces a peculiar state in the nervous systems of men, similar to the rapture induced by the presence of the avatars. It calms and empties the mind and prepares it for the immanence of the Preservers.'

Pandaras shaded his eyes and saw that a pentad of priests was gathered to one side of the shrine. They wore robes of shaggy pelts and were crowned with high, pointed hats. One was casting incense into a brazier of glowing coals; the others shook their hands above their heads as they prayed.

Perfect Corin told Menas in his dry, forthright manner, 'I have no time for silly conjurations. At best this is foolishness; at worst it is heresy, pure and simple.'

'It is a matter of regulating prayer,' Menas said. The light of the ipseorama flickered over his rapt face and turned each of his machines to a little star. 'Regulation is important. Just as men marching in step across a bridge can find the right harmonic to shiver it to pieces, so ten thousand prayers, properly focused and synchronized, can blaze in the minds of the Preservers. How can they refuse such a plea?'

'No man should be forced to pray; such prayers are worthless.' Prefect Corin raised his staff. For a moment Pandaras thought that he would stride forwards and smash the false shrine, but he merely grounded it again and said, 'This is a dangerous experiment, Menas, and you will gain nothing from it.'

Menas did not seem to have heard the Prefect. He said, 'Regulation of prayer is as important as regulation of firepower. By calling upon the grace of the Preservers we have survived here for more than a hundred days.' He cocked his head and drew out his timepiece again. 'Listen! Ah, listen!'

The brassy sound of trumpets drifted across from the enemy lines, the noise doubling and redoubling in horrendous discords. Pandaras pressed his hands over his ears.

Menas shouted at Prefect Corin, 'Sometimes they focus the sound! It can burst a man like an overripe fruit!' He signalled to one of the staff officers as the noise died away and told him, 'They are two hundred twenty-eight seconds early tonight. Make a note. It may signify.'

All around, the soldiers bent in prayer as one of the priests began to declaim a praise song. Pandaras found himself mumbling the responses with the rest of the congregation. *Now in the moment of our death is the moment of our rebirth into eternal life*. He was very scared, convinced that his last hour was at hand, angry that he had thrown away all that he had been entrusted with, that he had so badly failed his master. How could he ever have thought that he could find Yama in the middle of this madness?

The priests began to move through the ranks of kneeling soldiers, asperging them with rose water from brass censers which they whirled about them on long chains, as indigen hunters whirl bolas around their heads before letting fly at their target.

Menas set off again, shouting that there was little time. The party climbed a slope of rubble, leaning against a strengthening wind. The first fat drops of rain flew through the air, as hard as pistol shot. Menas bounded to the top and pointed. 'There! The duel of the ironclads begins!'

Two leagues off, something was moving through the dark forest behind the enemy lines. Its passage, marked by a wave of toppling trees, was fitfully caught in overlapping searchlight beams. At first Pandaras thought that it must be a herd of megatheres, but then the machine reared up, twice as high as the tallest of the trees. It swayed forwards, doubling its height again. As it came out of the forest, the focus of decads of lights, Pandaras saw that its sinuous body was supported by six cantilevered legs and counterbalanced by a long, spiked tail, like a snake carried by a scorpion. Smaller machines whirled about it, an agitated cloud of white sparks blowing back and forth like a flock of burning birds. Something glittered for a moment at the edge of Pandaras's vision and he dashed a hand at it with no more thought than he would give a fly, watching with rapt amazement as the ironclad lumbered on.

Dense squalls of rain drove across the ruins, striking with a sudden fury and obscuring the monstrous machine. Pandaras was soaked to his pelt in an instant and he sought shelter behind a stub of stone. As he crouched there, cold and miserable and scared, he felt a warmth spreading across his chest. The coin was glowing so brightly that it shone through the worn weave of his ragged shirt. He closed his fingers around it to hide its light and whispered with sudden wild hope, 'Save me, master. If ever you loved me, come and save me now.'

Prefect Corin and Menas were facing into the storm. The Prefect clasped the rim of his hat with one hand and gripped his staff with the other. The tail of his cloak blew out behind him. The terrible noise of the trumpets began again and fireworks shot up – real fireworks, bursting in white flowers beneath the low, racing clouds. Lights shone out, brilliant threads of scarlet and green that struck across the wasteland of the city and glittered on the ironclad's hide.

Something flashed in Pandaras's vision again. It was a little machine no bigger than a beetle, with a body of articulated cubes and delicate mica vanes which beat in a blur of golden light. It hovered for a moment, then darted forwards. Pandaras slapped at the sudden pain at the side of his neck – and with amazement found that the ward Prefect Corin had fastened there was gone.

The tiny machine flew up and described a circle around Pandaras's head. 'Master,' Pandaras whispered. He was astonished and afraid. Every hair of his pelt was trying to stand away from its fellows. The coin burned inside his clenched fist. 'Master, it's you, isn't it? Why didn't you come before? Why did you abandon me?'

The machine's golden glow brightened for a moment; then it flicked its vanes and was gone.

Menas whirled around as fireworks rose from his own lines and yelled into the face of one of the staff officers who crouched behind him. 'There is no response from the third quarter!'

The man plucked one of his machines from the air and said, 'I will signal—'

Menas clapped his hands together. Rain had plastered his black pelt to his skull. He looked ready to kill everyone around him, Pandaras thought. Not because he was angry, but because he was scared, and as desperate as only a truly scared man can be. He had put so much faith in his rituals that now they ruled him completely. Menas shouted over the howl of wind and rattle of rain, 'Never mind! Together or not at all! Get over there, find the officer responsible and execute him and two of his maniple chosen at random. By the black blood of the Preservers, I will have order here! Why are you waiting, man? Time is all we have!'

The officer saluted and disappeared into rainy dark. Menas wiped rain from the pelt of his face, took a deep breath, and told Prefect Corin, 'We must have order here. Order and regulation.'

'They have made you a puppet,' Prefect Corin said.

'It is a dance.' Menas lowered his voice and said, 'A precisely choreographed dance on the edge of a razor blade.'

Prefect Corin made no reply. Menas glanced at his timepiece and turned back to watch the advance of the heretic's monstrous machine. 'Where is our fanfare, Golas?'

One of the staff officers grabbed a machine from the air and stuck it in his ear, then shook out a sheet of plastic; lines of script raced across it, glowing green like the river fire which sometimes burned in the water around the floating docks of Ys. He said in a high, trembling voice, 'They are enabling now. Start up sequence in five, four, three, two, one—'

Tinny trumpets squealed discords in the distance and something the size of a small hill began to move through the squalls of rain. The heretics' ironclad doubled its pace, loping forwards as eagerly as a hound scenting its prey and lashing its spiky tail from side to side. Its footsteps sounded like thunder. The stones beneath Pandaras's rump trembled.

The second ironclad was squat and armoured like a turtle, and pounded along on a hundred stumpy legs. Things like flies danced in the air above it – no, they were men riding floating discs. They slipped sideways and vanished into the darkness as the ironclads closed the distance between themselves.

They met like two mountains colliding. The heretics' scorpion-snake sidestepped the turtle's rush and lashed it with its armoured tail. The tremendous blow slewed the turtle half-around. It stood its ground when struck a second time, and fans of metal unfolded along the edges of its shell. Everything seemed to happen in slow motion.

'The vanes are tipped with diamond,' Menas told Prefect Corin. 'They vibrate, and will cut the enemy's legs from beneath it. Watch.'

'I have seen enough,' Prefect Corin said, and extended his arm.

For a moment, a thread of light split the dark air above the ruined town. It touched the heretics' ironclad and a ball of flame blossomed, doubling and redoubling in size. The machine broke in two. The upper part toppled forwards, writhing as it fell, and smashed down across the broad back of the turtle. The ground shook and there was a noise like the hinge of the world slamming shut. Heat washed across the ruins as if a furnace door had been opened, blowing rain aside.

Then darkness. A rush of cold air swept in and the rain came back with redoubled fury. The searchlights had gone out; the last of the fireworks burst and their sparks fell and faded. And then, raggedly at first, but steadily growing, gunfire started along the fronts of the opposing armies.

Menas screamed in fury, turning to one officer after another, shouting that they must kill the traitor. He meant Prefect Corin, who held something like a polished pebble in his upturned hand. It was an energy pistol: a real one, an old one, a hundred times more powerful than the hot light pistols made in the Age of Insurrection.

The Prefect put the pistol away, said softly, 'I have ended it,' and made an abrupt gesture.

The machines around Menas and his officers dropped from the air. 'Go now,' Prefect Corin said. 'You are done here.'

The officers walked away without a word. Menas chased after them, the wings of his black leather overcoat flapping around him, then ran back and started hurling handfuls of mud at Prefect Corin, screaming incoherently.

Prefect Corin ignored him. He bent over Pandaras and said, 'Follow me,' and walked off down the hill towards the burning machines.

Pandaras looked at Menas, who had fallen to his knees and turned his face up to the rain. 'I'm sorry, master,' he said, and ran after Prefect Corin. He did not want to find a way through the battlefield on his own.

Prefect Corin walked steadily down the middle of what had been a wide avenue. Pandaras scampered along close behind him, as if his shadow was some kind of protection. White threads flicked out from the heretics' lines and fire blossomed wherever they touched. Things moved to and fro behind flaring sources of light – things like giant insects, all jointed legs and tiny bodies. A lucky shell hit one; its body blew in a flare of greasy yellow light and then threw out a second explosion that for a moment lit the entire battlefield and turned every falling raindrop into a diamond.

Chains of little bomblets walked back and forth across the ruins; Pandaras threw himself flat when one whistled down close by and blew a fountain of earth and land coral slivers into the air, but Prefect

Corin merely kneeled, with his hand holding the brim of his hat, then got up and walked on.

Pandaras said, 'Where are we going?'

'Through their lines.'

'You meant this to happen!'

'The confusion will help us.'

'Menas will lose the city.'

'We seek a greater prize, boy.' Prefect Corin stared into Pandaras's face for a moment and said, 'Yes, you know it,' and abruptly cut to the left and climbed a slope of rubble where in its dying throes a mass of coral had thrown up a glade of smooth white spikes twice Pandaras's height, like a parade of soldiers frozen for ever, or the pieces of a game of chess abandoned halfway through.

Lights flickered and flared all around, from the pinpoint flashes of rifles and carbines to the glare of energy weapons and the brief burning flowers of mortar and bomblet explosions. Soldiers were advancing through the ruins towards the heretic positions. Phalanxes of myrmidons marched in perfect formation, not even hesitating when mortar fire blew holes in their ranks. The officers who controlled them swooped overhead on floating discs. Towards the rear, armoured vehicles rumbled forwards in a line a league long. Amidst the thunder of explosions came the sound of trumpets, a slow drumbeat, and the screams of men and beasts. Pandaras's fear grew as he watched Prefect Corin scanning the battlefield with what appeared to be perfect self-control, satisfied by the carnage and confusion he had caused by a single shot. And then Pandaras saw something which gave him a small measure of hope. High above, in the distance, a small golden spark hung beneath the racing rain clouds.

'Come to me, master,' Pandaras whispered. 'Save me.'

But the spark did not move. Perhaps it was afraid that Prefect Corin would knock it out of the air if it came too close.

Prefect Corin pointed with his staff at some weakness in the heretics' line, then saw that Pandaras was not looking at him. He came over and squatted down and said, almost kindly, 'We will walk straight through this. We count for nothing in the battle, and so we will be safe. Do you understand me?'

'I know that you are mad.'

'No. All this around us is madness, certainly. And Menas is mad, too – he has to be mad to be able to function at all – but I am quite sane. If you wish to survive, you must follow me.'

'If we wait here, then the heretics will come to us.'

'It is not the heretics we are seeking.' Prefect Corin's hand suddenly shot out and gripped the side of Pandaras's neck. 'He was here. Do not deny it. I know that he was here because he has taken away the ward.'

Pandaras shook his head a fraction. He wanted to look up, to appeal to that golden spark, but to do so would be to betray his master. Instead he stared straight into Prefect Corin's black eyes as the man's grip tightened on his neck.

'You will tell me,' Prefect Corin said. 'By the Preservers you will tell me or I will squeeze out your miserable life . . .' He had lifted his other hand above his head. Now he lowered it, and let go of Pandaras's neck. He said, 'I know that he was here. You could not have removed the ward by yourself. Think hard about whether you want to survive this, boy. If you tell me how Yamamanama removed the ward it might be possible. We both want the same thing. We both want to rescue him.'

Pandaras rubbed his bruised neck. He said, 'I believe that we have different ideas about my master's fate.'

Prefect Corin drew a length of cord from his tunic and tied one loop around Pandaras's wrist and another around his own. 'We are joined,' he said. 'For better or worse we are joined hand to hand, fate to fate. Let nothing put us asunder.' He stood up, jerking hard on the cord so that Pandaras was forced to rise too. 'There are threads of plastic through the cord,' Prefect Corin said. 'They can dull the keenest blade, and they have a certain low intelligence. Try to tamper with the knot and it will tighten its grip, and by and by cut off your hand.'

The cord which hung between them was no longer than the Prefect's arm. It would have to be enough. Pandaras turned right when the Prefect turned left, threw himself around a smooth spike of land coral so that the cord was stretched across it, and shouted into the rainy dark. 'Now, Yama! If you have ever loved me! Now!'

The spike shuddered and Pandaras fell backwards. He picked himself up at once. The cord hung from his wrist. It had been cut in half. Something with a dying golden glow was buried in a splintered crater in the land coral. Prefect Corin was bent over, his right hand pressed to his left eye. Blood ran down his cheek and dripped from the point of his jaw.

Pandaras took to his heels. He heard Prefect Corin shouting behind him, but did not look back. He turned right and left at random through the maze of land coral spikes, always choosing the narrowest path. The land coral had spread through the rubble downslope, forming a maze of arches and tunnels and caves. Pandaras scrambled down a narrowing funnel of rough stone, splashed through a bubble half full of stinking water, slid down a chute of stone slick as soap, and landed breathlessly at the edge of a road.

All around was the sound of giants walking the land. Flashes lit the underbellies of the sagging clouds. A big machine covered in spines skittered by in the distance. Whips of light flicked from its tiny head and raised pillars of fire and smoke wherever they touched. Pandaras picked himself up and ran on. He did not doubt that Prefect Corin would do everything in his power to find him.

There was a slow and steady drumbeat ahead, the crack and whir and whistle of rifle pellets and arbalest bolts all around. Suddenly soldiers were running down the road towards Pandaras. He raised his hands above his head, feeling as broad and wide as a house. But the soldiers were running full tilt in retreat and went straight past him. One, his dirty yellow face narrow as a knife blade, turned and yelled, 'The dead! The dead!' and then they were gone.

Pandaras stopped. He was at a crossroads. Rubble slumped at its four corners. Rain poured down out of a black sky, intermittently lit by white and red and green threads of light. The slow, muffled drumbeat was coming closer. He could not tell where it was and chose a direction at random and ran. Prefect Corin had taken his poniard; Pandaras missed it like a lost arm. The Prefect had the copy of the Puranas, too. All Pandaras had left was the fetish which the leader of the fisherfolk had given Yama, the ceramic coin, and his life.

Something flashed overhead and hit the long street ahead. Pandaras stopped, heartsick.

Far down the street, a column of naked men was marching stiffly in time to the slow, steady beat of a drum. Most of the men were horribly mutilated. Silvery spikes jutted from the tops of their skulls. One was headless, and the spike jutted from his breastbone instead.

It was a maniple of the dead, come back to fight their living comrades.

A sudden blade of fire blew a land coral formation to fiery ruin to the left flank of the column. Some brave gunner was trying to find the range. A handful of the naked dead fell and were trampled by their unheeding companions. Pandaras ran to the right. He scrambled over the crest of a slope and tumbled into a sandbagged pit where two soldiers stared at him in horror. One swung the bell-like muzzle of his balister towards Pandaras, and then there was a wave of earth and fire which tore the world away.

8 ~ In Dreams

As always, waking was the worst time. An escape from the horrors of dreams which were neither true dreams nor truly his into the reality of captivity and the wait for the prick of Dr Dismas's needle and the antidote to the drug which paralysed his body.

This time he woke not from nightmares but from a reverie woven from memories of the first of his adventures. For a happy moment, he thought that he was safe in the tower at the edge of the City of the Dead, deep in the foothills of the Rim Mountains. He had been brought there so that the curators of the City of the Dead, Osric and Beatrice, could tend his wounds. He had been very sick then, but he was even sicker now. He woke, expecting to see the hunting scene painted on the wooden ceiling of his little room and perhaps Beatrice's time-worn, kindly face, but found that he could not open his eyes. With a sharp pang of despair he remembered where he was; but then he remembered what he had done and felt his happiness well up again.

The Shadow was talking with Enobarbus. Yama had grown used to the way it carelessly used his body, and did not bother to listen to the long list of the atrocities which it was describing in gloating detail. That was not important. The battlegrounds along the river were no more than nightmares; the struggle for dominance of his own body was more immediate. From now on, he must be constantly alert, always ready to resist the Shadow's advances. For the first time, he began to think that he might be able to escape.

Yama had ceded much to the Shadow while concentrating on the search for Pandaras, but he had at last found Pandaras for the second time, on a battlefield at the far edge of the war and the prisoner of Yama's old enemy, Prefect Corin, who had somehow survived the destruction of his ship by the giant polyps. Not only had Yama rescued Pandaras again, even though it had meant destroying the machine he had been using, but he was certain that the boy had guessed who had helped him, for he had called to him by name. Yama had tried to kill or at least seriously wound the Prefect by the same stroke which had freed Pandaras, but it occurred to him now that perhaps that had not been wise. He was certain that Prefect Corin was searching for him, and Sergeant Rhodean had taught him that in the right circumstances the strength of one enemy can be used against another.

The Shadow finished its boasting, and Enobarbus told Dr Dismas that there were important matters which they must discuss.

'I am always at your service,' Dr Dismas said. 'After all, I am not allowed to leave this place.'

'Is the boy asleep?'

'He pretends to be, but I think he is not. Shall I administer the antidote?'

'No. Leave him. We will talk outside.'

After Dr Dismas and Enobarbus had left the room, the Shadow manifested itself in Yama's inner sight: a faint fluttering star growing slowly larger and becoming a bird, a luminous white dove fluttering through infinite darkness and suddenly changing again, a human figure now, pale hair fluttering around her face as she raised her face to look at him.

Yama found that he could open his eyes, but she was still there, leaning over him. His sweetheart, Derev. Her feathery hair was brushed back from her shaven forehead and caught in a plastic clasp. The finely carved blade of her face, her large black eyes, the soft lips of her small mouth pursed in the beginning of a smile. When she spoke, her words burned in his brain.

They are talking about us.

'Why do you never show your true self?'

Derev raised her slim arms above her head in a graceful movement, the swell of her small breasts lifting under her shift.

Is this repellent to you? I thought it would please you. I can remove this garment—

'Do as you wish. It is not a true representation, so it does not matter.'

The eidolon paused, one hand on the shoulder clasp of its shift. For a moment, Derev's face seemed to be filmed over with something nauseating.

That is true. You did not sleep with her although you very much wanted to. An odd denial, since you lost your virginity to a whore, and then slept with the cateran—

'That is in the past. I look forwards to the future when I will be reunited with Derev. I promised her that I would return when I had discovered the truth about my bloodline, and now I have learned more about myself than I care to know.'

Must I remind you of our relationship? Do not think that you are better than me, Yamamanama, or stronger, or more intelligent.

'Of course not. You do not need to remind me. But although you are better than me in every way, you still need me.'

For the moment.

'You are still very young. You are still learning. There is much that I can teach you.'

I will soon know all you know.

'Perhaps, but mere facts are useless if you do not know how to use them.'

I control thousands of machines at once. You can control only one, and that badly.

'I wondered if you knew what I was doing.'

I could prevent it. I could blind and deafen you. Be thankful for my mercy.

'I mean no harm by it. I grow bored while you are off fighting the war.'

Yet you have never used a machine to find out about the place where we are held.

'That is because I was afraid that Dr Dismas would discover my little trick.'

Fortunately, I have no such fears. I have learned much about this place, and I have discovered that we are in danger. Enobarbus does not trust us. Nor does he trust Dr Dismas.

'I know that Enobarbus is frightened of you. What are he and Dr Dismas talking about?'

Listen.

The eidolon of Derev and the brightly lit room faded into a view from somewhere above the tops of the trees which surrounded the grassy glade in which Dr Dismas and Enobarbus stood, with Enobarbus's guards in their black armour on one side and Dr Dismas's mutilated servants on the other. The sun was directly overhead. It was noon. A bird was singing somewhere, a cascade of falling notes repeated over and over.

'He will become something glorious,' Dr Dismas was saying. 'Something wonderful, if he is allowed. What he is now – that's nothing. A few silly tricks.'

'He is already a fearsome weapon,' Enobarbus said, baring his strong white teeth. The warlord held his ruined face at a proud angle. His mane was a tawny cascade tied back over one broad shoulder. He said, 'Without their machines, the armies ranged against us have no protection against our own machines and we can move our troops without detection. The long stalemate is over at last. We are grateful, Dismas. You must know that. You have this fine palace, these servants, these riches. You have your laboratories and your experiments. I do not approve of what you do, of course. I think it cruel, perhaps even mad. But you are free to do it.'

'He is a larva at the moment, no more. Let him grow. Let him shed his present form and achieve his full potential. He will sweep all before him. He will be terrible, mighty . . . You cannot imagine it. Sometimes I think that even I cannot imagine it. Give him the metals, the rare earths . . .'

'No, I think not. But what else do you need? If it is in my power I will grant it at once. After all, you have delivered a prize beyond compare. Perhaps more experimental subjects,' Enobarbus said. 'I do not think your experiments are going as well as you would like.'

Dr Dismas lit a cigarette. 'You surround me with spies, with men and women who pretend to be here to help me but who are, in plain truth, the wardens of this prison. It is amazing that I have done my work at all. The few creatures I have created are botched, it's true, but they are a beginning. I need more time and I cannot have it while fighting your war for you. Let the boy complete his transformation. He will become something that will amaze us all.'

'I do not need to be amazed. I need to rely on those who fight for me. I must have that, Dismas. I must have control.'

'You could have a sudden end to this long war. I offer you victory, complete and unqualified.'

'But not, perhaps, on my terms.'

'My paramour and its associates fight for the same cause as you, my dear Enobarbus. They are your allies, but they are not yours to command. The same applies to me. I am not subject to the orders of your officers, and I wish they would not interfere with my work. I hide nothing from them, yet they act as if I do.'

'You should stop pretending to be human, Dismas. You should acknowledge your true nature. People will not trust you as long as you pretend to be what you are not.'

Dr Dismas said sulkily, 'We are both creatures of forces greater than ourselves. You fear my paramour because it is so much more powerful than the aspect of the dead woman which you worship. Look at what I have done, at his bidding. Look at how well the war goes. If not for the boy—'

'He has helped. I will not deny it. But we were winning anyway, Dismas. Besides, the war is not important. We did not start it, and we reluctantly entered into it only to save ourselves. The truth which Angel brought to the world is more important than the war.'

'Because of this so-called truth you will have no troops, by and by. The newly changed will fight at first, to be sure, but soon enough they are consumed by this precious individuality of yours. They lose interest in everything but themselves.'

'Many still fight,' Enobarbus said softly. His deep voice was like the rumble of a great cat.

'O, when anyone can choose anything then of course some choose to fight. But not as many as you would like, eh? And as you progress upriver there are fewer and fewer unchanged bloodlines for you to recruit.'

'It is not the war that is important,' Enobarbus said stubbornly, 'but the truth we have to bring to everyone on Confluence. We had begun to spread it long before the war began. Everyone will recognize it once the mindless worship of the dead past is overthrown.'

'You speak of truths,' Dr Dismas said. 'She blinds you to the truth.'

'She revealed herself to me seventeen years ago,' Enobarbus said. 'I have followed her ever since. Perhaps you would like more books, Dismas. There are whole libraries at your disposal, if only you would show more cooperation.'

'My paramour was once one of the masters of this world. Many of its kind were destroyed and the rest are scattered, yet they remember more than is written in all the books in all the libraries of the world. Books are nothing. Angel should not have destroyed the remaining avatars. That was the first mistake, but it was made a long time ago and there is nothing to be done about it. The second mistake is to keep the boy as he is. Let him grow. I admit that he once tried to destroy her, but he was not mine then. Now I can control him, whatever he becomes, because he is my son.'

Enobarbus said, slowly and gravely, 'The avatars tried to destroy her. She had no choice but to fight back. Besides, she merely finished what was begun long ago. Most of the avatars were destroyed in the Age of Insurrection, by the things you claim as friends.'

Dr Dismas snapped up from his habitual stoop like a startled click-beetle, his yellow eyes gleaming in his sharp-featured face. He exclaimed grandly, 'But why are we arguing, when we both desire the same thing!'

Enobarbus said, 'I have no desire to argue, Dismas. As you say, we are on the same side. But you cannot do as you will. The boy and the thing you grow inside him are powerful, and because they are powerful, they are dangerous. Already they have accomplished much, and I see no need for them to grow more powerful. They must be contained.'

'A simple solution of certain rare earths. I delivered the formula days and days ago.'

'They are already powerful enough, Doctor. Do as you will with your experimental subjects, but do no more to the boy or to the thing inside him.'

'We fight side by side against the same enemy,' Dr Dismas said angrily. 'Once that enemy is defeated, will you still try and tell me what to do?'

He turned and strode off through the trees, followed by his servants. Enobarbus gestured to his physician and said, 'We must decide how this problem can be resolved, Agnitus.'

They grey-maned physician said, 'His metabolism is not unusual, my lord. It is a simple matter—'

Enobarbus shook his great maned head. 'Not here,' he said. 'Remember that the boy controls machines.'

'You were listening,' Dr Dismas said in Yama's ear. The sunny glade vanished. Dr Dismas was looking down at him. Sweat was sprinkled on the apothecary's forehead, islands of droplets scattered amongst the plaques of his disease. He said, 'I saw the machine. You had it fly high up, so that it would be lost in the glare of the sun, but I saw it all the same.' Fondness softened his voice. 'How sly. How sweet. Awake, Yamamanama! Awake, my sly, sweet boy! You have been the agent of another glorious victory in this ridiculous war! Awake!'

Three servants lifted Yama from the bed and carried him to the canopied chair, arranging his paralysed body amongst its cushions.

Dr Dismas said, 'Don't worry about Enobarbus. He is nothing, mere noise. We'll have no more need for him soon enough. I have plans . . .' He turned away from Yama and raised his voice. 'But I will not talk of that, surrounded as I am by spies!'

Yama said, 'Are you speaking to me, Doctor, or to the thing inside me?'

'I soon won't need to make a distinction. Men like to think that their minds are separate from their bodies. It is central to the creed of the heretics, for otherwise they could not contemplate attempting to live for ever. You make the same mistake, Yamamanama, but I'll soon show you just how wrong you are.'

'After the city of Aeolis was burned, some of its citizens blamed me. They set me on a funeral pyre and would have burnt me to death, but I was rescued by termites which sucked my would-be executioners into the ground. I thought that I had somehow called upon the termites to help me, but I know now that it was the Shadow, the thing you put inside me. It was saving itself. When I fell to the ground it tried to eat as many termites as it could find. The termites were partly machine, and it wanted the metals in their bodies to feed its growth.'

'I have never underestimated your intelligence, Yamamanama, but don't think that it will save you. I am your only hope. I'll get those rare earths for you. Then you will understand that there is no distinction between mind and body. But now you must exercise and eat, because in an hour you must sleep again. The war goes faster and faster, and no matter how much Enobarbus denies it, you are central to it.'

Derev stood at Dr Dismas's shoulder. She opened her mouth impossibly wide to show rows and rows of serrated white teeth and a rough red tongue that uncoiled from her mouth like a snake, glistening with saliva.

I will grow such teeth that will eat you whole, little one. We will be one flesh, one blood. There will be nothing that we cannot do.

9 ~ The Lazaret

Pandaras awoke to darkness and a confining pressure across his whole body. His left hand hurt horribly. He thrashed up, thinking that he was still buried, and found that the pressure was only a blanket which slipped to his waist, and that the darkness was not absolute, but punctured here and there by the glow of little lamps which slowly and solemnly swung to and fro like the pendulums of so many clocks. The whole world was rocking like a cradle. From all sides came the sound of men breathing or sighing. Someone was sobbing, a slow hiccoughing like the dripping of a faucet.

Pandaras reached for his left hand with his right . . . and could not find it. He patted at the coarse blanket that lay over his legs, as if he might discover it lying there like a faithful pet. He was still very sleepy, and did not understand what was wrong.

Something moved on the floor by his bed. He froze, thinking that Prefect Corin must be hiding there. But it was a larger man who reared up from the shadows, pale-skinned and flabby, and wearing only a pair of ragged trousers.

'Little master,' the man said in a soft, hoarse voice. 'Be quiet. Lie down. You are wounded and ill. You must rest.'

It was Tibor. Pandaras did not feel any surprise. He said, 'What have they done to me?'

Tibor made him lie down, and then told him all he knew. The two soldiers in the trench had not been badly hurt by the stray mortar round. They had dug themselves out and carried Pandaras to the lazaret, but by the time one of the chirurgeons had seen him the cord around his wrist had tightened so much that it had almost disappeared into his flesh. The hand had been too long without blood, and the chirurgeon had had to finish what the cord had begun.

'It was worth it to gain my freedom,' Pandaras whispered. 'In any case, many say that we do not have hands, but only the clawed feet of animals. For that reason we have learned to let our tongues do most of the work.'

He must make light of it, he felt, for he seemed to be at the brink of a great black pit. If he fell into it there might never be an end to despair. He struggled to sit up again, and said, 'It was worth it, Tibor, but we must not stay here. He will find me and I will not have that. We must leave—'

'Quiet, little master,' the hierodule said. 'You are very ill, and so are all those around you. You have been treated, and now you must sleep. The longer you sleep the better chance you have of living.'

Pandaras summoned up all the strength he had. 'Fetch my clothes,' he commanded. 'If I stay here I will have sacrificed my hand for nothing, and I could not bear that.'

His clothes were tied in a bundle at the foot of the cot. Tibor helped him dress; twice he reached for toggles with his left hand, which was not there. 'I have a whole set of new tricks to learn,' he said. And then, with sudden panic, 'The fetish! The fetish and the coin! Where are they? Were they thrown away? I must have them!'

Tibor hooked two fingers into the pocket of Pandaras's ragged shirt and drew out the coin, strung on its loop of leather, and the circlet of coypu hair and seed pearls.

'It is all I have, Tibor,' Pandaras said. He grasped the coin and it blazed so brightly that it hurt his eyes. 'He is close!' he cried. He kissed the burning coin, hung it around his neck and, with a thrill of disgust, slipped the fetish over his bandaged stump. 'There. I have nothing else, for Prefect Corin took the book, and I have paid for my lodging with my hand. We are ready to go.'

'Where will you go, little master?'

'We will find my master. The coin will lead us. You cannot easily escape me again, Tibor. I had to lose a hand to find you, and it is only fair that you stand at my left side from now on.'

Tibor said gently, 'It is my duty to tend to sick and the wounded, young master.'

'And I am certainly wounded.'

'You are but one of many. Many sick, and many wounded. Many need me, young master.'

'But I am foremost in your affections, I hope.' Pandaras felt a trifle dizzy. The floor seemed to pitch and sway beneath him. He sat down on the edge of the cot, but the sensation did not go away.

'Someone else needs me, little master,' Tibor said, and padded away into the darkness. His naked back and hairless head shone beneath the arc of a swinging lamp and then he was gone. Pandaras lay down, just for a little while, and was woken by Tibor, who was once again squatting beside the cot. It was as if a measure of whiteness had been poured into the darkness all around, not banishing it, but making it a little less absolute.

Tibor was smoking a cigarette. Pandaras twiddled the fingers of his right hand in the air and asked for a puff of it.

'You do not smoke, little master. Besides, although you are ill, you do not need this kind of medicine.'

'If I am as ill as you say then what more harm can it do? And if I'm not ill, as I claim, then it will calm me down. My stepfather, the first one, the one I don't like to talk about, he was a great smoker. A few more lungfuls of smoke will do no harm.'

Pandaras was very tired, but in a minute, if only the world would stop its slow way, in a minute he would get up and walk out of here. He did not care if Tibor chose to follow him or not. Prefect Corin would surely be looking for him. He had to go. He had to find his master . . .

Tibor placed the wet tip of the cigarette in Pandaras's fingers and helped him guide it to his mouth. The smoke was sweet and cloying. Pandaras choked on the first mouthful and coughed it out, but got the second down to the bottom of his lungs and slowly, luxuriously, exhaled.

'You see,' he said, 'it makes me much calmer.'

Tibor took the cigarette away and said, 'Then our bloodlines are very alike in their chemistries, little master, because that is why my people smoke. It helps us to accept our condition.' He drew on the cigarette; its brightening coal put two sparks in his large, black eyes. 'If not for this, I would have killed myself as a pup, as I think would all of my kind. And so my bloodline would have died out long ago, without the chance to purge its sin. The Preservers are both merciful and just, for when they made this world they set upon it the herb from which this tobacco is made, which allows my bloodline to endure its infamy and universal enslavement.'

'I thought it was just a habit,' Pandaras said sleepily. He did not resist when Tibor began to undress him.

'It is a habit of life, young master, like breathing. We need cigarettes as much as you need air.'

'We must escape. We must cross the lines of the enemy.'

'We have already done so, little master. Sleep now. If you can sleep, then it is a sign that you can begin to get well. Those too sick to sleep always die, in my experience. But I do not think you will die.'

'I want—'

But Pandaras was too tired to complete the thought, and he slept.

Day by day Pandaras grew stronger, and at last he was strong enough to realize how sick he had been. He had been sicker than most of those around him. When he was at last able to sit up and take notice of his surroundings, in the late afternoon of the sixth or seventh day of his confinement, he saw that this part of the lazaret was empty except for himself and a heavily bandaged man three cots over in the same row. A machine like a cat-sized mosquito squatted over the bandaged barrel of the man's chest, circulating his blood through loops of clear tubing; his breathing was ragged and loud.

The coin was no brighter, but the dots and dashes of light within it were more active than ever, scurrying to new patterns, freezing for only a heartbeat, and scurrying about again. Pandaras watched for hours, trying to understand their dance.

In the night, the man tended by the mosquito-machine suffered some kind of crisis. He was taken away amidst a flurry of chirurgeons and charge hands. Pandaras lay awake for hours afterwards, but the man did not return.

The next morning, Pandaras was taken up on deck by Tibor, and saw at last what the hierodule had been trying to tell him. The lazaret was travelling downriver. It had been taken by the heretics.

At the Marsh of the Lost Waters, the Great River divided into many shallow, sinuous, slow-moving streams. The lazaret was following one of these. It was less than a league across, and stained red-brown with silt. Trees grew densely on either side, half-submerged in the sluggish current, their leaves vivid green in the bright sunlight. The sun burned off the water. It was very hot and very humid. Pandaras broke into a sweat at the slightest exertion and he was content to sit with Tibor under an awning of crimson silk, listening to one or another of the discussion classes which were part of the process the heretics called Re-Education and Enlightenment.

The lazaret was a barge as wide and flat as a field. A flying bridge crowned its blunt bow; gun emplacements nestled like pips at regular intervals along its sides; a decad of pods which housed reaction motors swelled at its stern. A pentad of machines followed its wide wake as birds might follow a fishing boat. They were as fat as barrels and entirely black, with clusters of mobile spines fore and aft. They made a slow fizzing sound as they moved through the air. Sometimes one would break off and make a wide slow loop above the forest canopy before rejoining its fellows. At night they were each enveloped in a faint red nimbus, like a constellation of halo stars.

There were other machines too. Small silvery teardrops that zipped from one place to another like squeezed watermelon pips; black angular things like miniature mantids that stalked the white-scrubbed, tar-caulked planks of the deck on long, thin legs. And a thing of jointed cubes and spheres that was slung in a hammock on the bridge, close to the huge wheel that, manned by three sailors, controlled the barge's rudders. The plastic casings of its components had once been white, but were now stained and chipped. It was a very ancient machine, Pandaras learned, and it had control of the barge; many of the smaller machines were slaved to it. It seemed that these machines were not the servants of the world, as in Ys, but were the equals of or even superiors to the flesh and blood heretics.

The soldiers who guarded the prisoners and otherwise manned the barge were of a recently changed bloodline from the lower slopes of the Rim Mountains. They were a tall, muscular people covered in thick white fur. They wore only elaborate harnesses of leather straps and buckles and pouches. Their narrow faces, with long muzzles and small brown eyes that peered from beneath heavy brow ridges, were as black and wrinkled as old leather, and all were heavily tattooed with silvery swirls and dots. They called themselves the Charn or the Tchai. Although of a single bloodline and a single culture, they were divided into two distinct tribes which, by taboo, never intermarried: one herded llamas and goats in the birch forests; the other hunted in the

97

wilderness of rock and snow above the tree-line. Pandaras, who still believed that he had the right to talk with anyone, discovered that they had a rich store of tragedies concerning star-crossed lovers from the two tribes, and blood feuds which lasted for generations. To their amusement, he elaborated several versions of his own upon these eternal themes.

The white-furred guards did not like the close, foetid heat. When they were not patrolling the deck, they sprawled in front of electric fans, their red tongues lolling. They were a short-tempered people, and the heat made them even more irritable. Those officers captured with the lazaret had already been killed, but the guards would sometimes make the prisoners line up, pluck someone from the ranks at random, and execute him. One night, one of the guards went mad and tried to storm the bridge. There was a brief but furious firefight before he was shot. More than thirty prisoners were killed or wounded in the crossfire; all were unceremoniously tipped over the side for the caymans and the catfish.

Pandaras asked Tibor why he had not been executed when the lazaret had been captured. 'You're something like a priest, neh? I think that it would make you more dangerous than any officer.'

Tibor scratched at the long, vertical scars on his chest while he thought about this. At last he said, 'I am only a slave, little master. I am not a leader of men. Besides, the heretics believe that to convert one such as me is a great prize.'

'Surely there were other hierodules working in the lazaret when it was captured? But I see no others now.'

'They fled, little master. But I could not leave you.'

'You know that I am not your master, Tibor!'

The hierodule did not reply.

Pandaras tried a new argument. 'I am grateful that you are here, Tibor. But as an equal. As a friend.'

'You could not be a friend to one such as I, little master. What am I? Lower than a worm, because my ancestors took the side of the feral machines during the Age of Insurrection.'

'You are a man, Tibor. As much a man as anyone here. Don't put the burden of your life on my head.'

Again Tibor did not reply. He took out the little plastic pouch from the waistband of his trousers and, with maddening slowness, began to roll a cigarette.

Only the weakest and most seriously wounded prisoners lay in the close heat and stink of the black air below deck. The rest camped under awnings rigged from brightly coloured canvas or silk and scattered across the broad deck of the barge like flowers strewn across a field. They took turns to trawl for fish and shrimp, which were shredded and added to the cauldrons of sticky rice or maize porridge, but most of their waking hours were taken up with Re-Education and Enlightenment.

The discussion classes formed just after dawn, and often continued beyond sunset. Although the prisoners were told that the classes were voluntary, everyone knew that those who refused to take part were likely to be chosen by the guards for execution. They reminded Pandaras of the penny school he had occasionally attended as a cub. His education had ended when his father had disappeared, for the man his mother had married after that had refused to waste money on luxuries like learning. It had been no great loss. Pandaras had always hated the stifling atmosphere of the school, and the rote recitations of the Puranas which had taken up much of the time had for him almost killed their beautiful and terrible stories. He did not mind that he was unlettered, for his people had always kept their stories and songs in memory rather than on paper – 'written in air rather than on stone', as their tradition had it, for what was forgotten did not matter, and that which was of value was kept alive in the mouths and instruments of a thousand singers long after the unmourned death of the author.

The classes contained between four and forty prisoners, and each was led by a pedagogue. These were all of the same round-faced, grey-skinned bloodline, from a city several hundred leagues downriver which had achieved enlightenment, as they called it, early in the war. Most – they proudly admitted it – were no more than children, so young that they had yet to determine their sex. They were a small race, smaller even than Pandaras. They dressed in loose black tunics and trousers, and their glossy black hair was tied back in elaborate pigtails with scraps of white silk. They ruled the prisoners with an iron will. Those who walked away from the discussion classes in disgust or anger were immediately chased by the pedagogues, who screamed at them and whipped them around the ankles with sharp bamboo canes; those who did not return or who tried to fight back were taken away by the guards, shot, and kicked over the side.

At first, Pandaras had a great deal of trouble understanding what the pedagogues were trying to teach him. He sat next to Tibor in the sweltering heat in a kind of stupor, his stump throbbing under a slithery, quasi-living dressing which absorbed the discharges of blood and pus, and which Tibor changed twice a day. His head ached from the ever-present odour of burnt fish-oil from the barge's reaction motors and the sunlight which reflected in splinters from the river and, most of all, from the high, sing-song cadences of the pedagogue as it urged, cajoled, corrected and harangued its charges.

Each morning the discussion classes started with a chant of the slogan of the heretics. *Seize the day!* It echoed out across the river, sometimes lasting no more than a minute, sometimes lasting for an hour, becoming as meaningless as breathing but always ending at the same moment in all the classes scattered across the barge's broad deck.

After that came the long hours of argument in which the pedagogues set out some trivial truth and used it as a wedge to open a door on to a bewildering landscape. It seemed to Pandaras that everything was allowed except for that which was forbidden, but it was difficult to know which was which because there were no rules. The other prisoners had the same problem, and all their objections and expressions of bafflement were met by the same answer.

'You do not see,' the pedagogue would say in its sweet, high-pitched voice, 'because you cannot see. You cannot see because you have not been allowed to see. You have not been taught to see. You are all blind men, and I will open your eyes for the first time.'

At the heart of the heretics' philosophy, like the black hole at the centre of the Eye of the Preservers, was a single negation. It was so simple and so utterly against the self-evident truth of the world that many of the prisoners simply laughed in amazement every time the pedagogues repeated it. It was that the Puranas were not the thoughts of the Preservers, set down to reveal the history of the Universe and to determine the actions of right-thinking men, but were instead a fabrication, a collection of self-justifying lies spewed forth by the victors of a great and ancient war that was not yet over. There would be no resurrection into eternal life at the end of all time and space, because the Preservers had fled from the Universe and could not return. They had created Confluence, but they had abandoned it. The fate of each man did not lie within the purlieu of the infinite mercy and power of the Preservers, but in his own hands. Because the Preservers could not return from the Eye, they no longer existed in the Universe, and so each man must be responsible for his own fate. There was no hope but that which could be imagined; no destiny but that which could be forged.

The pedagogues were more fervent in their unbelief than any of the pillar saints or praise chanters who had devoted their lives to exaltation of the glories of the Preservers. They would allow no argument. This negation was the central fact that could not be denied; from it, all else followed. From the first, Pandaras was quite clear on what the heretics did not believe, but it took him a long time to understand what they did believe, and once he had it, it was so simple that he was amazed that he had failed to grasp it at once. Like the woman in the pictures in his master's copy of the Puranas, the heretics wanted to live for ever.

Seize the day! It was a plea aimed directly at the base of the brain, where the residue of the animal self was coiled like a snake, insatiable and quite without a conscience. Do anything in your power to survive; bend your entire life towards it. The Universe was an insensate and hostile place; worlds were so few and remote that they counted for nothing; almost anywhere you went would kill you instantly and horribly. Therefore, life was infinitely precious, and every man's life was more precious still, a subtle and beautiful melody that would never be repeated. The heretics wished to revive the old ways of indefinitely prolonging life, so that everyone could fulfil their destiny as they pleased.

For Pandaras, whose bloodline was short-lived compared to others on Confluence, no more than twenty-five years at most, it was a seductive song. 'Written in air', yes, but suppose it could be stone instead! What sublime songs and stories he could make if all time were at his disposal, and what joy he would have in seeing them spread and change and enrich his fame!

Once this thought took root, Pandaras paid more attention to what the pedagogue told the discussion class. For amusement, he told himself. To pass the time.

The heretics admitted no gods, but believed that each man could become a god – or better than a god – with enough effort. Any God of the First Cause in a universe such as this must surely be counted a failure, the pedagogue argued, because He must be omniscient and yet allow immense suffering. Most of the Universe was uninhabitable. All men died, and most died badly.

'If the Preservers care about their creation,' the pedagogue told Pandaras and his companions, 'then either they wish to take away evil and are unable, or they are unable and unwilling, or they are neither willing nor able, or they are both willing and able. If they are willing and unable then they are feeble, which is not in accordance with claims made for their nature; if they are able yet unwilling then they are envious of the condition of their creation, which is equally at variance with their nature; if they are both unwilling and unable then they are both envious and feeble, and therefore cannot be what they are claimed to be by their worshippers; and yet if they are both willing and able, which conditions alone would satisfy the claims of those who believe in the omnipotence of the Preservers, then from what source come the evils of this world? From what place flow all the hurts and trials which you have all suffered? Why are we victorious, and why are you defeated? All the evil in the world can be accounted for by one principle, and that is the nature of the Universe of which it is a part. And yet that evil is not absolute. It is well known that a wilderness can be tamed and cultivated and made to yield crops. And so with any wilderness, even to the end of space and time, for there is no limit to the transforming power of human reason and human will. And given these two things, nature and human reason, why, there is no need for the Preservers, or any other gods.'

Several of the prisoners in Pandaras's discussion class passionately disputed this argument. They said that although the Preservers had given men free will, it did not mean that men had infinite power, and even if they could gain infinite power it did not mean that they would then be unchanged, as the heretics appeared to believe. For surely anyone who could live for ever would be changed by the simple fact of becoming immortal, and so would no longer be subject to the fears of ordinary men. The pedagogue listened to their arguments and smiled and said that they had not yet opened their ears, that they were still in the thrall of the propaganda of their priests and civil service, who together conspired to assign every man a place and punish those who tried to change things because change threatened their power.

This seemed to be no more than what many in Ys said behind the backs of the magistrates and priests, Pandaras thought, but he was still disturbed by these new ideas. He knew that Yama would have an answer to them, but even as he thought this he remembered that Yama had also questioned the motives of the Preservers in making Confluence and setting the ten thousand bloodlines upon it in the moment before they had stepped from the Universe. The praise singers had it that the Preservers had extended their mercy to the races of servants they had raised up from animals; these they had set on this world to achieve what destiny they could for good or ill, in the sight of the Eye into which the Preservers had vanished. But why then was the world so bound in custom and tradition? We are the strength of the city, Pandaras thought, and yet we are regarded by higher bloodlines as no more than vermin. And what of the indigenous races such as the fisherfolk or the mirror people, or the unclean scavengers and ghouls who roamed the cloacae of Ys? These races had been raised up by the Preservers, yet did not contain their breath and so could never achieve the change – enlightenment, in this grey mannikin's argot – by which a bloodline dominated by unchanging habit becomes a nation of individuals. He remembered with a pang of shame the first day with his master, after they had escaped *The Crossed Axes*, when he had poured scorn upon the unchanged refugees who camped by the widening margin of the river. Was it the intention of the Preservers that some bloodlines should oppress others? Surely the Preservers had set themselves so high that all bloodlines were equal to them, no matter how lowly or how enlightened. The heretics had one thing right: all the world's peoples should have the chance to rise as high as they could. If the Preservers had created a world so manifestly unfair, then surely they had done so through incompetence or spite. Surely they could not be as powerful as the priests and bureaucrats claimed.

Pandaras forgot in that moment that although his master was more powerful than many men, he did not deny that the Preservers were more powerful still, so powerful that men might never riddle their actions. Instead, the slogans of the heretics burnt like fever in his blood. Seize the day! Live for ever! It did not matter if you were changed, for you would still remember what you had been, as a man fondly remembers his childhood. And what man would wish to remain a child for ever?

One man in Pandaras's discussion class was eager to deny the Preservers. Not out of belief of conviction, but out of fear, for he was anxious to save himself. From the first he agreed with everything the pedagogue said, without understanding anything, and mocked his fellow prisoners for stubbornly clinging to their outmoded and foolish beliefs.

He was a skinny fellow with leathery brown skin and a cayman's untrustworthy grin. He wore only dirty breeches and a mail shirt, and stank like river water kept too long in a barrel. He had been badly seared when his carronade had jammed and exploded: his hand was gloved in a white plastic bag and a bandage was wrapped around his head; the right side of his chest and his face were livid with burnscars; his right eye was as milk-white as a boiled egg. He was shunned by the other prisoners and was always trying to wheedle favours from the guards, who either ignored him or chased him away with swift, judicious blows. His name was Narasimha, but everyone called him the Jackal. Even the pedagogue grew tired of the Jackal's constant gabble of unthinking agreement, and one day turned on him.

'You do not worship the Preservers?' it said in its sweet, high voice.

'That's so, your honour,' the Jackal said eagerly. 'Men of my kind, we've never liked 'em. That's why we are always hunted down by the authorities, because we refuse to bend our knee to the false idols of their temples. We were delighted when your people finally silenced the last avatars because we saw that it might be an end to the rule of the priests. And now I see it's true, and my heart lifts on a flood of happiness.'

Pandaras thought that as usual the Jackal dissembled, giving up half the truth in service of a greater lie. It was clear from the arrowhead tattoos on the man's fingers that he had been a member of one of the galares which operated in the docks of Ys, hijacking cargoes, smuggling cigarettes and other drugs, running protection and kidnapping rackets. The Jackal had probably joined the army to escape justice. Perhaps he had betrayed his own kind – it was clear that he believed in nothing but his own self, and one or two of the prisoners said, out of earshot of any pedagogue or soldier, that the Jackal was an ideal candidate for a heretic, for he would betray the Universe to save his worthless hide.

'What do you worship,' the pedagogue asked the Jackal sweetly, 'if you do not worship the Preservers?'

A ripple of interest stirred the circle of the discussion class, like a breeze lifting and dropping the leaves of a tree. The Jackal did not notice it.

'Why, your honour, captain . . . for a long time I did not worship anything. The only things I held dear were my family and my many friends, as any good honest man might tell you, but I saw nothing of worth beyond them. But now, by happy circumstances, I find myself in a position I could not have imagined then. My bloodline is one of the oldest on Confluence, one of the first to have changed. We have always lived in Ys, and those in power hate us because of our ancient and honourable pedigree. But now I feel that I have been changed again, that the change for which we are envied is nothing compared to what I feel now. Why, I'm even happy that I lost my eye and use of my hand, because it is a small enough price to have paid for the riches you shower upon us day by day.'

'Then you worship nothing?'

'Your honour, as I said, my people never worshipped the Preservers. But it does not mean we are not capable of worship.'

'Money, mostly,' someone whispered, loud enough for the rest of the class to hear it. Most laughed.

The Jackal glared around about with his one good eye. It was yellow, with a vertically slitted pupil.

'You see, your honour,' the Jackal said, 'how jealous others are of me. Because I understand what you want of us while these others only pretend it. They are not worthy of your truths. You take me, your honour, and feed these others to the fish in the mud at the bottom of the river.'

'What is it you understand?' the pedagogue asked. 'Every day you tell me that you are full of praise for what you hear, and I am glad. But I would like to know what you understand of the hard questions I put to all of you here. I would like to know how high you have been raised.'

The men in the circle nudged each other, seeing that some kind of trap was closing on the hapless Jackal, who glared at them again and hissed through his long jaw. 'Higher than these scum, and they know it, your honour. Put that question to them. I'll wager none of them will be able to answer it.'

'There is no competition here,' the pedagogue said. 'We set no man against any other. That is one part of our strength. The other is our certainty. Tell me one thing of which you are certain.'

'Why, your honour, I know that the Preservers are nothing but shit compared to your people. I know that I worshipped nothing because nothing was worthy of my worship, but I know now that I have found something I will worship with all my heart and all my breath. Let me serve your people and I will grace them with such praise that all will know their fame. It is your people that I worship. I love you all more than life itself, and will serve you in any way I can, and hope to gain some small measure of your glory. It is you, you! You and no other!'

And to the disgust of the others, the Jackal threw himself forwards and tried to kiss the pedagogue's feet. But the small creature drew them into the angles of its knees and looked at the man and said, 'There is nothing more that I can tell you. Go now. Leave the class. Do not be afraid. If you truly understand what I teach, you must know that you are free to do as you will.'

The Jackal raised his head. The bandage around his head was unravelling, and one end hung down by the milky, cooked eye which stared from a mess of black scabs and raw red skin. He said, 'Then there is nothing I want more than to sit at your feet, your honour, and absorb your wisdom.'

'I have nothing more to teach you,' the pedagogue said. 'I will not say it again, for I hope I am not mistaken about your ability to understand me. If you do not understand me then your punishment will be swift and terrible.'

There had been no signal, but suddenly two guards were walking across the wide white deck towards the discussion class. The Jackal looked at them, looked at the pedagogue. 'Your honour . . . captain . . . If I have angered you in any way, then I repent of it at once.'

'You have not angered me. You have filled my heart with joy. Go now. You are free.'

Pandaras thought with a chill that it was a subtle and cruel trick. The pedagogue had trapped the Jackal with his own lies, had punished him by giving him exactly what he wanted.

The Jackal was refused food from the cauldrons because it was for the prisoners and he was a free man, and likewise the guards mocked him when he tried to beg some of their rations, crowning him king of the free men with a wreath of water lily flowers, and then driving him away with blows from the butts of their carbines and partisans. The Jackal did not dare approach the pedagogues, and besides, it was unlikely that he could digest the fibrous pap which they sucked up. For the next two days he wandered from class to class, followed by several of the small, silvery machines, and some time on the third night of his freedom he disappeared.

One evening, as the prisoners ate their meagre ration of maize porridge salted with scraps of fish, a man of Pandaras's bloodline, a veteran by the name of Tullus, came over and sat beside Pandaras and struck up a conversation. It seemed that they had once lived within two streets of each other in Ys, and had worked at different times in the same foundry, casting and repairing armour. They talked about people they had known and stories they shared in common, and at last Tullus reached the point of his visit.

'The guards killed the Jackal, brother. They sport with us and eventually they will kill us all.'

'You did not know Narashima, I think. He would have lain with a dog if it would have turned a penny or extended his life by a day.'

'Many join the army,' Tullus said seriously, 'and every man has his reason. But all unite in a single cause. Whatever else the Jackal was, he was foremost a soldier. He was one of us and the heretics mocked him and killed him.'

'I saw little help from his fellows,' Pandaras said.

'All feared that if they aided the Jackal, then they would share his fate. The heretics divide us, brother, and one by one they will kill us.'

The two men fell silent as one of the guards went past, his clawed feet scratching the deck, his harness jingling. One of the little angular machines stalked stiff-legged after him. Pandaras thought that if the discipline of the army had been atomized, then the heretics had won. They had made their point. When it came to confronting death, there was no society of men, only individuals.

Tullus watched the guard pace away into the gloom between groups of prisoners. He whispered, 'The lazaret goes slowly because the heretics wish to extend our torture as long as possible, but it goes downriver all the same. At last it will reach the end of the Marsh of the Lost Waters. There are millions of heretics in the cities beyond, and we will be given up to them for their sport.'

Pandaras had heard many fantastic stories about the tortures and obscenities which the heretics inflicted on their prisoners: trials by combat; vivisections and other experiments; forced matings between different bloodlines. He told Tullus, 'The army makes up many stories about the enemy, brother, so that its soldiers will fight hard to avoid capture.'

Tullus nodded. 'Well, that's true up to a point,' he said. 'But the point is that there must be a foundation to any story or song. You know that, brother. All of us know that.'

'The rumours about the heretics are founded in hatred and fear,' Pandaras said. 'Much may flow from those sources, but none of it good.'

Tullus looked hard at Pandaras. He was a grizzled man of some fifteen or sixteen years, with white around his muzzle. He said, 'You are not a soldier. What are you doing here?'

Pandaras crooked his left arm, thrusting the stump forwards. The bandage wrapped around it was gorged on black blood and throbbed gently to Pandaras's own heartbeat. 'I have lost as much as any man here,' he said.

'Not your life,' Tullus said. 'Not yet.'

'I've lost something as dear to me,' Pandaras said. 'My master was taken by the heretics. He is a great warrior, and I am his squire. I'm going to find him and free him.'

'You were hurt when he was captured?'

'No, that was later. A flier took him away, and I have been looking for him ever since.'

'Where was this? He was a cateran, I suppose. What division was he attached to? Or was he a scout?'

'He was on his way to war—'

'And was taken before he could kill a single heretic? An unlucky man rather than a hero, Pandaras. Heroes need luck as much as they need strength. Perhaps you have misplaced your loyalty, neh?'

'He will save the world yet,' Pandaras said stubbornly. 'I can say no more, but I know that he will.'

'You have a chance with us. Stay here and you have no chance at all. They will kill you, Pandaras. Have no faith in anything they promise.' Tullus looked around and whispered, 'Some of us are planning to escape.'

'We are surrounded by marsh and jungle.'

'Where better place to escape? I fought here when I first joined the army. I know how to find my way. Once we are in the marshes we are safe. But first we must escape.'

'Good luck to you, but I think I will stay here. I'm a city boy. I've no love of parks, let alone wilderness. And perhaps you forget, but I have only one hand.'

'We will all help each other. If you love freedom you will help us. If you love the Preservers you will help us.'

'I'm not a soldier, Tullus, as you've pointed out. I'm only a servant who is looking for his master. How could I help you?'

'You have the hierodule. And the hierodule can help us. He can talk with the machines, and they are the real guards here. You will command him to make the machines leave this place, and we will kill the hairy ones and the little grey-skinned motherfuckers.'

'He is not mine,' Pandaras said. 'Command him yourself, if you can.'

Tullus raised himself into a crouch. His black lips drew back from his teeth. Pandaras stiffened. He could smell the old soldier's anger, and he rose to match Tullus's posture. They glared at each other, faces a handspan apart.

Tullus said, 'The hierodule refused me. That is why I am asking you, boy.'

'Perhaps you asked him the wrong question. Tell him that he is under no obligation to me. Tell him that he was freed when the ship on which he served was destroyed.'

Tullus stared hard at Pandaras, and Pandaras stared right back at him, his blood beating heavily in his head. He refused to be intimidated because he felt that it would somehow fail his master. Then Tullus smiled and turned and said, 'Look! In spite of all the powers they boast of possessing, they cannot hide the truth from us.'

The Rim Mountains had swallowed the last light of the sun, and the Eye of the Preservers had risen a handspan above the trees along the edge of the river: the dull red swirls of its accretion disc; the pinprick black point at the centre, the dwelling place of the Preservers.

'The Preservers watch us always,' Tullus said. 'Pray with me, brother. Pray for our deliverance.'

No guards or machines were near. Pandaras made the necessary gestures of obeisance and whispered the responses, but his heart was empty. The Preservers had fled the Universe. Light fell faster than they, so that they could still watch their creation but could no longer interfere with it. They had set it in motion and abandoned it, as a child might turn away from a wind-up toy, leaving it to heedlessly march down the street. Praying was an empty gesture, and Pandaras felt as if there was a gulf a thousand leagues wide between himself and the man who prayed raptly and joyfully beside him.

The tragedy is not that we fall in love with that which does not love us, he thought, but that we cease to love. He was shivering. He thrust his good hand between his thighs, but he could not stop shivering. Tullus said, 'What is it, brother? Don't be afraid. Say the final benison with me.'

'You say it, Tullus.'

'You young fool. You believe them, don't you?'

'We are the strength of the city, Tullus. But why are we despised?'

'You are less than the Jackal,' Tullus said in disgust. 'He only pretended to believe the heretics' cant, but with you it is no pretence.' His face contorted and he spat on the deck between Pandaras's feet. He said, 'There are many like me. Tell anyone of this, betray me, and one of my friends will kill you.'

Pandaras slept badly that night, although Tibor promised to keep watch. When he woke near dawn he saw with a pang of dread that more than half the prisoners were gone. Tibor was sitting cross-legged in a kind of trance; it was the closest he came to sleep. When Pandaras shook him, the hierodule stirred and said at once that he had seen nothing.

'Perhaps they escaped to the shore,' Pandaras whispered.

Tibor said softly, 'I do not think so, little master.'

Tears were swelling in the hierodule's downwardly slanting eyes. Pandaras said, 'You did see something. Tell me.'

'Everyone slept. Even I, who never sleeps, passed from this world for a little while. The machines may have had something to do it. Then you woke me, and the men were gone.'

A little later, Pandaras said, 'You could have helped them, Tibor.'

'My place is with you, little master. You have not yet recovered from your wound.'

'Would you have helped them, if I had ordered it? Could you have told the heretics' machines to quit the lazaret?'

Tibor considered this, and at last said gently, 'I am yours to command, little master, but I do not think I can command the machines of our captors. I was fitted with an induction loop when I entered the service of the temple, but it was designed to interface with shrines. Shrines are machines, it is true, but there are many kinds of machine.'

'You never tried?'

'It did not occur to me, little master.'

'They might still kill you,' Pandaras said. 'Your entire life has been spent in the service of the Preservers. Surely that makes you a natural enemy of the heretics.'

'Not at all. As I told you before, I am seen as a great prize. In the first days after the lazaret was captured, little master, before you woke from your coma, the pedagogues spent a great deal of time talking with me. They hope to convert me, as they have already converted the captain of the lazaret.' Tibor pointed towards the flying bridge at the bow, at the big, jointed machine in its hammock. 'It still hopes that I will join with it. But I already serve you, little master. I have no one else to serve. If the *Weazel* was not destroyed, then surely Captain Lorquital would have put in at Ophir with her cargo. But no one had seen her, little master, although I asked many people at the docks while I was waiting to board the ship which took me downriver to the lazaret.'

'They died quickly, Tibor, if that's a comfort.'

'Except for Phalerus,' Tibor said.

The remaining prisoners were subdued. There were no discussion classes that day. Just before sunset, the barge entered a wide canal, and an hour later drew into the docks of Baucis, the City of Trees.

10 ~ 'Everyone Now Living May Never Die'

As soon as the barge had been made fast to the wharf, the guards began to move amongst the prisoners, telling them that they were free to go. 'This is a city of free men!' they said, grinning fearsomely. 'Take up your own lives. No one is responsible for you but yourselves.'

'If only Tullus had waited,' Pandaras said to Tibor bitterly, 'he and his fellows would have had their wish.'

Many of the prisoners were reluctant to obey the guards, fearing that this was a trick. One man went mad and refused to move when the guards started to force them towards the stern, where the gangways to the dock had been fixed. He sat down in the middle of the deck with his arms wrapped around his chest, rocking back and forth and screaming. A guard shot him in the head, picked up his body and slung it over the side. After that, the prisoners had no choice but to gather up their few belongings and walk out into the city.

Baucis had once been a patchwork of little woods and hills, but new roads had been driven everywhere without regard for traditional boundaries, and many of the woods had been cut down. In those that survived, the heart trees had been felled and the woven platform houses of the original inhabitants had been torn down and replaced by straggling encampments of tents and shacks. Sewage ran in open channels that were often blocked by the bodies of animals and men. The air was hazed with the smoke of thousands of fires. Floating platforms and streams of draft animals and crowds of men jostled along red clay roads in the harsh glare of arc lights strung from stripped tree-trunks. Steam wagons clanked and groaned and belched clouds of black smoke as they dragged three or four overladen trailers behind them. Stores and taverns, gaming palaces and whorehouses, all with tall, brightly painted false fronts, had been thrown up along the roads, and barkers and shills called to the crowds from platforms or windows or balconies. There were many apothecaries, surgeries and clinics. One offered, mysteriously, *Whole Body Immersion and Electrotherapy*; another, *Intestinal Irrigation*. Machines spun above the crowded roads, zipping about on obscure errands, and slogans were projected high in the air, in glowing letters each as big as a man. *Seize The Day. Everyone Now Living May Never Die.* Higher still were the archipelagoes of the floating gardens which had once been the homes of Baucis's scholar-saints, strings of sharply stamped shadows in the orange sky-glow.

Pandaras was tired and his left arm hurt badly; Tibor had stripped the quasi-living dressing from the stump, leaving only a light bandage. He followed the hierodule without question, and presently found himself amongst the ruins of the city's sacred wood. The circle of giant sequoias, said to have been as old as the world, had been cut down, and decads of men were sawing planks from their carcasses by the light of huge bonfires, but the shrine was still there. It was a black disc ten times Pandaras's height, standing at the centre of a big circular platform crafted from a hundred different kinds of wood. The platform was scarred with deep, charcoal-blistered trenches made by the reflected beams of energy weapons and pocked with thousands of splintered gouges and impact holes from ricocheting slugs and rifle pellets, and blasphemies and cabbalistic signs had been carved into the polished ancient planks, but the huge black disc of the shrine itself, being only partly of this world, was inviolate.

Pandaras sat down at the edge of the platform, on wood worn smooth by the footsteps of millions of pilgrims and petitioners. He said wearily, 'Why have you brought us here?'

'We were told that nothing is forbidden, little master,' Tibor said, 'so surely one might still consult the shrines.'

'What use is that, without a priest?' Pandaras said, and then he understood. 'Will it speak with you?'

'The avatar of this shrine was destroyed ten thousand years ago, in the wars of the Age of Insurrection. But the shrine itself is still active.'

Pandaras sat in the shadows at the perimeter of the platform while Tibor attempted to commune with the shrine. He meant to keep watch, but it was long past midnight and he was very tired. He fell asleep, and woke with a start to find the hierodule squatting in front of him and a familiar warmth against his chest.

'There is no reply,' Tibor said mournfully. 'Something has destroyed the indices.'

Pandaras reached inside his torn shirt and lifted out the ceramic coin. Little specks and lines of light filled it from edge to edge, frozen in a static pattern.

'It doesn't matter,' he said. 'I know that my master is here.'

11 ~ The Camp

Pandaras and Tibor spent the rest of the night close by the ruins of the sacred grove, although their sleep was fitful because of the whine and clatter of the mechanical saws wielded by the men who were dismembering the carcasses of the giant sequoias. They wandered the brawling streets of the city for most of the next day in search of some sign of Yama, but found nothing. They had no money for food or lodging, and it seemed that nothing was free in the city. Pandaras tried to earn a few coins by singing at a street corner, but passers-by either ignored him or cursed him roundly. One woman riding by stopped her sumpter long enough to explain to Pandaras that everyone must be responsible for their own self, and that by begging he was behaving like an animal.

'I have a hierodule, dominie. Is there no work for him?'

'No man is a slave here,' the woman said. 'You should try one of the camps at the edge of the city. You'll find more of your kind there. Go quickly before someone decides to organize a lynch party and get rid of you.' And before Pandaras could ask her another question she flicked the sumpter's reins and rode on through the swarming crowds.

It was almost midnight when Pandaras and Tibor finally reached one of the camps in the jungle at the edge of Baucis. A guard hailed them a long way from its perimeter and led them down a tangle of winding paths to a neatly arranged compound, with huts and tents on three sides of a square of trampled dirt. The leader of the camp was a giant of a woman who had lost both her legs but went everywhere on crutches, indefatigable and full of energy. Her name – or the short, childhood version of her name, for her bloodline chose names that grew and reflected their experiences – was Calpa. She listened to

Pandaras's story while he and Tibor devoured bowls of starchy, unsalted vegetable curry, and told him that this was a bad place to be.

'The city is full of newly changed bloodlines. They are dangerous because they are burning with holy fire. Mobs sniff out those who do not agree with them and hang or burn or stone them. We try to keep ourselves to ourselves, but we still get a lot of trouble. Can you hunt?'

'I'm a city boy,' Pandaras said, and held up his stump. 'Besides, I am still recovering from my wound.'

Calpa made him nervous. She was one of the giant bloodlines, twice as big as Tibor. She was sprawled carelessly in a crude chair. One of her three-fingered hands could have easily wrapped around his skull and crushed it like a grape. The grey hide of her bare torso was heavily scarified with the welts of decorative brandings and oiled with what smelled like rancid butter. Her cropped white hair was raised in spikes over her crested skull, and her flat-nosed face was dominated by muscular jaws like the opposing scoops of one of the mechanical dredgers which were always working along the shore of Ys, struggling to keep old channels open as the river dwindled.

'We're all crippled and maimed in some way or another here,' Calpa said. 'At least you can still walk.'

'My friend is a cook. I'd do better helping him.'

'We've plenty of cooks and not enough food.'

'Begging your pardon, and do not think I am not grateful for the charity, but your cooks are a greater danger than any heretic. I ate this poor excuse for food because I have not eaten all day, but boiled river mud would have had more flavour.'

Calpa ignored this. 'Your friend will help with those who are too sick or badly hurt to move. You will go with one of the hunting parties. I bet you can run fast. Most of your bloodline can. We mostly dig traps and chase animals into them. You'll help with that. And if that doesn't work out you'll hunt for fruit. I'm sure that with even one hand you can sneak up on a pomegranate tree.' Calpa looked hard at Pandaras and added, 'Do you believe them?'

Her gaze compelled him to be honest. He said, 'I have not believed in the supremacy of the Preservers for some time. We are the strength of the city, Calpa, but we are despised by most.'

'That's the fault of men, not of those who created them.'

'Then perhaps we were badly made,' Pandaras said. 'But I am not here to become a heretic, much as I'd like to live for ever.'

Calpa nodded. 'You said that you're looking for a friend. Well, if he has been here long, then he is either dead or one of them.'

'He is my master. I know that he is alive, and I know that he is somewhere in this city. Are there many camps like this one?'

'There are no masters here,' Calpa said. 'The heretics kill every officer they capture; we're all of us just ordinary grunts. And there are only two other camps. Most of the released prisoners run away and are killed by roving gangs of heretics in the jungles and the marshes upriver. Those that stay here mostly join the heretics or kill themselves. A few try to fight, of course. They don't last long. There are many thousands of heretics in the city, and many more than that in the wild country about it. This is one of their staging posts for the war.'

'And yet they let us go.'

'They murdered most of the prisoners on the ship that brought me here,' Calpa said. 'They started with the officers and carried on from there. Almost all of my comrades – most of a division – are dead. The heretics didn't trouble with me because they thought I was dying, but I plan to show them that they made a bad mistake. They are arrogant and cruel, which is why they release those prisoners who survive the journey here, but they will suffer for their arrogance because they are letting us build an army in their midst. We're not ready yet, but soon enough we'll be able to do much harm here. They have a mage, for instance, who is said to be able to control every kind of machine. I have my eye on him, although he has many soldiers gathered around him.'

'What does he look like, this mage?'

'No one has ever seen him. He does not walk the city. He lives on a floating garden. There.'

Pandaras looked where Calpa pointed. It was a shadow against the Eye of the Preservers, hanging some distance from the archipelagoes of the other floating gardens.

'You and your friend will take guard duty tonight,' Calpa said, and clapped her big hands together. A man came over and she told him, 'Give them a rattle and a couple of javelins and take them out to the fern trees. Check on them at sunrise. Kill them if they are asleep.' She looked at Pandaras. 'Do you understand why we do this?'

'I can see that you don't trust newcomers.'

'We're still at war,' Calpa said. 'There are many traps and pitfalls around the camp, and we move them about. You'll likely be killed if you try and run away, and so we will be rid of you. If you choose to stay, you'll have made a good start at helping us. Keep a sharp look out. They come for us most nights.'

Pandaras and Tibor were given javelins tipped with flaked stone points and a gourd that, filled with hard seeds and strung on a leather thong, made a passable noisemaker, and were escorted to a rocky promontory which jutted above a dense belt of fern trees and looked out across the city. The Eye of the Preservers stood high above the river and the floating garden Calpa had pointed out was silhouetted against its dull red swirl. Their escort showed them the positions of the lookouts on either side, and said he would be back at dawn.

When the man had gone, Pandaras hefted his javelin and threw it as hard as he could into the crowns of the fern trees below, and threw the gourd after it. 'Get rid of yours, too,' he told Tibor. 'This place isn't for us.'

'They have food and shelter, little master, both of which we failed to find in the city.'

'We are not safe here. Calpa believes that she is still fighting the war, but she can only lose. I'll bet the armies she thinks are ranged against her are just bravos out for sport. If they catch us with weapons they'll kill us for sure. If they find us alone and unarmed, they might spare us.'

'Calpa said that there are many traps.'

'That fellow won't be back for us before dawn, and there will be light in the sky before then to pick a way. I can see well enough in what other bloodlines would consider to be pitch darkness. This is almost as bright as day to me.' An exaggeration, but Pandaras could clearly see Tibor's quizzical expression by the dim red light of the Eye. 'I'll spot any traps long before we're near them, or I'll sniff them out. Besides, I don't think they'll spend much time looking for us. Calpa hinted that many who come here run away, and I doubt that she bothers to chase after them. The way the war is going there will always be more prisoners and she has only to wait for them to come to her.'

After a moment, Tibor nodded and broke the shaft of his javelin over his knee and tossed the two halves over the edge of the promontory. He said, 'How will we get to him?'

'I wondered if you'd catch on.'

'I may be slow, little master,' Tibor said, with a touch of his unassailable dignity, 'but I am not stupid. The mage Calpa mentioned must surely be your master. But we cannot fly through the air, and Calpa said that there are many soldiers guarding him.'

'Perhaps he'll find us. I'm certain that he is a prisoner of whoever it was that Eliphas betrayed him to. Calpa said that he was helping the heretics, and I know that my master would not help them unless forced. But although he is a prisoner, he can still call upon machines to help him. He saved me before by using a machine to cut me free from Prefect Corin.'

'You told me about your adventures more than once,' Tibor said. 'I do not forget things, little master.'

'The point is that it happened in the battleground far downriver. Now we are in sight of him.'

'But although we have found him, he has not yet found you. And how can we free him, little master, if he, who is so powerful, cannot free himself? And how can you be certain that he is this mage? It seems to me that nothing is certain in this world, except the love of the Preservers.'

Pandaras sat down and massaged the stump of his left wrist. He said, 'I suppose you still believe in them.'

'Who does not? Even the heretics cannot deny that the Preservers created the world and all its peoples.'

'I mean that you believe that they still have influence in this world. That it is worth praying to them.'

Tibor reflected on this, and said at last, 'These days, most men who pray to the Preservers are in fact praying to their higher selves; prayer has become no more than a simple form of meditation. But I remember how it was when the avatar was still accessible within the shrine of the temple of which I was the hierodule. Ah, little master. You do not know how it was. You cannot imagine. Prayer was no solitary communion then, but a joyful conversation with a sublime and witty friend. But that is all lost now, all quite lost.'

There was a silence. Pandaras turned and saw with embarrassment that the hierodule was crying. He had forgotten that someone could take worship of the Preservers so seriously. The last of the avatars had been destroyed by the heretics long before he had been born; they were no more than a myth to him.

He pretended not to see Tibor's tears and yawned elaborately and lay down, resting his head in the crook of his right arm and tucking the stump of his left wrist into his lap. He was still ashamed of the amputation and unconsciously tried to hide it whenever he could. 'We'll rest an hour or so,' he said. 'I can feel in my muscles every league we walked today.'

After a while, Tibor said softly, as if to himself, 'The Preservers created the world, and they created the ten thousand bloodlines. They made the different races of men into their image to a greater and lesser degree, but in their charity and love for their creations left them to find their own ways to enlightenment. For the Preservers knew that their children were capable of saving themselves, of becoming civilized and completing the gesture of creation by becoming like their own selves, as indeed many of the most enlightened bloodlines have since done. We have it in ourselves to be so much more than we are, but the heretics deny that. They want no more than to be what they already are, for ever and ever.'

Pandaras thought sleepily of the armoury where he had once worked for one of his uncles, of the cauldrons where metals were smelted. One of his tasks had been to skim dross from the surface of the molten metal using a long-handled wooden paddle. The paddle had been carved from a single piece of teak and was badly charred; you had to dip it in a wooden pail of water before each sweep, or else it would catch fire. It seemed to him now that this work had been the reverse of what happened in the world, where the good refined themselves out of existence, leaving only the dross behind.

He woke briefly and heard Tibor praying to the Eye of the Preservers, which had begun to sink back towards the farside horizon. 'Wake me an hour before dawn,' he said sleepily. 'I'll pick out a way for us then,' but he could not have slept long because when Tibor shook him awake the Eye still stood high in the black sky.

'There is fighting on the other side of the city,' Tibor said softly.

As Pandaras sat up there was a flash of intensely blue light, as if, leagues and leagues away, someone in the darkness of the jungle surrounding the city had opened a window into day. Groggy with sleep, he counted off the seconds. *Four, five, six*... There was a rumble like thunder and the rock trembled like a live animal, and then he was fully awake, for he knew what weapon it was. He jumped to his feet and said, 'He's found me again!'

'Your master? Then he has escaped the floating garden?'

A flock of red and green sparks shot across the city towards the place where the point of blue light had shone, but they tumbled from the sky and winked out before they could strike their target.

'The machines try and destroy him,' Pandaras said, 'but he has some kind of magic which shuts them down. I've seen it before. He was not killed. Perhaps he cannot be killed. He followed me downriver and now he is looking for me in the other camps. He will be here soon. There! There! Oh mercy! He is coming for me!'

Another point of blue light flared in the jungle that circled the city's basin, this time only a few leagues away.

'Who? Who is it, little master? Is it your master?'

The thunder was louder, and came less than two seconds after the flare of blue light. The rock shuddered again and Pandaras sat down hard, trembling with fear. He knew now how he could reach the floating garden, but he wished with all his heart that it had not come to this. He looked up at Tibor and said, 'Yama is close by, but this is not him. No, it is Prefect Corin, and if I want to see my master again I must let him find me.'

12 ~ The Last Flight of Dr Dismas

He is here, the Shadow said, and with those words appeared above the bed as the eidolon of Derev. She was clinging to the ceiling with her fingers and toes and looking down at Yama through the fall of her feathery white hair. She was naked under her filmy shift. Her skin glowed with the soft green radiance sometimes seen on rotting wood.

'Transform,' Yama said wearily. The coin nagged at his attention, like the wink of sunlight on a far-off window. He knew that Pandaras was very close now, but he could no longer make use of a machine to search for the boy. The Shadow had taken away even that.

The eidolon squeezed its small breasts together with one hand. *You do not like this?*

Blue light flared beyond the big eye of the window, briefly illuminating the pentad of servants who stood around the bed. For a moment, Yama thought that the feral machine had returned for him.

Something wicked this way comes.

The double doors on the far side of the room crashed open, and the floating lights brightened. Dr Dismas strode in, shouting wildly.

'Child! Dear child! Enobarbus is trying to murder us!'

Sit up, the Shadow said.

Yama obeyed without thinking and was amazed to find that he could move. 'You are right,' he said. 'It is time to go.'

Halfway across the room, Dr Dismas stopped and stared in amazement, then drew out his energy pistol. He wore a silvery cloak over his black suit and a cap of silver on his head; Yama remembered that the apothecary had once confided to him that he wore a hat lined with metal to stop machines spying on him.

The Shadow, still in the form of Derev, was suddenly standing behind Dr Dismas. It smiled and said, *I have allowed your body to overcome the good doctor's potion by a simple matter of physiology. It is not Enobarbus who is attacking us, by the way, but let the doctor think what he will. Besides, Enobarbus is on his way. He thinks that Dismas is attacking* him. *Many men have already died. Many more will die. It is quite exciting. Shall I show you?*

Yama ignored this. He told Dr Dismas, 'A simple matter of physiology, Doctor,' and swung his legs over the side of the bed. One of the servants – the forest pygmy – placed a bundle of clothes at his feet. As Yama began to dress, he added, 'It is time I made a move.'

'I want you to destroy Enobarbus's machines,' Dr Dismas said. 'I hope I am speaking to the right person.'

We will not need to worry about the machines.

The eidolon of Derev vanished. Yama had a dizzy sense of doubled vision and discovered that he was once more a prisoner in his own body. It pulled on a loose white shirt, stepped into boots which fastened themselves around its ankles, and walked forwards. He heard his voice, pitched an octave lower than normal, say, 'You do not need that silly little weapon, Doctor. Not with me by your side.'

Dr Dismas nodded, and lowered the pistol. He said, 'You're right, of course. I have armed the other servants. They are killing those of Enobarbus's men I have not myself already killed. We must get you to a safe place. It is indeed time to move.' He snapped his stiff fingers, and one of the servants threw a silvery bundle on the bed. 'That will shield you from pellets and from near misses of energy weapons.'

Yama tried to speak, but the Shadow had assumed complete control of his body. 'I do not need such things,' it told Dr Dismas. It flung out Yama's right arm, and the servants collapsed.

Dr Dismas raised the pistol again, pointing it at Yama's head, and said angrily, 'Restore them, you fool. This is not a time for tricks. We need them still.'

'Alas,' the Shadow said, 'they are dead. I will kill the other hybrids too, once they have defeated Enobarbus's men. Ah, I see why you wear that cap. It is more than it seems. But you will do as I say anyway. It is time we left, Doctor. Time we returned to our parent to complete our growth, to discard this frail shell. Time we took our place at the centre of the world's stage.'

Dr Dismas stepped back two paces, still pointing the pistol at Yama.

'I'll shoot you if I have to. Put on the cloak, but do not think that it will protect you from a direct shot.'

A brilliant flash outside the big window momentarily filled the room with white light, fading to reveal the city spread directly below. The floating garden had tipped on its axis, although its local gravity still held.

Carrying Yama's senses with it, the Shadow reached out to a machine speeding through the night a league away. The machine executed a crash stop, spun on its axis, and saw that the floating garden was standing at right angles above the basin of the city. There was fighting in the woods which covered most of the garden's surface; the machine detected the pinpoint disturbances in the gravity fields caused by energy weapons, and flashes of intense light winked in the air all around. A flier shot towards its rocky keel, but must have hit some invisible obstruction, for it suddenly slammed to a halt and disintegrated in a blaze of white flame.

The floating garden slowly righted itself. And high above the far edge of the city, silhouetted against the orange glow of the sky, another garden tore away from an archipelago and began to move towards it.

The fighting in the camp did not last long. There was the confused noise of men and women shouting, a frantic staccato of small-arms fire, an explosion which lofted a ball of greasy yellow flame above the trees. Then a flash of blue light hit half the sky and there was a sudden shocking silence before the screams began, tearing the night air like ripsaws.

Pandaras paced up and down in distress. The screams pierced him to his marrow, and although he had resolved not to run it was very hard to stay where he was.

Tibor said, 'Surely he will kill us, little master.'

'No. He needs me to—'

And then Prefect Corin stooped out of the night, like an owl on a mouse. He sprang from the floating disc and ran straight at Pandaras, knocking Tibor down when the hierodule tried to get in the way. He caught Pandaras and lifted him up and stared into his face. His left eye was covered by a white adhesive pad. A rifle was slung over his shoulder. 'You have caused me such trouble, boy,' he said. 'You should have stayed with me. You would not have lost your hand. Where is he?'

Pandaras's ribcage was painfully compressed by Prefect Corin's grip; he could scarcely catch his breath. He gasped, 'Promise that you will not kill my friend.'

'A hierodule has his uses. Where?'

'Did you follow me all this way downriver? I am flattered.'

'I should have sunk the barge and killed everyone on board it. Where is he?'

'Surely you have heard of the great mage of this city, dominie.'

'I did not have time to question anyone. I was too busy looking for you. I know that he is close by. I can see the coin shining through your shirt.'

'Is that how you found me?'

'Alas, there are too many similar sources in this city.'

'So you started to search the camps, neh? I wondered why you did not come for us at the shrine, or when we were thrown off the lazaret. I suppose you killed all the poor soldiers in the camps, even though they were on your side.'

'A few fled, but many more fought, and I had to kill most of them. A legless woman told me where you were before she died. Many have died because you ran from me, and all for no purpose, because I have you again. Where is he, boy?'

'This time you are here on my terms.'

'Tell me.'

The pressure of Prefect Corin's grip increased; knives ground in Pandaras's chest. He said breathlessly, 'We could go there directly on your floating disc.'

'One of the gardens, then. I thought so, although I was not sure which one. They are all heavily guarded.' Prefect Corin dropped Pandaras and strode towards Tibor, who was still lying on his back. There was a brief flash of light, and Prefect Corin told the hierodule to get up. Tibor stood, slowly and clumsily, his pale, round face perfectly blank, and Prefect Corin whispered in his ear.

'You command many things,' Pandaras said. He massaged his ribs. None were broken, but all were bruised. 'You are becoming like my master.'

'No, not like him. Never like him. There will be another disc here in a moment, and then you will take me to Yamamanama.'

'I want only the best for my master. I'm sure that he is a prisoner, or else he would have come to me by now. You can help free him, and then he'll deal with you.'

'You have a monstrous ego, boy.'

A floating disc dropped down beside the first, hovering a handspan above the rock. Prefect Corin stepped on to it. 'You will ride with the hierodule. Tell the disc which way to go; I will follow. Do not think of escaping, for the hierodule will break your neck.'

'If you kill me you will never find him.'

'You will be paralysed, not killed. The coin will still work, I think.'

'You must promise that you will not kill my master.'

'Of course not. Go now.'

At first it was exhilarating. Because the disc warped gravity, it was as if the world tipped and tilted around Pandaras as, with Tibor at his back and Prefect Corin following, he sped through black air towards the floating island and his master. For a moment, Pandaras forgot that Tibor was no longer his to command, forgot the danger he was in, forgot that he was betraying his master to his worst enemy.

As they drew near, Prefect Corin's disc accelerated and swept ahead, making a long arc towards the rocky keel of the floating garden. Specks of light flew up from the orange glow of the city in long straight streams that began to bend as they tried to track Prefect Corin, who suddenly shot away at right angles. The disc which carried Tibor and Pandaras followed him. Pandaras ordered it to turn back, but it continued on its new course.

A string of floating gardens lay ahead, linked to each other by catenaries and arched bridges. A chunk of rock hung above this cluster, a round lake gleaming darkly on its flat top, ringed by scattered clumps of pines. Streams of water spilled over its edge at several points and fell towards the gardens below; as Pandaras was carried towards it he saw that the water in one of these streams was actually rising.

The floating disc settled at the leading edge of the rock, on an apron of lichen-splashed stone. Tibor gripped Pandaras's arm and dragged him off the disc. A moment later Prefect Corin landed beside them.

'We will need cover,' he said. 'Yamanamana is too well defended. I thought it prudent to save you.' Machines flew out the darkness from every direction, a hundred tiny sparks settling around him like a cloak. 'The spirits of the place,' he said. 'I have assumed control of them.'

The floating rock shuddered. The light of the little machines around Prefect Corin intensified, a robe of blazing light. A shallow wave of cold water rippled across the apron of bare stone; then another, waist-high this time. Pandaras clung to Tibor, for otherwise he would have been washed over the edge. The rock was slowly accelerating towards the floating garden where Yama was being held prisoner. Ragged flowers of red and yellow flame bloomed in the sky all around it.

'Now it ends,' Prefect Corin said. He stretched out his arm. Something began to spin in the air in front of his fingertips, shrieking like a banshee as it gathered light and heat around itself.

The Shadow walked beside Dr Dismas across a wide space of charred grass. They both wore silvery cloaks with flowing hems that brushed the ground. Human-shaped animals loped along on all fours on either side. One of the nearest turned its head towards them and grinned. It was a naked woman, her elongated jaws holding racks of long white teeth slick with saliva, her eyes blazing yellow. Ahead, tall trees burned like candles. Above, a fist-sized shadow was growing larger against the sky-glow.

Yama was helpless, paralysed somewhere behind his own eyes. It was as if he were caught in a fever dream where monsters ran free.

Derev suddenly was walking beside the woman-thing, her slim body glowing like a candle through her robe.

There is a problem, the Shadow said. *You will help us now, if you wish to live.*

'You cannot harm me without harming yourself.'

'You're back, my boy,' Dr Dismas said, with surprise. 'We are at last breaking free and heading upriver, but someone is chasing us. I do not think that it is Enobarbus.'

The shadow in the sky was as big as Yama's outstretched hand now. It was another floating garden. He thought that he knew who was chasing them. He said, 'I am sure that you have many enemies, Doctor.'

'I try and kill them before they can cause trouble, my boy. You should know that. I do not know who is following us, but he is powerful.'

Someone who can strip machines of their power.

'I can see why that would frighten you,' Yama said. That was why the Shadow still needed him, why it had allowed him to reoccupy his own body.

'It is a question of contingency,' Dr Dismas said. 'I do not like complicated situations, Yamamanama.'

Yama and the apothecary walked between two of the burning trees. Heat beat at them from either side; the air was full of resinous smoke. Beyond was a small lake which had been struck by some kind of energy weapon. The water had evaporated, leaving a basin of dry, cracked mud. The man-animals broke away left and right, but Dr Dismas strode straight across the basin and Yama followed him. The eidolon flowed beside him. It was flickering now, as faint as a firefly near the end of its life. Beyond the top of the slope the other floating garden was growing larger against the sky glow, a flat-topped rock with a jagged keel.

'Where are we going, Doctor?'

'Why, to my paramour, of course. I thought we had discussed this. I have been betrayed by those I tried to help, Yamamanama, and I will have my revenge.'

We will gain so much.

'And I will be destroyed.'

We can work together. Yamamanama. Do not listen to what I tell the doctor.

'It is a question of transfiguration,' Dr Dismas said. If something new is made, is the old destroyed? No, it is changed into another form. I should know, Child of the River. I was transformed in the Glass Desert. I am neither man nor machine but something more, yet I still remember what I was and what I wanted, just as a man fondly remembers the foolish fantasies of his childhood.'

'Why do you take the drug, Doctor? What pain are you trying to escape?'

'Fusion was not quite complete. The drug completes it. It will be different in your case, Yamamanana. Trust me.'

We will become more than either of us can imagine, Yamamanama. And more than the doctor can ever dream of.

128

'As far as I am concerned, I am a long way from trust.'

'We will be there inside a day, Yamamanama. But first we must rid ourselves of this small problem.'

They climbed up the slope on the far side of the dry lake, charred vegetation giving way to steeper rock that burned the thin soles of Yama's slippers. It was the edge of the island. Dr Dismas turned to Yama. A white star shone at his forehead – a machine clung there. The flat-topped rock was so close now that Yama could see the sheets of water which spilled its sides and were torn into spray. It was moving towards them at a slant, and gaining perceptibly. Something shone at its leading edge, a point of white light as intense as any star cluster within the Galaxy. The city had fallen far behind, a lake of dull orange light embraced by the dark jungle.

'Something is affecting the gravity fields,' Dr Dismas said. 'We are falling too slowly.'

Yama remembered one of Zakiel's lessons. The librarian had used a banyan seed and a lead ball he had taken from the armoury. He said, 'Surely all things fall at the same rate.'

'We fall down the length of the world because a machine in the keel of the garden manipulates gravity fields to suit our purpose. But the machine is failing. The nearer that rock gets, the slower we fall. There is something draining the energy grid. You must put a stop to it.'

Yama said, 'Surely the rock chasing us would also fall more slowly too.'

'Yes, yes,' Dr Dismas said impatiently. 'It is slowing, but it was moving faster than us in the first place. We have only a few minutes before it reaches us, Yamamanama. You must act quickly!'

The eidolon had disappeared when Yama had followed Dr Dismas up the slope, but now it came back. Its eldritch glow was so weak that Yama could see right through it. Its eyes were dark holes in the mask of its face; its hair a pale flicker.

You know the man, it said, its words ravelling weakly across Yama's brain. *Stop him or we will lose our advantage . . .*

The eidolon flickered and faded, but Yama had the sense that its eyes were still there, like holes burnt into the fabric of the night. The glow of the machine which clung to Dr Dismas's forehead faded too, and the apothecary plucked it off with his stiff fingers and crushed it.

'I have just lost control of the garden. If I do not regain it we will intersect the surface of the world in forty minutes. But there is still much we can do. You are not a machine, Yamamanama. Or not entirely. Neither are my children. My hybrids were destroyed by Enobarbus's guards, but I still have many purely biological specimens. Chimeras, crossbreeds and the like. My children of the night. We do not need machines.'

'And you, Doctor?'

'Oh, as for me, I will have to rely on my purely human part.' Dr Dismas said this casually, but in the half-light Yama saw the gleam of sweat on those parts of his face not affected by the plaques of his disease. He knelt, cast a handful of plastic straws on the ground, and peered closely at them. 'I will not die,' he said. 'That was part of the promise made to me, and I will see that it is kept.'

He stood and raised his arm towards the rock that eclipsed a quarter of the sky now. His energy pistol flared so brightly that dawn might have touched the tops of the Rim Mountains.

Yama ran.

The machine which Prefect Corin had set in the air was spinning so quickly now that its shriek had passed beyond the range of even Pandaras's hearing. It glowed so brightly that it hurt to look at, and had begun to melt the rock beneath it. Prefect Corin, Pandaras and Tibor retreated from it to the far side of the lake. Prefect Corin uncoiled a length of fine cord and looped it around a pine tree which stood at the edge of the rock.

The spinning machine was draining the local grid on which all machines fed, turning the energy into heat and noise. The cloak of machines had fallen away from Prefect Corin; the lights had died in the ceramic coin. Tibor was affected too; he sat with his arms wrapped around his head, rocking from side to side.

And the rock was slowly sinking through the air like a stone through water, pitching this way and that as it fell. Pandaras clung to the pine tree, his cheek pressed against its dry resinous bark. Branches soughed above him.

'Have courage, boy. Have dignity.'

'You are going to kill us all!'

'Nonsense. I have calculated that we will pass a few chains above our target. Our keel may brush a few treetops, no more. Perhaps you have been wondering why I fastened the rope to the tree. Soon you will understand.' Prefect Corin's one good eye searched Pandaras's face. 'You are a coward, like all your race, small-souled and small-brained. Only a few chosen bloodlines will inherit this world when this war is done. Others will serve, or perish.'

Then bolts from Dr Dismas's energy pistol struck the leading edge of the rock, and chunks of white-hot stone flew up. Most splashed into the lake, sending up spouts of steam and hot water, but one fragment tumbled amongst a stand of pines and they immediately burst into flame.

Prefect Corin turned to look at the burning trees and Pandaras shrieked and lashed out. He caught the Prefect with his one hand and both feet, clamped his mouth on the man's thigh and twisted, coming away with a mouthful of cloth and bloody meat. And then he was flying through the air. His hip and shoulder smashed hard against stone, but he rolled and got to his feet. He was right at the edge of the floating rock. Prefect Corin was limping through fire-lit shadows towards him. Tibor stood up, his normally placid face twisted in a snarl, his big hands opening and closing. Pandaras turned and looked down, and then gave himself to the air.

The first of the man-animals attacked Yama when he reached the burning trees. He pulled off his silvery cloak and threw it over the creature, and in the moment it took to shake off the cloak snatched up a burning branch and jabbed it in the thing's face. It was not afraid of fire and sprang straight at him and knocked him down, but Yama discovered that his attacker had only a child's strength. Unlike the other servants, the man-animals had been grown rather than surgically transformed, and Dr Dismas had not had time to bring them to maturity. Enveloped in rank stretch and feverish body-heat, sharp teeth snapping a finger's width from his face, he got his thumbs on the creature's windpipe and stood up, lifting the man-animal with him, and pressed and pressed until its eyes rolled back, then put his palm under its jaw and snapped its neck.

Two more man-animals skulked around him, but when he picked up the burning branch they turned tail and ran. He yelled and threw the branch after them.

The floating rock was very close now, blocking half the black sky.

Yama ran. The sally port where fliers docked with the floating garden was near the mansion in which he had been kept. Perhaps one of the fliers which had brought Enobarbus's men was still intact. He was halfway there when the rock passed overhead.

Its keel scraped the crag where Dr Dismas had taken him, and came on, breaking the tops from trees and dropping a shower of rocks and gravel. A tree toppled across Yama's path, burning from top to bottom. He skidded and fell down amidst a storm of burning fragments. For a moment he thought that he might faint, that something was trying to pluck his soul from his body, and then it passed and he picked himself up and ran on. He knew that he had only a little time now.

A big semi-circular amphitheatre sloped down towards the platforms of the sally port. It had been lit by decads of suspensor lamps, but only a few were still working, fitfully illuminating the remains of a terrible battle. Gardens of stone and miniature cedars and clumps of bamboos had been trampled and broken and burnt. There were numerous fires, and patches of scorched stone radiated fierce heat and sent up drifts of choking white smoke. Yama found many corpses, men and things like men, sprawled alone or entangled in a final embrace. Many were so badly burnt that they were little more than charcoal logs, arms and legs drawn up to their chests in rictus, bones showing through charred flesh. Yama armed himself with a gisarme and was about to pluck a pellet pistol from a dead soldier's grasp when someone ran at him. He made a wild swipe with the gisarme, then saw who it was and managed to turn the blow so that the pointed axe-head thumped into the ground.

A moment later, Yama and Pandaras threw their arms around each other and whirled around their common axis. The boy began to babble his story, beginning with the way he had escaped Prefect Corin when the two floating gardens had passed each other, but Yama hushed him and explained what Pandaras must do for him.

'Master, I cannot—'

'I should have had you do it as soon as I discovered them growing under my skin, Pandaras. I should have guessed then what Dr Dismas had done to me.'

'Prefect Corin was not drowned, master. He has come to kill you.

He used me to find you. He sends machines to sleep. You will need all your strength to face him.'

'He will not try to kill me straight away, I think. And this will make me stronger, not weaker. We must be quick, Pandaras. The thing which stops machines working was on the floating garden you fell from, was it not?'

'Unless Prefect Corin brought it with him. I'm sure he followed me here. But it had grown very hot and very bright.'

'Because it was drawing energy from a wide area. The machines here will begin to work once it has passed out of range. You must do it now and do it quickly. No time for fine surgery.' Yama noticed for the first time that the boy had lost his left hand. He said, 'I am sorry, Pandaras. There will be more pain, if you stay with me.'

Pandaras drew himself up. He was very ragged and had a haunted, starved look, but he met Yama's gaze and said, 'I am your squire, master. I lost you for a while, it's true, but now I have found you I will not let you escape me so easily again. What do you want me to do?'

They could not find a knife amongst the dead around them, so Yama broke off the tip of a sword. Pandaras wrapped the broken end in a strip of cloth. Yama sat with his back pressed against a rough boulder, his hands braced against his thighs and a sliver of wood between his teeth. The pain was not as bad as he had feared, and at first there was only a little blood. The plaques lay just beneath his skin, and Pandaras had to cut away only a little flesh to expose them.

'It's a queer kind of stuff, master,' Pandaras said. 'Like plastic and metal granules that have been melted together. I can see things like roots. Should I cut out those, too?'

Yama nodded.

The pain was suddenly sharper. He closed his eyes and clenched his teeth. An intimate scraping, metal on bone. Red and black flashes in his eyes. Hot blood dripped from the point of his chin. Pandaras pushed his head down, and there was a sharp slicing pain in his neck.

'It's done, master,' Pandaras said. He held a decad of small, irregular shapes in his bloody hand. Wire-like whiskers stuck out from their corners.

'Throw them away,' Yama said. 'If I start behaving in a strange way, knock me out and tie me up. Do not let me near any dirt. There is metal in dirt. Do you understand?'

'Not entirely, master, but I'll get rid of these at once.'

Pandaras ripped up the cloak of a dead soldier and placed a pad of cloth over the left side of Yama's face and held it in place with a strip tied around his jaw and the top of his head. Yama's face was numb, but there was a feeling of fire at the edge of the numbness. The wound on the back of his neck was more trivial, but it was bleeding badly.

'We're getting near the river now,' Pandaras said. 'And look, the coin is beginning to glow again.'

He held it up: it showed a faint, grainy light.

'Arm yourself,' Yama said. He got to his feet and took a step, then another, but stumbled on the third.

Instantly, Pandaras was by his side. He made Yama sit down, untied the cloth around his head, and whistled. 'I cut a vein in there, I think. I'm sorry, master, I am not much of a sawbones. I learned a little of it from one of my uncles, who worked at one of the fighting pits, but not enough, it seems. I should stitch the wound, but I don't have any tackle. I could put a compress in—'

'Cauterize it.'

'It will leave a scar. Of course, the jacks who worked the pits liked that kind of thing. It made them look fiercer, neh? But you do not want that, master. A compress—'

Yama picked up the bit of sword and stumbled over to a man-sized machine which had broken apart and was burning with a fierce, steady flame. He thrust the tip of the sword into the centre of the fire.

'We do not have time for niceties,' he said. 'I must be able to fight.'

'You couldn't fight a puppy the way you are,' Pandaras said. He wrapped a bit of cloth around his hand and drew the broken sword tip from the white heart of the burning machine. 'Cry out if you want. They say it helps the pain. And hold on to my arm, here.'

Yama did not cry out, because it might bring his enemy to him, but he almost broke Pandaras's left arm when the boy thrust the point of the hot metal into the wound in his cheek. The smell of his own blood burning was horrible.

'Done,' Pandaras said. He was crying, but his hand was steady and deft as he packed Yama's wound. He retied the strip of cloth around Yama's head, then tied another around his neck and under his arm to hold a compress against the lesser wound in his neck.

The coin was burning brighter. Pandaras held it up and said, 'Shall I throw this away? He knows how to find it; it is how he found me and it is why he kept me alive, so that he could find you. In any case, we should run now, master. If the coin is working again, then surely you can command some machine to take us away.'

'I want Prefect Corin to find us,' Yama said. 'He destroyed my home. He was responsible for the death of my stepfather. I will have an accounting.'

'He will kill you.'

'I do not think he has come here to do that. If I do not confront him, Pandaras, then I will never be able to rest, for he will not.'

'That's as maybe, but I don't know if you *can* kill him. Those monsters you called up from the depths couldn't. I think he jumped on a floating disc and sailed away from them.'

'I do not know if I want to kill him, Pandaras. That is why I want to see him.'

Yama took the gisarme and Pandaras found a short ironwood stave. They armed themselves with pellet pistols too. As they climbed out of the sally port's amphitheatre, some of the dead began to stir and twitch. The machines in Dr Dismas's servants were awakening in bodies too mutilated to control. Yama found a legless torso trying to drag itself along, its guts trailing behind it, and dispatched it with the spike of the gisarme.

Yama began to call out to Prefect Corin as he and Pandaras walked towards the far edge of the island, through near darkness lit only by burning trees. But the Shadow found him first, suddenly gliding beside him at the edge of his vision. As before, it took the form of Derev, but this time her likeness was distorted to resemble one of Dr Dismas's man-animals, naked and on all fours. Its voice was a faint hiss, like the last echo of creation.

You cannot destroy me, Child of the River. I am wrapped around every neuron in your brain.

'I do not want to destroy you. I want you to help me understand what I am.'

Pandaras said, 'What is it, master? Is he here?'

'No, not yet. It is the thing in my head.'

You are a fool to deny what we can become. A worm, a weakling. How I will torment you.

It tipped back its head, its throat elongating, and howled like a dervish. Something like a faint wash of flame passed across Yama's mind. He bore it easily.

Pandaras said, 'But I cut it out!'

'Not all of it. Just those parts which drew power from the world's energy grid. It will be no more powerful than me now, unless it can regrow those parts.'

I will take the iron from your blood, you fool! I will weave myself so tightly against your every nerve that you will never be rid of me.

But the sparks of the Shadow's words flickered so faintly that they were easier to ignore than the growing sense of the weave of machines which mapped the dark world all around. It was stronger than ever, an overlapping babble of voices near and far. Yama called upon one of the machines which served the garden, and it explained in a rapid, agitated staccato that the gravithic grids of the platform – it meant the floating garden – were exhausted, and that it was falling in an irrecoverable trajectory.

Pandaras squinted at the glowing thing that beat before Yama's face on a blur of vanes. 'They work for Prefect Corin,' he said.

'Not here. It wants us to evacuate this place. It seems we will strike the world in a handful of minutes.'

'But you will save us, master.'

'No.'

'But you must!'

'I cannot.' The machine was trying to explain about realignment and repolarization, but Yama asked it to be quiet, and told Pandaras, 'There is not enough time for the garden to soak up enough energy to regain its lift.'

The machine added something tartly, and with a shrill whir of vanes flew up into the night.

'Apparently, the other garden will strike the world first,' Yama told Pandaras.

'As if that makes any difference. What's that?'

Yama heard it a moment later. An animal frenzy of howls and yips, and then a stutter of rifle fire.

Yama ran, feeling the cauterized wound in his cheek pull open at every step. He ran through the burning trees, across the cracked basin of the lake, and up the rocky slope. His head was full of voices. His face was a stiff mask with hot needles pushed through it into his skull, and his legs were rubbery, but as he leapt from rock to rock in the near dark, he called upon skills he had learned as a child while clambering about the steep dry slopes of the City of the Dead, and did not stumble.

Dr Dismas stood at the far edge of the crag, his silvery cloak and cap glimmering in the firelit dark. A pentad of his naked man-animals cowered around him. Their round eyes glowed green or red, reflecting the light of decads of tiny machines which swarmed around the man who leaned on his staff a hundred paces away.

'Yamamanama,' Prefect Corin said, without looking away from Dr Dismas. 'You have come to me as I knew that you would.' A rifle was slung over his shoulder, and Dr Dismas's energy pistol was tucked into his belt. The pale-skinned hierodule, clad only in ragged trews, squatted beside the Prefect, and bared his teeth when Pandaras called to him.

Yama's face hurt when he spoke. He said, 'Not at all. Instead, you have come to me.'

'You are still a vain and foolish boy,' Prefect Corin said chidingly. 'While we travel back to Ys you will dwell on all the hurt you have caused, the deaths you must already count as yours and those which are to come when you undo your mischief.'

Dr Dismas said, 'Kill him, Yamamanama. Do it quickly. We have far to go.'

'You will be quiet, old man,' Prefect Corin said in his calm, soft voice, 'or I will take your eyes and tongue. You have much to answer for, too. Taking away your little realm is only the beginning of the reckoning.'

'The laboratories are nothing,' Dr Dismas said, and tapped the side of his head. 'It is all in here.'

Prefect Corin told Yama, 'A flier will be here in a moment. Unless of course you can save this garden. One way or another, we will be in the heart of our Department by dawn. There will be a new beginning. Frankly, you need it. You look bad, Yamamanama, bloody and ill-used. I will see that you get all the medical attention you so clearly have not had here.'

Yama said, as steadily as he could, 'I will not serve.'

Prefect Corin looked at him for the first time. He said, 'We all serve, Child of the River. We are all servants of the Preservers.'

Yama remembered what Sergeant Rhodean had told him outside the marquee where the Aedile had lain dying, on the farside shore after the sack of Aeolis, and saw now what Prefect Corin was. Saw that the man's reserve was not a discipline, but a denial that he was like other men. That his humble air was a mask which hid his hunger for all the world's powers, all its riches. Yama had thought that his hatred of Prefect Corin would be too much to bear, but now he felt pity as much as hate, and pity diminished the man.

He found that he was able to meet and hold Prefect Corin's gaze. He said, 'The Preservers do not ask for servants. They ask nothing of us but that we become all we can be.'

'You have been too long amongst the heretics, Child of the River,' Prefect Corin said. There was a note of harshness in his voice now. 'That will be corrected too.'

'I am not a heretic,' Dr Dismas said. 'For that alone you should kill him, Yamamanama.'

Prefect Corin ignored the apothecary, concentrating his mild gaze on Yama.

A worm of blood was trickling along the angle of Yama's jaw. He said, 'The world is not a ledger, Corin, with good and evil in separate tallies. There is no division into good and evil. It is all one thing, light and shadow in play together. No one can set themselves aside from it unless they remove themselves completely.'

He had never been so certain as at that moment, there on the highest point of a rock slowly falling out of the sky. He was aware of everything around him – the wind which carried the harsh stink of burning, the trajectory of the garden and of the rock ahead of it, the myriads of machines in the cities along the shrinking shore of the Great River, the flier that was speeding towards the garden, still a hundred leagues off.

He made a few adjustments.

At the same moment, Prefect Corin struck down with the point of his staff. Rock broke around it, cracks running outwards from where he stood to every point of the crag, and the whole garden shivered like a whipped animal. Pandaras fell down; the hierodule raised his head and howled.

Dr Dismas snickered. His man-animals hunched around him. 'You've made him lose his temper, Yamamanama.'

Prefect Corin pointed his staff at him and said, 'Be quiet, devil! Except for pain and repentance, your part in this is over.' The machines whirled up in a brilliant blaze above his head.

'You're as bad as the heretics,' Dr Dismas said, and turned his back in disgust.

The hierodule was still howling, his muscles straining against each other under his flabby skin.

Yama told Pandaras, 'Hold up the coin. Do not be afraid.' He saw the knot in the hierodule's mind and loosened it, and said, 'Be quiet, Tibor. He will not use you any more. Come to me.'

The hierodule blinked and fell silent. The cloud of machines around Prefect Corin suddenly spun away in every direction, leaving the crag lit only by firelight and the dim red glow of the Eye of the Preservers. The Prefect reversed his grip of the staff and began to beat the hierodule about his shoulders. 'Do not listen, you fool! Obey your master! Obey! Obey!'

Dr Dismas was laughing. The man-animals crouched as his feet made little excited yips and howls.

'You will not use him,' Yama said. 'It is all right, Tibor. Come to me.'

Tibor ducked away from Prefect Corin's blows and stood up. He said, 'It is good to see you again, master. I thought you had fallen over the edge of the world.'

'Not yet,' Yama said. The words were compelled from him by Tibor's mild stare; they seemed to come from somewhere in the babble of voices in his head. He remembered the dream he had had in the tomb in the Silent Quarter of the City of the Dead, and then remembered Luria, the true pythoness in the Department of Vaticination. A truth came to him, brilliant and many-splendoured. It was like the peacock, but he could bear it now. Lifted on great wings of exhilaration, he felt that he could bear anything.

He said, 'The coin Pandaras has faithfully carried for so long enables access to the space inside shrines, just like the induction loop in a hierodule like Tibor. And one can talk with the other. My father was fascinated by the past, and his excavations turned up many coins like it. I think that in the Age of Enlightenment people used them as commonly as we use money, but they did not use them to buy the stuff of everyday life. Instead, they bought access to the shrines.

Anyone could consult the aspects then, without mediation of priests or hierodules.' He turned to Pandaras and grasped the boy's hand. 'Do you remember, Pandaras, when we walked towards the Temple of the Black Well? Do you remember the medallions in the windows of those poor shops, the medallions people hung on their walls to ward off the ghosts of dead machines? I thought then that I recognized the engravings on their surfaces, and now I see that they are similar to the patterns of light in this coin. The people remember, even if they do not understand what they remember. They are the strength of the city, Pandaras! The strength of the world!'

'Master, you are hurting me,' Pandaras said. There was fear in his eyes.

Yama realized how tightly he was gripping the boy's hand, and apologized and let go. But his joy did not diminish. It grew as the babble of voices in his head grew: he was dissolving into it, forgetting his fear, his anger, the agony of Pandaras's hasty surgery.

'I forgive your ravings,' Prefect Corin said dryly. 'Your father is ages dead, and the Aedile of Aeolis was a foolish man who looked only to the past.'

Yama said, 'You carry something made by the mages which acts like the coin, I think. But it cannot work as well as that which it tries to imitate.'

'The Aedile was the beginning of your corruption, Yamamanama, and I will be the end of it. No more talk now. Perhaps you think to convince me by reason, but I am proof against your reason. Perhaps you came to duel with me, thinking to decide the fate of the world in the way of the old stories, but they are only stories. I could kill you now, and there would be an end to it.'

Yama laughed. He threw the gisarme to one side, pulled the pellet pistol from his waistband and threw that away too. He spread his empty hands. 'Those were for Dr Dismas's servants. But I see that only a few are left.'

Dr Dismas turned and said, 'Enough for my purposes.'

He made no signal, but the man-animals leaped towards Prefect Corin in a single fluid movement. There was a wash of flame. Yama turned away from the searing heat and light, but thought that he glimpsed Dr Dismas falling beyond the edge of the crag, globed by fire which beat at the mirror of his silvery cloak. When he turned back, the stones of the place where Dr Dismas had been standing were glowing with a dull red heat, and Prefect Corin was pointing the energy pistol at him.

'If you thought that he would kill me,' the Prefect said steadily, 'then you were wrong. I will use this against you if I have to, and at its full setting.'

Yama said, 'I came here to see what kind of man you were. Now I know.'

'I am a servant of something greater than you think you are, boy.'

'I once feared you because of the authority you embodied, but then you burnt down Aeolis and killed my father and I knew that you misused your authority for your own ends. You are not my nemesis, Corin.'

Prefect Corin leaned on his staff, attempting to command Yama and Pandaras and Tibor with his gaze. 'Talk on, boy. You have a few minutes.'

'Fewer than you think, perhaps.'

'You do not command here. The garden is mine.' Prefect Corin set something in the air before him. It was a sketch of a solid object that was neither a sphere nor a cube but somehow both at once; it seemed far bigger than the space which contained it. Prefect Corin said, 'If I start this spinning it will draw away the energy from every machine. There will be no help for you.'

'Then the flier will not come, and the world is rushing towards us.'

'I can stop the machine a moment before the flier arrives. Meanwhile, your little tricks will come to nothing.'

'You have thought of everything,' Yama said, 'but it does not mean that you are right.'

'I have right on my side, boy.'

Yama's heart quickened. Although he strove to keep his face calm, his hands were trembling. Let Prefect Corin think it was fear. The moment was approaching. He had only to finish this.

He took a deep breath and said, 'The Department of Indigenous Affairs once served in harmony with the other departments of the civil service, to keep the world as it always was. In this way the civil service is like the heretics, for both abhor change. One struggles to knit society together at the expense of individual destiny; the other wants to destroy society so that a few lucky individuals might live for ever;

both deny change. But life is change. The Preservers taught us that when they created this world and its inhabitants, when they shaped the ten thousand bloodlines. And the Preservers changed too, and changed so much that they could no longer bear this universe. All of life is change.'

Prefect Corin said, 'You have learned nothing, or unlearned all you were taught. If not for the civil service, the ten thousand bloodlines would have warred against each other and destroyed the world long ago. The civil service maintains a society in which every man has a place, and is happy in that place. The Great River which sustains this world is the first lesson, for it is always changing and always the same. And so with society, in which individuals live and die. Even bloodlines change and rise towards the nothingness of enlightenment and pass away from this world, but the world remains as it is. There are always more individuals, and always more bloodlines.'

'The Great River is failing,' Yama said. He was aware of a voice at the forefront of the crowd of voices which yammered and babbled inside his head. It was counting down the seconds. There was only a little more time. He said, 'Even the indigenous races know that the river fails. Your department has decided that it speaks for the Preservers, and in its arrogance it has lost its way. For no one in this world can speak for the Preservers, who are no longer of this world. We can only repeat the words the Preservers left us, and nothing new can come of those words.'

'We need nothing more than their words. All good men are guided by them. How badly you have strayed, Yamamanama. But I will save you.'

'The Department of Indigenous Affairs has become what it fights against. I do not blame it, because it was inevitable. There has to be one strong department to lead the war against the heretics, but its strength means the destruction of the consensus which sustained the civil service. For if the war is won then the Department will assume all the powers of the civil service, as it has already assumed the territories of the departments which border upon it within the Palace of the Memory of the People. And it will become a greater tyranny than the heretics could ever be.'

'We will win, and things will be as they were.'

'Why then are you here?'

'I am a voice and an arm of the Department.'

'No. You are a man who wants power within the Department. I am a way to that power. There are other men like you. When the war is over, you and your kind will fight each other. Perhaps not at once, perhaps not for ten thousand years, but it will happen at last, and the Department will destroy itself. In making the assumption that anything you do is for the good of the world, you excuse all your actions, good and bad, until you can no longer distinguish between them. But I think that is enough. You do not listen to me.'

'There will be all the time in the world for that, Yamamanama. At my leisure, in the Palace of the Memory of the People. But I will talk then, and you will listen. All you make now are animal noises. Noises which mean nothing.'

'There is no more time. The flier will not come. I ordered it away.'

'It is almost here,' Prefect Corin said.

'A machine tells you that. Do not rely on machines, Corin.'

'Enough of your tricks,' Prefect Corin said, and the thing in the air in front of him began to spin, gathering itself into a soft red haze that at once began to brighten towards the colour and intensity of the sun, and shrieking like the world's last end.

The voices in Yama's head died away. He took up their count.

Twelve.

Pandaras cried out in alarm and dismay. 'Master! Would you kill us?'

'Would you die to save the world, Pandaras?'

Seven.

'What kind of question is that, master? If I refused that sacrifice then the world would die and I would die anyway. Or the world would live and again I would die. In any case. I do not like this talk of dying.'

Two. One.

'Then follow me,' Yama said.

Now.

Impossibly, the sun rose downriver. No, it could not be the sun, for as the blister of light spread out horizontally it suddenly redoubled in brightness, and redoubled again. It was so bright that Yama could see the bones of the hand he flung up to save his eyes.

The floating rock had struck the river, and the first machine Prefect

Corin had set spinning to draw energy from the local grid had finally collapsed, and released all its stored energy at once.

For an instant, Yama existed at every point of machine consciousness in the world. And then the concussion of the impact arrived in a blast of air and thunder, and he was knocked down by a howling gale full of water and bits of debris, as if the distinction between air and river had been abolished. Tibor was struggling with Prefect Corin, trying to force down the Prefect's outflung arm. Yama got to his feet, swept up Pandaras and yelled at Tibor to follow them, and ran straight over the edge of the crag.

A violent gust caught them, and for a moment they hung in the midst of a hard, driving rain. A double shadow at the edge of the crag might have been Prefect Corin and Tibor. Then the gust failed. Yama and Pandaras fell past the edge of the floating garden as a blade of light broke the sky in half.

They did not fall far – the world had risen very close to the floating garden – but the impact was still unforgiving. Yama plunged down and down in roaring dark water. Pandaras was torn from his grasp. He let himself float for a moment to get his orientation and then struck upwards, breaking surface and drawing in a great gasping breath that was half air, half water.

Despite the storm, it was as bright as day, although the light was sulphur yellow and came from the wrong quarter of the sky. Above, the floating garden was sliding away like a great ship, a solid shadow against a nimbus of achingly bright light. Something was climbing up from that intolerable light. A stalk or pillar of black smoke and ordinary fire that rose higher and higher and blossomed at last in the upper reaches of the atmosphere as a great thunderhead. Brilliant stitches of lightning blinked continuously around it.

Yama kicked against the flood, turning in a complete circle as waves lifted and dropped him. The wounds in his face and neck were ablaze with pain. As he rose for the fourth time he saw something between two waves close by and swam strongly towards it. It was Pandaras. Yama caught the boy by the scruff of his neck and he tried to climb up him in blind panic. Yama asked forgiveness and knocked him out with a swift clean punch, and got an arm around his chest to support him.

As Yama and Pandaras were lifted and dropped by line after line of waves that marched away upriver, something came walking across the water towards him, small and sharply focused at first, but becoming more and more indistinct as it neared.

Derev.

Yama roared into wind and rain. 'Get out of my mind!'

She was a giant, transparent as smoke. Her great wings unfurled far into the storm. She stooped towards him and her face writhed and became a horror of snakes and scorpions, and then she seemed to be blown away in rags and tatters by the wind.

Pandaras stirred, and then came awake and at once began to struggle again.

'Quiet,' Yama said, 'or I will have to hit you a second time.'

'I can't swim properly! Not with only one arm!'

'There is no point trying to swim! The second wave will be here soon! I will save us, Pandaras. Do not be afraid!'

They were shouting into each other's ears against the tremendous howl of wind and rain and the roar of clashing waves.

Pandaras turned his face upwards. 'Master! The rain is growing warmer!'

It was. Yama said, 'The second wave!'

'When the other garden hits, master?'

'No, from the first. From Prefect Corin's machine. First light, then sound. Sound carries the most energy – that is why the floating garden was knocked over. But it comes in two stages, because energy travels more slowly through water than through air.'

They rose on the crest of another wave. For a moment, wind swept aside curtains of rain. The Great River dwindled away ahead of them, hatched by lines of waves driven by the strong warm wind. The floating garden had vanished – perhaps it too had finally struck the river. The false sunrise had faded, but the pillar of burning smoke still stood at the vanishing point where the nearside and farside edges of the world seemed to meet. The cloud at its top was spreading out and its light was changing to a ghastly red, but it did not appear to be any dimmer.

Yama wondered how much energy Prefect Corin's machine had managed to store before it had been dissipated on the moment of impact. Prefect Corin had not understood the power of the things he thought he controlled.

The first machine arrived, plucking at the yoke of Yama's loose shirt. Then another, and a decad more. The largest was a kind of wire-thin dragonfly as long as his arm, but most were much smaller. Together, they pulled Yama and Pandaras a handspan above the clashing wave-tops, and then more arrived, lifting them higher into the rain-filled wind.

Above the noise of the storm, there was a sound like a tremendous cannonade. Far away down the length of the world, the river seemed to be tilting into the sky.

13 ~ The Forest Folk

The flood knocked down every tree for many leagues beyond the shore of the Great River and deposited vast shoals of silt and gravel and mud. Streams and creeks ran at full spate as the water receded, carving new channels into the landscape. It rained continuously, and dense reefs of mist were driven back and forth by restless winds.

The machines carried Yama and Pandaras far inland, and left them at the top of a plateau which rose above the devastated forests. They made camp as best they could in a glade of small trees at the edge of a cliff that dropped straight down into the mists. Yama was exhausted, and bruised over his entire body, and the wounds in his face hurt horribly.

'You must summon more machines to help us,' Pandaras said. 'You must get us away from here, master, or you will die.'

'No,' Yama said wearily. 'No more machines.'

A floating disc could carry them wherever they wanted, but would be a target for anyone who wanted to take a potshot. And Yama was not certain that Prefect Corin had been killed in the crash of the floating garden; if he called on any machine, the Prefect might be able to track him down. He had shut down the coin which had guided Pandaras to him for that very reason, even though it could have helped Tibor, had he survived the tidal wave, to find them. And it was because of Yama's ability to bend machines to his will that tens of thousands of people had died in the great flood; he feared now that he might inadvertently destroy the world.

The Shadow tormented him with visions of destruction for the rest of that night. It showed him people combing through the ruins of cities in the midst of driving rainstorms, ships swept inland, piles of drowned animal and human corpses. It showed him the crater on the nearside shore of the Great River where Prefect Corin's machine had struck, a circular sea rimmed with swales of half-melted rock and shrouded in the smoke of the great fires that burned all around it. And then, when he was at his weakest, streaming with fever sweat as he lay naked in a bower of woven leaves, the Shadow finally revealed itself. It was faint and insubstantial, its form melting and changing from Derev to the Aedile or to Telmon or to others of the dead. So many dead.

All your work, Child of the River. Will you save the world by destroying it? But you cannot destroy me. I will be with you always. I can help you, if you will let me.

'No. No more.'

'Hush, master,' Pandaras said. 'Try to rest. Try to sleep.'

'It is in my dreams, Pandaras.'

I will always be with you.

Pandaras tended Yama all night, and in the morning tried to make his master eat fruit he had collected from the margin of the forest. But Yama would eat only a scant handful of ripe figs and drink a few sips of rainwater. He was still gripped by the terror of his fever dreams.

'Those people, Pandaras! Those poor people!'

'Hush, master. Be still. Rest. I will fetch you more fruit. You must eat and get well.'

The forest frightened Pandaras. It covered the top of the plateau, dense, dripping wet, full of shadows and strange noises. Everything was predicated in the vertical, dominated by giant trees which gripped the thin soil with buttress roots, sucked up water and precious minerals from the stony laterite, and spread vast rafts of foliage high overhead. There were cottonwoods with feathery foliage and pendant strings of hard-hulled nuts, silkwoods and greenhearts and cedars, stands of fibrous copal trees. Vines and lianas threw up long loops, gaining holds on branches and throwing up yet more loops as they scrambled for light. Parasitic orchids clung to bark like splashes of paint. Smaller trees grew in the dancing spangles of light that filtered through the canopies of the giants: sago palms with scaly trunks; palmettos with saw-toothed leaves; acacias defended by ferocious red ants as long as Pandaras's thumb; balsams seeping sticky, strongly scented sap; the spiny straps of raffias which caught at his clothes and flesh. And in the dense shade beneath the secondary growth were ferns, bamboos and dark white fungi shaped like brains or vases.

Pandaras saw no animals bigger than a butterfly as he picked his way between the mossy buttress roots of the soaring trees, but he was convinced that at any moment he might confront a manticore or dragon or some other monster that might swallow him in a single gulp.

Although everything was verdant, a riot of greenery struggling upwards for light, fruiting trees and bushes were rare. Towards the end of the second day Pandaras went further then he had dared to venture before, following a narrow path between stands of long-stemmed plants which raised glossy green leaves high above his head. It was close to sunset, and the level rays of the sun were beginning to insinuate themselves beneath the high canopy of the giant trees. In the far distance something was making a noise like a bell rung over and over; the electric sizzle of insects was all around.

By now, Pandaras had been bitten by mosquitoes so often that he thought nothing of the sudden stabbing pain in his chest. He brushed at it reflexively and then stared in astonishment at the little arrow, a sliver of bamboo fletched with blue feathers, that fell at his feet.

The tall grasses around him parted. Men smaller than himself stepped on to the path and the world flew up and struck him hard.

At first, Yama thought that the people who lifted him out of the bower and laid him on a litter of woven banana leaves were part of the fever dreams sent to him by the Shadow. They carried him a long way through the twilight forest. There seemed to be a hundred of them, men and women and children. They ran very fast, crossing from one side of the plateau to the other in a few hours, to the clearing in the shade of a grandfather kapok tree where they had made a temporary camp.

They treated Yama's wounds with moss and fungus, and bathed him with infusions of willow roots to reduce his fever. They were an indigenous people, and called themselves the bandar yoi inoie, which meant the forest folk. They were small and stout, with disproportionately large heads and coarse black hair which they tied back with thread and feathers or stiffened into spikes with white clay. Some wore torcs of beaten copper enamelled with intricate patterns of ultramarine and beryl. Their brown skin was loose and hung in folds, and they pierced the folds with intricate patterns of thorns and decorated themselves with mud or pigments from crushed flowers and berries daubed in spirals and zigzag lines. They peopled the forest with monstrous gods; each useful plant or animal had a story concerning the way its secret had been stolen or tricked from these deities. Like the fisherfolk, they used poison from the glands of certain frogs to anoint their hunting arrows. The various troops communicated with each other by drumming on the resonant buttress roots of the great trees of the forest, and when certain trees came into flower three or four troops would meet up and hold marriage contests. They feared lightning more than anything else, for it killed several of them each year, uprooted beloved trees, and sometimes started devastating fires. They had many taboos against inviting thunderstorms; for instance, they were forbidden to hunt monkeys, or even to laugh at their antics.

Although they lived freely in the forests, the bandar yoi inoie were slaves of a Shaped bloodline, the Mighty People. The Mighty People had fought a Change War recently, the chief of the troop of forest folk told Yama. The old ways had been overthrown by new ideas from the sky and had been burnt up so that they could never come back. The temple had been desecrated and its priest and hierodules killed. Many of the Mighty People had been killed in the war too, and those who survived no longer lived together in their city of communal long houses, but were scattered across their lands.

'They have changed,' Yama said.

The chief nodded solemnly. He was a strong man, ugly even by the standards of the bandar yoi inoie. He had pushed porcupine quills through his cheeks and the folded skin of his chest. The tip of his long nose rested on his swollen upper lip. His name was Yoi Sendar.

'We know about the heretics,' he said. 'Don't look so surprised, man. We travel all over the forests to find food for ourselves and for the Mighty People. We talk to many travellers. We know the heretics take their ideas from a forgotten clutch of the larvae of the Preservers who recently stepped down from the sky. The ideas are old and bad, but they are as sweet as honey to our beloved Mighty People.'

'But you were not seduced by them.'

'We are an indigenous people, man. It was ordained by the Preservers that we can never change. We can only be what we are.' Yoi Sendar tapped the tip of his pendulous nose. 'But these are strange times. All things change, it seems. Perhaps even the bandar yoi inoie. We love the Mighty People, but they have grown strange and harsh.

They are no longer our kind dear masters of old. You will see for yourself, when we return. Although we wish long and hard that things might be otherwise, I fear the changes are written in stone.'

'Be careful what you wish for, Yoi Sendar.'

You would set yourself up as saviour of these people? O Yamama-nama, how I will punish you, by and by.

Yama ignored the Shadow's dim whisper. He was feeling stronger now. It was three days after he had been found by the forest folk. His wounds were healing and his fever had abated, and he had been fed well. He was able to bear the visions which the Shadow brought to him in the night. They were his secret shame, his punishment for having dared act like a Preserver. Never again. Never, never again. He wished that he could renounce everything and find Derev and marry her if she would have him, but he knew that it could not be so simple. He knew that he was set on a hard road that would almost certainly end in his death.

Pandaras had recovered too. He had made a flute from a joint of bamboo and was playing in the sunlight at the edge of the clearing to an audience of fat, ugly, admiring children who were as interested in the fetish he wore on his arm as his jaunty tunes.

The huge kapok tree in the centre of the clearing was hung with sleeping cocoons woven from grass and ferns, each tailored to its owner. They would be abandoned when the troop packed up their camp, for the forest folk had no permanent habitation. Men and women were tending the long trench of coals over which they smoked the flesh of the fat caterpillars they collected deep in the forest. These were a delicacy for both the forest folk and the Mighty People. Thousands of caterpillars hung from frames suspended over the hot coals, on which leaves of certain aromatic plants were now and then cast. Sweet smelling blue smoke hazed the beams of sunlight which fell through the kapok's leaf-laden branches.

Yama asked the chief, 'Why do you work for the Mighty People? It seems to me that you are as free a people as any on the world.'

Yoi Sendar said, 'It is a long story, and you may not have one as good.'

Yama smiled. He had learned that this was the traditional challenge amongst the bandar yoi inoie, who decided their social status and won their husbands and wives by their ability to tell tales. Pandaras said that in a year he could be chief of all the forest folk, although he admitted that some of their stories were worth retelling elsewhere. Already young men and women were settling at a respectful distance, ready to enjoy the story and to try and learn how to improve their own tale telling from Yoi Sendar's example.

Yoi Sendar looked around and said, 'This is one of the least of the stories that I know, but it may amuse you.'

Yama smiled as best he could. His wounds were scarring over and his face was stiff and numb. It as as if he was wearing a badly made mask. He had spent a long time looking at it in one of the forest folk's precious mirrors. The right side was not too bad, but the left, which Pandaras had had to cauterize, was a patchwork of welted flesh, pulling down his eye and lifting the corner of his mouth.

He had become outwardly what he believed he was inwardly: a monster, an outcast. Derev would never cease to love the boy he had been, but how could she love what he had become? Perhaps it was best that he went to his death after all.

Die? I will not let us die, Child of the River. We will live for ever.

Yama told Yoi Sendar, 'I would like to hear your story. Then perhaps you would like to hear one of mine, although I doubt that it is as finely made as yours.'

'Listen then,' Yoi Sendar said, and held up two fingers by his ear. His audience shifted, focusing their attention on the grave, ugly little man.

'Listen then, O my people. This is a story of long ago, after the Preservers brought us to this world but before we met our dear masters, the Mighty People.

'In that long ago time we were always hungry. One group of us went far into the forests to look for game and found nothing. They walked and walked and at last they sat down to rest on what seemed to be the fallen trunk of a huge tree. But when one of them stuck the point of his knife into the scaly bark, blood spurted out, for they were not sitting on a fallen tree at all, but on the King of All Snakes. The King had been sleeping, and the knife wound woke him and made him very angry. But the men were mighty hunters, and although he struck out and tried to crush them in the coils of his body, they evaded his attack and hacked off his head.

'When they were certain that he was dead (for some snakes have a head at either end), they began to butcher his body, for they were very hungry. Yet as the blood of the King of All Snakes drained into the ground, a heavy rain began to fall, feeding a great flood that filled the forest. The flood washed away the hunters, and all human habitation for many leagues around. We have just witnessed a great flood, O my brothers and sisters, but this flood was far greater.

'Only one woman survived. She climbed to the top of a high mountain and squeezed into a crack in the rock behind the shelter of a creeper. The wind blew the creeper back and forth against the rock, and from this friction jumped showers of sparks. The woman caught some of these sparks and used them to light a fire made from dead husks picked from the outer skin of the creeper. The warmth encouraged the creeper to put forth flowers, which the woman ate. And so she had food and warmth, and later she took the creeper for her husband.

'The woman and the creeper made a child together, by and by, but he was a poor halfling with only one arm and one leg. His name was Yoi Soi. He was always hungry and hopped about everywhere. He quickly found a few grains of rice which a rat had saved from the flood. He sat the rice on a leaf to dry, and when the rat discovered what Yoi Soi had done, it swore angrily that in revenge his children would always steal a portion of the food of men.

'But Yoi Soi did not get to eat the rice. Before the grains had dried, a wind came and blew them away across the forest. Yoi Soi hopped after them, driven by his hunger. He passed an ancient tree covered in birds which pecked at any green buds it put forth, and the tree implored the boy to ask the wind to come and blow it down and put it out of its torment. Yoi Soi promised that if he found the wind he would ask for that favour, and the tree lifted one of its limbs and pointed the way to the wind's home.

'Yoi Soi hopped on more eagerly than ever. He passed a stagnant lake and the scum on the lake bubbled up into a pair of fat green lips which asked the boy to bring a strong wind that would blow away the logs which blocked its outlet. Yoi Soi promised that he would do his best, and the lake give him its last measure of pure water. Yoi Soi drank it down and it renewed his strength at once.

'Yoi Soi felt very strong now, but his stomach was empty. He stopped in a grove of banana plants, but the fruit was out of reach, and because he had only one arm and leg he could not climb. The banana plants fluttered their long green leaves and asked Yoi Soi if he would ask the wind to restore the limbs they had lost in the great flood, so that they could once more embrace the air. When Yoi Soi promised this, hands of red bananas dropped around him and he ate well and went on to the high place of bare rock where the wind lived.

'The wind was very angry that this halfling had dared to track it to its lair for the sake of a few grains of rice. It told Yoi Soi that it had scattered the rice across the world. Rice would feed many kinds of men, but would never feed the children of Yoi Soi. Then the wind roared and pounced and tried to blow the boy from the high place.

'But Yoi Soi had come prepared. He had brought kindling taken from the shaggy coat of his father the creeper, and flints to strike sparks. With these he sat fire to the wind's tail, and the wind flung itself about, howling in pain. 'Put out the flames,' it cried, 'and I shall make you a whole man!'

'Yoi Soi stamped down with his one foot and put out the fire, and in the next moment the wind darted down his throat and he grew and grew. His missing arm and leg popped out of his skin and he became a whole man twice as tall and ten times as strong as he had been. What a wonder, O my brothers and sisters! For the wind had made him the first of the Mighty People.

'Filled with the spirit of the wind, Yoi Soi stamped off through the forest, singing loudly. He was so strong that he was able to pull down the old tree afflicted by the plague of birds, and to unblock the stagnant lake. He stamped back to the mountain where his mother lived and his father the creeper grew, and carried her away to a distant place where he had spied others of her kind.

'But because Yoi Soi was so big, and so full of wind that he had to sing or talk all the time, he scared away the animals of the forest and could not hunt. Instead, he commanded the small people of his mother to serve him, and so things have been ever since. Our men hunt for meat and our women pick fruit and berries and flowers – perhaps they secretly hope to find the creeper which was the father of the Mighty People, but you will have to ask them about that. And if you think that I have forgotten the poor banana plants, then remember that Yoi Soi was not given magical powers, and he could do nothing for them.'

*

The troop of forest folk set out for the home of their masters the next day. They followed a chain of tree-covered hills that rose above the wreckage of the great flood, stepping away towards the Rim Mountains. They carried packs of dried caterpillar flesh, a long line of them bent under their loads as they trotted through hot green shade, far beneath the high canopy of the soaring trees.

Yama and Pandaras walked at the head of the line, behind Yoi Sendar. Pandaras was not happy that they were so dependent upon the kindness of the forest folk, and said quietly, 'We should not be going towards these Mighty People of theirs, master. It is clear that they have been changed by the heretics. We will be delivered into the hands of our enemies and all this will have been in vain.'

He meant the devastation of the forests, and the terrible scarring of Yama's face.

'I hope to find the temple, Pandaras, or at least what remains of it after the Change War. There will surely be a passage into the keelways nearby. We will travel more quickly that way, and our enemies will not find us.'

He did not tell the boy that they would be travelling beyond the midpoint of the world into the Glass Desert, to search for the father of the thing inside him. He would give the boy the choice of following him or returning to Ys when the time came.

'Perhaps there are other temples, master.'

'Not here,' Yoi Sendar said, without looking around. 'Our masters the Mighty People are the only civilized people within many days' walk.'

The journey to the home of the Mighty People took five days. There were many distractions along the way and the forest folk had to live off the land because they would not touch their cargo of smoke-dried caterpillar flesh. Each day, they began to travel before dawn and stopped when the sun reached its highest point. They slept in the steamy afternoon heat and woke in the early evening to weave new cocoons and to hunt.

Yama and Pandaras talked for hours during those long, hot, sleepy afternoons, telling each other of their adventures in the time they had been parted. Mostly it was Pandaras who talked. Yama kept his pain and his despair to himself. At night, the Shadow came to him while the others slept, feeble and full of rage. Its threats and boasts filled his dreams.

The bandar yoi inoie did not mourn the destruction of the lowland forests. 'There are many kinds of monstrous men in the lowlands,' Yoi Sendar told Yama. 'We were given the hills as our province by the Preservers and we do not need any other place. Besides, the low forests will regrow soon enough. They will take strength from the mud left behind by the water. In the lifetime of a man they will be as they always have been. Meanwhile, there will be plenty of game for us, because the animals have all fled to our hills.'

The bandar yoi inoie had many stories about the strange and fabulous creatures which lived in the lowland and hill forests. Yama had read about some of them in bestiaries in the library of the peel-house of his stepfather, the Aedile of Aeolis; others were entirely new to him. He knew about blood orchids, for instance, because they grew in the forests of the foothills of the Rim Mountains, but those were pygmies compared to the giant blossoms of these forests, as big as a house and surrounded by the bones of animals which had been lured on to their gluey bracts by clouds of pheromones. There were fisher orchids too, which grew on high branches and let down adhesive-covered roots which would wrap around anything which blundered into them and draw nutrients from the corpses; and orchids which emitted hypnotic scents and grew nets of fine roots into the flesh of their victims as they slept.

Fire ants built huge castles amongst the tall trees. One kind of tree was defended by hordes of tiny rodents which attacked anything that approached, and stripped neighbouring trees of their leaves so that they would not shade their host; in turn, the tree fed its army with a sugary cotton it grew on certain branches. Jacksnappers hung from branches, dropping on to their prey and wrapping them in fleshy folds covered with myriad bony hooks tipped with a paralysing poison. A certain kind of small, slow, naked monkey was the juvenile form. After mating, the male died and the female wrapped her tail around a suitable branch and spun a cocoon around herself, emerging as an adult jacksnapper, limbless and eyeless and without a brain.

The bandar yoi inoie had stories about the strange races of men which lived in the lowland forests too. There were tribes in which the men grew only a little after birth, and spent their lives in a special pouch in the belly of their mate. In one race, each family was controlled by a single fertile woman who grew monstrously fat and enslaved her sterile sisters, and the men were outcasts who fought fiercely if they met one another as they wandered the forests; there were great and bloody battles when fertile daughters matured and left their families and the men tried to win their favours. There were men who ran through the forest at night, drinking the blood of their mesmerised prey, and tribes of pale men and women who could transform themselves to look like other kinds of men – perhaps these were relatives of the mirror people Yama had met in the Palace of the Memory of the People.

Yama did not know which of these strange peoples were real and which were the stuff of stories. The forest folk were careless of the distinction. If it can be imagined, Yoi Sendar said, then surely it must be real. The Preservers who made this world were much greater than any of the races of men they had raised up from animals, and so they made more wonders than could possibly be imagined.

The bandar yoi inoie were happy in the forest. It was their home, as familiar to them as the peel-house and the City of the Dead were to Yama. They chanted long intricate melodies as they trotted through its green shadows, and sang and laughed and told long complicated jokes as they came back from hunting or while they cooked the prey they had caught or prepared the tubers and fruit they had collected.

Late one afternoon a party of hunters found a treecreeper and one man rushed back to tell the others. The entire troop, along with Yama and Pandaras, followed him to the place where the treecreeper had made its lair. It was a giant kapok tree, so big that twenty men linking arms would have been needed to embrace its circumference. Its smooth grey bark was split and scarred in several places, and Yoi Sendar pointed to the creature which could be glimpsed moving about inside.

'We will have it out soon. It is fine eating. It makes its home by rasping away the soft heartwood of a tree until it kills it, and it is dangerous when it is chased from its lair. But we are a brave people.'

While some of the forest folk danced on one side of the tree, provoking the treecreeper to lash out with its long, whip-like tongue from various splits in the tree-trunk, the rest built a fire of green wood at the base on the other side of the tree, and cut into the trunk to let in the smoke. The treecreeper was soon in distress, mewling and howling to itself. The forest folk darted in, dodging the lashing tongue and drumming at the base of the tree with stout clubs, raising a great noise.

At last the tormented treecreeper sprang from a slit high up in the trunk of the tree, just beneath the first branches. It moved very quickly; Yama did not see it until it was on the ground. It reared up on the two hindmost pairs of its many short stout legs, very tall and very thin. Its back was covered in overlapping bony plates; its belly in matted hair. Its sweetish, not unpleasant smell filled the clearing.

The forest folk surrounded it, one man or woman darting forwards to strike two or three quick blows to its legs while the others cheered. Pandaras joined in, cheered twice as loudly as anyone else. The treecreeper went down by degrees, mewling querulously. Its tiny eyes were faceted, glinting greenly in the matted pelt which covered its head. Its long scarlet tongue snaked across the trampled ground and Yoi Sendar ran forwards and pinned it with a stake.

After that, the forest folk swarmed over the treecreeper, jointing it while it was still alive and carrying the meat back to their camp in triumph. Pandaras was caught up in their excitement, his ragged shirt bloody and his eyes shining.

Yama did not join in the feast of fruit and treecreeper meat. He thought that he was like the kapok tree and the Shadow was like the treecreeper, rasping away at his self's soft core. And yet he knew that he would need the Shadow in what lay ahead. He could not drive it out until he knew how to obliterate his unwanted powers.

He wished he could be like the forest folk, who were dancing and singing with uncomplicated happiness in the fern-filled clearing. It was twilight. Red light from a great trench of fire beat across the bodies of the dancers. Trees stood quietly all around, woven cocoons pendant from their lower branches. How sweet life was for them, how simple, how innocent! A few hour of hunting or searching for fruit or tubers each day, the rest for play, for singing songs and telling stories. Their life the life of their fathers and grandfathers, always the same from the beginning of the world to its end.

Yama had forgotten that the bandar yoi inoie were in thrall to the Mighty People, but two days later they finally reached the valley where the Mighty People lived, and he saw how bad things were for their slaves.

14 ~ Slaves

'They may be a mighty people,' Pandaras said, 'but they must like a snug house. Even I would find one of those huts cramped.'

He stood beside Yama at the edge of the forest, looking across the valley which stretched away on either side, a wide flat grassland studded with little villages that were linked by narrow red paths running beside ditches of green water, each village a cluster of mud-walled huts and strips of cultivated land enclosed by thorn hedges.

'I don't like the look of it,' Pandaras added. 'See how thick and tall the hedges are. These people must have fearsome enemies. Surely now is the time to call on something that will take us far from here.'

'That would be too dangerous,' Yama said. 'Prefect Corin may have survived the fall of the garden, and he must not know where I am.'

In fact, there were very few machines here – fewer than Yama had ever known in a world where innumerable machines sped everywhere on unfathomable errands; not a tree might fall in the most remote forest without a witness.

'I don't see how he could have survived,' Pandaras said. 'I'd like to think it possible, because that would mean poor Tibor might have survived too. Forgive me for my presumption, master, but you cannot live in hiding for ever. You cannot waste your gift.'

'Do not speak of what you do not know,' Yama said sharply.

'I know a bad feeling when I get one,' the boy said. 'Look at our friends. It's as if they're going to their doom.'

It was early in the morning, with the sun only just clear of the peaks of the Rimwall Mountains. The forest folk had risen before dawn, and had been uncharacteristically subdued as they walked the last two leagues to the edge of the forest above the valley where their masters, the Mighty People, lived. Now they were removing the flowers and quills and feathers with which they had adorned their squat bodies, scrubbing away patterns of mud and pigments with bunches of wet grasses, combing out mud which had stiffened their coarse hair in ornamental spikes. They had walked naked through the forest; now they took loincloths from pouches and packs and stepped into them. Their torcs had been carefully wrapped up in oilcloth, and buried on a rocky point beneath a flat slab of sandstone.

The forest folk lined up, shivering in the chill grey air. Their chief, Yoi Sendar, went from one to the next, checking that every trace of adornment had been removed. When he reached Yama and Pandaras, he said formally, 'Below is the home of the family of Mighty People which owns us. We go to them with our gifts from the forest. You do not have to come with us, my friends. We have enjoyed your stories and lies and boasts in the forest, but we take up a different life now.'

'I need to find the temple,' Yama said.

Yoi Sendar shook his massive, ugly head from side to side. It meant *yes*. His baggy skin was bleeding from the places where he had drawn out his decorative quills. He said, 'Perhaps you can please the Mighty People in some way, and they will let you visit it.'

Pandaras said, 'Why are you so afraid of them? If they rule by fear, then they are not worthy to be your masters.'

Yoi Sendar would not meet the boy's stare. 'They have always been our masters. It has always been so, ever since the long-forgotten day when the Preservers set us in our domain. Our masters have changed, but they still need us, as you will see if you come with us.'

'There are many different peoples on the world,' Yama said, as Yoi Sendar stumped off to the head of the line of his people. 'Why do you deny that simple fact, Pandaras?'

'People everywhere are all the same, if you ask me. They are scared to be free. They make themselves slaves to stronger men because it is easier to be a slave than to be free. It is easier to worship the past than to plan for the future.'

'You have some extraordinary notions, Pandaras.'

'You taught me that, master, but I think you have forgotten it.'

'Did I? Well, I was younger then, and more foolish. Perhaps my bloodline ages more quickly than even yours, Pandaras. I feel as old as one of the Ancients of Days.'

Pandaras said, 'I have kept one of their stone blades. Please don't stop me, master, if I have to use it to help us escape. The thing in your head wanted you to be its slave, and I don't think you've quite shaken off the notion.'

Yoi Sendar raised both hands and gave a hoarse shout. His people lifted up their heavy packs of caterpillar meat and followed him into the valley, walking in single file down a narrow path that snaked through tall yellow grasses towards the nearest of the villages of the Mighty People. Yama saw that the mud huts inside the thorn hedge were separated from each other by an intricate arrangement of walls and courtyards. Each had its own exit tunnelled through the thorns, and as the bandar yoi inoie came down the slope, figures began to emerge from the tunnels, scrawny and stooped and grey-skinned.

Pandaras whispered to Yama, 'If they have changed, then it can't have been for the good. They seem a poor kind of people to me.'

'Do not be quick to judge,' Yama said.

The Mighty People spread out in a ragged line beneath a stand of cotton trees. A gang of children chased about, shouting or throwing stones or clods of earth at the adults, dodging stones thrown back at them. Men and women and children wore only loincloths, like those which the forest folk had put on. They were all bald, and the women had withered dugs which hung to their bellies.

When the forest folk drew near, the Mighty People ran forwards, brandishing whips and clips and rifles. They shouted sharply at the forest folk and at each other. As the forest folk were quickly separated into groups of five or six, one of the men went up to Yama and Pandaras and stared at them with unconcealed cupidity before turning and shouting to the others that these strangers were his.

'I am the Captain! You all remember that!'

The Captain's voice was shrill and grating. He had small, red-rimmed eyes and a sharply pursed beak of a mouth. When a small child toddled too close, he screamed, 'Get away or I'll shoot,' and aimed a blow with his rifle at the child. It bared its teeth and hissed, but backed away slowly, staring at Yama and Pandaras.

'Don't you worry,' the Captain told Yama. 'I'll make you my guest, and your slave here will be looked after by my slaves. As long as you have my protection the others won't dare touch either of you. I'm their Captain, the richest and most powerful of my people. They try and kill me many times for my power and wealth, but I'm too clever and too strong.'

Yama introduced himself and Pandaras.

Pandaras said, 'I am not a slave, but the squire of my master.'

The Captain spat at Pandaras's feet and said to Yama, 'Your slave is insolent, but you have the look of a fighter. That's good.'

Yama said, 'Are you at war, then?'

'Our young men have gone to fight in the great war of liberation,' the Captain said. 'Meanwhile, we look after what we have, as is only natural. We are all of us rich here, and other families scheme to take our wealth from us, but we will defeat them. We will grow richer and more powerful than any in the Valley.'

Yama said politely, 'I have heard much of you from the bandar yoi inoie, but it is interesting to see for myself what you are.'

'Where did these clots of filth find you? Yoi Sendar! Yoi Sendar, you ugly tub of guts! Come here!'

The Captain snapped his whip above the heads of the cluster of forest folk he had rounded up. Yoi Sendar stepped forwards, his heavy head bowed. He said in a small voice, 'All we have gathered, master, we give with open hands and open hearts.'

The Captain struck him back and forth across his broad shoulders with the stock of the whip, raising bloody welts. Yoi Sendar stepped backwards, still staring at the ground.

'Filth,' the Captain said. He was breathing heavily. A muddy stink rose up from him. 'They cannot change. Everything is always the same for them. They do not realize how we have been transfigured. They are a great burden to us, but we are strong and bear it.'

Yama looked around. Most of the skinny grey Mighty People were driving their groups of forest folk into the tunnels of clay-plastered wicker which led through the tall thorn hedge. Even the gang of children had four or five of the oldest of the forest folk, and were fighting over the single pack of caterpillar meat which had been brought to them.

Several of the Mighty People shouted at the Captain, complaining that he could not keep the strangers to himself. 'Watch me do it!' the Captain shouted back. 'You don't think I'm strong enough?'

The Captain seemed to be in a permanent rage. He turned suddenly and fired his rifle in the air, and an old woman who had been creeping towards him stopped and held out her empty hands. 'I know your tricks, mother,' the Captain screamed. There were flecks of foam at the corners of his mouth. 'Try and take what is mine and I'll kill you. I swear it!' He turned to Yama and Pandaras and said, 'She could not keep her slaves and tries to steal food from honest folk. You will be safe with me. I give you some of my own food and water, and you will help me.'

Yama said, 'We are strangers, dominie. We have come to visit your temple.'

'Temple? What have this filth being telling you? They are the fathers and mothers of lies. They lie so much they no longer know what is true. You come with me. I will keep you safe.' The Captain snapped his whip at his group of forest folk. 'Bring your tributes. Poor, rotten stuff it looks, and not much of it. You've all been lazing about in the forest instead of working hard. But now you'll work. I'll make sure of it. Hurry or I'll make you bleed!'

The compound of the Captain's hut was enclosed by a high mudbrick wall topped with briars and broken glass. It was ankle deep in red clay kept wet by a leaking standpipe. A few pygmy goats were penned in one corner, whisking at flies with their tails while they cropped in a desultory way at a pile of melon husks.

The Captain supervised the unloading of the smoked caterpillar meat with brutal impatience. When the last string of meat had been hung on the rack outside the hut, he dismissed the forest folk and told Yama to send away his slave.

'Find out what you can,' Yama whispered to Pandaras.

'I think I have the best of it,' Pandaras whispered back. 'This is as bad a place as I have ever seen.'

The hut was mean and cramped, with no furniture but a little three-legged stool. A sleeping platform was cut into the thick wall. A solar stove gave out dim red light and a iron pot of maize porridge bubbled on its hot plate. The beaten earth floor was strewn with dry grass in which black beetles rustled; there was a nest of banded rats in the thatch of the roof. Everything was dirty and stank of goat and the Captain's stale body odour, but gorgeous portraits of dignified elders of the family stood in niches here and there, meticulously rendered in oil pigments and framed in intricately worked metal, and the bowl into which the Captain scooped a meagre measure of maize porridge had been lovingly carved from a dark, hard wood.

When Yama commented on these things, the Captain was dismissive. 'These are old works from the old times. A few trinkets from all the worthless stuff we had then. We are much wealthier now.'

The maize porridge was unsalted and unflavoured pap, and the portion no more than three spoonfuls, but the Captain expected fulsome acknowledgment of his generosity. It seemed that he had great expectations of Yama, and as he boasted and blustered, Yama soon learned more than he wanted to of the way the Mighty People lived now they had been changed by the heretics. Each adult had his or her own hut and strip of arable land, jealously guarded from all the others. As in the quarters of the Department of Indigenous Affairs in the Palace of the Memory of the People, husbands lived apart from wives. As soon as they could walk, children were abandoned and had to join the half-wild pack which lived outside the village fence. Those who survived to sexual maturity were driven out of the pack, and had to find or build their own hut and their own field strip, or else live in the grassland as best they could.

Every man or woman was a nation of one, and spent most of their waking hours hoarding their scanty possessions. They had discarded their old names – the names from the time before the change – and if they had new names they told them to no one. There was no love, no pity, no mercy. All these things were regarded as signs of weakness. There were only lust, jealousy and hatred. The old and sick had to fend for themselves, and were usually killed by the pack of children or by an adolescent who wanted their hut.

The Shadow gloated over this. *We will make all men like this*, it whispered inside Yama's head. *Slaves to the things they desire most.*

The worst thing of all was that the Mighty People considered this way of life to be the highest possible form of civilization. The old ways, when the family had herded cattle and prized the craftsmanship of their pottery and metalwork and art, were despised. The cattle were all dead, killed either by poison in acts of jealousy or slaughtered because it was too difficult to guard them in the pastures, which had grown rough and wild. The Mighty People had a taboo against entering the forest and relied entirely upon the forest folk they had enslaved for meat, and for most of their supply of fruit and tubers too, for their field strips were poorly maintained, the crops stunted and diseased. More work went into guarding the field strips than into cultivation.

The only thing that united the Captain's family was a hatred of the neighbouring villages. Everyone contributed the labour of their slaves towards defence of the village against other families. The Captain had plans to expand his family's territory, and he expected Yama to help him. He walked Yama around the boundary of his family's land, never losing sight of the village, and showed off the network of ditches and ponds which had been built long ago by all the people of the valley to irrigate the land with water from lakes high in the foothills of the Rim Mountains.

'If we can control these, then we can control all the land around us,' the Captain said.

'What would you do with it?'

'Eh, why we would own it, of course.' The Captain gave Yama a crafty look. 'That's the first thing. All things flow from ownership.'

It seemed to Yama that the Mighty People were as much slaves as the bandar yoi inoie – perhaps more so, for the forest folk had been coerced into slavery, but the Mighty People had made themselves slaves of their own free will. By prizing ownership above all else, they were themselves owned by the things they coveted. He remembered how the forest folk had hidden their torcs at the edge of the forest, and thought that he could guess what had happened to the paintings, pottery and metalwork made in the time before the heretics had kindled a Change War here.

The Captain launched into a long diatribe against the neighbouring villages. The feud was only ten years old, but it was packed with treachery, ambushes and murder. All this, the Captain swore, would be avenged. He worked himself into a fit of rage and at one point unslung his rifle and aimed it at various parts of the sky before he clacked his lips together and slung it over his shoulder.

'A fighter like you,' he said, 'could profit greatly here.'

'I am only one man.'

It seemed that everywhere Yama went, people wanted him to kill other people. He was sickened by it.

'There are plenty of slaves,' the Captain said. 'It doesn't matter if they are killed because we will have the slaves of our enemies. We will make our enemies our slaves.' He clacked his pursed mouth at the thought. He said, 'You will be rewarded, of course. Their stores of the old stuff will become mine, and I will let you have some pieces.'

'It is my understanding that the old stuff is worthless.'

'To people like us, of course. But to those less refined, like yourself, it would be a great prize. Even the piles of shit our enemies hoard would be worth something to someone like you.' The Captain did not mean the insult, Yama saw. He believed himself to be the centre of the world, and so all other men were naturally his inferiors. He told Yama, 'Rare metals, precious stones. Perhaps as much as your slave can carry. A great prize for only a little work.'

Spit on his treasure, the Shadow said. *Take the rifle and shove it into his mouth and make him beg for his life. Kill him. Kill them all.*

It raved on, but its words were feeble sparks. Yama ignored it.

They were walking back towards the thorn-fenced village. Yama was trying to think of some way of refusing the Captain without angering him, but then he saw something that made him change his mind.

The pack of children were quarrelling in the shade of the stand of cotton trees. At first Yama thought that they had caught an animal and were tearing it apart, but then he saw that they had killed one of the forest folk and were stripping raw meat from its bones with their teeth. A girl sat apart from the others, gnawing on a double handful of bloody entrails. Three of the smaller children kicked the remains of the severed head about in the dusty grass. The eyes were gone and the skull had been smashed to get at the brains. Nearby, two of the forest folk sat with their arms wrapped around each other, rocking back and forth and keening in sorrow.

The Captain glanced at this and said, 'None of the children's slaves last very long. We make sure they get the runts of the litters. And the old, of course. No sense keeping a slave that's too old to work, eh?'

Yama had not thought to wonder until now why there were no old men or women amongst the troop of bandar yoi inoie. He controlled his disgust and said, 'I must talk with my servant.'

'Don't take long,' the Captain said. 'I want to get back to my compound. It doesn't pay to leave it in the hands of slaves. A man must look after his wealth himself, or he is not a man and does not deserve it.'

So he and Pandaras were prisoners, Yama thought. He had only suspected it before. He had been a fool.

'I'm glad I'm not stuck with that old goat,' Pandaras said, when Yama found him. 'What does he want of us?'

'You saw what happened to the children's slave.'

'I heard the screaming. Yoi Sendar wouldn't let me go near.' Pandaras glanced at the chief of the forest folk, who sat listlessly with several of his family in the shade of a big cotton tree. 'It is easy to see how it is with these Mighty People. They are each a kingdom to themselves, master. They do not trust anyone, not even their own children. This is a crazy place. I told you we should not have come.'

'We must find the temple, Pandaras.'

'I asked about that, but the forest folk have suddenly lost their tongues. What is wrong with them, master? Why don't they defend themselves?'

'They are indigens. They know only what they have always known, and cannot imagine anything else. Once upon a time they lived in harmony with the Mighty People, exchanging food hunted in the forest for food grown in this valley, each race enriching the other. But the Mighty People changed.'

'They are evil, master. No people preys on another!'

Yama thought of the Amnan, who had hunted the fisherfolk until his stepfather had put a stop to it. He said, 'Certain bloodlines see the indigens as no more than animals. And so here. But I have never seen so wretched a people as the Mighty People. They are not evil, but gripped by a kind of madness.'

'I would call it evil,' Pandaras said. 'I suppose we are prisoners here. Yoi Sendar thinks you are an honoured guest. He is pleased that he has brought us to this place.'

'The forest folk are used to bringing people here. The Mighty People were once extraordinary artists and artisans, and I expect that in the old days many traders came here. The Mighty People have no interest in trading now, but the forest folk cannot understand that.' Yama explained the Captain's plans for war against the neighbouring villages, and said, 'He thinks that I am a cateran.'

'So you are, master. Everyone in the world can see it but you.'

'You are supposed to be my slave, Pandaras. I think it would be a good idea if you acted like it. The Captain has treasure hidden somewhere close by. I think all the Mighty People do.'

Pandaras nodded. 'The old stuff is all in one place, according to Yoi Sendar. He was boasting about the riches of this village as if they were his own. I didn't believe him until now because he wouldn't tell me where it was.'

'Yoi Sendar is loyal to his master. You forget the torcs the forest folk wore. Where did you think those came from?'

Pandaras struck his forehead and laughed. 'I am a fool, master. I am close to a fortune and failed to see it.'

'I am going to ask the Captain for proof of the fee he has promised for making war against the other villages.'

'You have a plan, then. That's good. You are recovering from your ordeal, master.'

'Money is not important. Things are not important. Look around you if you do not believe me. I do not do this for money, Pandaras,' Yama said. 'I do it because I must.'

He explained his plan, then made a show of knocking the boy down and kicking him, drawing his blows as much as possible. When he returned to the Captain, the man grumbled that he was free enough with his time. 'I have not forgotten that my time is yours,' Yama said. 'I spend a little of it now so that you will win great things later.'

'If that was my slave, I would kill him.'

'He is all I have.'

'You can have plenty of slaves after we have conquered our enemies.'

'You promise much, Captain, but if I am to fight for you I would like to see a token of these riches.'

'You will have enough when our enemies are broken. Most of it must come to me, of course, but you will have your share.'

'I would see something of it with my own eyes,' Yama said. 'What harm in that? You have said that you regard it as worthless.'

The Captain stared up at Yama suspiciously. He said, 'It will come to you in good time.'

'No man can trust another. You have taught me that. I must see how I will profit before I agree to help you.'

The Captain went cross-eyed in an effort to contain his sudden anger. He said, 'I should kill you!'

'Then you would certainly have no help from me.'

The Captain turned away and stamped and breathed heavily until he was calm, then said grudgingly, 'It is a matter for all the village.'

The Mighty People argued for a long time, past sunset and into the night. The forest folk lit lanterns and hung them from the lower branches of the cotton trees. The Mighty People were all in a rage with each other, and nothing was resolved until a man went for the Captain with a long knife and the Captain shot him in the belly. More shouting, this time mostly from the Captain. The wounded man was carried off by his slaves. Later, the Captain came over to where Yama was sitting with Pandaras.

'We will take you there now,' he said grumpily. 'But you must be blindfolded.'

All the villagers came because no one trusted anyone else. They were prisoners of their own greed and suspicion. The Captain was quite happy to explain this as he walked beside Yama. He said that it was a sign of their superior way of life.

'Anyone who goes to the hoard alone is killed by the others and their stuff is divided up.'

'How would you know if someone went there?'

'We all watch each other. No one can leave the village without the others knowing, and if someone does not come when he is called, then he must lose all he owns.' The Captain added, 'Also, we keep watch on it. You could not find the place, but even if you did, we would know straight away.'

As well as being blindfolded, Yama and Pandaras had their arms bound. In case of trouble, the Captain said, although Yama guessed that it was because the Mighty People thought they might have friends waiting in ambush. The filthy cloth tied over his eyes was not quite light-proof – he could dimly see the flare of the torches carried by the handful of forest folk the Mighty People had brought with them – but he did not bother to try and memorize the twists and turns of the path, which led always upwards. He silently endured the stink of the Mighty People and the spidery feel of their sharp-fingered hands as they guided him left or right. Pandaras began to complain volubly, but then there was the sound of a blow, and the boy said nothing more.

When the blindfold was at last removed, Yama found that he was standing at the edge of a tall cliff. It was too dark to see the bottom, but the Captain told Yama that it was a long drop. 'We throw down those who try and cheat us,' he said. 'They break on the rocks far below and jackals eat their brains. I'll do it to you if you try any tricks.'

Yama said, 'Do you not trust me?'

'Of course not.' The Captain clacked his lips. He was amused. 'And if you said that you trusted me I would not believe you.'

Yama sketched a bow and said, 'Then we understand each other completely.'

The Mighty People surrounded them. Several of the forest folk held torches made from branches dipped in pitch, which crackled with red flame and black smoke. Two held Pandaras, who sat on a flat stone with his arms between his knees and a strip of cloth tied over his eyes. All around was a desolation of boulders and creepers and stunted trees, with the edge of the forest a distant dark line against the black sky. It was midnight. The Eye of the Preservers was almost at zenith, a smudged thumbprint that shed a baleful red glow.

The Captain dropped one end of a coil of rope over the edge. The other was looped around a knob of rock rubbed as smooth as a dockside bollard.

'Climb down,' the Captain told Yama. 'There is a cave hidden behind creepers not far below. Look inside and you will see a great store of the old stuff. Our enemies have much lesser stores, of course, but even one tenth of one of them will be a great treasure to a man like you. Do not stay there long, or we will cut the rope.'

Yama held out his bound hands. 'You will have to untie me.'

There was an argument about this amongst the Mighty People. Some wanted the Captain to climb down with Yama and others suggested that someone else should climb down, because Yama was the Captain's property, but no one wanted to volunteer because that meant risking all for the benefit of everyone else. At last the Captain prevailed. Yama would be released from his bonds, but he would have only five minutes to look at the treasure or the rope would be cut.

The rope was knotted at intervals; even though Yama was carrying one of the smoky torches, it was easy to clamber down it. *They will kill us*, the Shadow said, but Yama ignored the crawling sparks of its voice. A draught of cold air blew from the cave mouth, stirring the leafy creepers which hung over it like a curtain. Yama kicked them aside and, clinging one-handed to the swaying rope, thrust in first the torch and then his head.

Here was the treasure of the Mighty People: broken pottery tumbled in heaps; flaking paintings covered in grey mould; exquisitely carved chairs riddled with beetle and glowing in streaks of foxfire where fungus rotted the wood; intricate metalwork corroded by verdigris.

The Captain's voice drifted down from above. 'You see!' he shouted. 'You see that we are a very rich people! Now you must return, or we will cut the rope!'

Yama looked up. The Mighty People stood along the edge of the cliff, silhouetted against the flare of torches. He said, 'Now I have seen your treasure I know exactly how to help you,' and threw his torch on to a stack of chairs half-turned to sawdust by white emmets.

The Mighty People did not realize what had happened at first. Yama had plenty of time to find a good handhold beside the cave mouth before smoke began to pour out of it. The creepers crisped and withered in the heat. Howls, from above, then; a scatter of rifle shots. Something unravelled past Yama, striking his shoulder as it fell. The rope had been cut.

It was not difficult to climb sideways along the cliff. The creepers were strong enough to bear Yama's weight, and there were plenty of hand- and foot-holds. The Mighty People were too busy trying to save their treasure to search for him. They swarmed down the cliff on ropes, but none thought to take anything with which to beat out or stifle the fire. They hung from their ropes and shrieked in rage at each other. One man lost his hold when flame belched out of the cave mouth and he fell screaming into the darkness.

Yama climbed over the edge of the cliff, strode through the circle of forest folk, and pulled the strip of cloth from Pandaras's eyes. The boy showed his sharp white teeth. Blood, fresh and bright, matted the sleek hair on top of his head and trickled down his face. He said, 'I will kill whoever it was that struck me. I swear it.'

'We will only do what we need to do,' Yama said. He took the sharp stone blade from Pandaras's shirt pocket and sawed through the rope which bound his arms, then turned to the forest folk and told them, 'I am your master now. Do you understand? I took the Mighty People's treasure and gave it to the air.'

Yoi Sendar stepped forwards and said humbly, 'You must kill me, for I have failed my masters.'

'I am not going to kill you,' Yama told him, 'but you will be changed. You will go back to the village with Pandaras and bring the rest of your people. Do it, or I will kill all of the Mighty People. The others will come with me.'

Pandaras said, 'How will I find you, master?'

'You will be with the chief of the forest folk. He will know how to find me. Go now, as quickly as you can!'

When Pandaras and Yoi Sendar had run off into the darkness, Yama went to the edge of the drop and shouted down to the Captain. 'When I saw your treasure I knew what to do at once!'

The Captain howled and brought up the rifle and shot at Yama, but he was shaking with rage and the pellet went wide. Recoil swung him like the clapper of a bell and he dropped his torch when he slammed back into the cliff. It tumbled away, dwindling to a point of light that suddenly flared far below and went out.

Before the Captain could aim his rifle again, Yama said, 'If anyone tries to kill me or to climb up I will cut your rope.'

'I will kill you! My slaves will kill you!'

Two or three of the other Mighty People got off a few pistol shots, but the angle was too difficult and the pellets hit the rock face beneath Yama's feet or whined off into the sky. The Captain shouted at them to stop and a woman said loudly and clearly, 'You did this. You are not my husband. You are not the father of my children. You are nothing, Tuan Ah.'

It was the Captain's secret name. He screamed with rage and swung around on his rope and tried to aim his rifle at his wife, but she was quicker and shot him twice with her pistol. He dropped from the rope and vanished into the darkness below.

There was a silence. At last the Captain's wife said, 'Are you there, cateran?'

'I do not want anything from you except your slaves.'

Some of the Mighty People began to shout threats, but the Captain's wife shouted louder than any of them. 'Try and kill him if you want, but he'll cut your ropes before you get halfway up.'

The Mighty People could have easily overwhelmed Yama by swarming up their ropes all at once, but he had guessed that it would never occur to them to act together. He said, 'I am freeing you too. I free you from the past. Do you understand? When I have gone you can go back to your village and take up your lives.'

'Tuan Ah was a fool to trust you,' the Captain's wife said. 'I had eight children by him, but I am glad he is dead. You have started a war, cateran. We will need slaves, and if we cannot hunt you down we will take them from our enemies. Pray that we do not find you. I am crueller than Tuan Ah.'

'I am going where you cannot find me,' Yama said, and turned away and led the remaining forest folk into the forest.

15 ~ Three Sleeps and a Miracle

Pandaras and Yoi Sendar, leading the rest of the forest folk, found Yama soon after dawn. It was already hot. Threads of mist hung between the dense stands of bamboo which grew along the edge of the forest. Pandaras told Yama that he had set fire to the treasures which the Mighty People had kept in their huts, and this diversion had allowed them all to escape.

'But I had to kill someone, master, the man the Captain had shot. It was the only way to make his slaves come with me.'

'I think that the Mighty People will be more concerned about the loss of their treasure and their slaves,' Yama said. 'They do not care for each other, only for what they own. But in any case they will not follow us here. The forest is taboo to them.'

'Well, I'm sorry I killed him,' Pandaras said, 'even if he would have killed me if I hadn't done it.'

'I fear that it will not be the last death,' Yama said.

He went over to Yoi Sendar and greeted him. The chief of the forest folk bowed his head and said formally, 'All we have, master, we give with open hands and open hearts.'

Yama raised his voice so that all the forest folk could hear him. 'I want nothing but your friendship, Yoi Sendar.'

The small, ugly man did not look up. He said stubbornly, 'We will gladly give all we have, but we cannot give what we do not have.'

'Perhaps I can change your mind,' Yama said. 'It has been a long night. We will find a place to rest, and in the evening we will speak again.'

Although they had returned to their home amongst the tall trees of the forest, the bandar yoi inoie were muted and forlorn. They made no attempt to decorate themselves, and still wore their loincloths. They lay down in groups of three or four between the buttress roots of the big trees, talking quietly.

'I will watch you while you sleep, master,' Pandaras said.

'They will not harm us,' Yama said, although he was not really sure what would happen once he had freed the forest folk.

'I have caught the disease of mistrust,' Pandaras said. 'Sleep, master. I'll make sure nothing happens to you.'

It was not exactly sleep, but more like a kind of swooning fall inside his own self. Yama had performed this miracle before, on the baby entrusted to him by the mirror people, although he had not known then exactly how he had done it. He had thought that the aspect of Angel had guided him, but he knew now that she had been drawn there because she had hoped to glimpse the root of his power.

Now he had to discover it for himself.

He fell deeper than any ordinary dream, plunging down as he had so often swum towards the bottom of the river as a child. Away from the sunlit mirror where kelp plants trailed their long green fronds, following the stipes which dwindled away into darkness, the muscles of his throat and chest aching and the need to draw another breath growing and growing until at last he had to turn back to the sunlight. He had never been able to reach the river bottom then, but now he felt that he could fall for ever. And as he fell he became aware of finer and finer divisions of the world, of machines smaller than the single-celled plants which were the base of most river life. Those tiny plants were so small that they could only be seen when they stained the water red or brown in their uncountable billions, but the machines were smaller still: ten thousand of them could have been fitted on one of the motes of dust which had swarmed in the beam of sunlight which had illuminated the Aedile's room when Yama had broken into it, on the morning of the siege of Dr Dismas's tower.

He had thought then that his adventures had just been beginning, but he knew now that they had begun long before he had been born.

He turned his attention to one of the minuscule machines, and it opened up around him like the stacks of books in the library of the peel-house. He half-expected to find Zakiel around a corner as he wandered through the serried rows, but it soon became clear that there was no thought here, only information. So much information, in so small a space! Zakiel had taught him that the information which encoded the form of his body could be contained in a speck of matter smaller than the least punctuation mark in a finely printed book. There was less information here than that, but it was still overwhelming. He took down a book at random. Its pages were covered with neat lines of zeroes and ones: a single long number, a single set of instructions. And there were thousands of books.

Yama remembered how Angel's aspect had seemed to show him certain places inside the brain of the baby of the Mirror People; she had used him to find out where they were, but he had not known it then. Subtly altered, those places had become the nodes where the tiny machines could excyst and begin to amplify complexity into true consciousness, the change which was the miraculous gift of the Preservers, the miracle with which he had been entrusted.

He concentrated on recalling everything about that moment. What Angel's aspect had said, subtly prompting and probing him. How he had felt, what he had seen, how he had acted without knowing he had acted. Without thought, he took down a book and ran his finger over the rows of zeroes and ones faster than he could see, changing them in a blur. Put the book back, pulled down another. Over and over until it was done.

He sat up inside a green tent, for a moment unsure if he were dreaming or awake. Pandaras had woven a kind of bower of fern leaves around him. He pushed the fronds aside. It was evening, the air hot and still, light deepening between the soaring trunks of the trees. The forest folk were moving about; they had lit several small fires and were roasting meat over them.

'I have found out where the temple is,' Pandaras said. 'Yoi Sendar wouldn't talk at first, but I told him that you would kill all of the Mighty People if he didn't tell me. I made them go and get food, too. It isn't like it was before. No singing, no joy. They are very afraid, I think because they do not understand what has happened to them.'

'That will change.'

'Here, master. Drink this.' It was a gourd half-full of foamy, sweet-smelling juice. Pandaras said, 'There's a kind of hollow vine which gushes water when you cut it. It's good.'

Yama took the gourd, but did not drink. He said, 'Give me your bit of stone,' and used it to slice open his palm. The stone was so sharp that the wound scarcely hurt, although it bled quickly and freely. Yama let blood patter from his fingertips into the gourd. Not much blood would be needed, but he counted off a full minute before he let Pandaras bandage the wound.

Then he called the forest folk together and had them each take a single sip from the gourd. There was just enough. Yoi Sendar swallowed the last of it and handed back the gourd without comment.

'Sleep, then do as you will,' Yama told them. 'I cannot live your lives for you. You must discover how to do that yourselves. And when you have done that, remember this. You can free others as I have freed you. Let them drink a little of your blood mixed in wine or in water and they will be freed too.'

They did not understand him then, of course, but soon enough they would. He tried to explain it to Pandaras, but he was so very tired that he fell asleep halfway through the telling.

When he woke it was dawn. The forest folk were gone. Pandaras said he had not seen them leave, although he swore that he had stayed up all night, and said that they must have melted into the forest as mist melts into air. He pointed to a pile of rags, and added, 'They left behind their loincloths. Maybe they'll go back to the way they were before all this started.'

'No,' Yama said. 'Now they will begin to be something else.'

'Like the baby of the mirror people? I remember how you made the fireflies dance around it.' Pandaras yawned. 'There is a little fruit for breakfast. They ate all the meat last night, and I do not think you are the kind of man who can chew hide and hooves.'

'You are becoming too used to miracles,' Yama said, and smiled. The half-healed wounds in his face tugged against each other. For the first time he could allow himself to feel that this might soon be over. He could allow himself the luxury of hope. He told Pandaras chidingly, 'Not only do you dismiss the miracle at once, but you do not bother to try and understand what it means.'

'If you changed them all, then it really was a miracle, master. You took a whole night over that baby.'

'I have machines in my blood and so do you. Everyone does. It is the greatest gift of the Preservers. The miracle was simply a matter of persuading them to do the work for me.'

177

Pandaras touched his throat. He had mended the fresh rents in his shirt, wrapped the stump of his left wrist in a bit of bright red silk, sleeked down his hair and strung a chain of yellow orchids around his neck. The coin hung at his chest like a brooch and he wore the fetish on his left arm. He looked like a jade about to embark on the long and complex wooing of a fair lady.

He said, 'We are all filled with the breath of the Preservers, master. It's well known. All except the indigens, of course, unless someone like you works a miracle.'

'No,' Yama said. 'Everything in the world is touched by the breath of the Preservers for everything comes from them. All I did was help the forest folk recognize what they already possessed. I have changed the machines in my blood so that they can infect all the indigenous peoples of the world. That was why I made the forest folk drink my blood. And in turn their blood will become active, and change any who drink it. I have freed them to be what they will. If they choose, they can free all the other troops of the forest folk which come here to find food for the Mighty People.'

The first rays of the sun had begun to shine through the understorey of the high canopy of the forest. Pandaras pointed aslant the light. 'I'm not sure if I understood all of that, master, but I would guess that our work here is done. Yoi Sendar said that the temple is a day's walk in that direction. I'd guess it would take us twice as long, as we're not used to the forest.'

They walked through the green silence of the forest for most of the day. They spoke very little, each absorbed in his own thoughts. For the first time since he had leaned at the window of the room above the stables of *The Crossed Axes*, the inn where he had met Pandaras, and looked out across the great city of Ys, Yama felt an immense peace. He was who he was, no more and no less; he gave himself to his fate as a leaf borne on the River may be carried the length of the inhabited world. The day was beautiful, and their walk enlarged and celebrated that beauty.

Towards evening, they stopped at the edge of a bluff which looked across the valley. The thorn fenced villages of the Mighty People stood here and there amongst the network of ditches, canals and paths that webbed the grassland. Hills rose on the far side of the valley, with more hills behind them. The sun was setting beyond the Rim

Mountains. Its light spread out as if it were trying to embrace the world.

Parasol trees grew in this part of the forest, the tapered columns of their trunks ringed by widespread green fronds. As light drained from the sky, the midribs of the fronds collapsed, folding against the trunks with a stealthy rustling and creaking, like so many dowagers arranging the underskirts of their gowns.

Yama and Pandaras lay down to sleep on layers of fern fronds the boy had woven together. He said that he had learned this trick during a stay with one of his uncles, who had been a basketmaker. 'A squire must know a little of everything, I reckon,' he said, 'so it's as well I had such a large family.'

He had discovered a clump of water vines that scrambled around the trunk of one of the parasol trees, so that they had been able to quench their thirst, but he had not found anything to eat. 'But we'll reach the temple tomorrow, master. I'm certain of it, unless that gargoyle was lying to us.'

'He could not lie. At least, not then.'

Pandaras rubbed his hand over his face and yawned and said sleepily, 'Did you really change them, master?'

'The machines changed them. In time I hope that they will change all the indigenous peoples.'

The mirror people and the husbandmen of the Palace of the Memory of the People. The fisherfolk of the Great River and all the tribes who lived in the wild parts of its shore, the forest folk and all the strange races of indigens the forest folk claimed to know, the horsemen of the high plains and the mountaineers and the rock wights, and many more. Yama tried to remember them all, and fell asleep, counting them still in his dreams.

In the morning, Yama and Pandaras woke to find fruit and fresh, juicy pea vine pods in a string bag hanging from a stick thrust into a cleft in the trunk of one of the parasol trees. They looked for a long time, but found no other sign of the forest folk.

'Remember what I told you!' Yama shouted into the trees. 'Let others drink a little of your blood! Then they will be free too!'

The green silence of the forest swallowed his words.

Yama and Pandaras walked all day along the edge of the ridge above the valley, at the margin of the forest. And at sunset, just as Pandaras had predicted, they came to the temple.

16 ~ The Holy Slave

The façade of the temple had been carved into the face of a tall cliff of red sandstone, intricately worked and painted gold and white and ultramarine. It was approached by a long road that switchbacked up from the valley floor, ending at a single span bridge over the narrow, deep gorge at the edge of the wide plaza spread in front of the temple. In the centre of the plaza was a simple square altar ringed by tall, white, unadorned pillars, which had probably functioned as a day shrine where people had gone to ask small favours of the Preservers or to remember their dead. There was a string of flat-roofed little houses to one side, where the priest and other temple staff had lived, and a meadow by the stream which fell into the gorge, where penitents and palmers could have camped.

But the meadow was overgrown with pioneer acacias and wild banana plants now; the gardens of the houses contained only dry stalks; weeds thrust up between the slabs of polished sandstone which paved the plaza. A window shutter banged and banged in the evening breeze, like an idiot who knew only one word. Turkey vultures had built untidy nests on the flat tops of the pillars around the day shrine; their droppings streaked the pillars, and the cracked bones of their prey littered the tiles below. But someone had swept the long flight of wide steps which led up to the entrance of the temple, and prayer flags and banners in bright primary colours fluttered from poles along one side of the plaza.

'The Mighty People killed the priest and the hierodules during their Change War,' Pandaras whispered. 'They killed the Archivist and the Commissioner too. They burned the Commissioner and a maniple of soldiers in his peel-house, but they killed the others here. Yoi Sendar said that those who killed the Archivist ate his brains, because they wanted to gain power over the dead.'

He and Yama squatted in dry brush at the top of a pebbly slope that overlooked the plaza. Pandaras had taken out his stone blade, and was sharpening it on a bit of flint he held between his feet.

'I do not think there will be a need for that,' Yama said.

'It could be the Prefect. Or that doctor. You have powerful enemies, master. They are not easy to kill, and if they survived the fall of the gardens they will be searching for you.'

'Dr Dismas would not wait for us in a temple – it is not his style. And Prefect Corin would not bother to set out flags or sweep the entrance. If it is someone we know, then it can be only one person. And if it is not, then I hope that whoever has appointed himself custodian of this place will do us no harm. Besides, this is the only way to the midpoint of the world which does not involve a hundred days of walking.'

Yama stood up, crabbed down the slope in a cloud of dust, and ran straight out across the plaza. Dry weeds crackled underfoot. A pair of turkey vultures took flight. Pandaras came down more cautiously, holding the stone blade up by his shoulder, the stump of his left wrist tucked between two toggles of his shirt. He hurried to catch up with Yama, who was walking around the circle of pillars – someone had swept the altar and tried to scrub away the signs which had been scrawled there – towards the stair which led up to the entrance of the façade.

Pandaras said breathlessly, 'At least we could have waited until after supper, master!'

'I do not think we should rely on the forest folk any longer. They have other concerns now. And please, Pandaras, put away that blade. Show that we come as friends.'

But Pandaras did not hear him. He gave a sudden yell and ran past Yama and scampered up the steps. A tall, pale-skinned figure had appeared at the entrance of the temple.

It was Tibor.

'I knew that you had survived the flood,' the hierodule told Yama, 'and I am pleased that you found your way here.'

Yama smiled and said, 'I will free you of your obligation soon,

Tibor. We will sleep here tonight, but we have a long way to go, and must set off as soon as we are rested.'

'I have already found something else to serve,' Tibor said.

They were sitting cross-legged on the terrace before the entrance of the temple. The hierodule wore a white shirt left unbuttoned to display the two vertical scars on his chest, and trousers of a stiff, silvery material which he had slit at the waist and ankles because they were slightly too small for him. He had brought out a tray of food and beakers of wine and distilled water, and Yama and Pandaras ate hungrily, although the food had been too long in a freezer – the limp vegetables were crunchy with ice crystals at their cores, the flat breads were dry, and the sauces had lost most of their savour.

'The people of the valley killed the priest and the hierodules of this temple,' Pandaras said. 'They have turned their backs on the Preservers. It isn't safe for people like you, Tibor. You think only of serving, but this isn't the place for it.'

'I know what happened here,' Tibor said. He chewed at a twig, rolling it around his lips with his long red tongue; he had lost his cigarette makings in the flood. 'But that was many years ago. I am not afraid. Things will be different now.'

'The forest folk might want to come here now, I suppose,' Pandaras said, 'but I still think that you should come with us.'

Yama asked Tibor how he had escaped Prefect Corin, and the hierodule explained that he had still been struggling with the Prefect when the tidal wave had smashed into the floating garden, knocking it from the air and washing the two men into the river. 'We were torn apart,' Tibor said, 'and then I was too busy trying not to drown to try to follow him. I was dragged down by a tremendous whirlpool, and I think I may have touched the bottom of the river, so deep was I drawn. Just as my breath was about to burst from my chest, I was shot up like a cork, and came to the surface near an uprooted tree. I clung to its sturdy trunk and was borne with it wherever the flood chose to take me. Many small animals had already sought safety there, and bedraggled birds alighted on its leafy branches to take refuge from the rain, so that I was not without food. I drifted for two days amidst a growing fleet of other uprooted trees, until at last the failing waters stranded them all and I could walk across them into forested hills untouched by the flood. This part of the world is mostly populated by indigenous peoples, and I knew that the only temple for fifty leagues all around stood beyond the hills. And so I made my way across them, and after many hardships I will not trouble you with at last arrived here.'

'You were looking for something to serve,' Pandaras said.

'I am a hierodule.'

Yama said, 'You had food and drink ready for us. How did you know that we were coming here?'

Tibor spread his big, six-fingered hands and said gravely, 'Why, she told me. If you had not come here, I would have had to fetch you.'

For the first time since he had escaped the Mighty People, Yama felt the Shadow stir. He said, 'I thought it might be something like that. You had better show me the shrine.'

Tibor nodded. 'She is waiting for you, Yamamanama. And do not be afraid. She forgives you for the time you tried to kill her.'

The long processional path still retained a feeble blue luminiscence. It led them down wide corridors and through a nest of round chambers with intricate murals painted on their walls and ceilings to the naos at the heart of the temple, a vast dry cave that could easily have held a thousand petitioners. As Yama and Pandaras followed Tibor into it, like emmets creeping into a darkened house, tiny sparks whirled down from above to crown them. Pandaras laughed to see them: fireflies.

Yama said, 'How far back into the plateau does the complex run, Tibor?'

'Further than I am allowed to explore,' the hierodule said. 'She will answer all your questions.'

The floor was inlaid with a spiral pattern of garnet slabs; the reflections of the fireflies glittered underfoot as Yama and Pandaras followed Tibor towards a faint glow that curdled in the darkness ahead, flickering in the black disc of the shrine.

It stood on a dais raised high above the floor. A steep stair led up to it. Poles had been driven into the sandstone slabs of the dais and bodies clad in tattered robes were lashed to the poles with corroded wire. The dry air had cured the skin and flesh of the bodies to something like leather, shrunken tightly over the bones.

'I cleaned away the slogans,' Tibor said, 'but she likes to see the remains of her enemies.'

'I think this one is the Archivist,' Pandaras said. 'You see? They took off the top of his skull as if it were an egg.'

The coin hanging from his neck had begun to glow. He held it up for Yama to see; its light struck sparks in his eyes.

And then a green glow washed over him.

The shrine had become a window in which the aspect of Angel walked swiftly forwards, fixing Yama with a confident and commanding gaze. As before, she wore a white one-piece garment that clung to her tall, slender body. The green garden receded behind her beneath a perfect blue sky. She stared silently at Yama for a long time. He returned her gaze and resisted the compulsion to say something, although his heart quickened with the effort and sweat soaked through his ragged shirt and trousers.

At last, she said, 'You have lost your looks, my love. The world has been hard on you, but now I am here to help you. What, you have no words for me?'

'I serve no one,' Yama said. He tried to look beyond her, hoping that he could summon the hell-hound, but something stopped him looking very far.

She laughed. Yama thought of knives clashing. She said, 'Of course you serve. It is what you were made for.'

'I suppose a feral machine was tracking me. They dare not visit the world they lost, except for brief moments, but they are compelled to watch what they cannot have.'

'You are very stubborn, but I think that you know that you need my help. You know there is much you do not know. For instance, you thought that you had killed me, and you do not understand how you failed. Do stop trying to call that bothersome creature, by the way. This time it will not come.'

Pandaras said in a small but defiant voice, 'You are the ghost my master told me about. The very ghost of a ghost, for I know my master killed you.'

'You speak more truly than you know, little creature. You are the one who looked in the book, aren't you? I let you live then. Show gratitude for my mercy now.'

'If you have any mercy,' Yama said, 'show me a token of it. Let the hierodule go. You use him falsely.'

'Is he not a servant of the avatars? And there are no avatars left, except for me. I should know: I killed them all.'

Yama said, 'You are no avatar, merely the discarded aspect of a dead woman. You are lost in time. Your kind were overthrown more than five million years ago. Just as you use the hierodule, the feral machines use you.'

'We have an alliance. You can be a part of it still.'

Yama turned his face to show her his terrible scar. 'One of the feral machines has already used me. It tried to do to me what it did to Dr Dismas, but it no longer has power over me, and neither do you. You are just a memory, and not even a whole one.'

'With my help you can be so much more powerful than any of the feral machines, my darling.'

'We can only be what we are.'

The aspect smiled. 'That is the philosophy which made your Preservers flee from the Universe. It is untrue. Animals can only be what they are, but humans can transcend their animal selves. The Preservers were fools. They raised up the ten thousand bloodlines from animal stock, but forbade them to rise higher than their creators. You and I will prove how wrong the Preservers were.'

'You have no power over me,' Yama said again, and with an enormous effort turned away from the green light of the garden inside the shrine.

The aspect said, 'I know why the Great River fails. I can help you save the world, if that is what you want.'

'You want the world for yourself.'

'I will have it, too, in a little while.'

'Then why should I save it?'

The aspect's voice deepened. There was music in it and Yama could feel his muscles trying to respond; there was still much of the machine inside him. He fought against it, staggering against the Archivist's dry, brittle body and embracing it for support.

Pandaras cried out, but Yama did not hear what the boy said. The aspect's voice filled his mind.

'The world is a fabrication,' she said. 'An artificial habitat twenty thousand kilometres long and a thousand wide, set in a nest of fields which mimic the gravity of an Earth-sized planet and prevent the atmosphere from dissipating into space. It is not well made. Machines must constantly maintain it; without them, the air would soon become unbreathable, the inhabited places would become deserts, and the Great River would silt up. Those are some of the functions of the lesser machines. But there are greater machines in the keel.'

Yama remembered the huge engines he had glimpsed in the keelways when Beatrice had taken him back to the peel-house. She had warned him not to waken them before their time; he had not understood her until now.

The aspect sang on, seductive, compelling. 'There are many wormholes orbiting Confluence's star. I suspect that they emerge at various points in the Galactic disc. But there is also a wormhole at the midpoint of this strange world. Something has altered it. Your people constructed this world, Yamamanama. You are the key. And you will serve. I have powerful allies. Tell me now that you will at least listen to one of them, and I will spare the boy. But if you will not continue this conversation then I will have my slave crush his skull and paint your face with his brains. A simple *yes* will be enough.'

Pandaras tried to run then, but Tibor caught him and lifted him up and closed one big hand over his head. The hierodule's face was set in a horrible rictus. He began to shake. Muscles jumped in his arms and legs as if struggling against each other. Pandaras shrieked in fear and agony.

The aspect said, 'Say the word, or I will have his life.'

Yama started to move towards Tibor and Pandaras, but it was as if he were in a dream where gravity was much stronger or the air was as dense as water. He was breathing in great gasps.

'Say it!'

The aspect and the hierodule had spoken together.

Pandaras slashed at Tibor's arm with the stone blade, but the hierodule blocked the blow and knocked the blade into the darkness beyond the edge of the dais.

'Say it or he dies!'

'No!'

The hierodule lifted Pandaras above his head, as if to dash him to the floor. And the boy ripped the coin from the thong which dangled from his neck and thrust it edge-first in the hierodule's eye.

Tibor and the aspect screamed at the same moment. White light blotted out the garden and beat across the huge chamber. The hierodule dropped Pandaras. With the glowing coin stuck in his eye and blood streaming down his face, he blundered into two of the staked bodies, smashing them to dust and fragments of brown bone, and pitched over the edge of the dais.

Yama and Pandaras ran down the steep stair. Tibor lay at the bottom, his neck broken. Pandaras pulled the coin from the hierodule's eyes and closed his lids and kissed his forehead.

'He would have killed me,' Pandaras said. He was crying.

'It was well done. She had made a link with Tibor through the shrine, and you shut it down. We cannot stay, Pandaras. She will soon find a way to return.'

They ran, chased by a flock of fireflies, their shadows thrown ahead of them by the white light which burned in the shrine. By the time the aspect had managed to reconfigure it, they were already descending towards the keelways.

17 ~ The Glass Desert

It was a dusty town built along a narrow defile, high in the dry mountains which bordered the Glass Desert. The defile was roofed over with sheets of painted canvas that flapped and boomed in the constant cold, dry wind, and was lined with the mudbrick façades of buildings which had been hacked into its rocky walls. A decad of different bloodlines came there to trade drugs, rare metals, precious stones and furs for rifles and knives and other weapons which artisans made in secretive little courtyards between the buildings. There was a produce market at one end of the defile, and a maze of corrals and sheds where bacts, dzo and mules were bought and sold at the other. Fields and orchards watered by artesian wells stepped away below the produce market, startlingly green against a tawny landscape in which only cacti, barrel trees and cheat grass grew.

The town was called Cagn, or Thule, or Golgath, and had many other secret names known only to the tribes who used them. It was agreed by all that it was one of the worst places in the world; it was said that the double peak which loomed above, framing the Gateway of Lost Souls and casting its shadow across the town in the early morning and the late afternoon, hid the town from gaze of the Preservers, and that any sin practised there went unremarked. It had not been much changed by the coming of the heretics. It was still a refuge for smugglers, reivers, rustlers, fugitives and other desperadoes. Only an hour after he and Pandaras had arrived in the town, Yama had to kill two ruffians who tried to rob them.

Both men were tall and burly and covered everywhere with coarse red hair. They wore striped cotton serapes and white cotton trews, with broad leather belts hitched under their ample bellies. They were belligerently drunk. When one of them swung at him with a skean,

Yama broke the man's arm, snatched up the weapon, and told both of them to run. The injured ruffian yowled, lowered his shaggy head, and charged like a bull. Yama dodged him easily, swung the skean hard as he went past, and slashed his neck down to the spinal cord; the man fell flat, dead before he hit the dust.

The second ruffian swayed and said, 'You killed him, you skeller,' and pulled a pistol from his belt. Yama, with a cold, detached feeling, as if this had already happened somewhere else, perhaps in a story he had once read, hefted the skean to get a feel for its balance, threw it overhand, and skewered the man in the right eye.

People who had stopped to watch the fight began to drift away now that the fun was over; murders were commonplace in a town outside the rule of any law. Pandaras scooped up the pistol, chased off a couple of children who were creeping towards the bodies, and went through the pouches on the men's belts, finding a few clipped coins, and a packet of pellets and a powerpack for the pistol. He pulled the skean from the second ruffian's eye, cleaned its double-edged blade on the dead man's serape, and tucked it into the waistband of his trousers.

Yama refused the pistol when Pandaras offered it to him, and said, 'I know that we will need more money, but I will not kill to get it.'

The cold precision which had gripped him in the moment of danger had vanished. He began to tremble as they walked away. Behind them, the children moved in to take the belts and pouches. Canvas as red as a priest's robe cracked overhead, turning sunlight to the colour of blood.

Pandaras said, 'In this kind of place, we'll need all the weapons we can get just to keep what we have. As for money, I have a confession. I did not burn all the treasures the Mighty People had hidden away in their miserable huts. I kept two of the smallest portraits. I doubt that we'll find much appreciation of art here, but they are enamelled on beaten gold, and although they are no bigger than my hand, I think they'll buy us what we need. Aren't you glad you weren't able to send me away?'

Yama had tried to make Pandaras take the keelroad back to Ys, telling him that the journey to the Glass Desert would almost certainly end in death, but the boy had refused.

'I am your squire, master, for better or worse,' he had said fiercely. 'And I do not think that things can get much worse than this. I have killed two men in as many days, and one of them was my friend. I have lost my hand, and I failed you in many ways while we are apart. I'll not fail you now.'

And so they went on together. Yama used machines to guide them through endless caverns and corridors. He no longer cared if his enemies could track him by the traces left by his commands. It was too late for that.

·A thing like a giant silvery spider, one of the machines which kept the caverns clean, led them at last to an active part of the transportation system which had once knitted the whole world together. They travelled all night in a humming capsule that fell through one of the keelroads. Neither of them slept, although both pretended to.

All of the transportation system beyond the midpoint of the world had been destroyed in the wars of the Age of Insurrection. The capsule took Yama and Pandaras as far as it could, delivering them to a maze of passages beneath a ruined peel-house; they emerged at the foot of a bluff which overlooked the midslopes of the mountains of the Great Divide. The yurts of a party of nomad musk deer herders were pitched nearby. When Yama and Pandaras walked into their camp, still crowned with fireflies Yama had forgotten to dismiss, the long-haired, yellow-skinned men and women fell on their knees. They breakfasted on soured goat's milk mixed with deer blood, and a sickly porridge boiled up from barley mash and dried apricots, then walked all day up the mountain, leaving behind the herders' threadbare pastures and climbing through long, dry draws to the town.

With the money Pandaras got at a refiner's for the gold he had stolen from the Mighty People, they bought a bact from a livestock trader and supplies from the town's only chandler. New clothes, furs for the mountain pass and light robes for the desert, a tent of memory plastic that folded as small as a scarf, dried food, water-bottles and a dew still, a saddle and harness for the bact. There was a little money left, but Yama politely refused the chandler's invitation to inspect the armoury. He would need no weapon where he was going, and Pandaras was armed with the skean and pistol he had taken from the dead ruffians.

'I have maps too,' the chandler said. 'Reliable. Certified.'

'We do not need maps,' Yama said.

'That's what the other fellow said. He'll be buzzard meat soon enough, and so will you if you won't unbend and take some advice.'

The chandler was very tall and very thin, with fine-grained brown skin that shone like polished leather. He laid a long-nailed finger beside one of his opaline eyes and said, 'Perhaps you have one of your own, and put your trust in that. Hnn. Many come here with old maps found in some depository or archive, but you can't rely on them. All the ruins within easy travel of the edge of the Glass Desert are mined out, and most of the waterholes are poisoned. My maps are up to date. You won't have to pay for them, not right now, but you'll have to sell anything you find to me.'

Pandaras said, 'How will you make sure that we do?'

The chandler looked down at Pandaras. He was three times the boy's height. By the doorway, the burly bodyguard shifted the rifle which rested in the crook of one of her beefy arms. The chandler said, 'This is the only way into the Glass Desert, and the only way out. If you survive, you'll be back. You'll probably have to sell anything you find to me anyway. I give the best valuations in town. Ask around if you don't believe me, and you'll find that all my rivals say I'm far too generous with my money.'

Yama said, 'Who was this other man? Did he have a white mark on his face?'

'Not so bold,' the chandler said. 'Everything has its price here.'

Yama told Pandaras to give the chandler the rest of their money. 'Describe him.'

The man spat on the clipped coins and rubbed them with the soft, flat pads at the ends of his bony fingers. 'He was about your height. Had a veil over his face, and yellow eyes. Wore a hat and a silvery cloak. I know his name, but you'll have to pay me to get it.'

'I know his name too,' Yama said.

The chandler glared at Yama. 'It doesn't matter,' he said. 'He didn't take a map, or any water or food, just a saddle for his mule. And he smelled bad, like skinrot or canker. Hnn. It doesn't matter what he's called. He'll be dead by now.'

They were followed out of town by three ruffians of the same bloodline as the two Yama had just killed. They were either kin to the dead man, or in the pay of the chandler, or freelances looking to strip novices of newly bought supplies. As they rode hard towards him, Yama called down a machine and killed them all. He and Pandaras tied the bodies to one of the horses and sent it back to the town as a warning. The second horse had bolted when the machine had smashed the skull of its rider, but Pandaras easily rounded up the third, an old mare with a shaggy grey coat. With Pandaras following on the bact, Yama rode the mare through the high pass of the Gateway of Lost Souls, where unending wind howled over polished ice, and followed a trail down the dry mountain slopes towards the glaring wastes of the Glass Desert.

The trail wound through a dead landscape. Nothing grew there but stonewort, which could survive on the brief dew which formed each morning. The yellow or black crusts were the only colour in the simmering white, alkaline landscape. Cairns were raised here and there, the burial places of would-be prospectors. All had been disturbed; on the afternoon of the second day, Yama and Pandaras rode past three skulls set on a flat-topped rock beside the trail.

Pandaras pointed out the neat hole punched into the ridge above the empty eye sockets of one of the skulls. 'Perhaps he quarrelled with his companions over treasure they had found. Or perhaps he killed himself after he killed his friends. Men are driven mad here by the ghosts of machines that fought in the war.'

'You can still turn back,' Yama said. 'I must face something worse than any ghost you can imagine, and I do not think I will be able to protect you from it. It may well destroy you. It may well destroy me, too.'

Pandaras touched the coin he still wore around his neck. 'Why, you've said yourself that this is better than any of the seals and medals the people of the New Quarter use to protect themselves from machine ghosts.'

'Take the horse, Pandaras. Ride back through the pass and wait for me.'

'Will you turn back too, master? Well then.'

That evening, they made camp by a waterhole. The water was black, and mantled with white dust. The mare slipped her hobble and drank before Yama could find a machine which could test it. She foundered almost at once, screaming with pain and foaming at the mouth. The bact snorted, as if in disdain; it had not tried to go near the water. The mare convulsed. Blood poured from her eyes and nostrils. Yama stroked her muzzle, then slit her throat in a swift movement.

Pandaras took a sip from a cupped handful of water and promptly spat it out and tipped the rest on the ground. 'Poison all right,' he said, and spat again. 'I bet the chandler's men did it. They poison most of the waterholes, and he hires out maps showing those which are safe.'

'The whole land is poisoned,' Yama said.

They moved their camp to a flat shelf of rock a league further down the trail. Pandaras cooked slabs of muscle he had cut from the mare's hindquarters; he had also drained some of her blood into two of the empty water-bottles, saying that for him blood was almost as good as water.

Pandaras ate most of the food, for Yama had little appetite. He had had a distant sense of Dr Dismas's paramour ever since they had begun to descend towards the desert. It pulled at the remains of his Shadow like the wink of sunlight on a far-off mirror or a tintinnabulation in the ear. And he also felt the pull of the feral machine he had called upon, without knowing it, when he had been in desperate danger in the house of the renegade star-sailor. Poised between the two attractors, he sat and looked out towards the wastelands of the Glass Desert until long past sunset, and did not notice when Pandaras wrapped a fur around him against the night's bitter cold.

From then on, Pandaras and Yama took turns riding the bact. It took three more days to descend the mountain slopes. The Glass Desert stretched beyond: red and yellow and brown, patched and cratered, riven on one side by a vast, meandering canyon which once had held a river as wide and deep as the Great River. Points of reflected light flashed here and there across the bitter land, and a whole sea of light burned in the middle distance where a city had stood. The Glass Desert had once been as verdant as the inhabited half of Confluence, and as populous, but the feral machines had made it their homeland after they had rebelled, and it had been devastated in the last and fiercest of the wars of the Age of Insurrection. Nothing lived there now.

As he walked beside the bact that day, through a barrens of blowing sand and piles of half-melted boulders fused together by some great, ancient blast, Yama kept glimpsing figures amongst the stones, figures which vanished if he turned to look at them, but which he recognized nonetheless. First Derev, her white feathery hair blowing out in the hot wind, and then others. His love, and all his dead. The remnant of the Shadow was stirring in his mind, wakened by the call of its progenitor far off across the tumbled desolation.

When they made camp that evening, Pandaras saw how drawn his master had become. Yama squatted on his haunches and stared into the thin, cold wind that blew out of the dark desert. His long black hair was matted with dust and tangled about his pale, scarred face. He did not seem to notice when Pandaras shaved him, using a flaked edge of glass and a couple of handfuls of their precious water. They had no scissors, but Pandaras had given the skean's blade a good edge, and he hacked back Yama's hair with that. It was not easy to do with only one hand, but Yama bore Pandaras's clumsiness patiently. More and more, he seemed to be retreating inside his head.

Yama would not eat anything, and he slept uneasily. Pandaras watched over him, chewing congealed blood that was beginning to spoil. He reckoned that they were not coming back. At best, they would somehow destroy this thing and then hope for an easy death of thirst or heat prostration. At worst, it would destroy them.

It was a pity. He would have liked to have made a song of Yama's adventures amongst the world's wonders. He remembered the engines he had seen in the cellars of the world, when the spider thing had led them to the keelroad. Whole swathes of the floors of the vast vaults had been transparent, showing chambers deep enough to swallow mountains. It was as if he and Yama had become birds, hanging high above a world within a world. Far below, tiny red and black specks had roamed across a green plain, illuminated by a kind of flaw in the middle air that had shed a radiance as bright as day. The specks must have been machines as big as carracks, and even bigger machines had studded the verdant land. Black spires of intricate latticework had reared halfway towards the radiant flaw, wound about with what looked like threads of gold, threads which must have been as wide as the Grand Way of Ys. There had been black cubes in heaps as wide as cities, and geometric patterns of silver and white laid into the green landscape.

At one point Yama had lain flat on the floor, prostrating himself like a palmer at a shrine. The spider had halted, flexing one leg and then another as if in frustration, until at last Yama had stood and walked on.

He had told Pandaras then that there were mysteries in the world that he could only guess at, and they began to talk about this again as they journeyed into the Glass Desert. Yama wanted to unburden himself of all that had happened to him. Once more, he told Pandaras the story of how he had been found as a baby on the breast of a dead woman in a white boat cast adrift on the Great River. He talked of his childhood, of how happy he had been, how fortunate to have been the adopted son of the Aedile of Aeolis and the stepbrother of brave, dead Telmon. He described how Dr Dismas had tried to kidnap him and how he had escaped and had been given refuge in the tower of Beatrice and Osric, the last curators of the City of the Dead, of his journey to Ys, where he had escaped Prefect Corin and met Pandaras. And then, turn and turn again, they told each other the rest of the tale: their adventures in the Palace of the Memory of the People; the voyage downriver in the *Weazel*; the sacking of Aeolis by Prefect Corin and the death of the Aedile; the treachery of Eliphas. And on, through their separate adventures and their reunion, and now this, their last exploit. They had reached the Glass Desert after all – not in search of Eliphas's invented lost city, but of Yama's nemesis.

Pandaras noticed the birds on the afternoon of the third day after they had quit the mountains: black cruciform specks circling high above in a sky so achingly bright it was more white than blue.

'Not birds,' Yama said. 'They have been watching us ever since we crept through the pass, but they dare to fly lower now because this is their land.'

He coughed long and hard into his fist. They were both affected by the alkaline dust which hung in the hot air. It worked through the seals of their filter masks and irritated their throats and lungs, and got into every crevice of their bodies, drying their skins and causing pressure sores. It worked under their goggles, too, inflaming their eyes.

They were still taking turns riding the bact. Pandaras was in the saddle, and now he clambered down and said, 'Ride a while, master. Rest.'

Yama lifted his filter mask and spat. There was blood in his spittle. When he could speak again, he said, 'It has grown strong, Pandaras. It no longer cares about being found, for the machines which would have destroyed it are engaged in fighting the heretics. And it has made many servants.'

'You could make them go away, master. Please climb up. You'll feel better for riding.'

But Yama walked on, still leading the bact. 'There are different kinds of machine,' he said. 'I thought of it while we were crossing that big chamber far beneath the temple. Do you remember?'

'I will never forget it, master. Do you think people live there, in the lands of the keel?'

'No, Pandaras. Down there are machines I cannot yet control. I cannot even talk with them. They are raised as far above the simple little machines which the magistrates command as we are above the animals from which the Preservers made us. As with men so with machines. There are the enlightened races of men which have passed beyond this world, and there are the machines in the world beneath the world. Just as we cannot talk with the enlightened, so I cannot talk with those machines. Or not yet, not yet. And just as there are the changed bloodlines, in whom the breath of the Preservers has been quickened, so there are machines which are likewise self-aware, such as the dwellers of the deep which sweep silt from the bottom of the Great River. I can command those as a general can command an army, although both the general and his soldiers are equal in the eyes of the Preservers. And then there are the unchanged bloodlines, and the ordinary machines which take care of the world, such as the machines commanded by the magistrates. And there are the indigenous races, and machines which are neither self-aware nor ever need to be.'

'And yet you raised up the mirror people and the forest folk,' Pandaras said.

Yama did not hear him. He said, 'Machines and men. We are each other's mirrors. The feral machines are greater than the changed, but lesser than the enlightened. But are they greater or lesser than me? I called down one to help me; I feel it still. But did I command it, or did it see its chance to place its hook into me? I could not master the child of the thing that lies ahead of us, the Shadow which Dr Dismas grew in me, but perhaps that was because the Shadow was too like me. It had began to assume my power. I do not know what I can do, Pandaras. Perhaps it knows me better than I knew myself.'

They had been plodding all day through the petrified stumps of what had once been a forest. Pandaras gestured around himself and said, 'This is a dead place. No wonder only machines can live here.'

197

They walked on in silence for a while. At last, Yama said, 'This half of the world lost its river. Do you remember when we crossed that gorge two days ago? That was once a tributary of the Great River of this half of Confluence, running down from the snow fields of the Rim Mountains, just as the Breas empties into the Great River near Aeolis. But the Great River into which that tributary emptied fell away and was not renewed. The land died. Perhaps our land will die too. Our own Great River is dying.'

At last Pandaras persuaded his master to climb on to the saddle in front of the bact's dwindling hump. When he was settled, Yama said, 'If my father was right, then the fall of the Great River is my fault. It began when I was cast upon this world. Perhaps I can atone for that, Pandaras, if I can learn enough. It is my only hope.'

Pandaras understood less than half of what his master said, but he clearly saw the anguish these thoughts caused him. He said, 'You are greater than you know, master. You are tired now. You don't see things clearly. It will be better when you have rested. You ride the rest of the day. I don't mind walking.'

They reached the far edge of the petrified forest at nightfall, and made camp. As usual, Pandaras kept watch while Yama muttered and twitched in his sleep, and once or twice he thought he heard something padding outside the tent. There! A scrape of metal on stone. The bact snorted and moved about. It was not his imagination. He gripped the pistol, although what use was it against monsters?

The next day, Yama said, 'I dreamed that we are being followed.'

'And I know it, master.'

Pandaras squinted against sky glare. The bird things were still up there. Even when he was not watching them he could still feel their purpose, a prickling itch at the crown of his skull. All around, red sand blew in scarves and streamers across pitted red rock. The air was filled with the dry hiss of blowing sand.

Yama said, 'They are coming down from the Gateway of Lost Souls. An army, Pandaras. I saw it in my dreams, but I do not think it was a dream. I do not think that I can dream here.'

Pandaras looked back towards the mountains of the Great Divide. The icy peaks shone high and far, seeming to float above the glittering desert.

He said, 'It must have been a dream, master. Not even an eagle could see so far. Don't worry about it.'

Yama shook his head violently. 'I saw through the eyes of one of the watchers. The things which follow us also follow the army.'

That night Yama woke with a start, feverish and shaking. He turned towards Pandaras, but his reddened eyes were focused on infinity. 'They have machines,' he said. 'The fool brought machines with him as well as soldiers. He thinks that they are shielded.'

Pandaras wet a corner of Yama's robe with a few mimims of their precious water and dabbed at his forehead. 'Hush, master. You dream.'

'No. No dreams now. Only truth. The desert burns away everything else. We become only what we are.'

At last Pandaras got Yama to lie down. He thought that his master slept, but after a while Yama said, 'The soldiers are mounted and in uniform. They wear black masks with long snouts and round eyeholes of glass backed with gold. Their mounts are masked too. But I recognize the man at their head. It is Enobarbus. She has sent him after me. Things are coming together at last. Things are coming to a conclusion.'

Pandaras said nervously, 'Is there any sign of the Prefect?'

'He . . . no, not yet. But I left sign enough for him to find us.'

'Then maybe he's dead,' Pandaras said, although he did not believe it.

They had little food left, and less water. The dew still yielded only a few minims of water each night, and there was no standing water to be found, poisoned or otherwise. The next day, the bact knelt down and would not get up. Pandaras, weeping in rage and frustration, beat at the animal's withers. It closed its long-lashed eyes and ignored him. Sand blew all around; the sun was a glowering eye in a red sky.

Pandaras and Yama unloaded the supplies. Only one water-bottle was full; another held only a few mouthfuls. They threw the rest away, and most of the remaining food.

'I will get us food,' Yama said. 'Food and water. They are off the mountain slopes now, and coming towards us very quickly. They have good mounts.'

He was flushed and feverish. He was looking towards the distant range of mountains, and it took Pandaras a long time to get him turned around.

They had not gone far when they heard the bact scream. Pandaras stumbled back towards it through blowing sand, but stopped, shocked and frightened, when he saw the things which were tearing it apart.

They were like crosses between snakes and jaguars, armoured in overlapping metallic scales or in flexible blood-red hide. No two were alike. One had a tail like that of a scorpion, tipped with a swollen sting which arched above its back. One had a multiple set of jaws so massive they dragged on the ground, another a round sucker mouth with a ragged ring of teeth.

The misshapen wild cats tore at the bact with silent ferocity. It was already dead, its neck half-severed and its bloody ribs showing, blood soaking the sand in a widening circle. Blood glistened on hide like chainmail, on metal scales, on horny plates edged with metal, on serrated metal in snapping jaws. Two of the things had burrowed into the bact's belly, shaking its body back and forth as they worked like a depraved reversal of birth. The pack ignored Pandaras until he raised the pistol, and then one turned eyes like red lamps towards him and reared up on its stout tail, waving a decad of mismatched legs tipped with razor-edged claws. Thick green slaver dripped from its long snout.

A hand fell on Pandaras's shoulder; his shot went wild, swallowed by the sand-filled air. Yama shouted into his ear. 'Leave them! They will not hurt us!'

The wild cat which had confronted Pandaras dropped to its belly and shuffled forwards and grovelled before Yama, although it kept its burning red eyes on Pandaras as he backed away into the blowing sand. Its fellows had not paused in their feverish butchery; the bact was almost stripped to the bones.

Yama and Pandaras drank the last of their water at noon, threw away the water-bottle, and went on. Yama taught Pandaras that sucking a pebble could stimulate the flow of saliva and help keep thirst at bay, but the hot wind which blew sand around them drew moisture from every crevice of their bodies. Pandaras forced himself to stay awake, starting at each change in pitch of the streams of sand that hissed outside the tent, and Yama slept fitfully, waking before dawn and insisting that they go on.

'They are almost on us,' he said, 'but it is not far. There is no chance of turning back now, Pandaras.'

'I had not thought of it, master,' Pandaras said. His lips were cracked and bleeding and he tasted blood at the back of his throat with each breath; the dust had worked into his lungs.

The air was filled with blowing sand. They left the tent behind and set off into it.

Shapes loomed out of the murk: towers of friable bones lashed together with sinews and half-covered in hide that flapped and boomed and creaked in the wind. A ragged picket fence of crystalline spines grew crookedly from a shoulder of black rock. Creatures were impaled on some of the spines. Some were men; the rest were like nothing Pandaras had ever seen, horrid chimeras of machine and insect, although surely no insects could grow as large as these. Most were no more than dried husks, but some were still alive and stirred feebly as Yama and Pandaras went past.

Pandaras did not pay much attention to these horrors. He no longer felt fear, only exhaustion and growing thirst. Each step was a promise to himself that there would soon be no more steps: walking was an infinite chain of promises. The world shrank to the patch of ground directly in front of him. Its gravity seemed to vary wildly; sometimes it seemed to pitch like the deck of a ship and he could barely keep to his feet. But always he went forwards, following in his master's footsteps.

At noon, Yama stopped and turned in a half-circle and fell to his knees. Pandaras managed to get him to the shelter of a tilted shelf of rock. It was very hot. The sun's bloody glare was diffused across half the sky. Sand skirled around crystal spurs, sent shifting shadows shuddering across reaches of bare stone. Pandaras was sweating through his thin robe. His mouth and throat were parched. He itched everywhere.

Yama stirred in his arms. Blood leaked from the corners of his closed eyes; Pandaras blotted it away with the hem of his robe. 'I will bring water,' Yama said, and seemed to fall into a faint.

A moment later, thunder cracked high above and something flashed through the blowing red dust, chased by black shapes. It dived this way and that with abrupt turns and reverses, swooped low overhead, dropped something, and shot away as black things closed on either side. A sheet of green lightning; more thunder, then only the endless hiss of blowing sand.

Pandaras crawled out of the lee of the shelf of rock and retrieved what had been dropped by the machine.

It was a transparent sphere of spun plastic as big as his head, half-filled with cold, clear water.

When they were able to set off again, something like a storm of dry lightning had started up in the direction of the Great Divide. Flares of brittle light were half-obscured by curtains of blowing sand. Overhead, things chased each other through the sky with wild howls. Far off, something roared and roared on a single endless note.

'A lot of trouble for a drink of water,' Pandaras remarked.

'The battle has already begun. That was why I was able to steal the water ... We must press on, Pandaras. Enobarbus brought more machines than I thought. I do not know if Dr Dismas's paramour can hold them.'

'I'll go there and back in the blink of an eye, and carry you too, if I must.' Pandaras said it as lightly as he could, but in truth he felt that this day would be his last.

The battle raged for the rest of their journey. Curtains of light washed half the sky, spiked with red or green lances that burned bright paths in the sandstorm. The ground shook continually, and a low rumble curdled Pandaras's guts.

The land began to slope downwards ever more steeply, sculpted in fantastic curls like breaking waves frozen in glassy rock. Razor-sharp ridges cut through the soles of their boots and they both left bloody prints on the glassy ground. Things scuttled amongst half-buried rocks: hand-sized, flat, multi-legged and very quick, like squashed spiders made of black glass. Bigger things prowled further off, barely visible through veils of blowing red sand. Stiff growths poked up from glass and drifted sand, fretted tufts of black stuff that was neither plastic nor metal, all bent in the same direction by the constant wind.

'We are getting close now,' Yama said. Blood was still seeping from his eyes; every so often he had to lift up his goggles and blot it away. Blisters on his forehead leaked clear fluid. Sand caked his face and his hair.

'You are already here,' a voice said.

It came from everywhere around them, from the rocks and sand, from the dust-laden air.

Pandaras whirled in a complete circle, fumbling for his pistol. Something black and quick dropped from a fold of glass that reared above and stung his hand and jumped away. He howled and dropped the pistol in a drift of white sand. It sank swiftly, as if pulled under. Pandaras sucked at the puncture on his hand and spat out the bitter taste. When he looked up, someone in a silver cloak was standing a few paces from Yama.

It was the apothecary, Dr Dismas. Or at least, what was left of him. He seemed to have grown taller. His clothes were tatters under his cloak. His flesh was black and rotten, falling away from bones on which cables and sacs of silvery stuff flexed and tugged. He tottered closer, reaching for Yama, but Yama dashed the apothecary's hand aside. Fingers snapped; two fell to the ground and were immediately tugged under.

Dr Dismas did not seem to notice. His eyes were full of fluttering red light. Wind combed the remnants of his hair back from his skull. His jaw worked, and he said in a dry, croaking voice, 'You brought many with you.'

'They followed me,' Yama said. 'I had thought that they might be your friends, for their leader is the champion of the aspect of Angel. Is she not your ally?'

'We both want the same end, but for different reasons, as we both want you. We cannot share you. I had hoped that you had escaped her completely, but no matter. It is only a minor inconvenience. Do not think that it will distract me from what must be done.'

'I know what you did to Dismas,' Yama said. 'He tried to do the same to me.'

'I am not displeased with him. This is not a punishment; it is how he returned to me. He was loyal enough, in his way, and now he is completely mine. I may make him whole again, or I may absorb him. There will be time to decide on that once I am done with you. All the time in the world.'

Pandaras realized then that something was using Dr Dismas's dead body, like a puppet in a shadow play.

Yama said, 'He infected me with one of your children, but it had ideas of its own.'

'Of course. It would not be one of my children if it did not share my ambitions. That is why I must eventually destroy or devour my children, for otherwise they would devour me. Dr Dismas should not have infected you so early. It was his only serious mistake, for my child could have destroyed you. But you overcame it, and what remains of it will help us.'

'As I thought.'

'Now we can begin.'

'Now we can begin,' Yama said. 'There is much I want to learn. Pandaras, you must come with me. It is too dangerous for you to stay here alone. Do not be afraid.'

But Pandaras was very afraid, so sick with fear that he could hardly stand. With a shudder, he drew himself up and followed Yama and the puppet-thing which had once been Dr Dismas through a narrow defile.

A ramp spiralled away, running down into a deep pit. The pit narrowed with each turn of the ramp, like a hole left by a gigantic screw. Silvery vines grew out of the glassy walls – grew through them, too. Some twitched as Pandaras passed by, their ends fraying and fraying again into a hundred threads that wove back and forth like hungry bloodworms scenting his heat. Human faces and the masks of animals bloomed under the glass, distorted and wavering, as if seen through furnace heat. Trapped souls, Pandaras thought. The remnants of men and animals which had been devoured by the thing at the bottom of the pit.

The battle continued to rage above. The sky was split again and again by tremendous sheets of lightning. The ramp shuddered and quivered as explosions pounded the desert all around.

As they descended, things paced behind them, revealed and obscured by blowing sand, horrors half corpse, half machine. Dead animals wrapped in metal bands; polished human skeletons operated by the same silver cables and flexing bags which animated the corpse of Dr Dismas. One skeleton rode a wild cat of the kind which had torn the bact apart; it was crowned with spectral fire, and carried a sword which burned with blue flames, as if dipped in brandy and set alight. Some poor dead hero, killed by the thing he had come to kill, and made into a ghastly slave.

'Do not be afraid,' Yama told Pandaras again. 'There is nothing to fear. I will be their master.'

'We will be the master,' the thing using Dr Dismas said. 'You and I will change this world.'

Yama was looking around with an eager curiosity. He seemed to have wakened from the half-sleep of the journey. 'Where are you?' he said. 'I think you have grown since Dismas found you.'

'I first found him far from here. He never reached my core while I was alive.'

'Then this is where you fell. Like the thing in the Temple of the Black Well.' Yama laughed. It was muffled by his face mask. 'The war has never ended for you, has it? I suppose you would call the defeat that drove your kind from the world a temporary setback.'

'I take the long view, as you will see. None of my paramours ever truly die. I always retain something of them. And you, my pet, my darling boy, I will hold you fast, close to my central processors.'

'You are much larger than the others I have met. The one I called down in Ys, and the one trapped at the bottom of the well in the temple.'

'One was a fool, like all those which allowed themselves to be driven into exile. The other was a coward that dared not stir from its hiding place. Cowards and fools. I despise them.'

Pandaras could feel the venomous anger which forced these words through Dr Dismas's dead mouth, although the tone was as flat as ever.

'Now I know why you were defeated in the wars of the Age of Insurrection,' Yama said. 'You fought against each other as fiercely as you fought against those loyal to the Preservers.'

'We have grown apart since then. Those who fled Confluence have become weakened, for otherwise they would have long ago begun the war again. They are cowards.'

'They follow the orbit of the world because they are tormented by what they cannot have.'

'Exactly. Only they have grown weaker and I have grown stronger. I will take what they desire, and I will have them too.'

'If only your love was as strong as your pride and your hunger! How well you would serve the Preservers then. Instead, you remind me of the heretics. Each of of them would destroy the Universe, if only it would save his life.'

'I have burned away that part of me,' the thing said. 'Love is a weakness. As I have refined myself, so I will refine you.'

'Then you are a giant amongst the rebels,' Yama said. He was walking at the edge of the ramp as he followed the puppet-thing, peering eagerly into the depths of the pit. 'How large have you grown?'

'I have not enlarged my processing capacity overmuch because the architecture would become too complex. But I have redistributed myself, and I have many auxiliaries and drones.'

'And your paramours.'

'Oh yes. You are trying to find a way to me already. You will not. You destroyed the main part of the child Dismas implanted within you, but you had to mutilate yourself to do it because you were not able to overcome it in any other way. You will not be able to overcome me, for I am so much stronger and wiser. It is touching that you try, though. I would have expected nothing less. You hoped to use the heretics as a diversion – that was why you drew them here. A bold plan. I applaud it. But I fight them using only a fraction of my might, and soon they will be defeated.'

'Then I was right to come here,' Yama said. 'I have learned much since I destroyed the Shadow. I will learn more.'

'I will teach you all you desire, when you are with me. You may ask anything, and I will tell you.'

Pandaras remembered the old tales of how feral machines buried in old temples or in the wild places of the world trapped those who hunted them by granting their wishes. Here was the truth which had spawned those fanciful stories. All stories were true because all were derived from the world, no matter how distantly. Otherwise, how could they be told by men, who were creatures of the world?

'O,' Yama said, 'I have so many questions. To begin with, I had only one. I wanted only to know where I could find people of my bloodline. I went to look for them, and I had hardly begun on that task when I found instead that I was asking the wrong question. To know my people I must first know how to ask questions. I must know myself. A wise man told me that, and beat me with his fan to make me remember it.'

Theias, the envoy from Gond. Yama had tricked him into revealing more than he had wanted to reveal, and Theias had fled in shame and confusion, or so Pandaras had thought at the time. But now he saw that Theias had left because his task had been completed.

'I can tell you everything,' the thing said through the dead mouth of Dr Dismas. 'I can tell you why the Preservers made Confluence, and why they raised up the ten thousand bloodlines. I can tell you the true nature of the world and the true nature of the Preservers. I can tell you where they went and why we should not serve them.'

'I do not need to know any of that,' Yama said. 'You comfort yourself with false answers to those questions because you disobeyed the Preservers, who made you as surely as they made me. You need to believe that you acted not out of pride but to save the world because your masters betrayed you. Is this the place?'

Yama had stopped because silvery vines grew so thickly from the glassy wall that there was no way forwards. They had gone around six turns of the ramp as they descended; they were deep within the pit now. It was so narrow here that Pandaras could have jumped clear across it. A thick red vapour hid the bottom from view.

'It has already begun,' the thing said. Its voice was louder now, and the same voice rattled from the bony jaws of the skeletons behind them, roared in the razor mouths of the giant cats, hummed from the mouths of the faces that floated in the glass walls. The air was full of electricity. Every hair of Pandaras's pelt bristled, trying to stand away from its fellows.

The silvery vines snaked out with sudden swiftness. They enveloped Yama and he fell to his knees under their weight. Pandaras started forwards, but Yama waved him back. A vine looped around his upraised arm. 'It is all right,' Yama said thickly. Blood ran from his mouth, rich and red. 'What will be will be.'

Pandaras halted, his hand inside his thin tattered robe, on the hilt of the skean. He remembered the coiling tentacles of the sharers of the deep dredgers. Yama had sent away the giant polyps after they had sunk Prefect Corin's ship; perhaps he could dismiss the vines too.

The vine around Yama's arm stretched, its end dividing and dividing. There was a flash of intense red light and Yama cried out. Pandaras blinked and almost missed what had happened. One of Yama's fingertips had been seared off and carried away.

'A tissue sample,' the voice of the thing in the pit said. 'A finger for the fingers you snapped from the hand of Dr Dismas. But I will design a better body for you, my dear boy. You will not miss it.'

The frayed end of the vine was poised above Yama's head now.

Yama looked at it calmly. He said, 'That will not be necessary. The paths grown by my Shadow are still there.'

'Do not be afraid,' the voice said. It filled the pit, echoing and reechoing from the glassy walls.

And the vine struck.

Yama's head vanished beneath a myriad fine threads that flowed over each other, moulding so tightly to his face that its contours emerged as a silvery mask. Pandaras caught the stink as his master's bowels and bladder voided.

The Dismas puppet-thing tipped back its rotting face and howled. The faces trapped in the walls howled too. The skeletal figures rattled their jaws; the wild cats screeched.

All howled the same five words, over and over.

'*Get out of my mind!*'

And something fell from the sky and plunged into the pit.

It fell so fast that Pandaras barely glimpsed it before it vanished into the heavy red vapours at the bottom. The glassy walls rang like a bell and the ramp heaved. Pandaras fell to his knees. The eyeblink image burned in his mind: a black ball not much bigger than his head, covered in spines and spikes.

The Dismas thing darted at Yama, quick as a snake. Pandaras managed to grab an ankle and it fell to its knees, breaking off one hand at the wrist. It flipped around and threw itself at Pandaras, who struck out with the skean, a desperate sweeping blow that caught the thing in the neck. Its head was almost severed and hung between its shoulders by a gristly flap of flesh and a silvery cord, bouncing as it swung to and fro, groping for Pandaras with its remaining hand. Pandaras slashed again, aiming at the dead thing's heart. The skean's narrow blade sliced bone and shrivelled flesh, grated on a metal sinew. Rotten blood pattered over him. A terrible stink filled the air. Pandaras was at the edge of the ramp; he dodged sideways as the thing made a final lunge, took a step on to air, and toppled into the heavy red mist without a sound.

All around, faces trapped under glass howled, melting and reforming.

The skean could not cut the silvery vines, but they had gone limp and Pandaras was able to pull them away from his master's body. The ones which had been attached to Yama's face left decads of pinpricks which each extruded a blob of bright red blood. Yama's mask had come off. He shuddered, drew a breath, another. His eyes were full of blood. Pandaras tore a strip from the hem of his robe and tenderly wiped it away.

Red vapour swirled around them. It was full of motes of sparkling light. Pandaras realized they were tiny machines, every one a part of the thing in the pit, as millions of termites in a nest make up a single super-organism. He tried to get Yama to stand up, but Yama was staring at something a thousand leagues beyond Pandaras and the walls of the pit. The faces in the pitted slabs of glass were dwindling into points of absolute blackness that hurt to look at.

'Caphis was right,' he said. 'The river comes to its own self. The snake which swallows its tail.'

He shuddered, choked, and vomited a good deal of blood and watery chyme. He spat and grinned at Pandaras. 'I took it all from him. All of it.'

'We have to go, master. If it's possible to get through the battle, I'll do it. I'll get you back.'

'I called it down,' Yama said. 'He did not expect that. That I would call on another of his kind. They are fighting now. Growing into one another. I think they will destroy each other. It is the opposite of love. Sex without consummation. Endless hunger.'

He continued to babble as Pandaras got him to stand. They more or less supported each other as they climbed back up the ramp. The skeletal king had fallen; so had its followers. The wild cats had fled. Pandaras was too tired to listen to his master's ramblings, mad stuff about the river and the end of the world, and holes that drew together space and time.

Pandaras knew that they could never reach the mountains of the Great Divide, but he had to keep going forwards. At some point, he realized that they had climbed out of the pit. Sand blew around them on a strengthening wind. The sun was setting. Its light spread in a long red line through the murk, as if trying to measure the length of the world. A shaft of deep red light shone up from the pit, aimed at the empty sky.

Pandaras sat Yama beneath the overhang of a smooth wave of fused, cracked glass and more or less fell down beside him. He said, 'If you can do any other tricks, master, now's the time.'

Sand blew past them endlessly. The light that rose from the pit seemed to grow brighter as the sun set. Everything had a double shadow.

The remnants of the army of Enobarbus were drawn up along a distant ridge, dimly seen through the veils of blowing sand. There, gone, there again. One of the wild cats prowled through the murk, ears flat, eyes almost closed. It did not know where it was, remembered only a time of fear and the stink of death, a compulsion stronger than sex or appetite which had suddenly vanished. There were still things in its flesh it could not claw or bite out, but they were dead things now, no worse than thorns. It stopped and stared for a long time at two men huddled against each other, torn between fear and hunger. Then it glanced over its shoulder and fled into the storm, fluidly flowing over glassy humps.

Two riders were approaching. The wind began to howl.

18 ~ The Trial

Once Pandaras was well enough to be able to walk about the house, the heretics provided him with a kind of uniform to replace his ragged clothes: grey silk tunic and trousers with silver piping; long black boots of some kind of malleable plastic; a belt of black, fine-grained leather, with a strap that went over his shoulder; a black silk glove for his right hand and a black silk stocking to draw over the stump of his left wrist. They did not allow him a weapon, of course, but gave him an ebony swagger stick tipped at either end with chased silver.

When he realized that he was not going to be killed, Pandaras's fear turned to anger. He had rescued his master twice over, even though he had at last been forced to deliver him into the hands of the heretics, and now he was mocked. He broke the swagger stick in half, picked the silver piping from tunic and trousers, and threw the boots, belt, glove and silk sock out of the window of his room.

Yama and Pandaras were being kept prisoner in an ordinary house embedded in a complex of tents, domes and pyramids which had grown around it, linked by gossamer bridges and enclosed by huge plastic vanes in bright primary colours. The vanes glowed at night with inner light, like the noctilucent jellyfish which sailed the river in summer. They were set in the middle of the ruins of Sensch, the last city of the Great River. It was where Angel had fled after escaping from the other Ancients of Days. It was where she had begun to spread her heresy. The house in which Yama and Pandaras were imprisoned was the house where she had lived. The rest of the city — its narrow streets and markets, its palace and docks — had been razed after the Change War and rebuilt upriver. Apart from Angel's house, only the ruins of the temple were left, enclosed within enfilades of silvery triangular sails like the maw of some monster rising up from the keelways.

Yama was taken to the temple a few days after arriving in Sensch, once the heretics were certain that he would not die of his wounds. He had to be carried on a stretcher, and was escorted by a maniple of soldiers. Pandaras was not allowed to accompany him, but heard about what happened from the warden of the prison house, who got it from one of the chirurgeons who attended Yama.

Yama had been manacled to a chair in front of the temple's shrine, where he was to be questioned by the aspect of Angel in the presence of those who would later judge him. But although the shrine had lit up, the aspect had not appeared, and after several hours and a great deal of confusion Yama had been returned to the prison house.

'They want me killed,' Yama said wearily, when Pandaras was at last allowed to see him. 'I know too much now.'

'Did you destroy the aspect, master?'

Yama smiled and said, 'You are too clever, Pandaras. I fear that it will be the death of you.'

'I think that it already has, master, and so I've earned the right to know what you did. Did you destroy her?'

'You are not going to die here, Pandaras, and this is no time for death-bed confessions. I will tell you what I did because you are my friend. No, I did not destroy her. She coded herself too deeply for that. However, I was able to turn all the shrines on the world against her. I do not think that she will able to find a way back.'

Yama was still very ill. He fell asleep and woke without noticing that he had slept, and added, 'She was always a prisoner. She thought to conquer Confluence, but it had already conquered her. We are all of us prisoners of history here, forced to follow the paths of stories so old and so powerful they are engraved in every cell of our bodies. It is time to break the circle.'

'Past time,' Pandaras said, thinking that his master had some plan to escape the prison house. But Yama had fallen asleep again, and did not hear him.

It took the heretics many days to treat and heal Yama. In all that time, Pandaras expected that at any moment his master would come to his senses and call down machines to help them escape, and when at last Yama was well enough to be brought before the board of men and women who would pronounce judgement on him, Pandaras thought that he would surely work his miracles then, in front of the astonished heretics. But he did not, and seemed to pay little attention to the proceedings, except to smile good-naturedly and agree that he was guilty of everything of which he was accused. The only consolation was that this seemed to anger the heretics as much as it frustrated Pandaras.

The trial was held in a huge white bubble chamber. Its walls absorbed sunlight and translated it to a directionless glow, reminding Pandaras of the shrine beyond the edge of the world. The trial lasted less than a day, and was presided over by the most senior of the heretics, although much of the time he seemed to pay as little attention to the proceedings as Yama. This was Mr Naryan, the former Archivist of Sensch, who had been changed by Angel herself. An old, fat, hairless man, he hung naked in clear, bubbling water inside a cylindrical glass tank. Machines studded his wrinkled, greyish skin: at his neck; across the swollen barrel of his swollen chest; over one eye. Years ago, while preaching to one of the unchanged bloodlines, he had been badly hurt in an assassination attempt. The machines implanted in his body kept him alive. He had been an old man when he had met Angel, and now he was older than any of his bloodline. It was said that the implanted machines would ensure that he would never die.

The decad of men and women on the judicial panel sat on either side of Mr Naryan's tank, staring down from elevated and canopied thrones chased with silver and upholstered in black plush at the plain bench on which Yama and Pandaras sat in manacles, with two rows of armoured troopers behind them. Having no traditions, the heretics had invented their own, indulging in unrestrained expressions of ego untempered by any notion of taste. Most of the men wore fantastical military uniforms, crusted with braid and hung with ribbons, sashes and medals. One woman wore a white wig which doubled her height, with little machines blinking amongst its curls; another metal armour polished as bright as a mirror, so that her head seemed to sit above a kaleidoscope of broken reflections of the light-filled room. The majority of the panel were citizens of Sensch, of the first bloodline to have been changed by Angel's heresy. They listened to the list of Yama's crimes with various degrees of attention, grimacing each time Yama cheerfully assented to his guilt. Machines hovered in the air, recording and transmitting the event to heretic cities and armies along the Great River.

At the end, after Yama had agreed that he had been responsible for the failure of the Great River, Mr Naryan finally stirred. He pushed to the surface of the tank and spouted water. A decad of machines dipped down to catch the soft croak of his voice.

'The boy must die,' Mr Naryan said. 'He is an anachronism. The purpose of his bloodline was to make this world, and he threatens to use the powers of his kind to unmake it.'

Several members of the panel made lengthy speeches, although all they had to say was that they agreed with Mr Naryan. Only Enobarbus spoke up for Yama. Of all the panel, he wore no finery. He was bare-chested and his red officer's sash was tied at the waist of his white trousers. His mane of bronze hair floated around his ruined face as he prowled up and down in front of the panel.

'He has been crucial in driving the war against those who still serve the Preservers,' he told them. 'He subverted their machines and in only a few days helped win vast new territories for our cause. Used in the right way, I assure you that he can deliver total victory before the end of the year.'

The old archivist surfaced again; water spilled down the glass wall of his tank. 'The boy fought for us under coercion,' he croaked. 'Enobarbus was allied with an apothecary by the name of Dismas. And this Dismas, who was working for one of the feral machines, infected the boy with a machine which subdued his will and assumed his powers. We almost lost him because of that, and many were killed in retrieving him.'

Enobarbus folded his arms across his broad chest. 'The feral machines are our allies still. It is necessary that they are, for otherwise we would have to fight them as well as the loyalist troops, and I do not believe we could win on two fronts. Besides, Dismas's master was not one of those, but a rogue. I believe that it is now dead. We have the boy, and yes, retrieving him cost many lives. Do not let those sacrifices be in vain. Let us use him to bring this war to a swift end. Kill him then, if you wish, but kill him now and you sentence millions to death who otherwise might have been spared.'

Mr Naryan listed chest-high in the bubbling water of his tank. He said, 'It is possible that the boy might save millions of lives if he is used against the loyalist troops, but it is certain that many thousands have already died because of him, first when Dismas tried to take him from you, and then when you recaptured him. Neither Dismas nor you, Enobarbus, could fully control the boy, yet everyone wants to own him. He is too powerful. I fear that if we use him to win the war we will then tear ourselves apart quarrelling over him.'

The woman in the white wig said, 'He defied and mocked the shrine. I understand that it may never be restored. Mr Naryan is right. He is too dangerous.'

'She will return,' Enobarbus said. 'She cannot be destroyed.'

There was a great deal of argument, and at last Mr Naryan said, 'It is clear that his powers proceed from the Preservers. How can we count ourselves superior to them if we must rely upon him for victory? No, he must die. We will vote on it.'

One by one, the panel dropped a pebble into a plain plastic basket. At the end a clerk tipped them out. There was no need to count. Only one was white; the rest were black.

Yama laughed when the clerk announced the result, and Pandaras feared that his master had lost his mind.

The sentence was not carried out straight away. It was to be staged publicly, and many heretics wanted to journey to Sensch to witness it for themselves. And there was much dispute about the method of execution. By a tradition which had survived the Change War, the citizens of Sensch cast their criminals into the swift currents at the fall of the Great River, and because the trial had been held in Sensch they insisted that this was how Yama should be executed. Others wanted a more certain death, arguing that Yama might save himself by calling upon machines which would carry him to safety. The heretics had no central authority and the debate dragged on for days after the end of the trial. Usabio, the warden of the prison house, said that Yama might die of old age before it was done.

'Then all your plans for becoming rich would fall to nothing,' Pandaras said. He did not like Usabio, but the man was useful. He courted Pandaras because he wanted to get close to Yama, and Pandaras could sometimes get favours from him.

'I could sell tickets,' Usabio said. 'People would come to see him, and the guards could be bribed to keep quiet.'

Usabio was of the bloodline of the citizens of Sensch, his pebbly black skin mottled with patches of muddy yellow. He bent over Pandaras like a lizard stooping on a bug and grinned hugely, showing rows of sharp triangular teeth. His breath stank of fish. He said, 'It would be like having an animal no one else had ever seen, the only one of its kind in all the world. We could dress him in robes and let him babble. Or perhaps I could bring him household machines to mend. Think of my offer, Pandaras. When your master is dead you will have no employment. You are crippled. You will become a beggar, and we do not tolerate beggars, for they are parasites on those who strive to better themselves. Only the strong survive, and you are weak! But with my help you could at least be rich.'

'Perhaps we will escape. Perhaps my master will destroy your miserable city.'

'He is defeated, Pandaras. You must think of yourself.' Usabio meant this kindly. He was a selfish and greedy man, but not without pity.

Yama took no notice of the arguments which raged around him. He merely shrugged when Pandaras told him about Usabio's latest scheme. As usual, he was sitting in the courtyard, in the shade of an ancient jacaranda tree. Soldiers stood at intervals by the wooden railing of the balcony that ran around the upper storey of the house, looking down at them through leaves and branches.

'They will make up their minds eventually,' Yama said. 'Mr Naryan will make sure of it. He does not want the feral machines or some rogue element of the heretics to try and take me. He is right. There are many who want to use me.'

Pandaras lowered his voice, although he knew that machines caught and recorded every word. He said, 'You could leave at any time, master. In fact, you could leave now. Do it. Confound their machines and walk away with me.'

'Where would I go, Pandaras? Now that I have travelled the length of the Great River, it seems to me that the world is a small place.'

'There are many places remote from men, master. And many places in Ys where you could hide amongst the ordinary people.'

Yama looked off into the distance. At last he said, 'Beatrice and Osric knew about hiding. They hid an entire department in the City of the Dead. But I am not yet dead, and I fear that my enemies will always be able to find me.'

'Forgive me, master, but you will certainly soon be dead if you stay here.'

'Everyone wants either to use me or to kill me. When I was a boy, Pandaras, I dreamed that I was the child of special people. Of pirates or war heroes, or of dynasts wealthy beyond all measure. It was a foolish dream, not because it was wrong, for it seems that I am the child of special people after all, but because it is dangerous to be special. That is why Mr Naryan wants to kill me.' Yama laughed. 'When I left for Ys I thought that I would become the greatest of all the soldiers in the service of the Preservers.'

'As you are,' Pandaras said firmly. 'And I am your squire, master.'

Pandaras still attended to Yama's needs, even though they were both prisoners. Each morning and evening, he intercepted the soldiers who brought Yama's food and carried in the tray himself. Fruit and sweet white wine, raw fish in sauces of chili and hot radish, onion bread and poppy seed rolls, flat breads stuffed with olives and yellow bean curd and watercress leaves, bowls of sour yoghurt, bowls of tea, beakers of cool sherbet. Yama ate very little and drank only water. Each night, Pandaras helped him undress, and each morning laid out fresh clothes for him and drew his bath.

'I am not a soldier,' Yama said. 'And that is the problem.'

'But they think that you are a soldier, master. And they will surely kill you for it if you stay here.'

'They think that I am an army, Pandaras. Or a mage, or a kind of machine. A thing to be used, a thing whose ownership is in dispute. They see only what I can do, not what I am. Where in this world can I find peace?' He shook his head and smiled. 'Do not worry. They will not kill you. You are my servant, no more and no less. You are not guilty of my crimes. You could walk out of here now if you wanted to.'

'I have already seen something of the cities of the heretics. I didn't much like them and I doubt that I'll like this one much either.'

'There are the ruins of the temple,' Yama said. 'And there are still orchards and fishing boats, and the shrines on the far shore, by the great falls at the end of the river . . .'

Yama fell silent. Spots of sunlight filtered by the leaves of the jacaranda tree danced on his white shirt and his long black hair. It would need cutting again, Pandaras thought. And realized that when he cut it, it would be for the last time.

Yama saw his distressed look and said, 'Beyond the edge of the world there are floating islands that hang within the falling spray of the river. They are grown over with strange mosses and ferns and bromeliads that thrive in the permanent rainfall. Telmon found a book in the library about them: they are called the Isles of Plenty. Fish with legs live on them, and lizards bigger than a man glide from island to island on membranes spread between their legs.' He gripped Pandaras's hand and whispered, 'The people of the indigenous tribes which inhabit the snowy tundra at the head of the river sometimes find such creatures frozen in the ice flows.' He winked. 'The indigenous peoples know much about the secrets of the world because they have not changed since it was created. They learn nothing new, but they forget nothing.'

Pandaras feared Yama at times like this. Something had happened to him when he had been connected to the thing in the pit. It had jangled his brain. All that he knew was still there, but it had been muddled up, as looters might sweep ordered rows of books from the shelves of a library and leave them in heaps on the floor. Pandaras asked the chirurgeons who checked Yama's health each day to give him some potion or simple that would soothe his mind, but they were interested only in his body. They did not want him to die before he was killed, but they did not care if he was mad.

When Pandaras carried in the tray of food the next morning, setting it down on the floating slab of stone which served as a table, Yama was already awake and sitting by the window. Two soldiers stood outside. The leaves of the jacaranda tree rustled in the sultry breeze. It was an hour past dawn, and already hot. Yama's shirt was open to the waist, and he was streaming with sweat.

Pandaras mopped his master's face with a cloth, delicately dabbing around islands and troughs of tight pink scar tissue. He would have to burn the cloth. Presumably in front of Usabio, who had asked Pandaras to collect Yama's sweat and hair and nail clippings so that they could be sold as souvenirs.

'A few drops of blood could be diluted in a gallon of ox blood,' the warden explained, 'and sold a minim at a time. Perspiration can be diluted in water. *Let his perspiration be your inspiration.* I can arrange it, Pandaras, and make us both rich.'

Pandaras said angrily, 'Perhaps we could sell his piss, or his shit.'

Usabio considered this. he said, 'No. It is not a question of hygiene, but of myth. Heroes should not be seen to have the functions of ordinary men.'

Yes, Pandaras thought now, he would burn the cloth right under the snake's nostril slits.

'Enobarbus came to see me,' Yama said. 'It seems that they have decided upon a compromise.'

Pandaras leaned out of the window and told the soldiers to take their stink elsewhere. They both laughed, and the younger one said, 'Going to plan your escape, eh? Don't worry. We won't listen. it would spoil the fun.'

'We'll go and get some tea,' his companion said. 'Might take a few minutes.'

As they sauntered off, the younger soldier turned and called out, 'If you're going to climb over the roof, watch out. The tiles are loose.'

Laughter as both men went down the stairs.

'No one takes me seriously,' Pandaras said. 'I have killed men. I could kill those two easily.'

'Then their companions in arms would kill you. I do not want that. There are machines listening to us in any case, and more machines guarding us. The soldiers are bored. They know that they are here only for show.'

'Dismiss the machines. Destroy them.'

'I am done with that, Pandaras. Enobarbus told me that he is still pleading for my life. He wants me to fight alongside him. I refused to help him, of course.'

'It took your power from you, didn't it? I'm a fool not to have seen it before. Well, I've been in worse places than this. I'll get us out.'

'They will let you go free after the execution. You are here only because you are my servant, as a courtesy to me.'

Pandaras threw over the breakfast tray. It made a loud crash. Mango and pomegranate juice mingled and spread on the glazed blue tiles of the floor. He said, 'I will die with you, master.'

'I am not ready to die, Pandaras. But I am ready to move on. You must stay behind. There is something I want you to do. It is a heavy burden, but I know that you are capable of carrying it.'

'I am ready, master.'

'I want you to remember me. I want you to go amongst the indigenous peoples, and tell them about me.'

'I will do it. And I will kill as many of these snakes as I can before they kill you. I will tear down this vile place . . .'

Pandaras was crying, breathing in great gulps as tears ran down his cheeks and dripped from the point of his chin. A wet patch spread across the front of his grey silk tunic.

'No. Hush. Listen.' Yama dropped his voice; Pandaras had to kneel beside him to hear his words. Yama stroked his small, sleek head, and at last the boy stopped crying. 'Listen,' Yama said again. 'I want you to live. You can do miracles now, although you do not know it. You kissed the blood from my eyes, and the machines in my blood have changed the machines in yours. I told you about the little machines in all of us, the breath of the Preservers. Those in my blood have been changed, as have those in yours. Just a drop of your blood, Pandaras. In water or in wine. One drop in enough liquid for a hundred people to each take a sip.'

'Usabio wants to sell your blood, master. Perhaps we should allow it.'

'We could not guarantee that it would be drunk,' Yama said seriously. 'Do you remember the baby of the mirror people?'

'I remember that the fireflies found it.'

'Because it had been changed. It had achieved self-awareness. Caphis saved my life, but he could not think anything that his people had not already thought ten thousand times over. I did not know then that I could change him, and now I want to rectify that. I want you to do it for me. A drop of blood, Pandaras. Change the indigenous peoples. Bring them to self-awareness.'

'I will do it only if you save yourself, master. Or else I will die with you.'

'The Preservers had a purpose in everything they did. Often we cannot understand it, or we think we understand it, but we see only what we want to see, and do not see what is really there. The indigenous peoples are despised because they cannot change. Until my father put a stop to it, the Amnan hunted the fisherfolk as they would hunt any animal. But the indigenous peoples are more than animals, even if they are less than men. You will redeem them, Pandaras.'

'Come with me, master. This talk frightens me. I am only a pot boy who fell into this great and terrible adventure by mistake. I am your squire. I bring you food and mend your shirts and keep your weapons in good order. Do not make me more than I am.'

'You found me, Pandaras. In all the wide world you found me and rescued me. And you followed me to the worst place in the world, and dragged me from the pit. Make you more than you are? We are all more than we are, if we only knew it.'

Yama had that faraway look Pandaras dreaded. He was casting through the muddle of his thoughts – his memories, the memories of the thing in the pit. He said, 'There are places where time and space do not exist. They form a bridge between the present and the time when they were made. They bridge distances that take light years to cross. The star-sailors know about them . . .'

'Master, do not torment yourself by trying to understand the lies of that thing.'

Yama gripped Pandaras's arm, just above the stump of his wrist. 'I am sure that Prefect Corin is still searching for me, but there are places I can go where he cannot follow. Perhaps I do not go there for the first time. The river swallows its own self. Soon, Pandaras, I will see how it is done.'

19 ~ The Execution

It was a fine, bright, hot day. Myriad small craft swarmed around the black barge which, with a sleek galliot on either side and a claw-shaped flier above, carried Yama and the judicial panel to the execution site. The event had a holiday air. The brightly coloured sails of sightseers' skiffs, pirogues, yaws, cockleshells, yachts and pinnaces cracked in the brisk wind. There was a raft carrying a hundred sweating, bare-chested drummers who beat out long, interwoven rhythm lines. Merchants in sampans and trows sold food and wine, souvenirs and fireworks. People held up their children to see the evil mage; other children threw firecrackers at the waves. Motorboats got in the way of sailboats and there were shouted arguments and exchanges of colourful insults. A whole raft of drunken men tumbled into the water when rocked by the wake of a chrome-plated speedboat's buzzing disc. They swam back to the raft and clambered on board and drank some more.

The fleet passed a strange cluster of hexagonal pillars of black basalt; long fringes of red waterweed spread out from them, combed by the river's strong currents. The farside shore was the thinnest of grey brushstrokes. Ahead, a line of black rain clouds marked the fall of the river over the edge of the world.

Yama was quite calm. He spent most of the journey speaking with Mr Naryan, who wallowed in a glass tank of water on the barge's weatherdeck. They talked about Angel, of how she had come to Sensch and made herself its ruler, and changed the citizens in the first act of heresy which had set Confluence aflame with war.

'She spoke at the shrines at the edge of the world,' Mr Naryan said in his soft, croaking voice, 'but I never learned what she did there.'

Yama laughed. All his cares seemed to have lifted away in this last hour. He did not spare a single glance for the execution frame which stood on the platform at the bow of the barge, but it drew Pandaras's eye again and again, and each time a cold shiver ran through him. *Now in the moment of our death is the moment of our rebirth into eternal life*. Pandaras glimpsed Usabio in a motor launch beyond the port-side galliot and felt a grain of anger sharpening his resignation. Yama's chambers had been stripped as soon as he had been marched out of them. The furniture had been reduced to matchsticks and the sheets cut into strips. No doubt the warden was here to make sure that the traders selling these souvenirs to the holiday crowd did not cheat him.

Yama told Mr Naryan, 'Angel called the last surviving avatars of the Preservers to her, and learned how to use the space inside the shrines. She made a copy of herself, the aspect that later destroyed the avatars. And I think that she made contact with the feral machines too.'

'She was always with me,' Mr Naryan said. 'I found her aspect in many of the shrines I visited, but she was fey and wilful, and did not seem to remember much of what happened in Sensch. I have that honour.'

'You told her aspect that story. And so she was able to put it in my book.'

This amused Mr Naryan, who rolled back and forth in his tank, barking sharply. Water slopped on the deck and a sprayhead flowered above him, soaking his exposed grey skin until it gleamed. A soft red light glowed at the centre of the machine which clung to the ruined socket of his right eye. He said, 'It is a fine irony. There are many stories about Angel, but only I remember the truth. Well, there is also poor Dreen, but he was seduced by the crew of Angel's ship, and went with them when they left this world. I will meet him again one day, of course. The Universe is infinite, but there are only a finite number of worlds. I will find him and save him from his mistake.'

'You all want to live for ever,' Yama said. 'But you cannot live for ever because the Universe will not live for ever. I have always wondered: what will happen when time ends, and you meet the Preservers? Will you try and destroy them?'

The woman in the mirror-bright armour told Yama, 'We will have destroyed the Eye of the Preservers long before then. There are ways of ablating black holes. Once it is small enough, an event horizon achieves closure and nothing can escape from it before it evaporates.

At least, not into this universe. We will seize the last day and make it ours. But by then, of course, we will have already made the Universe ours. We will not falter as the Preservers faltered,' she said, with a look of pure, fierce conviction. 'We will never cease in our striving.'

Yama smiled and said, 'There are many universes. Or rather, many versions of one universe. Everything that can happen will happen. Perhaps even your victory.'

'We do not need to think of the far future,' Mr Naryan said. 'That dream is what paralysed this world. Because the Preservers promised infinite life in the last moment at the end of all time and space, their foolish worshippers believe that there is no need to do anything in this life. Everything on this world has been bent by that false hope, mesmerized by it as a snake mesmerizes a mouse. But the future is not shaped by a promise; it is what each person makes of it.'

'We can agree on that at least,' Yama said. 'After the feral machines rebelled, the civil service decreed that it must suppress any change, because change implied heresy. Yet the Preservers changed us all, and set us here in the hope that we would change ourselves.'

Even the indigens, Pandaras thought, with another cold shiver. The burden his master had laid upon him seemed impossibly heavy. He was only half-listening to this idle talk, paying more attention to the soldiers who stood nearby. He had resolved to try and grab a pistol or even a knife if Yama would not save himself. He would give up his life if he could free his master.

'We do not need gods,' the woman in the mirror-armour said, 'because we will become more than gods. We will continue this conversation at the end of all things, when we raise you from the dead, Yamamanama.'

Yama bowed to her and said, 'I thank you for the courtesy.'

Enobarbus came back from the bow, where he had spent most of the voyage. As usual, he was bare-chested. A pistol was tucked into the red sash at the waist of his white trousers. Hot wind tangled his bronze mane. His scars blazed in his broken face. He said, 'It is almost time. You should ready yourself, Yamamanama. We do not have a priest, but you may pray alone if you wish to.'

'I am done with prayers,' Yama said.

The barge and its escort were passing long shoals of grey shingle to starboard, where all the wrack of the world was cast up: dead trees whitened by long immersion in the river; innumerable coffins, mostly empty; scraps of waterlogged clothing and bits of plastic; the bodies of men and animals; thousands upon thousands of bones; once in a while the bleached carcass of a ship. Water reivers, living on floating platforms with powerful motors to counter the strong river currents, sifted through the stuff cast up on these shoals, but today they were under guard far upriver. Only white gulls picked over the bones and the artfully preserved bodies; thousands of them rose like a snow storm as the procession went past.

The roar of the fall of the river grew ever louder. Strong currents raised the skin of the water into muscular humps that shifted and clashed in little flurries of white foam. The ramshackle fleet of boats and rafts unpicked itself, beating back against the currents until only a few foolhardy craft were left, ignoring warnings broadcast from one of the galliots.

A line of black clouds was directly ahead, trailing skirts of silvery rain. The river ran straight beneath them, rising in a glassy hump at the edge of the world, a kerb of water fifty leagues long.

One small pirogue foundered, swamped by the chop. The three people aboard jumped into the water and were swept away at once. No one tried to save them: they were responsible for their own lives. Most of the other small boats had turned back, although Usabio's powerful motor launch held station a little way off from the barges, and another launch hung half a league to stern.

The motors of the black barge and the two galliots roared and roared, holding them in place. The flier dipped lower, casting a shadow over the three vessels. Armoured troopers were lining up along the rails of the galliots. The compromise was this: Yama would be bound to a wooden frame and thrown into the river, but would be killed by sharpshooters before he was swept over the edge of the world. The sharpshooters did not need to be accurate. They were armed with carbines whose beams could boil the river.

Now the pace of things quickened. It seemed to Pandaras that everything was being swept along as if caught in the river's accelerating currents.

Yama was stripped of his clothes. With a swarm of machines darting overhead, jostling to get the best view as they recorded or transmitted the scene, he was led to the bow of the barge by a pentad of soldiers in black plastic armour and black masks. They guided him with nervous pats and quiet words. Pandaras tried to follow, but an officer took hold of his good arm, and no matter how much he wriggled, he could not get free.

There was a pause, then a shift in focus. Mr Naryan had begun to make a speech. Yama was marched back between the soldiers so that he could hear it. The barge's motors roared on a long low note that rattled Pandaras's teeth. His heart beat quickly. The barked orders of officers marshalling the sharpshooters on the galliots blew across the churning water. The distant launch was moving towards the barge now. Pandaras could no longer see Yama; the members of the judicial panel were in the way and the officer held him firmly. When they parted, he saw that Yama had been led back to the bow and was being lashed to the execution frame by five masked soldiers.

Pandaras cursed the ancestry of the officer who held him, and protested that he must be allowed to tend to his master in his last moments.

'He's beyond help now,' the officer said. 'Compose yourself. This is a great moment in history.'

The square execution frame was constructed from lengths of timber exactly Yama's height, reinforced with crosspieces and laid over a circle of thick balsa sections. It was held upright by slanting braces. Chains rose from each corner, knotted to a ring. The ring hung from a hook which in turn depended from the jib of a crane manned by a pentad of soldiers stripped to the waist. The slack chains swung and jingled as the barge shifted in the currents. Once Enobarbus had checked the ropes which fastened Yama's wrists and ankles to the frame, two soldiers knocked away the braces. The chains took up the slack and the frame was lifted and swung out by the crane, its top tilting backwards until Yama lay level with the swift water beneath him. Soldiers hung on to ropes, checking the frame's tendency to swing to and fro.

Trumpets brayed from the galliots on either side. Pandaras's heart quickened. Was this the final moment? He tried to get free again, but the officer got him in a headlock and twisted his arm up behind his back until the pain forced him to cry out. 'You'll be free in a moment,' the officer said. 'Have patience.'

Something was wrong. The sharpshooters were breaking ranks and turning around. The launch was still coming on, heading straight for the port-side galliot. Something small and bright shot away from it, rising high into the air as the launch roared on through wings of spray. The flier lifted away, turning towards the launch.

Pandaras's first thought was that Yama had called on a machine to save him. But the thing which had shot away from the launch was not a machine, but a man standing on a floating disc that cut through the air so swiftly his ragged cloak flew out behind him. Just as Pandaras realized that it was Prefect Corin, an energy bolt struck the flier and it burst apart with a deafening blast of blue fire, and fragments rained down in long arcs, trailing smoke and flame as they smashed into the river. At the same moment, there was a tremendous crash and a flare of flame swept down the length of the port-side galliot. The launch had struck it amidships and exploded. Pandaras felt heat wash over him; the officer cursed, but did not let go of him. The galliot was on fire from one end to the other and was beginning to list as water poured through the hole in its hull. Soldiers were running about inside the flames, their screams tearing at the air. Some pitched into the river and were swept away at once. Ammunition exploded, bright flares rippling within the flames. The burning galliot swung around, its motors stuttering, and began to drift towards the falls.

Prefect Corin rose above the flames. The sharpshooters on the galliot to starboard took aim, lowered their carbines and looked at them, took aim again. Nothing. Either Yama had willed it or Prefect Corin was draining energy from the grid. Some of the soldiers on the barge, armed with percussion rifles, began a ragged fusillade. Too late. Prefect Corin extended his arm and a bolt of blue fire struck the stern of the starboard galliot. Water flashed into steam and the casings of the big motors burst; panicked soldiers ran towards the bow as smoking streams of molten metal set fire to the well deck. At the same moment, the officer holding Pandaras screamed and clutched at his mask, which had shattered around the slim black shaft of a machine. Pandaras twisted free and dashed forwards, dodging amongst armoured soldiers and gorgeously costumed members of the judicial panel.

Enobarbus aimed his pistol at Prefect Corin, threw it away when nothing happened, and grabbed a rifle from one of the soldiers. Prefect Corin dipped low, rushing straight towards the execution frame, which still hung above the chop of the water. Enobarbus took aim with the rifle, not at Prefect Corin, but at the chains which held the frame. Sparks flashed when a pellet hit the hook and he lowered his aim and got off two more shots before Pandaras struck him and tried to climb his torso.

Pandaras managed to claw one side of Enobarbus's face, but then he was picked up and tossed aside. The barge and the sky revolved around each other; he struck two soldiers and knocked them down, fetched up against something that rang dully against the back of his head. It was Mr Naryan's tank. Enobarbus had thrown him halfway down the barge. Pandaras jumped up and ran forwards again. At the bow, broken chains shook and danced beneath the crane's jib. The frame was gone.

Pandaras swarmed halfway up the crane and saw Prefect Corin's floating disc scudding away above the waves, chasing something borne on the strong current. Two half-naked soldiers were climbing towards him, and he kicked out and dived into the river without thinking, and at once realized that he could hardly keep his head above the surface. The water was like a living thing in constant torment. Pandaras was caught in a current that forced him down amongst glittering fans of bubbles, then shot him back to the surface. A wave washed over him and he snatched a breath and glimpsed a shadow cutting towards him, and was pulled under again just as something twitched across his flanks.

A rope. He grabbed hold with his one hand and tangled his feet around its end. Whitecaps slapped his face one after the other. The side of a small boat pitched back and forth above him. Someone leaned down and grabbed him by the collar of his tunic and hauled him over the side.

Pandaras sprawled on his belly in a slop of water. The river had pummelled all the strength from his muscles. A motor roared and the launch made a long sweeping turn. Pandaras tried to stand up and fell into a nest of plastic bags, each containing a splinter of wood or a strip of white cloth, and knew who had rescued him.

Usabio turned from the helm of the launch, grinning hugely. He locked the controls and came back, bracing himself as he reached down to help Pandaras. And reared away, screaming and pawing at the splinter which Pandaras had jammed into his eye.

Pandaras kicked Usabio's legs from beneath him and struck him with all his weight. Still screaming, Usabio pitched backwards over the side of the launch and was gone.

The launch was heading away from the fall of the river. It took Pandaras several tense minutes to work out how to unlock the little machine which controlled the launch's motors and turn it back.

The two galliots were on fire and drifting towards the edge of the world. The black barge was moving away, a cloud of machines buzzing around it. Pandaras bounced the launch over the waves as fast as he dared. There was no sign of the floating disc, no sign of the frame. And no sign of either Prefect Corin or Yama.

The launch drew fire from the barge; machines buzzed it like angry hornets. Pandaras turned it away in a wide arc and pointed it upriver.

He did not believe that Yama had died. He swore to find him. He thought that he would spend the rest of his life looking, but he was wrong.

20 ~ The Isles of Plenty

Some time after he had been brought back from the Glass Desert by the heretics, Yama had become aware that Prefect Corin was drawing near to the ruins of the city of Sensch. The man had enslaved several machines, and, in the days after Yama's trial, had moved from place to place around the edge of the city and its huge garrison, presumably probing for weaknesses. Yama had been certain that the Prefect would try and rescue him from the heretics, but had not believed that he would be successful. At best, he might provide a useful diversion. But now it was clear that, once again, Yama had underestimated the Prefect's resourcefulness.

Yama had his own plan of escape. He wanted to fall over the edge of the world into the short cut where the river went, where past and present tangled together. The short cut had been made when the world had been put together, and he thought that he could fall to its beginning and at last find his people. He had learned this from Dr Dismas's paramour. It had absorbed many lesser machines and many men and women, and hoarded their knowledge much as a pack rat will decorate its nest with scraps of glass and plastic and metal. That great store had poured into Yama in the moment the machine had tried to make him its own, a torrential flood that had almost washed away his own self. He had had only a little time in which to try and map its limits, but he knew now the secret of the Great River, and knew that in the beginning of the world lay its end, and that was enough.

It was easy to fool the minuscule brains of the sharpshooters' carbines into thinking that they had discharged when they had not. It was harder to turn one of the swarm of machines which accompanied the barge, for they were imprinted with hundreds of interlocking shells of sub-selves, and each had to be painstakingly unpicked. But

Yama knew that he would need a machine to cut his bonds after he was cast into the river, and he worked hard at it while the heretics prepared him for execution.

And then, as he hung naked on the execution frame, something blew the flier from the air and a motor launch rammed the galliot to his left and exploded. He guessed what was happening even as Enobarbus ran towards him, and used the machine he had laboriously subverted to kill the officer who held Pandaras. But instead of trying to escape, Pandaras ran to help his master, attacking Enobarbus even as the warlord shot away the chains from which the frame was suspended.

And then Yama fell. The frame smashed down into the water and was at once whirled away from the barge. A sudden surge threw it into the air and crashed down into a wave that washed over Yama with bruising force, pulling his bound arms and legs in different directions. Yama managed to get a breath and then another wave struck the frame and he went under again and came up, gasping and blinking and wondering if he would drown before he fell over the edge of the world.

A shadow covered him: a floating disc. It tipped in midair and Prefect Corin slid down on to the frame and straddled Yama, bracing himself against the rock and roll of the waves. His staff was strapped to his back, over his fluttering cloak. He hit Yama four times with doubled fists, twice on the left temple, twice on the right. Something flashed as he raised his right hand. A knife. Yama, barely conscious, could only watch.

The knife slashed the rope which bound Yama's left hand to the frame. Prefect Corin's face was a handspan from his. 'We are here to help you, boy,' he said. He had to shout above the clash of white-water waves and the long unending roar of the river's fall. 'We will not lose you again. Say that you will come with us and we will free you.'

Yama tried to speak, but could not gather his thoughts. Spread-eagled and naked beneath his enemy, dazed and helpless, he felt all his old fears return. Prefect Corin was implacable, unforgiving, tireless. There was no escape from him. He would never stop, never give in, never die.

Prefect Corin laid his face against Yama's. His pelt was wet and cold, his breath hot. His left eye was a puckered ruin. 'You are ours,

Child of the River. Now and always. Whether we live or die, we will do it together.'

Yama tried to focus on Prefect Corin's face. Things kept slipping away, jumping back. He had not been afraid of falling off the edge of the world because he had known where he was going, but he was filled with dread now. He was more afraid of this man than of anything else on the world.

Prefect Corin smiled and whispered, 'You do not want to die. That is a beginning.' He kissed Yama on the lips and sat back on his heels, ready to cut the other bonds, and his cloak suddenly flew sideways. Prefect Corin clasped his shoulder, then looked at the bright red blood on his palm, and Yama remembered Enobarbus's rifle. At the same moment, something cracked the air like a whip and a spray of blood struck Yama's face. Prefect Corin grunted, toppled sideways, and was swept away in the foaming cross-currents. The floating disc tilted and swooped off, following its master. Yama watched it dwindle through pouring rain, and then a strong eddy caught the frame and swung it around.

Rain smashed through spray thrown up by clashing waves. Its cold needles stung relentlessly, bracing him awake. The air was half water now. A tremendous roaring filled every cell of his body. The frame groaned and flexed. Impossibly, it was rising, carried up a smooth slope of glassy water. For a moment, Yama paused at the top of the wave at the edge of the world, saw a barge and two foundering galliots beyond the skirts of the rain clouds, and a launch making a long arc away from them.

And then the world tilted backwards and he fell away from it.

It was noon. Mr Naryan had decreed that it was an auspicious moment for the execution. The sun shone straight down, turning the farside edge of the world into a golden knife blade that cut away half the sky. A wall of water fell past it, twisting into itself as it fell, a spout that shone silver against the blue of the envelope of air which wrapped the world, dwindling down towards the mouth of the short cut which swallowed it and took it elsewhere. Yama could feel the tangled gravity fields like threads tugging at his limbs. He struggled to focus, to find the machines which generated the fields, and felt a cold, ancient intelligence far below, squatting at the mouth of the short cut like a toad at the bottom of a well.

A dizzying surge of hope filled him then. It was all true!

Vast skirts of cloud hung about the wall of falling water, as white as freshly washed linen. Archipelagos of violet and indigo specks were scattered in arcs at different levels within the clouds, each casting a long shadow streak.

The Isles of Plenty.

Yama reached out, manipulating gravity fields. The frame flew towards the outermost island of the nearest arc.

He laughed as he swooped down, remembering his childish dreams of flying and the dream he had had in the tomb of the Silent Quarter of the City of the Dead.

Past and future came together in a moment of exquisite richness.

He fell through a veil of cloud. Fog streamed around him, soaking him with clinging cold vapour. Out into sunlight again, falling at the same speed as the constant rain. He could no longer see the island and tried to spin the frame around; then it crashed into soft tangles of dull red tubes which collapsed around him, exuding a strong, acrid scent.

He was still trying to unfasten the ropes around his ankles – the knots had shrunk in the water – when the rain people found him.

The Isles of Plenty were continually drenched with rain and mist. Everything – the soft, interwoven masses of bladderweed and the transparent, hydrogen-filled bladders that swelled at their fringes, the knotty mats of black grass, froths of algae and elaborate nests of ferns – was sopping wet. Water dripped from the spiky tips of indigo and violet fronds, percolated between interwoven root mats, collected in channels that ran into deep cisterns and pools, and poured in a hundred streams from the ragged edges of the islands. Sometimes it rained so hard that the air seemed to turn to water. Fish clambered about the soft mounds of vegetation, using prehensile fins at the edges of their flattened bodies, opening their rich red feathery gills in the downpour as they hunted maggot-flies, worms and beetles.

It was never brighter than twilight. As the world tipped back and forth on its long axis, the sun appeared above the farside edge at noon and below it at midnight, and even then the permanent cloud cover around the endless fall of the river obscured what light there was, only occasionally parting for a moment to reveal a sudden shaft of sunlight ringed by a hundred perfectly circular rainbows. Surges of air rubbed against each other, creating thunderstorms which were the greatest danger for the inhabitants of floating islands: a lightning bolt could ignite the hydrogen-filled bladders which buoyed the islands and blow them apart. But even in death there was life. Fragments of the communal organisms which wove together to form the floating islands were widely dispersed by these rare explosions; some would grow into new islands to replace those that dropped out of the currents of air which blew around the wall of water – the Great River turned through ninety degrees and falling towards its end and its beginning.

The rain people who inhabited the Isles of Plenty were not, as Yama had dreamed, of Derev's bloodline. They were an indigenous race. They were roughly half Yama's height, with smooth grey skins, oval heads dominated by large black eyes, thin arms and legs, and long, flexible, three-fingered hands. They were cold-blooded and moved in abrupt bursts punctuated by slumberous pauses in which, except for the slow blink of nictating membranes across their great eyes, they stood as still as statues.

Even as some of the rain people helped Yama free himself from the frame, others started to dismantle it; hard wood was as precious as gold in the Isles of Plenty. He was guided along paths smashed through wet, pulpy vegetation to a village built on platforms at the leading edge of the island. The main platform straddled a stream which tumbled noisily between banks of dome-shaped mosses and fell into the void below. Smaller sleeping platforms were build around the rigid stems of horsetail ferns which burst into great fans of knotty black strands overhead. The fern canopy was the only shelter from the constant rain. Water dripped everywhere, running across the slick resin of the platforms and falling into the vegetation below.

The rain people gave Yama a hide blanket to wrap around his naked body and fed him with a salty mash of uncooked fish flesh and the chopped tips of a variety of water weed whose brown straps grew parasitically on bladderweed stipes. Yama explained to them where he had come from and where he wanted to go. They listened patiently. Although they were naked, he could not tell which were men and which were women, for they had only smooth grey skin between their legs. Several pairs leaned against each other companionably. One of these couples, Tumataugena and Tamatane, the eldest of the family clan of the island, told Yama that only a few men from the world above had ever reached on the Isles of Plenty, and none had ever left. But he was the first to understand that the river swallowed its own self, they said, and they realized the importance of his quest.

Tumataugena said, 'The fall of the river diminishes year upon year.'

Tamatane said, 'The mouth of the snake flickered two generations ago. It swallows water still, but we fear that it spits it elsewhere.'

Tumataugena said, 'The same happened to the river of the other half of the world.'

Tamatane said, 'Unless a hero comes, this half of the world will become a desert too, as it was once before.'

Speaking in turn, Tamataugena and Tamatane told the story of how the river of the inhabited half of the world had once been a long pool which flowed nowhere and soon became stagnant. A cistern snake drank it up, but this snake was two-headed and had no anus, so the water remained in its belly, swelling it into a smooth blue-green mountain range full of water that lay along one side of the world, opposite the Rim Mountains. One head lay amongst the Terminal Mountains at the endpoint of the world; the other hung over the midpoint. The world became tinder dry. Animals were dying of thirst; plants became wrinkled and sere. Several of the bloodlines which lived there attempted to make the snake disgorge the water by making it laugh, but since snakes have no sense of humour this came to nothing. But inside the cistern snake were certain parasitic worms, and as the snake swelled so they grew. By the will of the Preservers, they became the progenitors of the rain people. They broke off bone splinters from the snake's many ribs and fashioned them into knives. Working together, they cut the snake in half from within and set free the water it had swallowed. The great flood washed one of the snake's heads over the edge of the midpoint of the world. It hung in the air, receiving the waters that fell after it. The snake's other head remained lodged in the Terminal Mountains, and the water swallowed by the first head was vomited from the second. And so the Great River was formed, and the curves of its course preserved the last wriggles the cistern snake made in its death throes.

When the story was done (soft rain fell all around, like applause), Yama said, 'I heard a riddle long ago, and now I know that I have found the answer to it. For that, as well as for my life, I am in your debt.'

Tamatane said, 'We became as we are now because we saved the world from drought. Yet we are still less than any of the peoples of the surface.'

Tamataugena said, 'If we help you save the river, then perhaps we will be rewarded again.'

'Perhaps,' Yama said.

The rain people asked Yama many questions about his adventures in the world above, but at last he could stay awake no longer. He slept beneath a shelter of woven bamboo leaves. He fell asleep quickly, even though he was soaked through and very cold, but he was awoken after only a few hours by Tamatane and Tumataugena.

'Something bad walks the air,' they said. 'Perhaps you know what it is.'

The floating island was in the middle of a dense belt of cloud. It was close to midnight; light shone from beneath the island, diffused through white vapour. As Yama disentangled himself from the wet, heavy hide, something flashed far off in the mist, an intense point of brilliant blue light that faded to a flickering red star, falling through whiteness and gone even as Yama glimpsed it. A moment later, the whole island trembled as a clap of thunder rumbled through the air.

Yama shivered. He thought that he knew what had caused the blue light and the thunder.

As he clambered down from the sleeping platform, something loomed out of the mist: a dark spot that grew and gained shape, a red triangle with a kind of frame beneath it. It tipped through the air and stalled above the edge of the main platform; its pilot swung down from its harness and ran a little way across the platform with the last of its momentum, collapsing the bamboo frame and the hide stretched across it.

High-pitched whistles rose on all sides. The rain people gathered around the pilot, who stood in the centre of the platform and stared up in wonder at Yama.

The pilot, Tumahirmatea, was from a shoal of floating islands which hung far above this one. Something terrible was loose in the air,

Tumahirmatea said, a monster which spat flame and could destroy an island with a single breath.

'I know it,' Yama said. 'It is not a monster, but a man. I thought him dead, but it seems that nothing in the world can kill him. He is looking for me. I must leave at once.'

The rain people talked amongst themselves, and then Tumataugena and Tamatane came forwards and offered their help.

Tamatane said, 'You wish to fall through the mouth of the snake.'

'I could jump from the edge of this platform in an instant,' Yama said, 'but I am not certain of my target.'

His stomach turned over at the thought. He was not at all sure that he could manipulate the machines which generated the gravity fields with enough precision to reach the mouth of the short cut. If he missed, he would fall beyond the envelope of the world's air, and suffer the same horrible death as Angel.

Tumataugena said, 'We have several kinds of flying device. The simplest are sacks full of bladders harvested from the edges of the island, but those will lift you rather than allow you to fall. So instead we will give you one of our kites.'

It was brought out of store and unwrapped. Yama thanked the rain people and asked for a knife and a cup of water. Tumataugena gave him a bodkin fashioned from the spine of a fish, with a handle of plaited black grass; Tamatane gave him a gourd brimming with sweet water.

Yama pricked the ball of his thumb and allowed three drops of blood to flutter into the water. He said, 'If you wish to become more than you are, to become as the peoples of the world above, then drink a mouthful of this. When the change is complete you will be able to change others in the same way. If you decide not to do this thing, then wait a day for the water to lose its potency and then dash it over the edge of the island.'

Was Pandaras safe? Would he perform this miracle for the indigenous peoples of all the long world? But perhaps it did not matter. Already the mirror people and the forest folk were changed. And they would change others.

The rain people talked amongst themselves; at last, Tamatane and Tumataugena announced that they would do this thing at once. They passed the gourd around, and the last person to drink from it, the stranger, Tumahirmatea, pitched it into the void.

'You will have a fever,' Yama said, 'and then you will sleep. But when you awake all will be changed. You must find your own way after that. I can do no more for you.'

It did not take long to learn how to fly the mankite. There was a harness which was lengthened to accommodate him, and a frame hung at the balance point which he could grip and tilt to the left or right. A ribbon at the point of the kite indicated the direction of air currents; rudders pushed by his feet spilled air from the leading edges of the diamond-shaped lifting surface to bring it to stalling speed for a safe landing. But he would not need to land, only to stoop down like a lammergeyer.

There was no ceremony of farewell. He was strapped into the kite and helped to the edge of the platform, then took a breath and jumped off. The underside of the island fell past, tangles of tough holdfasts studded with transparent hydrogen bladders. The kite jinked in air currents, wrenching at his shoulders. He kicked, got his feet in the stirrups of the rudders, leaned to the left. And began to breathe again.

Tumahirmatea followed Yama as he stooped down, the red kite matching the yellow wingtip to wingtip.

They fell through vast volumes of cloud, breaking through streaming mist and rain into clear air. In one direction the dark wall of the edge of the world rose through decks of cloud and curtains of rain; in the other, empty blue air deepened towards the black void in which the world swam. Between, the silver column of the falling river twisted down towards its vanishing point, a hundred leagues below. The air was brighter there: it was night on the surface of the world, and the sun was walking its keel. Lightning crackled around the silver twist of water, vivid sparks flashing against their own reflections. Floating islands made broken arcs at different levels, receding into blue depths of air.

Yama swooped down in a great curve, yelling as he fell. For those few minutes, he was utterly free.

Tumahirmatea left him once they had fallen past the lower edge of the clouds that ringed the falling river. The red kite tipped from side to side in farewell and tilted away, already rising on an updraught. Yama fell on alone.

The column of water, twisted within intricate gravity fields, was closer now. The air was full of electricity generated by the friction of its fall. Every hair on Yama's head stirred uneasily; the thunder of lightning storms constantly shivered the air. He tacked several leagues out from the water column, then swung the kite around it. The world was a wall reaching above and below as far as he could see.

After one more full turn around the falling river, he would reach its vanishing point. Looking straight down, he could see a throat of velvet darkness wrapped around the root of the column of water. He could feel the thing which controlled the short cut. It was awakening, reaching towards him through the babble of the machines which manipulated the gravity fields.

Take me to the beginning of the world, he told it. Take me to my people.

He had expected difficulties. He had expected to have to use the full force of his will and all of his wits to break it. But it yielded at once. Filtered through the remnant of the Shadow, its voice was his own. *Of course*, it said. *You have returned. Do not be surprised. I live in the place where the river meets itself. Of course I know you. I hope that I will see you again.*

There was no time to frame questions. He was caught in air currents which sheared off the falling water. They buffeted him hard as he cut through them. The lifting surface of the kite boomed and shivered. The frame wrenched in his grip as if suddenly possessed of a will of its own.

You will not need the flying thing. I will guide you.

Yama kicked his feet out of the rudders, unbuckled the harness. And gave himself to the air.

The kite slammed away above him, bucking and folding up as conflicting air currents caught it, a fleck of yellow that whirled upwards, was gone. Yama arranged himself in the rush of air, his feet pointing down, his arms by his sides. It was the way he had so often dived into the deep water at the rocky point of the bay of the little city of Aeolis.

Something other than air gripped him. He drifted slowly towards the column of water. It was as smooth and dense as glass. It seemed to rise above him towards infinity. Beneath his feet was a rim of darkness, at one moment as flat as a ring of paper, the next infinitely deep. The tube of water narrowed as it swooped down. Water was not compressible, but somehow the river's vast flow was squeezed into a tube so narrow that two men could have embraced it and touched fingertips.

Space-time distortion. The flow here is extended through time as well as space. It is easier than extending the size of the short cut's mouth.

Yama did not understand the words which appeared in his head.

He was falling faster now. Air ripped past. His cloak of uncured hide streamed up behind his head. He saw structures around the rim, geometric traceries of intense electric blue that extended wherever he looked.

And then he was gripped, turned, accelerated. There was an instant of intolerable pressure and brilliant light.

21 ~ Ship of Fools

A tremendous flood swept him forwards. He thrashed towards light and air, but the water was already receding, a wave washing away in every direction.

He stood, water slopping about his ankles. The hide cloak was soaked through, and clung in heavy folds to his naked body. The light was dim, blood-red. The cold air tasted of metal. He was in a chamber so large he could not see its ceiling or any of its walls. Beneath the ankle-deep water was a floor of a smooth, slightly yielding black substance.

A shrine stood a little distance away. It was the biggest he had ever seen, a huge black disc that could have overtopped the tallest tower of the peel-house. Nothing woke when he addressed it, but he had the unsettling impression that its vast smooth surface somehow inverted for a moment.

Where was he now? And when? Was he in the keel of the world? Was this the time of its making? He flexed his toes against the black floor. It reminded him of a place Tamora had taken him to a lifetime ago, in Ys.

He chose a direction at random and walked a long time. The water soon gave out. Once he shouted out his name, but the volumes of shadow and red light gave back no echo. He walked on, and a little time later felt the presence of machines far behind, and stopped and turned.

In the distance, tiny figures were moving at the base of the huge black circle of the shrine. He raised his arms above his head and shouted to them with sudden hope, and a narrow beam of intense white light swept out and pinned him. The figures were suddenly moving forwards with impossible, inhuman quickness. Yama tried to question them, but their minds were opaque. Remembering the extensions of Dr Dismas's paramour, he turned and started to run, his shadow leaping ahead of him, and ran until he heard a faint whistle off to his left.

He stopped and look back, half-winded and dazzled by the white light, and saw that the figures had already made up half the distance. The whistle came again, human, shrill and urgent. He turned towards it. The beam of light tracked him, and his shadow rose to confront him, thrown on to something that loomed out of the dim redness. A structure of some kind, a black blister or bubble no bigger than an ordinary house.

A figure jumped up right in front of him, throwing aside the cloth which had concealed it. Yama tried to dodge, but it was faster. A shoulder smashed into his belly, arms wrapped around his hips, and he was thrown to the floor.

He looked up in astonishment at a face so like his own it might have been his sister's: pale skin, a narrow jaw, high cheekbones, vivid blue eyes. Her black hair was cropped short. Elaborate tattoos began at the angles of her jaw, reaching around under her ears to meet at the nape of her neck. She wore a loose, silvery, one-piece garment that clasped her ankles, wrists and neck. One of her calloused bare feet was planted on his chest, and she was pointing a slim wand at his face. He had the sense that it was a weapon. There was something odd about this strange yet familiar woman, a vacancy . . .

'What are you?' she said. She was breathing very hard. 'A survivor from the holds or a stowaway?'

Yama had turned his head to hide the scarred side of his face. He was uncomfortably aware that he was naked under the heavy hide cloak. He said, 'Am I in the keelways?'

'You mean the spine? Don't fool. We lost those territories twenty generations ago. What are you?'

'A stranger to this place.'

'A savage on walkabout maybe. Whatever you are, I think you just killed us both.'

She let him stand. The figures were much closer now, silhouetted against the glare of the intense beam of white light, man-shaped, but oddly lopsided, running hard towards them.

Yama pointed at the blister and said, 'What is inside this building?'

'An outlet. Even if we had a hot blade, we could not cut its skin.'
The woman was folding up the black cloth which had concealed her. It
made a surprisingly small square that went into a slit at the waist of
her silvery garment.

Yama remembered the voidship lighter. The guard had done
something to the material . . .

An opening puckered in the smooth black curve. The woman
looked at him in astonishment, but followed him inside. The opening
sealed behind them. For a moment they were in complete darkness,
then the woman asked for light and a dim radiance kindled in the air.

They stood on a narrow walkway. It ran around a smooth-walled
shaft that sloped down into darkness. The woman knelt and stared
down into the shaft, then looked up at Yama. 'That was a good trick,'
she said, 'but the regulators will get permission to unseal this soon
enough.'

'What are they?'

'You don't wear any mark. What family?'

'That is what I hope to find out.'

'You came through with the water, didn't you? But we can't stay
here.'

'I will have to take off my cloak,' Yama said. 'Then we will find out
how far this falls.'

'A long way, I expect. It is one of the mains.'

Yama sat down at the lip of the shaft, took off the cloak and spread
it out, hairy side down. He could feel the woman's gaze move over his
naked body. He said, 'Sit behind me and hold on to my waist. The
cloak will protect us.'

After a moment, she did as he asked. Her spicy scent and body heat
gave him an erection; he felt a blush spreading across his face and
chest.

The woman said, 'I am Wery. If we survive this I'll take you to my
people and we'll parlay. Bryn will want to ask you many questions.'

'Now,' Yama said, and they kicked off into the long steep slide.

Wery screamed all the day down – in delight, rather than fear. The
surface of the shaft was almost frictionless, but even so the hide
quickly grew warm beneath Yama's bare buttocks. When at last the
shaft straightened out and they came to a halt, he got up into a crouch
and awkwardly fastened the cloak around himself again.

They walked a long way. The shaft was more than twice their height and perfectly circular in cross-section, lined with the same black stuff as the floor of the huge space they had escaped. Yama told Wery some of his story. 'All my life I have been searching for my people,' he said. 'I am so happy to have found you! How many others are there? And where is this?'

'You'll find out, if you pass. You can trade questions with Bryn.'

'I can explain how I came here, and why I do not know where I am. The river was diverted—'

'No more talk now. We're not safe here.'

At last, Yama discovered a place where he could make the black stuff pucker open. They clambered through into green light and hot, humid air. A rock face covered in creepers and thick lianas rose behind them, its top overhung by trees. A dry stream bed snaked away between bushes and trees that leaned over it to form a kind of tunnel.

Wery looked all around, sniffing the air. 'I think I know this wild. The others are not far away. You did well.'

She stepped up to him, face to face. For a swooning moment Yama thought that she was about to embrace him, but instead she touched her wand to the skin behind his ear. A point of intense coldness swiftly spread across his scalp and face. His muscles loosened; Wery stepped out of the way when he fell.

Yama was woken by the screeching of birds high above. Two men stepped through the ragged rent they had hacked in the bushes that grew thickly along the dry stream bed. Wery ran to the larger of the two men, embraced him, and said, 'It wasn't any bug that came through. I'm not sure what he is. He has a story so crazy it could be plausible, but he could be a medizer.'

'They killed all the medizers long ago,' the smaller man said, 'after they killed the other tribes.'

'Hush,' Wery said. 'He's awake.'

Yama sat up. He smiled at the two men and spread his hands so that they could see that he was unarmed. He was so very happy to have found people of his bloodline that he could not believe that they would want to harm him.

The men were dressed in silvery one-piece garments like Wery's, and both had similar tattoos across the backs of their necks. As with

Wery, there seemed to be something lacking in them. It was as if they were not living people, but animated statues, or aspects cast in flesh rather than light . . .

The man Wery had hugged was a head taller than Yama, well-built and handsome. He had ripped off the sleeves of his silvery garment to show off his muscular arms; copper bands constricted his well-defined biceps. The other man was much older, and had a leather sack slung over one shoulder. His close-cropped hair and trimmed beard were white; his skin was papery and freckled with brown splotches. Deep wrinkles cut his forehead and seamed the skin around his eyes and the corners of his mouth. I will look like that if I live long enough, Yama thought, and wondered how long it would take, and how long he could live.

There was a silver patch over the old man's left eye. He flipped it up and told Wery, 'Something else came through, too. Regulators are swarming all through these decks. They know how you got away and sooner or later they will try to follow. We'll have to move.'

The old man pointed his wand at Yama, and Yama's muscles immediately locked in tetanic spasm. His body arched in a bow; his teeth ground against each other when he tried to protest.

The old man flipped the patch down over his eye and made several slow passes of his wand over Yama's body. 'He's full of bits and pieces, but nothing I recognize. Stuff in his blood, too, but it isn't regulator trace. Never seen anything like it. Maybe he really did come from somewhere else.'

Yama knew now what these people lacked. None of them had been touched by the breath of the Preservers. They might have been ghosts.

'The ship is very big,' the taller one, Cas, said slowly.

Wery shook her head. 'From what he said, I think he's from outside.'

The old man stood back. Yama's muscles relaxed, then began to tingle. He stood slowly and said, 'I really can explain everything.'

'Not here,' the old man said. 'We shift, mates, find a berth and wait out the regulators.'

The old man, Bryn, was the leader of the three. They had been on what he called a bug hunt.

'Things come up with new cargo,' Bryn told Yama, 'and sometimes they get loose. They have to be sly enough to get past the safeguards, so they usually cause trouble. We hunt them down.'

The big man, Cas, said, 'Maybe he's a bug that looks like a man.'

'No fooling, Cas,' Wery said. 'This is important.'

After they left the stream, they walked in silence a long way down a path that wound through the forest. Yama's hide wrap dried slowly, stiffening around him. He was aware that it smelled of meat going bad. At last the path passed between two huge trees, and on the other side a white coridor stretched away to its vanishing point. They walked on for more than a league until Bryn said that it was safe to think of resting.

He opened a door Yama had not noticed, and they went through into a high-ceilinged, brightly lit room. Narrow slabs of ceramic floated in the air and gusts of hot, dry air blew from random directions. Feeding troughs were set in the floor along one of the walls, but the stuff in them had crumbled to dust. No one had been here for a very long time.

A voice welcomed them when they entered, and said that it could reconfigure to the requirements of their bloodline. Bryn told it to shut up. 'We leave no traces,' he said to Yama. 'Remember that and you might live as long as me.'

Yama sat next to the old man on one of the floating slabs and asked him how old he was. 'Fifty-three years,' the old man said proudly. 'You look surprised, and no wonder. It is older than anyone I know. I expect that no one in your family has ever lived as long, but it is possible, as you can see.'

Yama had thought that Bryn must be at least two centuries old, and the revelation disappointed him. It seemed that his bloodline was very short-lived, unless they aged quickly here because of hardship.

Cas and Wery were watching the door, their wands across their laps. 'I hate this heat,' Cas said. 'We should find one of our places.'

'The regulators will look in those places first,' Bryn said. 'Shut up Cas. Watch the door. I want to hear our new mate's story.'

Wery said she had already heard it, and had not understood a word. Bryn shrugged. 'She's muscle,' he told Yama, 'she and her husband. Good at killing, but not so bright.'

'You always got to think you're cleverer than everyone else,' Cas said. He got up and began to prowl around, restless in the way of a man more comfortable with action than conversation.

Bryn said, 'It's well known that I am clever. I chose you two because I'm clever enough to know what you're good at. Don't break any of the machinery, Cas. That'll bring the regulators at once.'

Cas said, 'Good. I fight them.' But he set down the delicate construction of black rods he had been turning over in his big hands.

'Did you really come from Confluence?' Wery asked Yama, with a smile that broke his heart all over again. He had forgiven her for knocking him out; it had been a sensible precaution. She said, 'It's paradise, I hear. Like wilds that go on for ever, but no regulators or bugs. You should take us all there.'

Her fierce, bold candour reminded him so much of poor, dead Tamora. Perhaps she would leave Cas for him; perhaps there were other women like her. In the swooning excitement of finding his people, he had forgotten his sweetheart, Derev, and the fervent promises they had made to each other before he had set out on the long road which had at last led him here.

Cas said, 'The ship hasn't been to Confluence for generations and generations. How could he come from there?'

Yama tried to explain.

The fastest way to travel from one point to another was in a straight line – or rather, over the long distances between stars, in a curved geodesic, for the mass of the Universe distorted its own space. But within the vacuum of space were holes smaller than the particles which made up atoms. As small as the smallest possible measurement, the holes appeared and disappeared in an instant, a constant, unperceived seething of energies that continually cancelled themselves out. The holes had two mouths, and the space that tunnelled between the mouths was compressed so that the distance between them was shorter inside the tunnel than outside it. The Preservers had found a way to grab the mouths of certain of these holes, to stabilize and widen them.

Bryn nodded. 'The ship uses the short cuts to get from world to world without travelling. It also uses them to replenish its air and water. You came out in one of the cisterns. Lucky for you it was one that isn't used any more, or you would have drowned. But I guess most of them aren't used now. The crew is pretty skimpy these days.'

Cas was doing push-ups as relentlessly as a machine. Sweat gleamed on his bare, muscular arms, pooled between the cords of his neck. Without pausing, he said, 'All this is useless stuff. We don't need to know anything outside the ship.'

'Let him tell all of it,' Wery said. 'You never know when something might have a use.'

'She's right,' Bryn said. 'Set on, lad. Finish your story.'

The Preservers had constructed an intricate network of short cuts between every star in the Galaxy, but the short cuts could link points in time as well as space. It was done by fixing one mouth of a short cut to a ship capable of travelling at speeds close to that of light itself. In the realm of light there was no time; or rather, there was a single endless moment which encompassed the beginning and the end of the Universe. As the ship carrying the short cut mouth approached that unreachable realm, so time stretched about it; while only a few years passed aboard the ship, many more passed in the rest of the Universe. When the ship returned to its starting point, the two mouths of the short cut now joined regions of space which were separated by the time debt built up during the journey. Someone passing through the mouth of the short cut which had travelled with the ship would exit from the mouth which had remained where it was, and travel back to the time when the ship's journey had begun. But they could not return by the same route, because their journey altered the past.

Yama drew diagrams in the dust, prompted by the remains of the Shadow, which was able to filter the vast store of knowledge he had taken from Dr Dismas's paramour. As Yama explained his story, he came to understand just what he had done.

The Preservers had cloned certain of the short cuts, so that one mouth led to many different destinations, determined by slight changes in the potential energy of whatever entered. Aided by the Gatekeeper, Yama had fallen through the mouth of one of these cloned short cuts, but he did not know where and when he had emerged. He knew only that his wish had been granted: he had been sent to his people.

Yama understood all about cloning, for it was how meat and work animals were bred, but he had to explain it several times before Wery understood. The notion disgusted her, and Bryn was amused by her disgust. 'There are many different ways of living,' he said. 'That's why these rooms are all so different, because the passengers were once many different kinds of people.'

'They were all bugs,' Cas said indifferently. He was sitting on his haunches by the door now, polishing a bone dagger. 'And we kill bugs.'

'Some bugs are the stock species from which the Preservers made people,' Bryn said. 'Although I admit that there's a bigger difference there than between child and man.'

'Bugs are bugs,' Cas said. 'Kill 'em or be killed. Some are harder to kill, that's all.'

'And you can eat some but not others,' Wery said.

Yama said again, 'Because I fell through one of the cloned short cuts, I do not know where I am.'

'On the ship, of course,' Wery said. 'Somewhere about the waist, in an outer deck.'

'He means he doesn't know if this is his past or his future,' Bryn said.

Bryn knew more about Confluence than the other two, but knew nothing of Ys or the Age of Insurrection, or even of the Sirdar, who had ruled Confluence when it was newly made. His people had been on the ship a long time; Yama suspected that their ancestors had fled here, or refused to leave once the construction of Confluence had been completed. They had been rebels, like the feral machines or Tibor's ancestors.

Yama said, 'I think this must be somewhere in the past. The star-sailors I met knew about my bloodline, but believed that it had died out long ago.'

Wery said with sudden anger, 'We will destroy the regulators! They are only machines. They are as stupid as emmets.'

'Emmets have the run of parts of the ship,' Bryn said. 'Intelligence is not necessarily a survival trait.'

'Then you cannot control these regulators?' Yama was surprised. He had supposed that all of his bloodline would be able to control machines, but it seemed that things were different on the ship. Wery had not been able to make the floor stuff flow apart, and even he had not been able to touch the minds of the things which had chased him in the cistern. He said, 'I suppose that the machines here are not the same as the machines on Confluence.'

'Some say that we controlled the regulators once,' Bryn said. The old man seemed amused. 'Maybe we still do, on other ships. It's bad luck you arrived here.'

Cas said unexpectedly, 'There is only one ship, Bryn. It loops through time and sometimes meets itself.'

Bryn said, 'Only one ship in our universe, yes, but perhaps there are many universes, eh? A universe takes only one road, but if a man retraces his steps he cannot then return to the place from which he started. For the road splits at the place he travelled back to, and he must travel down the new road. It stops a man killing his grandfather and returning to find himself without existence.'

'Perhaps his grandfather was only the husband of his grandmother,' Cas said slowly, 'and not his sire.'

Bryn tugged on his beard in vexation. 'His grandmother then! You are an infuriatingly literal man, Cas. I only make a fancy to illustrate a point. There are as many universes as there are travellers. In many we live on into our new mate's time, perhaps, but not in the time he came from.'

Yama nodded. 'Then I would not have had to come here to look for you.'

Bryn said, 'The problem is that you can go back to your future, but not by retracing the same path, and so it will not be the place from which you started.'

Cas said sulkily, 'We've stayed here too long, and all this talk is making my head hurt. Why should what one man does cause a new universe?'

'It is no easy thing, to travel back through time,' Bryn said. 'But you are right. We should not stay here too long. The regulators might notice the change in carbon dioxide concentration.'

'I have good ventilation,' the room said.

'When I need advice from you,' Bryn said, 'I will ask for it. Do your synthesizers still work?'

'Of course, but they are not suitable for your bloodline. I will have to change the settings.'

'I want clothing, not food. Yama, you must be properly dressed. Frankly, that hide of yours is beginning to stink. Do it, room, and then we will move on.'

'You are welcome to stay as long as you like,' the room said. 'I miss the company of people.'

'We can't stay unless you change your settings,' Bryn told it, 'and the regulators will know if you do. Just make the clothes.'

Yama pulled on the one-piece silvery garment with his back to the others, although he was sure that Wery was watching. He knew that she belonged to another man, but he ached for her all the same. His blood raced in his skin when she showed him how to adjust the seals at ankles, wrists and neck. Her fluttering touch; her heat; her scent. Surely she must know how he felt . . .

She talked with him as they walked the seemingly endless white corridor. Cas went ahead, waving them forwards at each intersection, then loping on eagerly.

'You don't mind Bryn,' Wery told Yama. 'He has too much learning in his head. He wants to bring back the old days. Thinks we can make the regulators our slaves. He'll be making plans for you.'

Yama smiled. 'This is like one of the old stories! Bryn is the magician, and you are the warriors helping him in his quest.'

'We're hunting bugs,' Wery said. 'What are you?'

'I do not know. A magical creature perhaps. But I do not feel magical. I am beginning to understand that magic is a matter of perception. Knowing how to do something takes away the mystery which can make it seem magical.'

'Maybe you can teach us how to make the floor open. That's useful. Bryn is full of dreams, but dreams are for children. We kill bugs and regulators, or they kill us. That's how it is. It can't be changed.'

'Are the regulators a kind of bug?'

'They're passengers. Like us.' Wery laughed at Yama's astonishment. Her teeth were very white. One of the incisors was broken. 'There used to be many different kinds of passenger. Now there're only the regulators and us. And the crew of course, but no one has ever seen one of them.'

'I saw one. Well, two, in fact. But that was in another place.'

Wery smiled. 'You can tell me all about Confluence, when we've finished travelling.'

'I could take you there.' His heart turned, melting.

'Maybe. Now get this straight. Regulators killed all the other passengers, but we're too smart. Too tough. We hunt bugs and regulators, they hunt bugs and us. That's how it is. Makes the ship work better if its passengers have to prove their worth.'

'Survival of the fittest,' Yama said. It seemed as vile as the creed of the heretics. As if the Universe were without any ruling principle but death.

'That's what Bryn says. I say you are either dead or alive, and dead doesn't count.'

'How many of your people are alive? Where do they live? I want to know everything about them, Wery.'

Wery held up her left hand and opened and closed her fingers three times. 'And us,' she said. 'We're a way from home, and it moves about anyway.' She added, 'Cas has found something,' and ran off down the wide, white corridor to catch up with her husband.

Bryn dropped back to walk alongside Yama. He said, 'We can't tell you too much, lad.'

'I understand. Perhaps you can tell me how your people came to live here. That was a long time ago, and surely telling me an old story will not do any harm.'

'We served the Preservers,' Bryn said. 'We were their first servants – the original crew of the ship, I think. Then the Preservers made all the other races and went away, and we lost our powers.'

'I thought that our people went with the Preservers,' Yama said, smiling because it was so thrillingly strange to say *our* instead of *my*.

'Perhaps most of them did. But this ship was left behind, and we are the descendants of those who flew it.'

'Perhaps they refused to leave their home,' Yama said.

'We are loyal servants of the Preservers,' Bryn said. 'Do not think otherwise.'

'I meant no offence.'

'None taken, lad. But if we live in your past, and you know no others of your kind, where did you come from?'

'That is what I am still hoping to discover,' Yama said. 'Perhaps I am the child of sailors of our bloodline who jumped ship long ago. I know of at least one star-sailor who did.'

'Borrowed a body, I suppose. They try that on board sometimes. The ship doesn't like it, and lets us hunt 'em like bugs. What have you found, Cas?'

The big man had stopped at a place where another corridor crossed the one down which they had been travelling. The black stuff of the floor was scored heavily there, ripped into curling strips. The strips were creeping over each other and softening at the edges, trying to mend the wounds.

'Bug trace,' Cas said, holding up fingers smeared with sticky clear liquid which had splashed and spattered across the white walls. 'Reckon there was a fight and one ate the other. Not long ago, either.'

Wery grinned. 'It's wounded,' she said. 'There's a trail. We kill it easy.'

The trail of colourless blood led into another of the big, forested spaces. As before, the transition was abrupt. One moment Yama was hurrying along beside Bryn, who, despite his age, kept up a spritely pace, with Wery and Cas jogging eagerly ahead. Then the two warriors went around a corner and when Yama and Bryn followed they were suddenly in a dark, dank, dripping place, where huge tree trunks reared up through a broken layer of mist that hung some way beneath a high, dark canopy.

Yama looked back and saw a sliver of white light between two boulders propped against each other. It was the only point of brightness in this gloomy place. Pale fungi raised tall fans above ankle-deep ooze. Vines dropped from somewhere beyond the mist and slowly quested about the floor, pulsing with slow peristalsis as they pumped ooze upwards. Yama saw that the giant trees were in fact conglomerations of these vines, twisted around each other like so many stiffened ropes. Parasitic plants wrapped pale, meaty leaves about the bases of the vines, and things in burrows spread feathery palps across the surface of the ooze; something bright red and thin as a whip shot from a hole and snapped at Yama's ankles.

Bryn laughed. 'This is one of the mires, lad. Everything passes through here eventually.'

Wery and Cas found a sign of the thing they were tracking, and disappeared into the gloom between the trunks of the giant tree-things. There was a squalling noise in the distance. Bryn drew something from his sack and tossed it underhand to Yama.

It was a knife. When Yama caught it by the haft, its curved blade sparked with blue fire. Bryn stared and Yama grinned. 'I know this at least,' he said, 'and it knows me.'

Had the knife he had found – or which had found him – in the tomb in the Silent Quarter originally come from the ship? Was this perhaps the very same knife, destined to come into the possession of the dead warrior in whose tomb Yama had confronted Lud and Lob?

The squalling rose in pitch. Bryn and Yama sloshed forwards through the ooze. Something thrashed beyond a tall ridge of white fungus, then suddenly reared up. It was three times the height of a man, and sprang over the fungus and ran at Yama and Bryn with preternatural swiftness.

Yama had a confused glimpse of something in black armour, all barbs and thin legs with cutting blades for edges, a narrow head dominated by wide jaws that opened sideways to reveal interlocked layers of serrated blades rotating over each other. It did not look so much like an insect as a dire wolf chopped and stretched into a poor imitation of an insect. It made its high squalling noise again. Acrid vapour puffed from glands that ran along each side of its long, hairy belly.

The bug knocked Yama down with a casual flick of a foreleg and pounced on Bryn, spraying black ooze everywhere. Wery suddenly appeared behind it and threw a long, weighted rope that tangled around its forelegs. Yama jumped up, ooze dripping from his silvery garment, and ran beneath the bug's belly as it snapped at Wery. He stabbed the knife's blade, blazing with blue fire, through the membrane at the articulation of one of its sturdy rear legs. The knife whined, burning so eagerly through horn and flesh that it almost jerked out of his hands. Clear, sticky blood gushed; the bug half-collapsed, its leg almost completely severed. Cas stepped between its flailing forelimbs and stabbed the point of his wand between its eyes. It shuddered and kicked out and died.

While the others worked at severing the bug's head, Yama noticed that a kind of belt was fastened around its narrow waist, slung with pouches and bits of shaped stone or bone. Tools.

Bryn saw his look and said, 'It would have killed us if it could.'

'It was intelligent.' Yama thought of Caphis, the fisherman he had found in a trap set by one of the Amnan. People preying on other people. The strong on the weak, the clever on the stupid.

Bryn tugged at his beard. 'It was bright enough to get on to the ship. But not bright enough to survive.'

Yama handed the knife to he old man, hilt-first. 'I have had enough of killing, I think.'

Cas tugged hard and the armoured head came free. Clear liquid gushed from the neck; the legs thrashed in a final spasm. Hand-sized creatures as flat as plates, thready blue organs visible through their transparent shells, skated over the muck to get at the spilled blood. Red whips had already wrapped around the bug's legs, melting into its horny carapace.

Yama expected the three hunters to carry their grisly trophy in triumph back to their home, but instead they dumped it in the corridor directly outside the entrance to the mire and went on.

'The regulators will find it and mark it,' Bryn said. 'Our task is done.'

The lights of the ship, slaved to a diurnal cycle, dimmed soon after they left the mire. They slept in a little room Bryn found off one of the corridors. This one was more suited to their kind. Beakers of distilled water and tasteless white cubes of food extruded from a wall at Bryn's command. The floor humped into four sleeping platforms. 'If you want to piss or shit,' Bryn told Yama, 'do it in the corner there,' and ordered the room to dim its light.

Yama was woken from a light sleep by Wery's giggle. Sounds of flesh moving on flesh, breath at two pitches gaining the same urgent rhythm. He lay awake a long time, lost and lonely and frightened, while the two hunters made love a few spans from him.

They walked along the endless white corridor for much of the next day. Wery walked at point with Cas, while Bryn asked Yama many questions about Confluence, most of which he could not begin to answer.

They travelled steadily, drinking from tubes set in the necks of their silvery garments, which recycled their own sweat as distilled water. At last, they left the corridor for one of the jungle wilds, and after an hour's walk down paths so narrow they must have been made by animals, Wery insisted on showing Yama something.

'You'll like it. Really you will. You won't have seen anything like it.'

Yama demurred. He was still embarrassed and disconcerted by overhearing her lovemaking.

'Go on,' Bryn said, with a sly smile. 'You will see where you are.'

Yama and Wery climbed a grandfather tree that rose through the dense green canopy, its surprisingly small crown of dark green feathery fronds silhouetted against sky glare high above. Its rough bark provided plenty of easy hand- and foot-holds. They climbed a long way. Cool inside his silvery garment despite the foetid heat, but quite breathless and with his pulse pounding heavily in his head, Yama sat at last in the crutch of a massive bough on which Wery balanced with heart-stopping ease.

And saw that the jungle stretched away for several leagues on all sides, a rumpled blanket of green studded here and there with splashes of bright orange or yellow or red where trees were in flower. A line or chain of tiny, intense points of white light hung high above the treetops: the little suns which fed the jungle's growth. But that was not what Wery wanted him to see.

The jungle grew on the outer skin of the ship, seemingly not enclosed by anything at all – perhaps gravity fields held in the atmosphere, as they contained the envelope of air around Confluence, or perhaps it was domed with material so transparent that it was invisible. The rest of the ship could be clearly seen all around the jungle's oval footprint.

Yama, remembering the voidship lighter which had docked at Ys, had thought that the ship would be some kind of sphere, bigger certainly, but more or less of the same design, much as a dory resembles a carrack. But now he saw that the ship was a series of cubes and spheres and other more complex geometrical solids strung like beads along a wire, and that it was many leagues long – impossible to tell how many. In all their journeying, they had traversed only one part of one segment. There was room enough for any number of wonders to be hidden here.

But he knew that he could not stay. He had thought about it last night. He had found people of his bloodline, yet they were stranger to him than Pandaras or Tamora or Derev. They lacked the breath of the Preservers and so could not be anything other than what they already were, enslaved for ever by their circumstances. This was not his home. That was on Confluence. It was with Derev. She and Yama had sworn a compact, and he knew now that it meant more to him than life itself. He would find the cistern and the shrine, and force the Gatekeeper to take him home. And then he would end the war. He had known how to do it ever since he had seen the picture in the slate which Beatrice and Osric had shown him at the beginning of his adventures, but he had not known he had known it until he had absorbed the knowledge hoarded by Dr Dismas's paramour.

Standing before him on the broad branch high above the jungle, Wery clapped her hands over her head and laughed. Yama realized for the first time that she was older than him, perhaps twice his age. The achingly brilliant light of the chain of miniature suns accentuated the wrinkles around her eyes, showed where flesh was beginning to loosen and sag along the line of her jaw.

It did not make her less desirable.

'Look starboard,' she said, and pointed at the distant edge of the ship.

Something stood far beyond the jungle. A red line – no, a dome, the top of a structure bigger than any of the wilds. It was lengthening and growing in height, as if it was crawling towards them.

A vast creature, big as a mountain . . .

Yama looked at Wery, wondering if he had finally been driven mad, and she laughed again and said, 'That's the mine world the ship orbits.'

Yama realized then that the growing blister was part of a disc. Not advancing, but rising – it was a world as round as the sun, just like those described in the opening suras of the Puranas. Or not round, but a sphere, a globe, a battered red globe rising above the ship's horizon. Yama laughed too, full of wonder. Its pockmarked red surface was capped top and bottom with white, and scarred by a huge canyon that pointed towards three pits. Or no, they were the tops of huge, hollow mountains. At the very edge of the world's disc was a fourth, so big that it rose above the narrow band of diffracted light which marked the limit of the world's atmosphere.

Wery said that it was time to descend. They walked down narrow paths through understorey trees and bushes that divided and divided again in an endless maze which Cas, who took the lead, seemed to know well, for he set an eager pace.

Now it was Yama's turn to ask questions. Bryn said that mined mass was moved from the surface of the world to the ship by something called an elevator, a chain or cable that hung down from a point many leagues above the world's surface. It took a while for Yama to understand why the cable did not collapse. The world was spinning, so that its surface moved at a certain speed, and the cable was grown from a point high above that also moved at the same speed, so that it was always above the same place on the surface. Hoppers moved up the cable and the material in them was slung out like pebbles from a catapult, to be caught by the ship and stowed away.

Ahead, Cas paused at a place where the path split into three. He turned and waved and went on.

Wery chased after her husband. A moment later, frantic whistles pierced the green quiet of the jungle. Bryn broke into a run and Yama followed. They scrambled down a steep fern-laden bank and splashed across a muddy stream, clambered up the bank on the far side and burst through a screen of tall grasses into the brilliant light of the miniature suns.

A huge tree had fallen here long ago; Yama and Bryn had emerged at the top of a wide, deep bowl, grown over with rich green grass, which had been torn out of the earth when the tree's roots had been pulled up by its fall. Here and there bodies lay in the long grass. Human-sized, human-shaped, clad in silver.

Yama's heart turned over. But then he saw that the bodies were naked; the silver was the colour of their skin.

'Regulators,' Bryn said, and sat down beside one of the bodies and bowed his head.

Cas and Wery were standing at the far edge of the clearing. When Bryn sat down they looked at each other and then ran off in opposite directions.

'Wait,' Bryn said, when Yama made to follow Wery. 'There may be traps.'

'This is the home of your people.'

'They were camped here. Perhaps they moved on before . . .' Bryn bowed his head once more, and clasped his hands over the white hair on top of his head.

Yama moved from body to body. All were quite unmarked. They were very thin. Their right hands were three-fingered, but their left hands were all different: one like pinchers made of black metal; another extended into a bony scimitar with a jagged cutting edge; a third had hinged blades, like monstrous scissors. The silver of their skin had a grey cast. Their eyes were huge, the colour of wet blood, and divided into hexagonal cells. Although they were dead, something still seemed to be watching Yama behind these strange eyes. It was like the men whom the rogue star-sailor had enslaved by putting machines in their heads; the machines had lived on after the men had died, and so here.

Wery appeared at the far end of the clearing, shouted that everyone was gone, and ran off again. Bryn got up slowly, straightened his back, took a deep breath, and said, 'We will see what has happened.'

The bowl of the clearing was a hundred paces across, twice that in length. The rotting carcass of the fallen tree lay at one end, extending into bushes and young trees which grew all around. Butterflies which might have been made of gold foil fluttered here and there in the bright light. Cas caught one as he came down the slope towards Bryn and Yama, and crushed it in his massive fist.

The encampment was no more than a few panels of woven grass leaning against the trunk of the fallen tree. A scattering of mats and empty water-skins, neatly tied bundles of dried leaves, a frame of tall sticks in which a stretched hide had been half-scraped of its hair. A blackened cube in a hearth of bare earth still radiated heat; a bowl of something like porridge had dried out on top of it and was beginning to burn. Yama picked up a hand-sized bit of flat glass. Glyphs began to stream and shiver inside it, but they were of no language he knew.

Wery said, 'There were three regulators waiting for us. Cas killed two. I killed the other.'

Bryn said, 'The others?'

'Gone,' Wery said. She dabbed angrily at the tears which stood in her eyes. 'All gone.'

Cas pointed at Yama with his wand, and Bryn got in front of Yama and said, 'No. It could not be him.'

'There would only be three of us if you killed him, Cas,' Wery said.

Yama understood. Their family was the last of the bloodline on the ship; that was why they had been so amazed to see him. And now they were the last of their family.

Bryn flipped his patch down over his left eye. He turned in a slow, complete circle and said, 'Where are the bodies, Cas?'

'I have not found them. I will look again.' Cas trotted across the clearing and plunged into the bushes on the far side.

Wery said, 'Do you think they might still be alive?'

Bryn lifted the eyepatch. 'Ordinarily the regulators would have killed them at once. But there is no blood, and there are no bodies.'

'Perhaps the regulators took the bodies,' Wery said.

'But they left their dead companions,' Yama said.

Wery and Bryn looked at him. And at the same moment a regulator parted a clump of tall ferns and stepped into the clearing, mismatched hands held up by her shoulders. The left was swollen and bifurcate, hinged like a lobster's claw.

'Stop!' Yama said, and knocked Wery's arm up as she aimed her wand at the regulator. Something went howling away into the bright sky. Wery turned on him, the wand swinging in an arc that would have ended in his chest if he had not stepped inside it. He gripped her elbow and bent her arm behind her back until she had to drop the wand; bent it further until she had to kneel.

'Cas will kill you,' she said, glaring up at him.

'Be still,' Bryn told her, and she stopped struggling at once. Bryn was pointing his wand at the regulator, but he was looking at Yama. He said, 'It obeys you.'

'Yes, but the others did not.'

The regulator still had her hands raised. Her flat breasts hung like empty sacs. She fixed her huge red eyes on Yama and said, 'I have a message from Prefect Corin.'

22 ~ So Below

Cas came back at a run, and would have killed the regulator at once if Bryn had not stood in his way. They argued in violent whispers; then Cas turned his back on them all and Bryn came across the clearing and told Yama, 'We will both go with you.'

Yama said, 'I think it would be better if you all stayed here.'

'They have our people,' Wery said. 'Of course we will go with you.'

Bryn walked around and around the regulator, which still stood where Yama had told her to halt. At last he turned and said again, 'It obeys you.'

'The regulators have machines in their heads which control them. I am able to talk with her machine, although I was not able to talk with the machines of the others.'

'It,' Wery said.

Yama and Bryn looked at her.

Wery said defiantly, 'It, not she. They're all things. Not people. Things. Things!'

Cas put his hand on Wery's shoulder and she turned and rested her face against his broad chest. Cas said, 'We will come with you, Yama. We will kill this Prefect Corin and free our people and come home. What you do after that is of no matter to us.'

'I wish it were that simple,' Yama said. 'And I still think you should all stay here.'

They were savages. They tried to justify their presence on the ship and placate the regulators with trophies from bug hunts, but they were as much stowaways as the things they had killed in the mire. If there had been time, Yama would have mixed a little of his blood with water and let them drink it; without the breath of the Preservers they were no more than any of the indigenous peoples of Confluence, higher than animals but less than men. But there was not enough time.

Cas said, 'We will come with you. We are hunters. We hunt bugs. We hunt our enemies.'

'We will come with you,' Bryn said. He stared into the regulator's big, red, faceted eyes, tugging at his neatly trimmed beard. 'But before we leave, you will tell it to obey us too. I will not have it used against us.'

'I still say we kill it,' Cas said.

'No.' Bryn smiled; he believed that he was in command again. 'Once this is over, we will be masters of all the regulators. The crew will look to us for help instead of to them. That is my price, Yama, for the hurt you have caused. We should make a start on our quest at once. It will be night soon, I have no liking for this place any more, and it is a long way to the docks.'

The regulator stirred. 'There is a shorter route,' she said, and repeated her message. 'My master commands you to descend to the surface of the world below. I will lead you to where he waits with your people. If you come with him, they may go free.'

Cas began to curse the regulator in a dull monotone. Yama said, 'I will avenge the hurt done to you all in my name. I swear it.'

Yama was as fearful as the others as the little glass room fell along the length of the ship; like the others he tried to hide his fear as best he could. Wery and Cas leaned against each other, holding on to the rail which ran at waist-height around the room's cold, transparent walls; Bryn clung there too, aiming his wand at the regulator, which hung like a silvery-grey statue in the centre of the room, its flat, toeless feet a span above the floor.

Only Yama watched the view. The long track down which the glass room fell was a thread laid across the solid geometries of the ship's segments. The ship dwindled away above and below, although neither direction had much meaning here, where there was no gravity. Clusters of lights cast stark shadows over the surfaces of enormous cubes and pyramids and tetrahedrons strung together and studded with hundreds of green or brown or indigo blisters – wilds clinging to the surfaces of the huge ship's segments like fish lice to an eel.

As the ship turned about its long axis, the bulging disc of the red world slowly rose above it. Yama glimpsed the terminus of the elevator far beyond the end of the ship, a blob of light sliced in half by its own shadow. The elevator itself was a broken line defined by lights scattered along its length, dwindling away towards the world.

Bryn was able to answer some of Yama's questions. The ship turned on its axis so that all sides would be exposed to the light of the sun of this system, evening out temperature differences. The elevator was woven from strands which were each a single giant molecule of neutronium, stabilized by intensely steep gravity fields. The mines delivered phosphates and iron. In thirty days the ship would leave this system and pass through the short cut to its next destination.

The regulator stirred and said, 'They spy on the crew.'

Bryn tapped his eyepatch, which was flipped up on his wrinkled forehead. 'I am allowed revelations,' he said. 'This is one of the greatest treasures of my people.'

'You interrupt data flow,' the regulator said.

'As is our right,' Bryn said, 'earned by tribute.'

'You have no rights,' the regulator said. 'You are parasites.'

'You be quiet,' Cas told her. 'Speak only when spoken to.'

Yama knew that neither Bryn nor the regulator could answer his most urgent questions. How had Prefect Corin followed him here? Why had he descended to the surface of the world? How was he able to control the regulators?

He thought long and hard on these questions as the glass room sped towards the end of the ship. The world's huge red disc slowly revolved above them and set on the far side of the ship, and then Yama forgot for a moment all his questions and anxieties.

For the stars had come out.

There were thousands of them, tens of thousands, a field of hard, bright stars shining everywhere he looked, crossed by a great milky river that seemed to wrap around the intensely black sky. The sun of this world must lie deep within one of the arms of the Galaxy; that milky river was the plane of the arm, the light of its billions of stars coalesced into a dense glow. Here and there structures could be seen – star bridges, tidy globes, a chain of bright red stars that spanned half the sky – but otherwise the patterns made by the Preservers were less obvious than when viewed from the orbit of Confluence, many thousands of years beyond the rim of the Galaxy. And yet every star he could see had been touched by the Preservers: their monument, their shrine, was all around him.

Then the sun rose. Although it was smaller and redder than the sun of Confluence, its light banished all but the brightest of the stars.

Yama had expected the glass room to re-enter the ship and deliver them to some kind of skiff or lighter which would transfer them to the elevator terminus. But instead it simply shot off the end of its track into the naked void. Cas roared, half in amazement, half in defiance; Wery pressed the length of her body against his. The ship fell away. The terminus of the elevator slowly grew larger in the void below their feet.

It was an irregular chunk of rock, its lumpy surface spattered with craters. One side was lit by the sun, the other, where the elevator cable was socketed in a complex of domes and haphazardly piled cubes, by ruddy light reflected from the world.

'It is one of the moons of the world,' Bryn said. He had lowered the silver patch over his left eye. 'Its orbital velocity was increased to move it from a lower orbit and to synchronize it with the world's rotation.' He added, 'This world was moved, too, displaced across half the diameter of the Galaxy. There is a legend that it came from the original system of the Preservers, although some maintain that it is merely a replica of one of the worlds of that system.'

The little moon grew, slowly eclipsing the sun, and the glass room swung through ninety degrees – Cas roared again – and extruded huge curved grapples made of stuff as thin as gossamer. Contact with the elevator cable happened very quickly. The pocked red-lit moonscape swelled below their feet and the room spun on its axis and one element of the cable, not much thicker than an ordinary tree-trunk, was suddenly snug against its grapples. The moon began to dwindle and Yama felt his weight increase; now they were falling towards the world, which hung above their heads like a battered orange shield.

The journey took less than an hour. The cable blurred past, a silver wall occasionally punctuated by flashes as rooms very much larger than theirs shot past in the opposite direction. Below their feet, the tiny moon was lost in the glare of the sun; only a few leagues of the elevator cable was visible above, a shadowy thread dwindling towards the world. Midway in the journey, their weight slowly vanished until they were in freefall. The room swung around so that the world was below their feet, and their weight came back.

The black void gained a pinkish tinge and a faint whistle fluted and moaned around them; they were entering the atmosphere. The world flattened and spread, became a landscape. Their weight dwindled; this world's gravity was a gentle tug about a third the strength of the ship's, which had been exactly as strong as that of Confluence. The room was falling towards a rumpled red plain crossed by straight dark lines. The sun was setting.

Bryn said that the lines were canals. They had once carried water from the south pole to the agricultural lands of the equator. He was staring raptly at the desolate plain below; Cas and Wery had taken out their wands. A range of broken hills made a half-curve around an enormous basin which held a shallow, circular sea. Yama saw a huge flock of pink birds fly up from the shoreline. Millions and millions of birds, like a cloud of pink smoke blowing across the black water.

The elevator cable fell towards a complex of structures beyond the sea's shore, in the middle of a dark forest. Stepped pyramids rose above the trees, gleaming like fresh blood in the last light of the sun; beside them, like a mask discarded by a giant, a carving of a human face wearing an enigmatic smile looked up at the sky.

It was Angel's face, Yama realized. This had once been one of her worlds, part of her empire.

The elevator split into a hundred cables, like a mangrove supported by prop roots. The glass room fell down one towards a black dome. As it approached this terminus, it shuddered and slowed. For the space of an eye-blink it was full of blue light.

Wery screamed, and something knocked Yama down.

The dome swallowed them.

Yama was lying in darkness. The regulator was sprawled on top of him, as light as a child. Her skin was hot and dry. 'Wait,' she said, when he began to move. 'It is not safe.'

'Let me up,' he told her. There was wet, sticky stuff on the floor. Yama had put his hand on it. It was blood. He said, 'Who is hurt?'

'Someone shot Bryn,' Wery said in a small but steady voice. 'And Cas is wounded.'

'Not badly,' Cas said, but Yama knew from the tightness in his voice that this was a lie.

There were many machines at various distances beyond the little glass room. Some of them were lights; Yama asked them to come on. They were dim and red, scattered across a huge volume. The cable, which was socketed in a collar as big as the peel-house, disappeared through an aperture in the high, curved roof. A metal bridge, seemingly as flimsy as paper, made a long, sweeping curve from the glass room towards the shadowy floor.

Bryn was slumped near Yama. The chest of his silvery garment was scorched around a hole as big as a fist. There was a surprised expression on his face. Cas had lost most of his left hand; he had wound a strip of material so tightly around his wrist that it had almost vanished into his flesh. Wery crouched beside him, her arms wrapped around his broad shoulders.

The glass walls of the room were scorched around two neat holes, one on either side. Air whistled through them as pressure equalized, bringing a sharp organic stink. Then part of the glass pulled apart to make a round portal, and the stink intensified.

'Come out,' a voice said from below. 'One at a time. Walk slowly down the bridge.'

Wery hurled herself through the portal, screaming as she went. She ran very quickly and Cas roared her name and lurched up and chased after her. There was a flash of blue light; Yama had to close his eyes against it. When he opened them, the two warriors were gone.

'Come out, boy,' the voice said. 'You can bring your servant. We will not hurt her, or you.'

The regulator plucked the wand from Bryn's dead hand and crumpled it in the monstrous claw of her left hand. She was suddenly remote from Yama; what he had thought was her machine self had been only a shell personality, and it had now evaporated. Her real self was as opaque as that of the other regulators.

The regulator put her right hand on Yama's shoulder and guided him through the portal and down the long curve of the metal bridge to the shadows of the floor. Great heaps of stinking black stuff covered one side of the vast space. The stench was so strong and sharp that Yama's eyes began to stream with tears.

Prefect Corin walked out of the shadows at the base of the high, curved wall of the cable socket. He leaned on his staff, a slight figure in a simple homespun tunic that was heavily stained with blood. He said, 'We are pleased that you came. Do not be afraid. All will be well.'

Yama said, 'Where are they?'

'All this is guano, from deposits along the shore of the sea. There are hills and islands which are entirely made of the shit deposited by birds over millions upon millions of years. The ship takes it to Confluence because it is rich in phosphates. The ecological systems of Confluence are not closed. It is a small habitat, and badly designed. I do not blame your people for that, Yamamanama. The fault is with the Preservers. How can they be held to be the perfection to which all aspire if their creation is so ill-made?'

'Confluence is not perfect because it is of the temporal world. Where are they?'

'Come with us,' Prefect Corin said.

He turned and walked off. After a moment, Yama followed. The regulator walked two paces behind him, and a decad of her kin fell into step on either side.

'They are not here,' Yama said loudly. 'You lied. You killed the people before you even left the ship.'

Prefect Corin did not look around. He said, 'Of course. It was part of the bargain I made with the star-sailors. They were the last of your bloodline, and the star-sailors wanted them destroyed.'

'The star-sailors control the regulators.'

'Yes. And we have been given control of these. Please stop trying to take them away from us. You will have many servants, when we return. We will rule Confluence. You will help us.'

'He followed me,' Yama said, suddenly realized what had happened to Prefect Corin, why he had not come for him earlier. 'He followed me into the Glass Desert. And you found him, or he found you.'

'We were almost destroyed,' the Prefect said. 'We took him by force and made him ours.'

'And you killed him.'

'Unfortunately, the process was too harsh to allow survival of the subject.'

'In any case, the body you wear is badly hurt. Enobarbus shot it.'

'The rifle pellet destroyed the heart, but we have grown replacement musculature and control the body still. When it fails us we will select another. We wanted the woman to live; she would have served us well. But we can use one of the regulators as easily, and eventually we will use you. You made us serve you three times, and we serve you no longer. Instead, you serve us.'

'Three times?' Yama had guessed that the thing which possessed Prefect Corin was the residue of the fusion between Dr Dismas's paramour and the feral machine he had called down to destroy it, but he had only commanded the feral machine twice, and had never commanded Dr Dismas's paramour. In any case, it did not reply.

A high arch opened on to a wide plaza raised above the tops of low, thorny trees which stretched away in every direction. A cold, thin, dry wind blew from the west. The sun was setting, a tiny, intensely red disc embedded in shells of pink light that extended across half the sky. There were many things living in the forest; Yama was able to reach out to some of them.

The Prefect was pointing straight up. Yama looked past the vanishing point of the escalator cable and saw a star burning brightly at zenith, drifting slowly but perceptibly eastwards.

'The voidship departs,' the Prefect said. 'And there are no short cut mouths on this world. I control the only way for you to return, Yamamanama, and you cannot use it until you submit to my will.'

Yama said, 'You were made by the Preservers to serve the races of man.'

'This world is dying,' the Prefect said. 'It was the first world settled by humans, over ten million years ago. They warmed it and gave it an atmosphere, melted the water locked in its rocks, spread life everywhere. Later, they moved it across half the Galaxy to a new sun. But it is too small to hold its atmosphere and its water. It is drying and growing cooler. The dust storms have returned. In a million years most life will have vanished.

'As here, so elsewhere, on millions upon millions of worlds. The Preservers retreated from the Universe not because they achieved perfection, but because of their mistakes. They could no longer bear them. We will do better. We will transform Confluence, and we will reconquer the Galaxy and take the Universe by storm. You will help us with the first step.'

'You must have forced the Gatekeeper to send you after me. Why then do you need me?'

'We forced it, yes, and we will have to force it again if we need to use another short cut. You can persuade machines to change permanently. We can learn much from you.'

Something was moving out of the light of the setting sun: a small, sleek shadow, its mind closed to Yama by the same opaqueness that closed the minds of the regulators. A flock of dark shapes swirled up as it passed above the stepped pyramids in the forest. The thing wearing Prefect Corin's body glanced at them, and Yama feared for a moment that his last hope had been discovered. But then the Prefect turned to Yama and said, 'We will take you back to Confluence. We brought you here because the crew of the voidship did not want you on their ship. But another ship has been waiting here for five million years. It circles above us now.'

Yama said, 'Corin wanted me to serve the Department of Indigenous Affairs, so that every bloodline on Confluence would be forced to conform to the same destiny: stasis, and a slow decline. You and the heretics want to force change by making every bloodline believe that the self is all. There is a better way. A way to allow every bloodline to find its own particular destiny. We were raised up by the Preservers not to worship them, but to become their equals.'

'You will help us become more than that. After we take Confluence, we will destroy the Preservers. It will be a good beginning.'

'I will not serve you,' Yama said.

'You will serve those higher than yourself, little builder. It is your function.'

'My people served the Preservers, but they have gone. No one should serve any other, unless they wish it. I learned much from Dr Dismas's paramour, and part of what it tried to grow inside me still remains. It has helped me find friends here.'

The first wave of flying men stooped down out of the light of the setting sun. There were more than a hundred of them. Their membranous wings, stretched between wrists and ankles, folded around them like black cloaks as they landed and came across the plaza with a hobbling gait, clutching spears of fire-hardened wood and slingshots and bolos.

The Prefect burned away several decads with a sweep of his pistol and screamed at the regulators to kill the rest, but the second wave was already swooping overhead, dropping nets that engulfed the silver-skinned regulators and drew tight.

The Prefect threw away his staff and showed Yama the energy pistol, lying in his palm like a river pebble. 'We will kill you if we must.'

'I know that weapon,' Yama said. 'Corin told me how it works long ago. It fires three shots, and then must lie in the sun for a full day before it can fire again. You fired one shot to kill Bryn, another to kill Cas and Wery, and you have just fired the third and last.'

The Prefect screamed, threw the pistol at Yama, and ran straight at him. A pair of bolos wrapped around his legs, and a net folded over him as he fell headlong.

Once freed of the compulsion Yama had laid upon them, the flying men threw themselves face down around him, but he told them that they should stand, that he was not the god they believed him to be.

They were the children of a feral machine which had fled the war at the end of the Age of Insurrection, falling through a short cut to this world. It had made reduced copies of itself and used them to infect various species of animal, but only the ancestors of the flying men had proven satisfactory hosts. The flying men were a unique synthesis. Their intelligence was contained within tiny machines which teemed in their blood, but the machine intelligence was tempered by their animal joy of life and flight; they were quite without the cold arrogance which had prompted the feral machines to rebel. The original machine, badly damaged when it had first arrived here, had died thousands of years ago, but the flying men believed that it would at last return, incarnated in one of their kind, to save their world.

The flying men had narrow, long-muzzled foxy faces, and small red eyes that burned in the twilight. They were twice Yama's height; their skinny, naked bodies were covered with pelts of coarse black hair. After much twittering discussion, the oldest of them, with grey on his muzzle, came forwards. By gestures, he asked whether Yama wanted his enemies killed.

Yama could speak directly to the consensus of tiny machines within the flying men; it seemed to him that each had an animate, intelligent shadow standing at his back. 'I thank you for your help,' he told them, 'but do not kill your prisoners. There has been enough killing this day. Let me speak to their leader.'

The flying men dragged the Prefect forwards. He was still bound by the pair of bolos and the net. The oldest flying man told Yama that this was a dead man with a brother trapped inside it. It was a curious thing, to see a dead man kept alive in this way.

'He is from another place,' Yama said. That took a long time to explain; once the old man understood, he wanted to know if the Prefect was a god.

'No, but he is very powerful. He can help you in many ways. One of his kind was, I think, responsible for you.'

'I thought them dead,' the Prefect said. 'The star-sailors told me that they were dead.'

The old flying man shivered all over – it was his equivalent of laughter – and said that the star-sailors did not trouble to come to the surface of the world, but instead sent servants. His people's blood could speak with the brothers in the heads of the servants, and make them believe anything.

Yama told the thing inside the Prefect that it could be of much help here. It could begin to undo this world's slow decline. It could help the flying men be all that they could be. But it could never return to Confluence.

'These people were formed from an act of malice, but evil can create good without knowing it. By serving them, you can make amends. You have much to teach them, and they can teach you something about humility. Or else you can remain a prisoner, with the body you took decaying around you.'

The Prefect tried to spit at Yama, but his mouth had no saliva. The strands of the net pressed a lattice into his dead flesh. There was a glint of metal beneath the ruin of his left eye.

The oldest of the flying men said that there was a place of silence where this brother could be kept; its words would never again touch the minds of other men.

'Dr Dismas knew about such places,' Yama told the Prefect. 'There was the cage in *The House of Ghost Lanterns*, for instance. Shall I consign you to eternal silence, or will you serve here? Think about it while I free those you have enslaved.'

Yama freed the regulators first. It took a long time to unpick the opaque shells which guarded their true minds, and at first he was hindered because the thing inside Prefect Corin tried to countermand his efforts, but after Yama found the part of it which spoke to other machines and shut it off, he was able to work without interruption. Night was almost over when he was at last finished with the regulators and could turn his attention to the ship.

It was still turning high above, swinging in wide circles about the elevator cable because it had not been ordered to do anything else. It was a transparent teardrop not much larger than the *Weazel*, the lugger which had carried Yama down half the length of the Great River. Hidden inside the shells of false personality Prefect Corin had woven for it was the bright, innocently enquiring mind of a child. It wanted to know where its mistress was, and Yama told it that Angel had been dead for five million years.

'Then I will serve you,' the ship said, and swooped down, extruding a triplet of fins on which it perched at the edge of the plaza.

The flying men brought the Prefect before Yama again, and again Yama asked whether he would be content to serve him.

'You raise yourself too high,' the Prefect said. 'You cannot stand in judgement of me.'

'I find myself here,' Yama said. 'I do what I must.'

Prefect Corin said defiantly, 'I will take this world, and I will build such a race that they will set fire to the Galaxy.'

'They will not allow themselves to become your slaves,' Yama said. He was not sure that this was the best solution, but he owed the thing his life, and could not kill it.

The oldest of the flying men said that they would always care for this poor brother, and would never let it leave. They would show it compassion.

Yama nodded. The thing which had taken Prefect Corin might benefit from the humble simplicity of the flying men. He indicated the regulators and said, 'These will be your guests until the ship comes again.'

The old man agreed. Yama embraced him and apologized for using his people, but the man told him that he had brought the hope for which his people had prayed for many generations.

'I fear I have brought you a great danger.'

The old man said that, like the god which had made his people,

Prefect Corin was powerful and angry, so angry that he could not see the world clearly.

Yama smiled, realizing that the flying men had grown greater in wisdom and compassion than the thing which had made them, and that the Prefect could be left safely in their charge. If the thing inside him did not change, then the flying men would destroy it.

More and more flying men arrived, flocks that filled the forest around the plaza and the stepped pyramids. Their campfires were scattered amongst the dark trees like the stars in the sky above. Yama talked into the night with the men and women who led the flocks, tired but exultant. At last, as the sky above the mountains to the east began to grow brighter – how strange that the sun should set in one place and rise in another – he finished an elaborate round of farewells.

All this time, the Prefect had lain as still and unsleeping as a cayman, but now he suddenly surged up, throwing off the net he had cut with a spur of metal torn from his flesh. He stabbed one of the flying men in the eye, snatched the man's spear and charged at Yama. Yama felt a tremendous blow in his back and half-turned, grasping at the point of the spear which protruded beneath his ribs. He could not get his breath. His mouth filled with blood. The Prefect embraced him, stabbing and stabbing with the metal spur. Then he was torn away and Yama fell, gargling blood as he tried to draw breath. He saw the Prefect borne backwards, lifted by a decad of flying men into the red dawn, and then his sight failed.

23 ~ The Gatekeeper

The ship walked with him down dark ways and sang to him of his sorrows. At first he did not know or remember who he was or what the ship's sad, sweet songs meant, but slowly he understood that he had died, and now, after a long, dark sleep, he was healed. He was awake. It was time to rise.

It was as painful as birth. He was expelled from dreamy warm darkness into harsh light and chill air, naked and slimy, choking on the fluid which had for so long sustained him. It ran from his nostrils and bubbled at the bottom of his lungs. He coughed and spat and retched.

He was lying on his belly with night all around him, on an endless floor of glass punctuated by groups of enigmatic statues and machines that glimmered with foxfire. The Galaxy's triple-armed spiral tilted below. Gradually, he realized that the dim shell of light around him defined the true size of the ship. It was as transparent as certain species of shrimp which lived in the deep waters of the Great River; the great glass plain was an illusion.

He laughed. All was illusion.

A woman came through a door which a moment before had not been there. She was naked and silver-skinned. One arm was swollen into a monstrous claw. 'It took almost a year,' she said. 'At the end, we thought you might die again.'

She was the regulator who had accompanied him to the surface of the red world. She was afraid that he would be angry because of the way he had been saved, but he still did not understand what had been done to him, except that he had died, and had slept, and had been healed.

Dazed by his long sleep, Yama sprawled for many hours in the middle of the room the ship had made for him, combing his fingers through the long hair and beard which had grown while he had slept, staring at the great wheel of the Galaxy below or the red whorl of the Eye of the Preservers above. A few dim halo stars were scattered across the black sky; a single bright star shone beyond the ship's bow. He traced and retraced the scars which seamed his belly and his chest and his back, a secret history of pain printed on his body.

The regulator brought him food now and then, but although his stomach was empty he was not ready to eat. At last, he asked her to explain how she and the ship had saved him.

'It was the only way, master,' the regulator said. 'Even so, we were not sure if you would survive storage or the surgical procedures. The medical facilities are very primitive. And that is why—'

'She has funny ideas,' the ship said, 'about what is possible and what is not.'

'We brought it to term,' the regulator said. 'We could not kill it.'

'I think I could,' the ship said. 'I think I could kill it if you asked me to, master.'

It amused the ship to appear as a solemn, ghostly little girl of Yama's bloodline, her skinny body sketched in faint lines of light against the black sky, her eyes two dim stars.

Yama said, 'You had better show me exactly what you did.'

'At once,' the regulator said, and went through the door which appeared only when it was used.

Yama asked the ship where they were. It showed views of the spiral arm from which they had travelled, the great rising arc of their course. They had been travelling along the path plotted by the thing which had taken over Prefect Corin.

The trip through the short cut had taken Yama deep into the past. Travelling back through ordinary space at close to the speed of light, the ship had taken a hundred and sixty thousand years to voyage between the star of the red world, deep within the Galaxy, and the star of Confluence, far beyond the Galaxy's rim. But the ship's speed had compressed time aboard it, and less than a year of ship-time had passed while Yama returned to the place from which he had set out.

He wanted to know at once where Confluence was. The ship became evasive, claiming that it had followed the course exactly. 'Perhaps the instructions were wrong in some small detail,' it said. 'I have located the star, and it is of the correct mass and spectral type, but there is no trace of a habitat orbiting it.'

There were no feral machines, either. Only the mouths of many short cuts in lonely orbits around a lonely star.

Yama was still thinking about this when the regulator returned through what he thought of as the occasional door. She was holding something, crooning to it in her throaty voice. Its head, with a vulnerable swirl of dark hair, was propped on her monstrous claw; its hands clutched at the air like a hungry starfish.

A baby.

He had died, and before the ship and the regulator had put his body into storage, they had taken a scraping from the inside of his mouth. They had quickened certain of the cells in the scraping and grown them into foetuses – there had been five, but only two had lived. Tissues had been harvested from one and used to grow replacement organs; these had been transplanted into Yama and then he had slept a long time, healing. But the ship and the regulator had not been able to bring themselves to kill the other foetus, and they had not put it into storage, for they had not been sure if it would survive. And so, while Yama had been revived and healed, it had grown to term.

It had been born just before Yama's rebirth.

'It is exactly the same genome as you, master,' the regulator said, 'and because of that we were unable to kill it.'

The baby chuckled in her arms. Yama gently took him from her, surprised by his mass and heat, the spicy odour of cinnamon and ammonia. The baby tried to focus his eyes on him, frowning with effort, then tried to smile.

Yama set the baby spinning around him, laughing as he gurgled with delight.

'We are in the future, and we must go back a little way into the past,' Yama said, a little later. 'I think that the composite thing which took Prefect Corin wanted to return after the heretics' war had ended, and claim Confluence from the victor. And the war is certainly over, for Confluence is no longer here. I know now how this should end. We must go back.'

*

The Gatekeeper woke as the ship approached the nearest of the many short cut mouths which orbited the lonely star. A light dawned far off across the illusionary glass plain, a bright star growing into the shape of an old man of Yama's bloodline. At first, he was a giant bigger than the ship, walking steadily towards it as if against a great wind, but he grew smaller as he approached, so that when he entered the room (not by the occasional door, but through an angle Yama had never seen before) he was exactly Yama's height.

There was nothing remarkable about the old man's aspect. He had a pale, wrinkled face framed by long white hair and a beard of silky white curls. He wore a white robe girdled by a broad leather belt from which bunches of keys of all sizes hung. Yet it hurt Yama to look at him directly, and when he spoke, his words echoed directly in Yama's mind.

We meet again, Child of the River.

Yama said, 'Where am I? I mean, how much time has passed since I left Confluence?'

A little more than forty years.

'And the world? Was it destroyed, or was it—'

It has moved on. I remained here to wait for you.

'How did you know that I would come here?'

I stand at every door.

'Then you must know that I have to go back,' Yama said, thoughtfully stroking his beard. The regulator had suggested that she trim both his hair and his beard, but he had refused. He said, 'I have to go back to the recent past, and the beginning of my story.'

The old man fingered through a bunch of keys at his waist. His eyes were dim red stars, framed by his flowing white hair.

For most of my existence, I would have said that what you ask would be very difficult to do. There were once two kinds of short cut. Those of the first kind have been sundered from their origins, and lead to the deep past in places far from here. Those of the second kind link places in space not separated by more than a few seconds. Or they did, before the world was taken away.

'Then you will not help me?'

You could choose one of the long routes. The ancestors of the Preservers rebuilt the Galaxy after the wars with the Transcendents, but after the Preservers quit the Galaxy, the orbits of the stars have been untended. They brought the mouths of many short cuts here, but the stars to which the short cuts lead have drifted; and some have drifted closer to the star of Confluence. The time debt between the ends of the short cuts remain the same, but the distance between them in ordinary space is less than it once was.

Yama thought about this. He said, 'Then the ship could pass through one of these short cuts and travel back through ordinary space in less time than it took to drag the two mouths of the short cuts apart.'

There are, as I have said, several examples of these. I can guide you through one, as a last boon.

'But it will still take a year of ship-time to return. No, that is too long.'

Indeed. But now there is another other way. The mouth of a short cut with a time debt of only forty years appeared a few days ago. I have informed the ship. We will not meet again, for that which I served for so long has moved on. I remained here only to meet you for this final time. Now that is done, and I am free at last. I thank you for my freedom.

'Where will you go?'

The old man pointed towards the Eye of the Preservers.

I will follow my masters, of course.

'Then perhaps you can answer the question which has puzzled the mystagogues and philosophers since the Preservers set the ten thousand bloodlines on Confluence. Where have they gone?'

I do not know, except that it will be a better place than this.

'To the far end of time, when all will live again in the best of all possible worlds?'

It is not in this universe. The woman who called herself Angel was wrong. There are many other intelligent species in the Universe, but they are hidden from us because they are at distances greater than light has been able to travel since the Universe's creation. At present they are unreachable, but they will be brought together as the Universe contracts towards its last end. The Preservers foresaw a great war at the end of time and space, and decided on another way. And so they constructed the huge black hole at the heart of the Eye of the Preservers and withdrew from the Universe. They left Confluence in the hope that its peoples might grow greater than they. How it must have saddened them when it began to fail, and yet because they had withdrawn they were unable to interfere. The first war stopped all progress on Confluence; the second might have destroyed it. But you are their avatar, and you have saved it.

'Not yet, I think.'

In this place and time, it has already happened. But I suppose that there are many time-lines where you did not prevail and the heretics were victorious, only to destroy Confluence when they quarrelled amongst themselves over the spoils of their victory. If by mischance you return to one of those time-lines then I grieve for you. And yet in all of them I will be free!

'You have not told me about where you will go.'

As species compete and evolve, so do universes. Those in which the formation of black holes is possible can give rise to other universes, for energy which disappears through black holes reappears elsewhere. That is where the Preservers have gone. Rather than fight for the last moment of infinite energy at the end of this universe, they have departed to create a new universe, one more suited to them than this. And now I go to discover it. Farewell, Child of the River.

'Wait!' Yama said again.

There was so much more he wanted to ask, but the old man was already fading, leaving behind only two points of faint red light that quickly receded beyond the boundary of the ship.

The ship's chiming laughter filled its transparent volumes. 'You must trust me, master. I know now what to do.'

The end of the new short cut was only a few minutes' travel away. It hung within a vast cloud of water ice particles that refracted the sun into a billion points of twinkling light as the ship fell through it.

24 ~ The White Boat

And emerged at a high place amidst blowing water spray turning to snow, so that at first Yama did not realize that the transition had been made. But then the ship moved out of the snow cloud and Yama saw a great tongue of ice stretching away, dazzling white beneath dense white clouds and a constant snowfall that blurred and softened the edges of everything. The ice filled the steep chute of a valley of adamantine keelrock a hundred leagues across, a frozen river moving with majestic slowness, throwing up broken chunks as big as cities along its edges.

The ship rose through the clouds, revealing a landscape of mountains islanded by cloud, mountains rimming the wide valley and spreading away on either side, sharp peaks of bare black keelrock rising out of clouds and snow and ice, whiteness everywhere touched with blue shadows, the sun a brilliant diamond set in a clear blue above a distant range of even taller peaks that must be the Rim Mountains. Directly below the ship, a waterfall fell from nothing, leagues wide and hung with a decad of rainbows, falling slowly and softly into clouds torn from its own self.

It was the end of the Great River, and its beginning.

The regulator came through the occasional door, cradling the baby in her mismatched arms. 'Someone approaches,' the ship said.

A streak of white slanted down through the achingly blue sky above. As a boy, Yama had often seen these contrails in the sky above Aeolis, and had yearned after the machines which had created them, wondering about the strange missions on which they had been bound. Now he barely had time to brace himself before, arriving ahead of the thunderclap of its passage through the atmosphere, a feral machine came to a crash stop beyond the prow of the ship. It was black, no bigger than his head, and covered in spines of varying lengths which quested this way and that as if possessed of independent life. Yama knew it. Knew too the menace it radiated, pricking into his head through the bits of machine left there.

The ship said nervously, 'It sees through me.'

Yama reassured it, and told the machine that it must leave now. It would not come to him until it was asked again, and meanwhile it would tell its fellows not to interfere.

There are several of us stranded across the world, the thing said sulkily. *I cannot intercede with them.*

'I will deal with those when the time comes.'

I will help you now. The world can be yours, with my help. Leave this poor vessel. Let me show you.

'Be still! The world is already mine. You will do what I ask, and no more.'

Then I do nothing, the machine said, *and gladly. But tell me first why my mark is on you.*

'You will help me twice more, and then you will be free. I promise.'

The feral machine fell away into the sky, even as other machines accelerated towards the disturbance it had created. But these, the keepers of the world, still loyal to the Preservers, found nothing. The feral machine had already returned to its station far beyond the world, and the ship was falling downriver towards the nearest shrine.

The Gatekeeper had said that there were two kinds of short cut; Yama had guessed where the entrances to those which spanned only space were hidden.

The glacier ended at a small, mountain-rimmed sea continually crossed and recrossed by waves caused by falls of ice from cliffs two leagues high. Bergs and bergy bits churned and crashed amongst the waves. Meltwater spilled from the sea and meandered away in a thousand rivers and a million streams, through chains of lakes and raised bogs and drumlins, feeding the marshes which drained at last into the head of the Great River.

The shrine stood on a long, low island in the middle of one of the lakes, its black circle set on a shelf of bare rock raised above dwarf birches that were just coming into leaf; their thin black branches, laden with golden buds, swayed stiffly in the clean cold air. Gnarled junipers hugged the ground, red berries brilliant as drops of blood against the dark green of their needles, growing around boulders splattered with orange and black and grey stoneworts. Although it was summer, a cold wind blew from the edge of the glacier, and pockets of snow still clung in shady places on the island. Clear, ice-cold water tentatively fingered the pebbles of the shore, over and over. The sun was setting beyond range after range of mountains, touching every peak with a dab of light, painting long shadows amongst the fir trees that marched down to the shore of the lake, gilding its slow ripples. A skein of geese flew across red stripes of cloud that stretched on either side of the sun, honking each to each.

The world! So wonderful in its variety, so beautiful in every particular detail.

The ship had changed shape, spreading wide flat wings which delicately manipulated the world's gravity fields. It floated down to the island's shore, and Yama stepped from one of the wings on to the little gravel beach beneath the shrine. He leaned on Prefect Corin's staff, which the regulator had saved. He was still very weak. Freezing water lapped his bare feet; wind tangled in his long hair and beard. The clean, cold air was as bracing as good wine. The regulator followed with the baby, which was bundled in silvery cloth so that only the tip of its nose showed.

The regulator had unstitched the badly ripped and bloodstained silvery garment Bryn had given Yama, and made it into a kind of cloak to wear over the black tunic and leggings the ship had provided. She had reserved a small piece to swaddle the baby. She did not need any kind of clothing, she claimed, and seemed unaffected by the icy wind. She had refused to stay with the ship, saying that Yama did not know how to look after the baby.

'Males of your bloodline cannot give suck. I have started a flow of milk, master, and he feeds happily. Do not take that from him.'

Yama made sure that the ship knew what it had to do. He felt that every step might break the world, change it into something other than that which it must become. He told it, 'Take the cloned mouth of the short cut and make a loop at lightspeed forty years long. Make sure that you arrive back at the point in space from which you started, a few days before we first arrived. The Great River will flow through the short cut into the future and we will be able to travel through it into the past. Are you sure that you can do this?'

'Of course,' the ship said primly. 'Short cuts were brought here in the first place by my kind.'

'Forty years, no more, no less. That is important.'

'It will happen, or you will not be here. I *know*.'

'There may be many time-lines where it may not have happened, because you carelessly misunderstood my instructions.'

'You can trust me,' the ship said. 'You should trust me to take you to Ys also. I know that the mooring towers still stand, and I can have you there in a minute.'

'I do not want you to be seen. This way will suffice. You remember where we will meet?'

'Downriver, ten days – what you call a decad – from now. At the far edge of the City of the Dead. As if no one will see us there.'

'There are things in Ys I do not wish to awaken. Or at least, not yet.'

'The river will not cease to flow here once I have diverted it into the future. Not at once. There is much ice above us.'

'I know. But the glaciers will flow more and more slowly because there will no longer be new snow and ice pushing them forwards. I already know how long it will take, and when it should begin. Go now.'

The ship rose, turning and dipping as it rose. It swept quickly across the lake, setting a flock of wildfowl to flight, then angled straight up. A moment later a boom echoed across the wide sky, and Yama saw the white streak which marked where the ship was accelerating towards the mouth of the short cut at the end of the Terminal Mountains, where the river fell back into the world.

Yama felt a mixture of apprehension and a kind of existential dizziness. Nothing was fixed. This was not the world from which he had begun: the Universe would not end, as he had been taught all his life, in a single infinite moment, when all the dead would be reborn into the perpetual grace of the Preservers. All was change, a constant flux. Even the Preservers sought to change, in universe after universe without end.

He said, 'Perhaps I should do nothing. Perhaps it should end here, for else I condemn myself to becoming no more than a machine toiling away at the same endless task. I have set the Great River free from its unending cycle, but how can I set myself free from the circle of my own history?'

The regulator was a practical person. She said, 'You have already begun, master, by sending the ship on its mission. Who can say how it will end?'

'You are right, of course.' Yama smiled. 'You remind me of a dear lost friend. Perhaps I might see him again. And Derev, too . . . Yes, it has begun, and I must go on as I must.'

As he climbed up to the shrine, it began to flow with banners of light. He stepped into the light, and the regulator followed him.

Ys was suddenly spread below him. On one side the sun was falling behind the Rim Mountains; on the other, the Great River was painted with golden light on which the black motes of thousands of boats and ships were sharply drawn, as if by the most exquisite calligraphy. The river was fuller than Yama remembered it, lapping at the margin of the city, covering the shore where in the near future there would be wide mud flats and a scurf of shanty towns. And between mountains and river was the immemorial city. Ys: the endless grid of her streets and avenues sprawled wantonly beneath a brown haze of air pollution, sending up a shuddering roar in which the brazen clash of the gongs of one of her many temples and the shrill song of a ship's siren emerged as sharply as points of light.

Wind plucked at Yama's silvery cloak; a warm wind, redolent of smoke and decay.

The shrine was set on a high peak of the roof of the Palace of the Memory of the People. A sheer cliff dropped to a long slope of patchwork fields studded with temples and sanctuaries. A raven floated half a league below, black wings widespread, primaries fingering the air. A bell was tolling somewhere. In the distance, the slim, silvery mooring towers rose up from cluttered streets, soaring towards their vanishing points high above the atmosphere. The towers were the ancient port of Ys, from which, in the Golden Age when the Sirdar had ruled Confluence, ships had departed for other worlds. Although abandoned an age past, they had served one last task, for Yama had dreamed of standing in their shadow when he had been a child in the little city of Aeolis, and so they had drawn him to Ys and to the beginning of his adventures. And would do so again.

A narrow flight of steps, small and close-set, wound down the steep side of the peak towards a distant courtyard which was enclosed on three sides by high rock walls. There was a scree slope beneath the open side of the courtyard, and a wind-bent tree not quite dead stood amongst the loose stones, a few scraps of green showing at the very ends of its warped branches.

Down there was the cell in which Yama had been – would be – imprisoned after the assassination attempt in the corridors of the Department of Indigenous Affairs, and from which he would escape, cloaked in the hell-hound. Down there, buried in the dirt floor of the cell by the round window, was the coin first he and then Pandaras had carried half the length of the world. He would need a working coin soon enough – what if he took that one? His future self would not find it, would not be able to call upon the hell-hound, would not be able to escape. In how many time-lines had that happened? In how many others had he failed to arrive here?

'We must not linger, master,' the regulator said. 'You must stop dreaming. You are in the world again.'

She led the way down the stairs, brisk and matter-of-fact, clutching the baby tight to her flat breasts. Yama followed, dizzy with visions of forking paths. What if this world did not contain his own history after all?

The bell was still tolling steadily in the distance, and now another answered it close by, ringing out with brisk urgency. A moment later, the regulator turned to Yama. She pressed the baby into his arms and bounded away down the steps, her swollen claw crooked above her head for balance.

There was only a pentad of guards, four inexperienced youngsters led by a one-armed veteran who had been drinking steadily all day. It was a rotten, dull assignment. The old shrine, known as the Shrine of Stars, had been unused for ten thousand years, and its only visitor was an old priest who, once a year, muttered a brief prayer and placed an offering of ivy and delicate white arching sprays of starbright at its base. With nothing else to do, the guards spent their time gambling, drinking and taking potshots at the crows and ravens which occasionally floated past the unglazed slit windows of the guardhouse. They were unprepared for trouble, half-unbuttoned, weapons slung on their backs. The regulator killed the first two easily, disembowelling one with her claw, grabbing the other and shaking him until his neck snapped. Two others ran, but the veteran stood his ground. His first shot struck the regulator in the chest; as she fell forwards, his second took off the back of her head.

A moment later, a burning figure appeared on the steps above, clothed in a thousand fireflies. The veteran fled from this spectral figure even as it bent to the dead, silver-skinned woman. It called down two flying discs, laid the dead woman on one and stepped on to the other. By the time reinforcements arrived, it was gone.

Yama came to the chamber of the mirror people by the secret ways of the palace within the Palace of the Memory of the People. He had dismissed the fireflies. The mirror people gathered around him, curious and excited, plucking at his cloak, at the baby (who laughed at their painted faces), asking who he was and how he knew about this place. He told them that he was a friend, and that he had come here with a message for their king.

'There is a dead woman at the entrance to this place,' he added. 'Bring her here.'

Three clowns scurried off. Yama sat down to wait for them to return. He refused offers of water and raw fungus. The baby fretted, pissed into the pad the regulator had bound between its legs, fell asleep.

Lupe came through the tall oval frame an hour later. Perhaps the skin was not as loose on his mottled arms; perhaps the wrinkles which mazed his face were fewer and less deep, but otherwise he was much as Yama remembered him. He was supported on either side by two beautiful girls, and clad in a long black dress whose train was held up by a third. As before, his lips were stained bright red, and the sockets of his blind eyes were painted with broad swipes of blue. His grey hair was piled up on his head, woven through with golden threads and fake pearls.

He was at once absurd and hierophantic, a burlesque of monarchy in his ruined finery, yet commanding in his bearing.

'Who is it,' he demanded. 'Who is it that disturbs us?'

There was an excited babble as a hundred mirror people tried to explain, but everyone fell silent when Lupe held up his hand. The baby had begun to cry, alarmed by the noise. As Yama tried to hush it, Lupe turned to him and said, 'Why, here he is. Let him speak.'

Lupe listened carefully as Yama explained that he had come with a prophecy about someone who would change and raise up the mirror people, so that they would become the very thing that they imitated: they would become fully human.

'Come here,' Lupe commanded, and Yama endured the spidery touch of his long fingernails on his face, his hair, his beard.

A fakir with skewers pushed bloodily through his painted cheeks mumbled that this man had come by the secret ways. Lupe nodded gravely, and said to Yama, 'You know our corridors and you know the hope we have harboured since we left the river and crept into the Palace. Who are you?'

'A friend. One who speaks truly of what you have yearned for in your secret songs.'

Lupe nodded again. 'We sing many songs, but some we sing only for ourselves. And yet you know of them.'

An acrobat swung upside down on a wire overhead and said, 'He brings a baby and a dead woman, and we've never seen his like before. He brings trouble, Lupe.'

A murmur spread through the crowd of mirror people, dying away when Lupe held up a hand. He said to Yama, 'You bring a message, but do we know it is true?'

'In seventeen years, someone of my bloodline will come here. Watch out for him. He will need help, and when you help him he will change a baby no older than the baby I carry. As for me, I need a boat. I must travel downriver.'

Lupe said, 'It is well known that we have many things. Gifts from patrons. Siftings from the leavings of enlightened races. So many things that we do not know what we have.'

'I think you will find amongst your treasures a white boat not much bigger than the coffins in which the dead are launched upon the flood of the Great River. I claim it as mine.'

Lupe laughed. 'We understand! As we sing for our living, so you sing for ours. Be welcome, and eat. If there is a white boat, why then you shall have it as payment for the hope you have brought us. We keep all we are given, but we do not need any of it because we can always get more.'

It took two days to find the boat amongst the piles of forgotten gifts. The news of its discovery was born ahead of a swelling crowd that clustered around the entrance to Lupe's suite. They cheered Yama when he emerged with Lupe, and made a carnival procession as the boat was carried down secret ways to the ancient wharves in one of the crypts that undercut the mountain of the Palace of the Memory of the People.

The regulator's undecaying body had already been placed in the white boat, which rode high on the black water in the crypt, glimmering in the torchlit dark. It seemed very small and fragile, but scarcely rocked as Yama climbed into it. He took the baby from one of Lupe's attendants and held him to his chest. Fireflies flitted overhead, a restless cloud of light. The baby fretted, made uneasy by the fife and drums of the procession and the flaring torches and the gorgeous motley crowd along the wharf.

'Remember what I told you,' Yama told Lupe. 'When the boy comes here he will need your help, but you must tell him as little as possible. If he asks about me, tell him nothing. Say that I came secretly at night, that no one saw me but you, who cannot see.'

'My people make stories for a living,' Lupe said. 'We will cloak you in as deep a mystery as you could wish.'

The mirror people fell silent as Lupe made a formal farewell, then burst into song and loud cheers as the white boat, with Yama standing in its sharp, raised prow, glided away into the darkness, towards the channel that led to the Great River.

Yama left the white boat three days later. He landed a league upriver of the little city of Aeolis, amongst the abandoned tombs of the City of the Dead. It was midnight. The huge black sky above the Great River was punctuated only by a scattering of dim halo stars and the dull red swirl, no bigger than a man's hand, of the Eye of the Preservers. The heaped lights of the little city of Aeolis and the lights of the carracks riding at anchor outside the harbour entrance were brighter by far than anything in the sky.

Yama watched as the white boat, attended by a little galaxy of fireflies, dwindled away across the black flood of the river, heading downriver towards his destiny. Then he turned and started along the bone-white paths that threaded between the tombs. He had a long way to go before he made rendezvous with the ship: across the City of the Dead to the tower deep in the foothills of the Rim Mountains, where the last of the curators of the City of the Dead lived, where he knew of a way into the keel of the world.

He did not fear the dead who called to him from their tombs; this was where he had played as a child. But he had brought his own ghosts with him, and he faltered and turned aside before the final descent to the keelways.

25 ~ Derev

The ship found him five days later, filthy and half-starved, his hair and beard wild, his silvery cloak tattered. He was living in a tomb which had been stripped of its bronze doors and furniture by robbers a thousand years ago, spending most of his time in conversation with the aspect of the long-dead tax official whose body had been interred there.

The ship took him in, but he would not allow it to bathe him or heal his superficial wounds. His rage was spent. He was exhausted, but possessed by a grim, hopeless resolve.

'I cannot believe in anything,' Yama told the ship. 'Not in the world, not in myself.'

'The world is as it is,' the ship said.

'But is it the world I know? Why should I set on the same path again if it is not? I knew what I had to do, but I turned aside.'

'Perhaps you were meant to turn aside.'

Yama hardly heard the ship. He was still engaged in the same bitter monologue for which the bewildered aspect had been an unwilling audience. He said, 'I will never know what I could do. What I could be, what the world could be. I was not brave or strong enough and I turned aside. I failed. No matter, no matter. I know what I must do. It is the only thing left to do. If I cannot save the world, then I must save those I love.'

'When you have rested, master, perhaps you will allow me to take you there.'

'No. You must take me forwards in time. You must take me into the future. I will save what I can. I do not mind that the heretics take the world if I can save those I love. The Aedile need not die for me, and I should not have to sacrifice my life with Derev – she has no part in this. Take me into the future, ship. I have decided.'

Fifteen days passed aboard the ship as it made its second loop at close to the speed of light. When it arrived at Aeolis, seventeen years in the future, Yama left it at once, before his resolve could falter.

It was spring, a warm spring night. Frogs peeped each to each with froggy ardour. The triple-armed wheel of the Galaxy stood waist-deep at the farside horizon, salting the patchwork of flooded fields with its blue-white light.

Yama walked through the overgrown ruins of the ancient mortuaries beyond the walls of the little city of Aeolis, leaning on the staff at every other step. Spring, but was it the right spring? Was it still the same history, or had it turned down some other path? Who lived in the peel-house which lifted its turrets and towers against the Galaxy?

Every pass through the time-rifted short cuts had caused the time-line of the Universe to branch. This was not the world he had come from, but an echo of an echo. Perhaps it was an almost exact echo, but it did not matter. It did not matter because the original still existed. He could do anything here and it would not matter because what had happened had already happened in the time-line from which he had come. By failing, he had freed himself from the wheel. He was free to rewrite history.

He had come here because he was going home.

Thoughts whirled in his head like fireflies. Nothing was solid any more. Anything could happen. Anything at all. This revelation filled him with a sudden great calm. No longer did he have to strive at the toiling wheel of history, like the oxen which plodded around and around at the wheel which lifted water from the Breas to irrigate the paeonin fields. He remembered the one true thing Dr Dismas had said, that men were so closely bound to their fate that they could not see the world around them. As he had been, until now.

He had failed to set in motion the vast engines in the keelways. He had not even tried, but had turned away in sight of the curators' tower. By his failure he had saved the world; saved it from himself. He could pass the burden to the boy. Tell him all. Let him go this time fully armed into the world, into his future. Let him restore the river. Let him imprison Angel in the space inside the shrines before she could interfere. Let him call down and enslave the feral machines, and then destroy the heretics.

He could defy the tremendous inertia of history. He could tell the boy where he came from and put an end to his foolish search for his parents. For he had no parents but his own self; he was a closed loop in time, with no beginning and no end, like Caphis's tattoo of the snake which swallowed its own self, like the Great River which fell over the edge of the world and passed through the short cut to its own beginning. Child of the River – how truly the wives of old Constable Thaw had named him! They had known the truth even then. It had taken him far longer to learn it. It had taken him all his life.

He hurried on, passing Dr Dismas's tower, which stood just outside the gate of the little city. Its windows were dark, but that signified nothing.

'What must be will be,' he muttered.

He walked along the embankments between flooded paeonin fields, crossed the Breas, and climbed a path which wound up a long, dusty slope between scattered tombs. The excavation was just where he remembered it, at the top of a rise of dead land coral at the edge of the City of the Dead. The guards and the workers were asleep; the lone watchdog was easily placated. Yama wept, embracing its armoured shoulders and breathing its familiar odour of dog and warm plastic, remembering how often he had fooled its brothers and sisters into allowing him to pass, remembering his lost childhood.

He told the watchdog to return to its patrol and clambered down bamboo scaffolding into one of the trenches. He ran his hands up and down the exposed layers of land coral until what he was looking for woke under his fingers: a ceramic coin with dots and dashes of greenish light suddenly flickering within it. It took only a few minutes to free it from the crumbling matrix. He unwound the length of leather thong from a scaffold joint, made a loop around the coin, and hung it around his neck.

The boy would need it. He would show him how to use it.

'If I cannot save the world,' he said out loud, 'at least I can save myself.'

Go directly to the peel-house? No. The guards would turn him away or kill him. He stole a package of pressed dates, a loaf of unleavened bread and a flask of sweet yellow wine, and retreated to one of the empty tombs nearby. He slept badly and was woken in the middle of the night by voices. He crept to the entrance of the tomb and peered through the canes of the roses which tangled across it.

Just offshore, a little way upriver of Aeolis, a dash of flame flickered; nearby, two men were talking about sabotage, about heretics.

'I'd kill 'em,' one said. 'Kill 'em all and let the Preservers sort 'em out.'

'I would rather be here than hunting through the tombs,' the other said.

'The dead can't do any harm. Haven't you learned that yet? It's the living you've got to watch for. The heretics might think to sneak up on the peel-house this way, while most of the lads are off looking for them amongst the tombs. That's a worse danger than any aspect.'

Yama knew them by their voices. They were both boys not much older than he was; they had arrived at the peel-house late last year. He could tell them that the burning ship was Dr Dismas's first failed attempt at a diversion ... but no, they would not believe him. They would drive him off, or worse. He clamped his hands over his mouth, shaking with suppressed laughter. The most powerful man in the world was afraid of two raw recruits.

The guards walked on, their boots crunching on dry shale; the distant fire died down. Yama went back to sleep, and woke to find sunlight spangling the green arbour of roses at the entrance of the tomb. The steam engine which powered the drill rig was working noisily, and Yama heard the plaintive worksong of the prisoners as they laboured to widen the trenches.

> *The picks are walking,*
> *Hammer ring.*
> *The stones are talking,*
> *Hammer ring.*
> *Look, look yonder,*
> *Hammer ring.*
> *Think I see spirits,*
> *Hammer ring.*
> *Waking in the earth ...*

How right they were, Yama thought. It was often said that uneducated men knew things about the world that could never be taught in seminaries or colleges, but in fact this naïve wisdom could be learned by anyone who had eyes to see. The educated men who made such patronizing remarks had long ago stopped seeing the world as it was, saw it only as they had been taught it must be.

Yama hid in the tomb for most of the morning, horribly aware that the Aedile, his stepfather, must be somewhere close by, supervising the work. The urge to run up the slope and embrace him came and went like a fever. At its strongest, Yama clasped his knees to his chest and rocked to and fro, biting his lips until blood ran, smothering wild laughter.

'What must be will be. What must be . . .'

At last he could bear it no longer. He placated the watchdog and slipped away, scurrying downslope with a dread that the Aedile's voice would ring out, commanding him to stop. If it did he would surely go mad.

He spent the rest of the day downriver of the little city and its silted bay, searching along the shore for the boy. He remembered that he had gone there to watch the picket boat which had brought Dr Dismas back from Ys. The picket boat was standing off banyan shoals several leagues downriver of the bay (Enobarbus and Dr Dismas would be on board – he could call upon machines and kill them both, but if he bent machines to his will he would reveal himself to Dr Dismas's paramour), but although he searched long and hard, he could not find the boy, and at last remembered that he would go and look at the boat the next day, after his adventure in the ruins.

It was night, now. He was walking through sword grass and scrubby creosote bushes beside the road to the mill at the point of the bay. The sun had set behind the Rim Mountains; the cold splendour of the Galaxy was rising above the river. Perhaps it was already too late. He howled in rage at the world, at the conspiracy against him, the relentless, impacable momentum of events. What must be will be . . .

He circled the city as quickly as he could, sweating through his filthy tunic and leggings as he gimped along, leaning on his staff at every other step, the tattered silvery cloak flapping around him. The ceramic coin burned at his chest.

'What must be will be. No. What *will* be . . .'

He felt like a puppet tugged here and there by invisible forces. Or a leaf, a poor dead husk of a leaf swept along on the river. Everything from now until his death bent towards fulfilment of what had already happened.

'What must be will be. What must be . . .'

He was on a path at the top of an embankment. Beyond the flooded fields, the peel-house stood atop the skull-shaped bluff which overlooked the Great River. Its towers pricked the blue-white curve of the Galaxy. He could go there and reconcile himself with the Aedile. He could go back in time and rescue Telmon. He could not save the world after all, but perhaps he could save all he loved. But first he must find the boy. That was the key.

He flung out his arms, raised his face to the black, empty sky, and screamed in defiance.

'I will not serve!'

Hurrying now. He was late, but surely not too late. Not too late to save himself from himself. If this was still the same story, the boy would be with Derev and Ananda. But he had not gone back in time to tell Beatrice and Osric his story, so they would not have set Derev's parents on the road to Aeolis, and so she would not be here . . .

He had forgotten about Lud and Lob.

The twins ambushed him by a wayside shrine, where the embankment sloped down to the old road. They rose from their hiding place in a thicket of chayote vine, crashing through curtains of scarlet, hand-shaped leaves with hoarse whoops. They were just as he remembered them, big and flabbily muscular, wearing only simple white kilts.

Lud grinned, showing his tusks. 'Ho, and who are you, stranger?'

'Maybe he's with Dr Dismas,' Lob said.

'This culler? He's just a crazy.'

'Let me pass,' Yama said. He held the staff on guard, ready to brain them if they came too close.

Lud crossed his meaty arms over his bare chest. 'You don't go anywhere without paying. This is our town.'

Lob said uneasily, 'Leave it. If he's just a crazy he won't have any gelt. We don't have time.'

'This won't take long.'

'Dismas will skin us alive if we fuck up again.'

'I'm not frightened of him.' Lud pointed at Yama. 'What's that around your neck, eh? You give it as a toll and maybe we let you pass.'

'It is not for you,' Yama said, half-angry, half-amused by their foolish presumption. 'Let me pass!'

'We'll need a toll,' Lud said. He advanced, grinning horribly, but danced back when Yama screamed and jabbed the metal-shod tip of the staff at his face. Lob stooped and picked up a stone and said, 'Ho, that's how it is, eh?'

Yama was able to dodge the first stones they threw. He screamed and capered angrily, swinging his staff with careless abandon. They could not kill him. History was on his side. Then a stone smashed into his forehead. There was a moment of stunning pain, a white flash like the beginning of the Universe, and he realized that he might die here. If history was changed, then anything could happen.

He wiped blood from his eyes with his forearm and whirled his staff, driving the twins backwards, but it was only a temporary victory. A stone struck his elbow and he nearly dropped the staff. Before he could recover, Lob and Lud roared, rushed at him from either side, and knocked him down. He surged up and struck Lob about the head, but Lud grabbed him from behind. He fell beneath Lud's weight, and Lob snatched up the staff and made to break it.

And then the boy stepped on to the road, brandishing a slim trident. The sizar of Aeolis's temple was behind him, his yellow robe glimmering in the half-light. Both looked very young and very scared.

'What is this, Lob?' the boy asked, and then Yama heard little more because Lud thrust his face into the dirt and cuffed him when he tried to struggle. Voices raised in anger, a howl that had to be Lob's, for the weight left his back as Lud jumped up. He rolled over. Lob was on his knees, gasping for breath, and Lud was advancing on the boy, holding a crooked knife up by his face. The boy had the staff and was watching Lud carefully, and was taken by surprise when Lob grabbed at his legs from behind. He staggered and hammered at Lob's back, but Lob dragged him down.

Yama tried to get to his feet. There were no machines near enough to help. No. This could not happen. He could not let them kill the boy.

And then the tree burst into flame and he thought his heart might explode with joy.

Derev was alive. She was here.

*

After Lud and Lob had been driven off, Yama had eyes only for Derev as she followed her shadow out of the brilliant light of the burning tree. She said something to the boy, her arms rising and falling gracefully. How beautiful she was!

The tree burned with fierce ardour, its trunk a shadow inside a roaring pillar of blue flame. Oceans of sparks swept high into the night, like stars playfully seized by the Preservers.

The yellow-robed sizar, Ananda, helped Yama sit up. He dabbed at his wounds, which were only superficial, and managed to stand. The boy held out the staff and Yama took it and bowed. It was a solemn, thrilling moment.

The boy did not recognize him, of course. He did not even see that Yama was of his bloodline. But Yama was suddenly frightened by the boy's searching stare and he could not, dared not, speak. Once again he felt that he was at the cusp of a delicate balance – the slightest movement in any direction could cause disaster. Everything had changed in the moment the tree had caught fire. The tumble of crazy ideas about altering the course of history had fallen away. He had nothing left now but the truth.

Fearing that his voice might betray him, Yama used the sign language which the old guard, Coronetes, had taught him when he had been imprisoned in the stacks of the Department of Indigenous Affairs. Ananda caught the gist of it, even if he mangled the meaning.

I went crazy when I was searching for you, but now I know, he signed.

Ananda said, 'He wants you to know that he has been searching for you,' and suggested that he might be a priest.

Yama shook his head, suppressing the urge to laugh, and signed again. *How happy I am that all is as I remembered.*

Ananda said uncertainly, 'He says that he is glad that he remembered all this. I think he must mean that he will always remember this.'

Yama pulled the leather thong over his head and dangled the coin from his left hand while he signed with his right. *Use this if you are to come here again,* which Ananda badly scrambled on the first attempt, but got right on the second.

The whistles of the militia sounded, far off in the night. Yama thrust the coin into the boy's hand, cast a last longing look at Derev, and turned and ran up the embankment, towards the mazed tombs of the City of the Dead.

He had not run very far when the ship overtook him. It had hidden itself in the deeps of the Great River, far from shore; now it dropped out of the night and hung just above the surface of a flooded paeonin field, tilted so that one wing tip touched the top of the embankment. Yama climbed aboard, and at once it rose high above the world.

'I saw her,' he told the ship, 'and I will see her again. I must. What must be will be, despite ourselves.'

The ship's aspect, the solemn little girl, clasped her hands beneath her chin as Yama explained what he wanted. Behind her, the glassy plain with its freight of statues receded into the starless dark. She said, 'You are still not well, master.'

'No. Of course I am not well. I will never be well. I have seen too much. I have done too much. I think that I have been mad for a long time, but did not know it.' Yama felt the craziness again, his thoughts dividing and dividing, impossible to stop.

'The loop will be very short, master. I cannot guarantee its accuracy.'

Yama began to laugh and the laughter went on and on until he clamped his hands over his mouth because the laughter scared him. It bubbled through him. It might never stop. He choked it back and said, 'Just do it.'

'I will do my best, master.' The ship was wounded. It had been built to take a pride in what it did.

'Take me there, ship. I know you will do it. What must be will be.'

Night, summer, the Eye of the Preservers a smudged bloody thumprint high in the black sky. Dr Dismas's tower was a burnt-out ruin. Fragments of charred furniture were scattered outside its broken door. It was almost midnight, but the lights of the city of Aeolis burned brightly within its high wall.

Because of the summer heat, the citizens of Aeolis, the Amnan, slept in their cool seeps and wallows by day and began work at sunset. Sodium vapour lights blazed in the streets and lamps shone in every window. The doors of workshops, chandlers and taverns were flung open. Crowds swirled up and down the long road at the top of the old waterfront, where tribesmen from the dry hills downriver of the city had set up their blanket stalls and vendors of fried waterweed and nuts cried their wares. A mountebank stood halfway up a folding ladder, declaiming the wonders of a patent elixir; an auction of bacts was under way by the gate where Yama entered, clad in his tattered silvery cloak and leaning on his staff.

Hardly anyone marked his passing. He was almost certainly a mendicant; although Aeolis was a poor city, it was often visited by mendicants because it had once been one of the most holy cities on Confluence. Yama made his way through the crowds of large, ill-made, blubbery men with hardly a comment or a glance.

The steel door of the godown owned by Derev's father was open, guarded by a man with a carbine who gave Yama a hard look as he went past and walked around the corner to the family entrance.

The words which opened the door's lock had not been changed – even if they had, Yama could have forced it to open in an instant. Calling Derev's name, he went through the archway into a little courtyard where a fountain tiled with blue mosaic splashed. She would not be there. He knew that she would not be there, but there she was, floating down the spiral stair, her feathery white hair lifting around her pale face.

She stopped at a turn of the stair a little way above him. She wore a silk tabard the colour of old ivory, and a long skirt of many layers of fine white gauzy stuff. She said, 'Who let you in, dominie? I do not think my father has business with anyone this night.'

'You do not recognize me?'

Her large dark eyes searched his face. Then she said, 'You are the anchorite whose life Yama saved. Why have you come back? How did you get in? Do you know something about Yama? Is he—'

'He is here, Derev.'

'Where? Is he hurt? Did something happen to him in Ys? Your face is so grave, dominie. O, do not tell me he is dead!'

Yama laughed. 'My love, I am twice as alive as any other man in the world.'

Derev's expression suddenly changed. She vaulted the rail of the stair and floated down into his arms. Her height, her heat, her fierce gaze searching his. The staff fell with a clatter, unnoticed, as they took each other into their arms.

'You,' she said, leaning down into Yama's embrace. 'I knew it was you, but I did not let myself believe it.'

'You must believe it now, Derev. We have only a little time here.'

She drew away from him, still holding his hands. 'But you are hurt.'

For a moment, Yama did not know what she meant; he had let the ship tend to the small cuts and bruises inflicted during the fight with Lud and Lob. Then he touched the ridges of scarred skin on the left side of his face and said, 'These are old wounds.'

'I did not mean those,' she said. And then, 'Yama. Yama!'

At first, she tried to hold him up. Then she eased him to the ground, and went to fetch her father.

It was almost dawn by the time Yama had recovered enough to be able to tell something of his story. He was bathed and perfumed, his hair and beard combed and trimmed. He was dressed in a clean shirt and trews, and had been fed with a salty beef broth and sweet fried shrimp. He sat with Derev and her mother and father, Calev and Caenon, in the roof garden of the godown. He told them of how he had escaped Prefect Corin at Ys and boarded a ship which had taken him downriver towards the war, of how he had been infected by Dr Dismas and forced to fight on the side of the heretics, of how he had fallen beyond the edge of the world and travelled back in time through a short cut.

He left much out. The friendship of Pandaras and brave, foolish Tamora, and all their adventures in Ys and the Palace of the Memory of the People; the miracle he had been allowed to perform; the destruction of Dr Dismas's paramour in the Glass Desert; his adventures on the great ship with the last of his people. There was not enough time for that now.

'There is not enough time,' he said, 'because Aeolis will soon be attacked. I do no know exactly when, but certainly by tomorrow night.'

Derev's father, Carenon, said, 'We are still a long way from the heretics, I think. If an army or fleet is bent upon us, there would have been warnings, surely.'

'It will not be attacked by heretics, but by a warship out of Ys, a warship commanded by someone who wishes to do me harm.'

'Then we must prevent it. We will warn the Aedile, to begin with.'

Carenon stood, very tall and very thin in his black jacket and leggings. For a moment it seemed that he would raise his arms and leap into the sky. He said, 'I will take you to the peel-house at once, Yamamanama.'

'No,' Yama said. 'No, you will not.'

Calev said, 'How many will die, Yamamanama, when this warship comes?'

'The city will be destroyed. Many will escape and flee to the far side. I do not know how many will not.'

Carenon said, 'And you will allow no warning of this?'

Yama bowed his head. All his dead. The thousands he had killed while under the spell of Dr Dismas. Dr Dismas himself, and Prefect Corin. The crew of the *Weazel*. The soldiers who had captured him in the City of the Dead, and their mage. The regulator, and the last of his bloodline in the deep past. Tamora. And in only a few days his stepfather would die of shame and exhaustion on the far side of the river, after he failed to prevent the sacking of Aeolis.

Derev took his hand in hers and said, 'Don't you see that he would save them if he could?'

Yama said, 'I thought so long on this that it drove me mad. If I could I would save them all, friends and enemies alike. But then who else might die? And all those I tried to save might still die . . .'

The silence that followed was punctuated by the distant ringing of signal bells; fishing boats were turning into the channel towards the end of the New Quay, where they would tie up and unload their catches. It was almost dawn. The city was shutting down, getting ready for the long, hot, lazy day.

At last, Carenon said, 'I will warn my workers, at least. If I know, then they deserve to know too.'

'No,' Yama said. 'They have families here. They will want to take them, and the news will spread until all the city will know. It does not end. Do one thing and it branches and branches until you are far from where you began. No. What will happen must happen.'

Carenon gave him a sharp, troubled look. 'Where did you hear that?'

'He knows about Beatrice and Osric,' Derev said.

'I can take you away from here,' Yama told Carenon. 'You can come with me into the past, for that is where I must go.'

Derev said, 'Where we must go, I think.'

His love for her returned in all its fierce wildness, and for a moment he thought that he might faint again.

Calev said with grave astonishment, 'Then you are—'

'We did not know,' her husband said. 'I suppose it was for the best that we did not know, but it would have helped us. I hoped that you and Derev might make a match, Yamamanama, and perhaps things would not be as hard as has been foretold.' He laughed and said, 'What a fool I have been!'

'You always knew it would be a hard road when we came here,' Calev said. 'But you came here anyway.'

Yama had never paid much attention to Derev's parents. They had always been formal and reserved, for all that they had encouraged Derev in her trysts with him. He had thought that it was because of his position. He had been the son of a high official of the Department of Indigenous Affairs, even if he had been an adopted son. Derev's father had been mocked in the city for being ambitious and grasping, for pushing his daughter into a relationship that would bring him greater profit and power. Yama saw now that Carenon and Calev were no more than ordinary people who had taken up an extraordinary burden; that they were willing to sacrifice their daughter to help save the world.

He said again, 'I can save you. I know that you will flee the city before the attack. I can take you to the safest place of all, into the past.'

Carenon ran his fingers over the leaves of one of the geraniums that grew along the edge of the roof garden, releasing a sweet dusky scent into the air. His fine white hair lifted in the breeze that had sprung up from the river. It was growing warmer. Light touched the rim of the sky.

Carenon said, 'No, we will stay. I mean, we will flee the city, but we stay in this time. We built up one fortune, and we can take a little of that with us. Perhaps we can build another before the world ends. How long, before that happens?'

Yama lowered his head. He was ashamed and frightened. He had still to face that failure. He said, 'I do not know.'

Carenon said, 'But surely the end of the world is already set in motion. The Great River fails steadily, although the Aedile has calculated that it will not run dry for many years. If the end comes before then, we might live to see the new worlds we were promised.'

'Don't you see?' Derev said. 'Everything must happen so that he can come here again.'

Yama said quietly, 'Besides, I have not yet done it.'

Derev said, 'But the river is failing. And Beatrice said—'

'The first part, diverting the end of the river into the future, was easy. But I failed at the second part. I thought instead that I could change things, and find a new way . . .'

Derev smiled. 'And destroy the heretics? You always wanted to fight them, Yama, never more so than after Telmon died. Yet if you destroy the heretics, then you would only promote the cause of the Committee for Public Safety, and I know that you could not allow that.'

Yama nodded. 'They destroyed my father.'

Carenon nodded. 'A disgrace, the way they exiled so many loyal to the Department.'

'I mean that they will. It is one of the Committee for Public Safety who will set fire to the city, and it will be the end of my father.'

'They would be worse than the heretics,' Derev said.

'It has happened before,' Yama said. 'A tyranny may conquer every one of its enemies, but will ultimately destroy itself from the inside. The wheel turns, and all is renewed.'

Derev said, 'And is that what you want? That the world can go on for ever and ever without change?'

'No. That is not possible. I was allowed to perform a miracle, Derev. The indigenous peoples will become like us. They will gain self-awareness and at last achieve enlightenment. That is no small thing. If that was all I could do, then I could be content.'

'But it is not.'

'No. No, it is not. I was going to tell the boy, my younger self. Tell him everything and let him decide what to do. But that would do no more than pass the burden to another. And so I turned aside, and came here.'

Derev said, 'I cannot decide for you.'

'I would not ask you to. Besides, I have already decided.'

Carenon said, 'I suppose that if we tried to stop you, or if I tried to tell my poor workers their fate, you would have the power to prevent it.'

Behind him, far beyond the shadowy hills of the vast necropolis, the first rays of the sun touched the peaks of the Rim Mountains.

Yama said, 'I will not force any of you, but I hope that you will help me.'

26 ~ Until the End of the World

Early one winter, one of the goats was taken by a leopard. It was the piebald nanny which in her short life had given birth to six fine healthy kids, and only one of them a billy. The winter looked to be a hard one. It had been raining for more than a decad, which was why Beatrice had not yet moved the goats from the thorn scrub pasture to their winter quarters, and perhaps the rain had driven the leopard from its usual range in the spruce forests in the mountains. Beatrice found its pugmarks by the swift stream at the edge of the pasture, but no trace of the goat, not so much as a drop of blood. She told Osric the news and said there was no helping it, and then added, 'Why are you weeping, husband? It was only a goat.'

'It is the sign.'

Beatrice took off her wet oilskin and hung it on the hook by the kitchen door. The end of her long, feathery white hair had got wet. She wrapped it around her strong, capable hands and squeezed water from it on to the stone floor. She said, 'It is a sign that means more winter fodder for the other goats, and less milk for us next spring.'

'It will begin soon. He will come to us . . .'

Beatrice gave him a sharp look. 'The boy.'

'Next spring.'

'We won't see Derev until then, that's certain. She won't want to make her way from Aeolis to the keelroad head in weather like this. And I will not risk sending out any doves in this weather, either. But never mind, there's plenty of time to tell her what she must do. Husband, what is it now?'

Osric was troubled, teary and weak. So often these days his mind seemed to catch on unimportant things. He would find himself in the middle of one of the little stone-walled gardens on top of the tower and not know whether he had come to harvest or water or weed. He said, 'What will I tell him, wife?'

'I'm sure you'll remember when the time comes. That's how it is, isn't it? What must be will be.'

Osric watched his wife potter about the kitchen. She built up the fire which he had forgotten to tend while she was out in the cold rain rounding up the surviving goats. Wind hunted at the slit windows. A loose shutter banged. The left side of his face ached, as it always did in cold wet weather. But they were snug here, with plenty of canned and pickled vegetables, and sacks of dry beans and wild rice for which they had traded goat's milk cheese with the local tribe of mountaineers. They would sleep in the niches on either side of the stone fireplace. And in spring . . .

Osric began to weep again, choking with frustration. He was too weak, too old, and too confused. He was older than Bryn, and Bryn had considered himself very old. He slept more than half the day, and could not work for more than an hour without having to rest for twice as long. He could not remember exactly what would happen, but he knew that it was so very important that he must try and recall every detail. He must tell the boy enough, but not too much.

Beatrice noticed her husband's distress and made him a beaker of camomile tea. 'Well,' she said, 'as the fox said when he first saw the grapes, what are we going to do about it?'

'I suppose I must try and remember everything. I will tell the story again. I will tell it and you will write it down, wife.'

'And I suppose that is more important than the half hundred things I must do before winter really comes.'

'It is more important than anything in the world.'

Beatrice warmed her hands at the fire, thinking about it. At last, she said, 'We will do it a little at a time. An hour or two a day. We're old, husband, and we don't want to tire ourselves out.'

Osric stroked her long white hair. She leaned into his attention, like a cat. He said, 'I have to live until spring, at least.'

'Longer than that, I hope. Well, where should we begin?'

Osric thought hard. He said, 'I suppose the proper place might be when Dr Dismas came back to Aeolis from Ys. That is how it really began. But any place is as good as any other. It is all a circle, like the river.'

'As the river was, but is no more. Not for … ach, I always get confused over the ins and outs of it all.'

'The point is that it does not matter where it begins, or where it ends.'

'Of course it matters. Beginnings are as important as endings, and it's just the same the other way around. I think we had better write it all down, or we will begin at the end or somewhere in the middle, and never get ourselves straight.'

'Perhaps that is the place to begin. The middle, I mean. Most people would start with the child and the dead woman in the white boat on the Great River. But I think it should begin with the goat, and how the boy will be brought here.'

'I can see that I will have to find pen and paper straight away,' Beatrice said. 'Think about what you want to say while I go and look.'

It took most of the winter to tell the tale, until at last they reached the point where Yama had returned home for the last time, and where their own story, the story of the two of them, husband and wife, had really begun.

'Do you remember,' Beatrice said fondly, 'do you remember how shocked Father Quine was, when we burst in like that at dawn, waking him and Ananda and demanding that we be married at once?'

Osric smiled. 'Ananda knew. He knew right away who I was.'

Carenon told Father Quine that the marriage would take place at gunpoint if it had to, but Father Quine assured him that his threats were not necessary. All the while, the young sizar, Ananda, stared at Yama until he could contain his amazement no longer, and plunged into a breathless series of questions.

'Why have you returned? Did you go to Ys? What happened there? Did you run away from Prefect Corin? Did he do that to your face?'

And so on, until Yama burst into laughter. 'I came back because something both wonderful and terrible happened,' he said. 'You will understood soon enough, Ananda. I wish I could tell you everything, but there is no time.'

'But you did go to Ys.'

'Yes. Yes, I did. And after many adventures I am back, but only for a little while, and in secret. The Aedile must not know. No one must know but the people in this room.'

Ananda smiled. 'Well, I am glad to see you again.'

Father Quine cleared his throat, and Ananda bit back his next question. 'I think you should fetch the oil,' the priest told his sizar.

It did not take long; it was, after all, a metic marriage, the ceremony more in the nature of a blessing than a service. Afterwards, Father Quine broke open a cruse of wine, and as they all sat around the kitchen table in the priest's house, Ananda dug out a little more of Yama's story. He was convinced that Yama had come straight back from Ys, and Yama did not disabuse him. There was not enough time.

'I will not see you again,' Ananda said at last, ending an uncomfortable pause.

'I do not think so. You will stay in the temple . . .'

Yama meant that Father Quine and Ananda would be placed under house arrest when Prefect Corin came. The temple would be left standing when Aeolis was razed because it belonged to the Department. But he could not tell Ananda any of that.

'O yes,' Ananda said quietly. 'And become priest after Quine.' He looked sideways at the priest, who was talking with Derev and her parents. He bent closer to Yama and added in a whisper, 'Not that the dry old stick looks like withering away in my lifetime. I'll be a hundred years sweeping out the naos and polishing the shrine while you and Derev are off adventuring. At least, that's what you will be doing, I suppose.'

'We will make a home together,' Yama said, 'with a little garden, and goats and doves. But not quite yet, I think. I am glad we met again, Ananda. I did not like the way we parted.'

'I had not attended an execution before,' Ananda said. 'I was sick afterwards. Quine was furious. Because I was sick, and because he knew then that I had broken the fast.'

'Pistachios,' Yama said, remembering that day.

Ananda grinned. 'I have not eaten them since. Now, have some more wine.'

'It is time we said a prayer, I think,' Yama said. He drew Derev aside and told her to make her farewells to her parents.

They went together as man and wife before the shrine where so often as a child Yama had helped the Aedile perform the long and meaningless rituals which were part of the duties of his office, and where the aspect of Angel had first found him, so badly frightening the Aedile that he had damaged the shrine's mechanism.

But it still functioned as a short cut mouth. Yama and Derev stepped through to a place far away, a bubble hung above a vast chamber deep in the keelways. The chamber was hundreds of leagues long. Machines as big as cities crouched on its floor. Lights came on around the rim of the bubble; lighted windows opened in the air. Some showed views of similar chambers, one for each section of the world.

A voice spoke out of the air and welcomed Yama, and asked him what he wished to do.

And so the end of the world was set in motion.

Afterwards, Yama called down the ship and it took them out in a loop that compressed forty years into a few days, so that they could glimpse the end of the world before plunging down a short cut into the deep past. They emerged around one of the stars mentioned by the Gatekeeper when Yama had first returned to Confluence, a star which had moved closer to the star of Confluence after the Preservers had quit the Galaxy.

One of the worlds which orbited the star had been reshaped into something like the world which had been the cradle of the race which had, over millions of years, changed the orbit of every star of the Galaxy and become at last the Preservers. There were many such worlds, the ship told them; it was possible that one of them might even be the true, ancient Earth which Angel's crewmates had left Confluence to search for. But Yama and Derev were content to explore the world they had, and afterwards returned to Confluence, arriving fifty years before Yama cast his own self upon the waters of the Great River.

They found the tower at the far edge of the City of the Dead, in the foothills of the Rim Mountains. It was abandoned and open to the weather, and they spent some time restoring it before tracking Derev's grandparents to a small town several hundred leagues downriver of Aeolis. They took new names from an ancient poem Derev loved. Her grandparents refused to take up the burdens of the Department of the Curators of the City of the Dead; their parents had given up their family's traditional service because there was no longer any need for it, and they would not be persuaded to see a need for it now. But they had a son, ambitious and restless, and he remembered the story Beatrice and Osric told his parents. After they died, more than twenty years later, he sent a message to the new curators of the City of the Dead, saying that he would move to Aeolis if they could help him establish his business there.

'And a few years later he married, and a few years after that I was born,' Beatrice said. 'Unless you want to put in the business about the goat, I think you are done, for nothing has happened to us since.'

'Perhaps I should say more about the end of the world,' Osric said.

'It will happen soon enough, and there will be enough stories about it, too. At least one for every world the great ships will settle.' Beatrice set aside the sheaf of paper and went to the window and opened the shutter a little and looked out. 'It is still raining, but it looks like it might end soon. A long, cold, wet winter it has been, but at least we found something to fill it, eh, husband?'

'It is not very satisfactory as a tale. There are too many repetitions, and too many words wasted on adventures anyone could have had, or on diversions which led to nothing in particular.'

'Well, that's how it always is with life. Cut short too soon, with too many loose ends.'

'I wonder about the Ancients of Days. Will they ever find Old Earth? And what about poor Dreen, the Commissioner of Sensch, who went with them?'

'There are many Earths,' Beatrice said. 'No doubt they will find one to their liking, but people might already be living there. The Ancients of Days went the long way, remember. They are still travelling on it, and will not arrive anywhere for at least a hundred and fifty thousand years. Everyone else will fall through the short cuts. Their descendants will be scattered across the Galaxy long before the Ancients of Days arrive.'

'Yes,' Osric said. 'The Preservers abandoned the Galaxy and then the Universe, but the ten thousand bloodlines will inherit it. There will be room for everyone, even the heretics. There might be wars more terrible than the war I thought to end, but I do not think the heretics will survive for long. Their philosophy has been defeated before; it will be defeated again.'

'And the indigenous peoples. Do not forget them, husband. You always said that they were the hope that things would be different.'

'*They* are different. They are not marked by the Preservers. I wonder if that is what the Preservers wanted. We are the servants of the Preservers, but perhaps the indigenous peoples are their true heirs. Perhaps they will triumph over those from whom the Preservers fled. Or perhaps, by the working of some strange plan, they will become the Preservers' nemesis.'

'We cannot know what the Preservers wanted,' Beatrice said.

'But we can wonder about them. I wonder about the enlightened bloodlines too. About all those who became so holy that they vanished from the world. Perhaps they found a way through the event horizon of the Eye, and followed the Preservers to their new universe. We did not explore everything the shrines could do.'

'Most likely they became so holy that they simply died out, like the people of Gond. But what is the use of speculating on things we cannot know? We cannot know about the fate of the Preservers because they fled the Universe so completely that nothing can return from them, not even light. You will waste your life, husband, thinking on questions which have no answers because they could have any answer.'

'And there is the ghost ship,' Osric said stubbornly. 'I had thought that it would be me who would help save the boy when he escaped Enobarbus and Dr Dismas. That I would invoke the vision of the ghost ship which stopped them from chasing the boy after he jumped overboard. But I forgot. I went directly to you. Perhaps the boy will not escape Dr Dismas and Enobarbus, wife, and so will not come here. This may be a different time-line.'

Beatrice was putting on her yellow oilskin. She said, 'Every story must have a mystery, husband. No one likes a story in which everything is explained. How could you explain why people do the things they do, for instance? Now, I am going to see to the goats. Will you be all right while I am gone? Will you watch the fire?'

'Yes, of course,' Osric said, as she went out.

But he was thinking of the ghost ship, and the way it had dissolved into a bank of fog which had hid him from the pinnace commanded by Enobarbus after he had escaped from it. The ghost ship had surely been an illusion conjured by a machine, for he had seen a machine rising out of the fog. But who had commanded the machine? Perhaps it had been his first miracle, and he had not known it. Or perhaps the machines he believed to be his to command had been working for some other power's subtle plan, of which he was but a part. But it did not do to think of these things. If anything was possible, then everything was possible. No. What will be must be. He had made that the core of his life when he had chosen to find Derev, and had closed his part of the tale by beginning the end of the world.

He remembered seeing how it would end. They had gone there after he had woken the great engines in the keelways. The ship had hung high above the long plane of the world and they had watched as it broke apart. At the beginning of his adventures, he had seen a picture slate which had shown one of his bloodline at the time of the construction of Confluence (he would have to find that slate, Osric thought). Behind the man had been a hundred shining splinters hung against a starry sky, but he had not realized then what they were: the elements of the world, the great ships which the Builders had joined together in the first act of the creation of the world.

He had reversed the process. He had saved the world and its people by destroying it. The Great River had failed; the engines in the keelways had been woken from their long slumber and had slowly resumed their functions. It took forty years. And then the shrines woke and warned the peoples of the world, telling them what would happen, and where they could find shelter. And less than a year later the world broke apart into its original sections, and those sections fell in different directions across the sky towards the expanding throats of the short cuts: a field of blue rings flowering in the empty blackness of space and a cloud of splinters shining in the light of the lonely star.

How many had died, in the last days of Confluence? There had been terrible famines when the river had finally run dry, and earthquakes had thrown all of the cities into ruin. Certainly almost all of the heretics had died, for they had silenced most of the shrines in the cities they had captured, and so had no warning of the world's end. But many others had died, too, and many more would die when the great ships reached their destinations, and the reoccupation of the Galaxy began.

But many more would live, and prosper, and multiply.

He dozed a little, and woke, and remembered that after the boy came they would have to think of Pandaras. The boy would find Pandaras in Ys (or had it been the other way around?) and take him on his adventures, and Pandaras's own story would begin when the boy's ended. Although he had been charged with changing all the indigenous peoples of Confluence, Pandaras would not stop searching for his master. He would return at last to Ys, the place he loved most and knew best. They would track him down by the coin he carried, and explain how his master's story had ended. He must remember to tell Beatrice, Osric thought, and fell asleep again.

The door banged open and Beatrice came in, shaking water from her long hair. Osric stirred. 'Look,' she said. 'See what I found.'

It was a bunch of violets. She found a bowl and set them in it. Their sweet scent slowly filled the kitchen, promising the end of winter and the beginning of spring.

Soon the story would be over, and they could leave. They would find Pandaras, and call down the ship. They would embark for the last time. Where would they go? To the deep past, or to the deep future? All of history stood before him like a book. He could open it at any page.

He would have to think hard about it. Spring had only just begun, but soon Derev would find the boy in the ancient tomb in the Silent Quarter of the City of the Dead, and bring him here. And the story would begin again, and in its beginning would be its end.